What the Sea Wants

a novel in two parts

by

Karin Cox

First published 2016 by Indelible Ink Press
Copyright © Karin Cox 2015
ISBN 978-0-9873602-9-8
Edited by Theo Fenraven

This book is a work of fiction. People, places, events, and situations are the product of the author's imagination. Any resemblance to actual persons, living or dead, to place, or to historical events, is purely coincidental.

To enjoy special offers, newsletter and fan discounts, sign up to Karin's new-release mailing list at *http://eepurl.com/vk_bP*

Follow the author on Facebook at *www.facebook.com/KarinCox.Author* Or twitter @Authorandeditor or follow her blog at *http://www.karincox. wordpress.com* or *http://www.karincox.com*

For all the stars

who've already burnt out.

PLAYLIST

All songs available from iTunes, except for "Drowning" by Uri Avi, available by emailing the author.

"Wash Away" by Matt Costa
"Beach" by San Cisco
"Dandelion" by Tom Curren
"Secrets" by OneRepublic
"Wave Machine" by Martha Tilston
"Bonfire Heart" by James Blunt
"1983... (A Merman I Should Turn To Be)"
    by The Jimi Hendrix Experience
"Drowning" by Uri Avi & Karin Cox
"Constellations" by Jack Johnson
"When Summer Has Passed" by Howard Eliot Payne
"Stranger" by Angus & Julia Stone
"Sunshine" by Matt Costa
"Better Days" by Pete Murray
"Grey Ocean" by Lior
"Scare Away the Dark" by Passenger
"Starry Night" by Patrick Park
"These Arms" by Matt Costa
"Come Save Me" by Jagwar Ma
"I Won't Let You Go" by James Morrison
"Life Is Wonderful" by Jason Mraz
"Thinking Out Loud" by Ed Sheeran
"This Love" by Taylor Swift

Author's Note

I feel I should warn readers straight up that while *What the Sea Wants* is a romance novel, it probably isn't a relaxing beach read! It is set around a fictional surfing community on Australia's east coast, where sun and surf don't just come with hot, shirtless surfers but occasionally come with other hazards too.

Like the sea, this story is sometimes turbulent and never static. It isn't always chronological, nor does it follow the rules (when will I learn!). It's a tale of befores and afters, of how we look to the future, believing we might predict it, even if we really can't. But mostly it's a reminder that perhaps we shouldn't try.

So, as you read this novel, remember that not all who are missing are lost. Sometimes life sinks us, and sometimes it throws us a lifebuoy.

I trust that international readers will forgive Aussie spellings, punctuation, and slang. As an Aussie, I felt the novel would lose authenticity if I Americanised my characters and their words to suit the US market, but I'm also a proud Aussie who wanted to share my country's many quirks with overseas readers. For those who find themselves "lost at sea", some terms are linked to a glossary in the back.

Happy reading.

Karin

PART I

Before

We are such stuff as dreams are made on,
and our little life is rounded with a sleep.
WILLIAM SHAKESPEARE

CHAPTER 1

"There's something about me you need to know, something I'm not sure I can tell you." I let a handful of sand trickle between my fingers and closed my eyes, doing my best to stop the flickering show reel in my head, each image a vivid reminder I shouldn't even be having this conversation. Was I really going to share this with him? And if I did, how could I be sure that if something happened between us, something to end this wonderful dream, Ash Gordon wouldn't turn around and spill? If he did—maybe even *when* he did—I knew what it would mean.

I'd seen the looks on people's faces before. The crinkling, narrowed eyes, the quirked eyebrows, the faux smiles. Long ago, back before I closed up shop and stopped letting people know I was different, back when I still made an effort to make friends and explain, I'd seen those expressions. But this was now, and I knew what most people would think. The same thing sceptics always thought about people like me: another one for the funny farm.

Ash took my hand, pressing my sandy palm to his lips. "Babe, nothing you say can change how I feel about you."

"Nothing?" Doubt made my voice quaver, or was it the intensity of his eyes—multi-faceted, brilliant, gleaming with the inner depth that was the wellspring his songs burst forth from.

I turned away, focussing on the horizon, on the sun drowning in the sea.

"Nothing!" he promised, shaking his head, his tousled, dirty blond curls escaping from his sunglasses where they were pushed up on top of his head. "I'd love you even if you'd been born a dude."

I laughed, but I couldn't stop myself from readjusting my bikini top, momentarily self-conscious of my lack of curves. He'd been joking, of course, but I still worried. Worrying was my thing, after all. "Really?"

He shrugged and winked. "Hey, a cute arse is a cute arse, I always say."

I wrinkled my nose at him, and he revealed that perfect, crookedly confident smile that had me hooked from the get-go.

"Next on the list." He checked off another finger. "I'll love you even if you're a reptilian alien masquerading as a human."

"Like Trump?"

"Nah, like Bieber."

"Ha. Nice! But I'm not an alien." At least I didn't think so. Sometimes I did feel like I came from another planet, though. Planet Fucked Up. My secret, the secret I was struggling to tell Ash, had made me wary. It kept me silent. It made me wonder what was real and what wasn't. But most of all, it made me anxious. It kept me up at night. I chewed my fingernails, scrolled news websites for hours, or withdrew from the world for days. It made me afraid to dream. And right now, it made me wonder how to tell Ash.

"Right. Next guess." He folded down another finger. "I've long suspected you're actually an angel."

I rolled my eyes. "Nice line, Romeo. I'm no angel."

Ash gave a disbelieving *pffft*. "That's bad news. Means you're a demon." He gave my bikini strap a tweak. "An angel in the streets and a demon in the sheets…?" He waggled his dark eyebrows. "I gotta say I'm kinda wishin' for that."

"Perv." I slapped his hand away. "I'm not a demon."

But maybe it was a kind of possession. I'd often wondered where it came from, from what dark place. Wherever it was, I'd spent most of my life wishing it would go back there. For sixteen years, Yiayia made the sign of the cross every time I stepped over the threshold of my grandparents' house in Melbourne, but her efforts had done nothing to ward off whatever darkness had latched onto me.

Ash caught my arm and pulled me down on top of him, kissing the tip of my nose. "I'm just messin' with you. Spill it, babe. No more secrets." His eyes darkened and his tone, while not dismissive, was guarded, despite his reassurances. "I'm sure I've heard worse. How bad can it be?"

The last time he'd said that, it had been bad.

Droplets of water from my surf-wet hair trickled onto his shoulders as I wriggled off him and sat up, resuming my slow funnelling of sand. I was afraid to look at him, anticipating his disbelief.

"No secrets," I repeated softly. Then I did it. Said it. "Ash, I … I see things sometimes—terrible things."

His brow furrowed. "That's it?" He sounded half-disappointed. "Like what? Hallucinations? Is it some kind of... condition or something? "

I shook my head. "No. More kind of *The Sixth Sense*."

"You see dead people?" He jolted upright.

"No." I swivelled the beaded bracelet on my wrist, the one Yiayia had given me believing it to be some kind of lucky charm. "I see people die."

CHAPTER 2

Blood paints the water with a filmy swirl, crimson curling into blue like smoke evaporating into air. I want to scream but can't. My mouth feels too full—of teeth, of water, of words I want to holler but can't choke out through the grit of sand and panic.

But someone is screaming, high-pitched as a siren, as the fin carves the waves, dissecting them like a surgeon's scalpel amputating a limb. Something dark and sleek, gunmetal grey and deadly as a pistol, hurtles toward a lone surfer.

Time slows for the propulsion of its zeppelin body and blunt nose. My eyes are fixed on its pale, bored eyes, on its crowd of jagged teeth.

Everything thrashes.

Everything churns.

The water squeals and sings and parts in terror as the beast launches forward. And then there is nothing but blood. Legs churn to walk on water, to rise above a visceral, crimson hell. And with every jerk, more blood. More fear. More death.

CHAPTER 3

"Hey! Hey! Are you okay?"

Strong fingers gripped my shoulder, and a resonant voice drowned out the soundtrack of screams in the fading dream.

I sat up and shivered, as if to shake off the gauzy vision, but its mood clung to me like the caul I'd been born with. My Greek grandmother insisted the thin, shawl-like membrane that had wrapped my newborn face was the portent of a seer, the sign of one who had the *mati*—Yiayia's word for evil eye. To ward it off, she'd muttered a prayer at my birth; the *xematiasma*, she called it. It didn't appear to have worked, or not for long.

The first dream occurred when I was four, and I'd been having nightmares ever since, although I'd never had one after falling asleep on a public beach before. If I wasn't still so terrified, I'd be fire-engine-red with embarrassment.

"I was watching from the tower."

My eyes moved to the face of the guy gesturing to the yellow-and-red lifesaving tower down the beach, and my embarrassment gave way to abject humiliation. I almost wished a shark had eaten me, just so I wouldn't have to deal with fact that the hottest guy in Willow Bay now thought I was a lunatic.

Ashley Gordon was a senior in the year above me at Willow Bay High. He was one of the "cool kids," a surfer with a huge entourage and no lack of girls throwing themselves at him, and probably under him.

"Looked like you were having some sort of fit." He ran a brown hand through his loose curls. "You were yelling and thrashing around."

How embarrassing. "I'm fine." I waved him away. "I fell asleep. It was just a bad dream."

I usually paid the surf scene little attention, but it was difficult for anyone, even a loner like me, to not pay attention to Ash Gordon.

Loser, not loner, some at Willow Bay High might have termed me, but whatever. I had my bestie and my books, and most of the time I liked imaginary people a lot more than I liked real people—and a heck of a lot more than I liked dead people.

I shivered again, shoving thoughts of the dream from my mind and concentrating on his handsome face instead, on the high cheekbones and angular jaw, the squarish chin, the dimples, and the long, straight nose. Anything but his eyes.

My first glance at them had plunged me into depths so intensely blue-green, I couldn't even come up with a word for them, and I was a card-carrying word-nerd, a bookworm who devoured romance novels as fast as my fingers could one-click them. I could think of a synonym for almost any word, but Ash's eyes weren't readily describable. They weren't azure or cerulean or sapphire or aquamarine. They weren't Pacific blue or Indian Ocean green or Atlantic grey or Artic ice. They were just amazing. Concerned and curious and sparkling with an indescribably oceanic clarity. They made my heart constrict, and I wondered whether I'd just had a stroke and drifted away into the blue sky or drowned in those glorious eyes and been sent straight to fantasy-book boyfriend heaven.

"Hey." His voice was thick with concern, his quads tanned and taut as he crouched by my side, resting his elbows on his thighs. "You sure you're all right? Need me to call an ambulance?"

I shook my head, and he gestured toward a four-wheeler that was cruising the beach, selling ice creams and cold drinks. "Can I get you anything?"

Not trusting myself to speak again yet, I shook my head again. "Take a deep breath," Ash instructed, placing a cool palm on my forehead. "If you need first aid, I'm your man."

My man.

The kiss of life ought to do, I thought, my gaze fixed on the cushion of his full bottom lip.

I did as he instructed, cautioning myself to function. *Breathe, Juliette. Yes, Ash Gordon is touching you. But just remember to breathe. Deep breaths. Atta girl.*

The heat of his palm made me flush like a boiled lobster, and he withdrew his hand. His dark eyebrows knit together, creating a furrow between those intoxicating eyes. "You're hot."

Right back at ya.

"I-I'm on the beach," I stammered, groaning inwardly at having morphed into Captain Obvious.

I was only on the beach because Jazmin, my bestie since preschool, had insisted I accompany her. She was only here because of Dylan Hoffstede. Willow Bay's very own Rip Curl Pro contender had become my best friend's newest obsession. Dylan was two years older than us, and when he wasn't surfing, he was under a car at Shifty's Mechanics on Bloom Street, which was where Jaz had met him. She didn't say a word the entire time he explained her hand-me-down Corolla's automatic transmission needed a complete do-over, which was how I knew Jaz had a mega instalove thing going on; Jaz was never quiet. Her mum joked that Jazmin Piper had entered the world, screaming like a banshee, and hadn't yet stopped to take her first breath. Still, I had to hand it to her: Dylan was hot. He wasn't Ash Gordon's thigh-parting, jaw-dropping, blond, ocean-eyed surfer perfection with a smile that could melt hearts the way pavement melted flip-flops hot, but he was still cute as. Handsome enough to turn Jaz mute for half an hour. After he fixed her car, Jaz had driven straight to Anchorage to buy a boogie board and begged me to accompany her to the beach.

"A boogie board? Like that's going to impress a surfer."

"It's called a body-board, and it's cheaper than putting my car in the shop all the time."

Which was true.

The body-board. A current pulled through me. *The shark!* Residual panic from the dream surged into something new as I swung my hand up to shield my eyes and squinted out at the water, looking for Jaz.

She was out deep, her arms and torso stretched over the board, waiting for a wave. The crescent shape of a fin rose from the darker water behind her.

"Shark!" I screamed, trying to rise but finding my legs still shaky from the dream. "Jaz!" I toppled on my butt in the sand. "Shark!"

Ash's head snapped around to the waves, but within seconds he turned to me with a relieved little chuckle.

"That's just Bitten." His bright-white grin disappeared into dimples in his cheeks, making him look all the more like the poster boy for the Australian Dental Association or *Surf Weekly* or something, if there was such a thing.

"A bottlenose dolphin," he explained, extending a hand to help me up. "Every surfer in Willow Bay knows Bitten."

Silver streaked beneath the surface before the dolphin appeared again on the crest of the wave.

"You can tell by the chunk out of its fin." Ash pointed. "That's how he got his name. Met something that didn't agree with him, poor fella. Probably a great white." He watched for a moment, smiling, before turning back to me. "He's kind of a celebrity. Loves hanging out the back with the surfers. Sometimes, he comes so close you can almost touch him. He's good luck. Keeps the men in grey suits away."

"Men in grey suits?" I mumbled, feeling like an idiot for having to ask.

"Sharks." He said matter-of-factly, as if it was the most obvious thing in the world. "I reckon there's more chance of Bitten keeping them away than the stupid shark nets the council wants if that big development goes ahead." He scoffed. "Look at this place. As if it needs banana boat rides and crap, let alone shark nets on these beaches. Dolphins are bound to get caught up in them."

"Shark nets?" *Nice one, Juls. You've completely forgotten how to speak in sentences!* Blood began flowing again now I knew Jaz was safe, but the dream still disoriented me. I sat down a little too quickly, sending up a puff of fine white sand and grunting with the effort.

Ash was staring out at the ocean, hands on his hips. "I'm trying to start a petition against the nets, but Mayor Aldershot's being a—" Breaking off, he crouched beside me again, his smile fading. "Anyway... you sure you're okay? You gotta be careful in the heat. Sunstroke can be a killer. You should get some water into you, or an icy-pole, some electrolytes."

I pointed to a bottle of now-tepid water tucked into my beach bag. "I'm fine."

"Good. Stay hydrated, okay? On a sizzler like this, I'm almost hopin' someone gets into trouble so I can go in for dip, and here you are wearing jeans." Ash gestured to my inappropriate beachwear, which Jaz had already scolded me for earlier.

Great first impression, Juls.

Desperate to change the subject, I pointed out that Jaz was about to be engulfed by a massive wave. "Jazmin isn't in trouble enough for you?"

He laughed. "Nah, she's getting the hang of it."

The wave crashed over her, and he shrugged. "Kinda. Jazmin, huh? I've seen her around."

Ahhh. Of course you have.

It wouldn't be the first time a guy I fancied had fallen for my best friend. Jaz had a confident, caramel-blonde appeal and a dairy farmer's-daughter frankness guys seemed to appreciate. And boobs. I had none of those things, especially the last. I was stuck with a mouthful while Jaz owned the whole milk bar. Mum kept reassuring me I was just a late bloomer, but at nearly seventeen, surely the puberty fairies had come and gone. I took after Dad in that respect. Another thing to thank the bastard for.

"Yeah. Jazmin Piper," I answered after a moment, trying to keep the disappointment from my voice. I picked up the book I'd been reading and wiped sand off the cover. Given my recent attempts at conversing with a real live human male, I considered it might be best to return to a fictional guy.

Ash was still staring out at the surf, taking note of kids bobbing in the shallows and watching Jaz and a few other surfers. A girl strutted past, lithe and tanned in a bikini. "Hey, Ash," she called.

He returned her wave, and I couldn't help but peer over the top of the book. No one could have helped noticing her impressive booty. I suppressed a small sigh. Who was I kidding? This guy was buff and brown and toned and sparkly eyed and washboard-abbed and basically perfect. And I...? Well, I was Juliette Evangelina Papavasilou Brewer. Too thin, too quiet, and just a little bit paranormal.

"Seeya at Drew's party." She blew him a cute little kiss. "It's going to be *fantastic!*"

That's when I recognised her.

The Fantastics was the term Jaz had coined for a gaggle of popular girls in the grade above us. They wore so much makeup they resembled Bratz dolls crafted in the image of D-list celebrities, and to them everything was "fantastic" but especially themselves. I'd noticed a group of them earlier, smearing coconut oil on skin so fried it would've made a hot barbecue chook proud and kept Cancer Council Australia in business. They hung around the surfers, giggling and preening like a flock of rainbow lorikeets, or used fake IDs to swoop on visiting Rugby League stars at Swaggers, Willow Bay's only nightclub.

I did my best to stay out of their way. It was no secret the Fantastics could destroy anyone who challenged their position at the top of Willow Bay High's pecking order.

Fashion, makeup, and backstabbing were never really my style anyway. I had better things to do than sizzle on the beach, plotting to bring down my competitors—usually reading, studying, or horse-riding with Jaz out on the farm. The Fantastics, on the other hand, avoided book smarts like they were a communicable disease—not that some of them didn't have *those* either, or so the rumour mill had it. I told you they knew how to destroy a girl!

Of course, they weren't all like that. Some were agreeable hippy chicks like Lisa Rubin or the neglected children of affluent, jet-setting parents with palatial homes high on Hume Hill, overlooking the bay. Jaz and I had gone through primary school with some of them, but most paid little attention to the bean-pickers and farmers' daughters from Bannockbrae or Roeburn, or the reserved ethnic daughter of the local hairdresser. The truth was, I had too much dirt the Fantastics could dig up if they really wanted to get their shovels out. Best I kept my head down—and firmly attached to my neck.

"Watcha reading?" Ash jogged me out of my reverie by gesturing to the paperback I was still clutching.

I held it up, blushing.

"*Simple Perfection.*" His bowed lips moved over the title. "Seems like you got the right book."

I frowned, wondering what he meant. He'd better not be laughing at my genre choice! I didn't always read romance. I liked classics too. Literary fiction, fantasy, romantic suspense, young adult, paranormal romance. Anything with words. If it had a plot, I read it; sometimes I'd read it even if it didn't. My main criteria was that I could lose myself in it for a little while, escape my own reality.

Right now, the reality was that Ash's blue-grey-green-whatever-they-were eyes were sparkling, and his smile was so charming I didn't feel the need to be in any other world than this one.

Indicating the cover again, he said with a wink, "Just like you—simple perfection."

"Oh." I blushed. If he only knew how complicated my life was, how far from simple, Ash Gordon might have turned and run then and there.

The perfect girl in the crew Ash hung with was good at sports, tanning, selfies, applying eyeliner, drama, and twerking. The list was probably longer than that, to be fair, but I was pretty sure being able to predict disasters wasn't on it. Heck, being an avid reader wasn't even on it. Horse-riding, natch. Rom-coms, probably not. To the popular kids, most of my pastimes were a surefire ticket to Loserland. Do not pass go. Do not collect two hundred dollars.

Ash's tongue crept out to wet his lips, then he pouted. "Was that line too cheesy for you?"

"Uh. No. Ah. A li'l bit," I admitted. I buried my face back in the pages, staring at a jumble of ink. Actually it just made me feel odd, hot and embarrassed and strangely electric. I could tell he was still watching me, and the thought made me anxious. The type no longer resembled words; whole paragraphs jumped around with a skittery, heart-rate monitor effect.

"Well, I tried," he said with a laugh, turning his piercing, indescribable gaze to the ocean. After a minute, he added, "You still seem flustered. I can walk you up to the clubhouse, if you like. Get you back in the air-conditioning."

Of course I was flustered. Ash Frakking* Gordon (*not his real middle name) was talking to me. He was probably even complimenting me... maybe... unless he was just taking pity on a girl with a roo loose in the top paddock. I slid the book back into my bag and stood, wobbling a little. "All cool," I insisted, my demeanour belying my words. "Anyway, I gotta..." I gestured toward Jaz. I could hardly nick off without letting her know where I'd gone.

"I don't think it's a good idea for you to go in the water yet," he said, with a sexy, low undercurrent of authority. "Not because of the *shark*." He emphasised the word, grinning. "And it would cool you down, I guess, but because you've been kind of, well, I wouldn't want you to faint or have a fit out there."

That wouldn't happen. I had no intention of entering the water. Not only because of the dream, but also because I wasn't wearing swimmers beneath my Levi's. I was far from the fainting type, too, although I certainly wasn't about to admit that if it meant having to 'fess up to being somewhat more para than I was normal.

"If I get into trouble out there, I guess you'll come save me and get that dip you wanted." I smiled, trying to divert his attention from my dream.

"I'm a surfer." Ash laughed. "We try not to save body-boarders if we can help it." Tugging the collar of his bright yellow lifeguard uniform, he added, "Just joshin'. It's kind of a requirement of the job. But surfing's heaps more fun than body-boarding. Look at Dylan out there, carving it up." He pointed out past the breakers. Dylan's legs were bent, his long hair flying as he showed off an impressive display of abdominal muscles and surfing prowess.

"You know him?"

"Dyl? Yeah. Been best mates since we went to Nippers together. I can't promise to teach you to surf as well as he does, but if you decide you want to learn, I'll set you up with the basics." He raised one eyebrow, as if in challenge. "You wanna put your mate Jaz to shame, you gotta learn to ride a real board. How about it?"

"Me? Surf?" I didn't even own a bikini. "Now? Oh, I don't—"

He laughed. "Maybe not *right* now. I'm on duty." He inclined his head toward the tower. "But soon. It'll be fun, and it's the best way to get up close to a dolphin. What're you doin' Saturday morning?"

"S-Saturday…?" My schedule for Saturday certainly didn't involve doing anything with anyone as hot as Ash Gordon—maybe a book boyfriend, courtesy of one of my favourite authors, but no one who existed in real life.

I'm… reading? Bup-barm! Wrong! I struggled to think of an answer, staring blankly at his lips. *Think, Juliette!*

"Nothin'?" His cheeks creased into dimples again. "Excellent. It's a date! Meet me at Piers Beach at eleven." He gestured to my jeans. "You might want to wear a bikini this time, though." A smirk twisted his lips, and I spent a long second fantasizing about how they'd feel against mine. Ash leaned close, his hand warm on my forearm. "I mean we *could* skinny-dip, but there's heaps of ankle-biters here on weekends. Probably best you wear a bikini."

I nodded, my mouth drier than the sand dunes behind us.

Skinny-dipping? I couldn't even…

Don't imagine him nude. Don't imagine him—too late.

My face reddened at the thought. What had I just agreed to?

Ash waved down the beach to the lifesaving station, where another lifie was gesturing for him to return. "Time to head back to the tower of terror," he said. "Seeya Saturday."

He spun on his heel, bare feet crunching in the sand as he strode off. I watched him go, mentally undressing his broad shoulders, slim torso, and well-muscled behind.

After a few metres, he turned and busted me spying. "Hey, I forgot. What's your name?"

"Juliette." I waited for the inevitable Shakespearean reference.

It never came.

"Juls," he said simply, with a nod of confirmation. "I like it. Suits you. Saturday." He clicked his index finger and thumb together. "Don't be late. I'm gonna teach you how to ride the wave."

And he did. I just never expected to be dumped by it so cruelly.

CHAPTER 4

I don't know how I see death coming, or where or when the tragedies that crowd my skull will happen in real life; sometimes they don't, and I long for those dreams that don't come true, dreams I can believe are only your garden-variety nightmare, although I can never really be sure they didn't happen somewhere else either. Maybe I hadn't watched the news closely enough that week.

The very first time, Mum thought it was just a bad dream.

I'd woken up screaming for Dad. As was always the case, Mum came; Dad was unreliable like that.

"What's wrong, *paidi mou?*"

Dad was more Aussie than a meat pie, but Mum was from Melbourne, Australia's cultural melting pot. She'd spoken English since she was a kid, peppered liberally with Greek.

I curled myself around her like a vine, my mauve-and-green-striped cotton pyjamas wet at the collar with sweat. "Tell Daddy not to go," I sobbed.

"Shhhh." Mum patted my damp back. "Listen to that snoring. He's not going anywhere except the Land of Nod."

"No! Tell him not to go."

"Oh, *koritsi mou.*" Mum stifled a laugh. "Land of Nod just means sleep. *Hypnos.* It's make-believe. He's just asleep." She lifted my clinging weight up off the bed. "Come on."

In their bedroom, my six-foot father was curled around a pillow, partly covered by a blue doona and snoring fit to burst.

Dad snorted, sat up, and kicked off the covers as soon as the wedge of light from the open door hit the bed. "What's all the racket? For Pete's sake, I'm trying to sleep here."

I flung myself at him, clinging to him like a koala joey.

"What's up, baby doll?" he muttered.

"Don't go," I sobbed. "Don't leave."

"Hey, I'm not going anywhere." Dad ruffled my hair. "It was only a nightmare." His voice was scratchy, crumpled with sleep.

"What about the debt?" I asked through trembling lips, stumbling over the word.

Mum shook her head and re-plumped her pillow. "*Ai ai ai.* Where did you hear that word? No worrying about adult things, *entaksi?* Okay? We're not in debt. *Ola kala.* It's all good."

I started to sob again. "But I saw him leave. It was the debt. I heard you yelling it."

"A nightmare," Dad insisted. He turned to Mum. "For Chrissake, Ada, take her back to bed. I've got to get up early, yanno." He rolled over and shut us out. It wasn't the first time.

Dad left within months. Turns out, he'd racked up more than twenty grand of gambling debt on three credit cards Mum hadn't known about, not to mention borrowing money from other shady characters to try to pay back the cards. Mum only found out when a debt collector came around to break one of Dad's legs with a baseball bat.

Dad left. We sold the house, and Mum and I moved to Willow Bay.

They tried to reunite again once after that, when I was six. It lasted sixteen months before Dad shot through, vanishing into the blue one day. "Gone to Queensland," like all the characters who departed Ramsay Street did on *Neighbours.*

I got a birthday card made out to "My beloved Juls" the following year and fifty bucks in a princess card for "Baby doll" the next, and then he joined the ranks of deadbeat dads, or maybe that should be "live beats." He was still alive, as far as I knew. But in any case, he'd abandoned us, and I couldn't blame him. Who'd want to stay with a freaky kid who dreamed shit that got you in trouble and kept a running list of tragedies in her head? I guess he blamed me for Mum finding out. Most days, I blamed myself.

I hoped the shark dream I'd had on the beach was one of those nightmares I never saw on the news or in the papers. Only a few had been like that, like the recurring dream I called the "Hanged Man"—a dark, unrecognisable figure swinging from a rope in a shed doorway, backlit by the sun.

The surfer in the dream had been out too far for me to recognise, the dream too dark around the edges. Maybe it was a tourist passing through, rather than a local from Willow Bay or Figtree. Maybe it wasn't even in Australia. Maybe Hawaii or perhaps Bali. Yet although I couldn't make out a face, whenever I shut my eyes, I saw the movement of the board, the hair tied back, the bloodied teeth.

It came again that night, still overwhelmingly real. Blood in the water, the beast thrashing—not a great white, but a bull shark that appeared out of nowhere. It had the effect of increasing my nervousness about Saturday's surfing lesson.

The next morning, I rang the surf lifesaving club anonymously. If they shut the beach, I might get out of this surf-date thing with Ash Gordon. My entire body tingled at the thought of seeing him again, but the idea of him watching me try to surf was cringe-inducing.

"What's that, love? A shark? Saw one, did you?" Phil Cochrane, the club manager, asked down the line.

I cleared my throat and mumbled, "Sort of. On Piers Beach yesterday. Maybe you want to shut the beach for a coupla days."

"No need. Seen a few about lately. But those fellas tend to mosey on pretty quickly. Coupla shoals been coming in shallow, looking for a feed, then they'll be on their way. I'll tell the lads to keep a lookout."

"Thanks."

"Cheers for calling it in. Better to be safe than sorry."

They didn't shut the beach, but nor had the dream come true. Not that day, not the next.

Perhaps it wouldn't. I hoped it wouldn't.

Looking back on it, it makes me wonder why, if I'd seen Dad leave, and the shark, and the Hanged Man and all the other things, I hadn't seen the one cataclysmic thing that was coming for me.

The thing that would rock me.

The thing that would wreck me. Ruin me.

The thing that would send me under.

Through all the other dreams, it had been there, waiting to happen. And all the while, I'd been blissfully oblivious.

CHAPTER 5

Shrieks form a terrible choir in my head. Young and high-pitched, they're cut with the grind of metal, the screech of brakes. Sparks jump from the corkscrewing road like firecrackers. The bitumen twists around a signposted curve that could be anywhere along the coast high road from Willow Bay to Anchorage or beyond.

Nothing is familiar, only that unstoppable slow motion that comes as the white bus launches itself toward the drop. Robbed of its velocity, it careens up on two fat wheels. It pauses against the backdrop of forest, the way a roo might before blinding headlights. It teeters there a moment, then shudders and plummets. Rattles add to the din. Splicing metal rents the air.

The screamers tumble with it, dragging their shrieks behind them until the crashing swallows them.

A small blond boy, a Lightning McQueen backpack with the initials HJ scrawled on it in permanent marker, tumbles head over feet, screaming, face smashing against the smeared, cracked glass. Revolutions of green, red. Branches. Blood. The pale flash of faces contorted with fear.

Twisted metal shears off the white arms of ghost gums, bones and branches snapping like twigs. Kids—just little kids—bleeding, breaking, dying. The cacophony becomes a whimper. The whine of the still-functional, upturned engine an accusation. Smoke and sweat and diesel fill my nostrils, but the backpack still clings to the boy's body, its racing red colour turned burgundy with his blood. And there, on a glitter of windscreen glass, the driver's severed head eyeballs me accusingly. A mop of grey hair above lifeless blue eyes stretched wide, as if jolted from sleep.

"Look away!" screams my brain. But I cannot. My eyes are closed.

I wake up howling, sheets squeezing my torso like a fist, and my pillow drenched with tears.

CHAPTER 6

"Hey, Juls, wait up?" Ash's low, melodic voice sent a pulse of anticipation down my spine.

"Oh my glob," Jaz whispered, flinging her school bag over her shoulder. "Ash Gordon just called out to you."

Not wanting to look too eager, I numbly followed her to the bus queue, trying to heft my backpack onto my shoulders.

"Hey, if it isn't Little Miss Simple Perfection," Ash teased. He pushed through the line with a "'Scuse me," ignoring the grumble of a guy behind us, and followed it with "*Oomph!*" as my bag slid off my shoulder and whacked him in the chest.

"What've you got in here?" he said, easily taking the bag from me. "Rocks?" The weight of it made his biceps bulge, and I could barely tear my eyes from his arms as he ushered Jaz and me onto the bus.

"Books, right?" He winked.

I nodded.

"Thought so. Mum's got some poor sap on detention, so she's staying late, which means I'm catching the bus today. Plus, I wanted to ask you something."

The line of students behind pushed us forward, and he bounded up the steps after me.

"Your mum's a teacher?" I finally found my voice.

"Not here. At Figtree Heads. She'd have me on detention all the time if she knew what I got up to here."

Jaz turned, eyebrows raised, but I threw her a *Don't you dare say a word* look and prodded her in the back to hurry her down the aisle. She plonked her bag under a seat and slid in next to Lisa Rubin, leaving our usual seat free for me to take the window and Ash to settle next to me in the aisle. He set my bag down, kicked his Billabong backpack beneath the seat in front, and casually laid one arm over the seat, his fingers dangling near my shoulder.

"So, you amped for tomorrow?"

Amped?

Jaz tittered behind me.

"I guess so. If by amped you mean nervous."

"There's nothing to be nervous about."

Maybe not for Ash, but there was plenty for me to be concerned about. Getting on a bus today was enough to make my synapses snap. The only thing I knew for sure about last night's dream was that kids were involved, like it was a school bus or something. I glanced around anxiously. It was all high-schoolers on this one, no primary school kids, but as the hydraulic doors shut, burping a *whoosh* of warm air, my chest tightened with sudden, claustrophobic panic.

Swallowing the metallic taste in my mouth, I focussed on the back of the driver's head. It was a woman, her brown ponytail tied with an orange elastic. The dream flashed into my mind again. The male driver's watery blue eyes accusing me. The boy's backpack. I rubbed my temple with one thumb and closed my eyes for a second, willing it to stop. *Dammit. Why can't I make them stop!*

"Nervous? She's shitting herself," Lisa whispered to Jaz behind me.

I opened my eyes to Ash's worried stare.

"Still worried about sharks?" He leaned closer and murmured, "Because we won't be going that deep. Not our first time."

I exhaled, realising I'd been holding my breath. *First time…?* Why did everything he say make me tingle in strange places?

He wasn't to know about the dream, or how much it terrified me. "No. Not sharks," I lied. "Drowning. Or totally sucking at surfing." I waved offhandedly. "Or wearing a bikini."

Ash gave a low chuckle and patted my shoulder. "Everyone sucks their first time," he drawled.

It had to be deliberate, that magnetic gaze, and the low, slow manner that made everything sound like filthy innuendo.

His words were followed by another giggle from Jaz and Lisa.

"Plus"—he flipped my braid back over the seat—"I'm sure you'll look incredible in a bikini."

"Smooth," Jaz muttered.

My stomach somersaulted. Was that what this was—just a flirtation?

Of all the girls Ash Gordon could have chosen to teach to surf, I had no idea why he'd picked me. I could hardly even look at him;

yet all that week at school, wherever I'd gone, Ash had been right around the corner, watching me with those winking, teal-turquoise, frustratingly changeable eyes. And when pinned by a stare from them, I discovered I had no chance of looking away. Absolutely no chance.

When we'd first entered senior high, Jaz's older sister, Zara, had warned us about a group of boys calling themselves the V-team. Their mission was to deflower junior girls and brag about it, even keeping a tally. Jaz and I had laughed about it, considering it total bullshit at the time. As if!

But during break period two days ago, when I'd told Jaz about meeting Ash, my bestie's generous mouth had set in a tight little line. We were sitting under a tree near the basketball courts, eating our lunch, and my attention was constantly wandering to the far end of the courts, where Ash and his friends were playing HORSE. I'd little choice but to confess. It was hard to hide that something was up with me.

"Ash? Ash Gordon? THE Ash Gordon?" Jaz gestured in his direction, clearly unconvinced. "I leave you alone for one hour on the beach, and this is what happens?"

I nodded, fixated as Ash smoothed his tawny hair back, trying to trap it in a ponytail. It wasn't quite long enough, and he dropped it, easily catching the basketball Troy Pearson had attempted to hurl at his head while he was distracted, before tossing it neatly into the net.

I could feel Jaz's eyes boring a hole into my profile as she watched me ogle him.

"Hey!" Jaz poked me in the ribs and sniffed the air. "Do you smell smoke?"

"Huh?" I spun to look around us.

"Because I think your bush just burst into flames." She mimed spraying a fire extinguisher at my crotch. "You need an evacuation plan, Juls. Fast."

"Hilarious." I rolled my eyes. "I've barely even spoken to him. He was nice, but—"

"*Nice*," she mimicked, flipping one long golden curl over her shoulder. "Lisa Rubin is nice. Ice cream is nice. Ash Gordon is not nice. He's hotter than a Queensland summer, but that boy is not nice, Juls. First, he's shagged half of Willow Bay, probably all of Figtree, and a quarter of Anchorage. You see where I'm going with this? I mean he's gawkworthy, sure. Those eyes—hello! But get a load of him." She pointed to the end of the court, where Ash was dribbling past a simpering group of juniors. With the balance and grace of a surfer, he launched himself into the air, shoulders rippling with cords of muscle as he grabbed the ring and slam-dunked before dropping down on lean, brown quads.

"See?" Jaz said. "He's a total poser. Anyway, last I heard, he was dating Renee Aldershot. That's the kind of chick he goes for—bimbos with bolt-ons."

"Bolt-ons?" I watched his cheer-squad on the sidelines. All blonde. All giggling. All stacked.

"Zara told me Renee's mum took her to Phuket to get her girls done. That's why she hasn't been in school the last few weeks. Probably needed to have her nipples sewn back on."

I groaned. "Jaz, what on earth are you on about?"

"Renee's boobs!" she muttered. "How else do you think they got so huge?"

I looked down at my barely there chest. I couldn't imagine getting plastic surgery to remedy it, but the Fantastics were a different breed. It was possible, I supposed, but knowing Jaz, it was probably just gossip.

"Like you can talk." I indicated the buttons straining the front of her white school blouse.

"One hundred percent natural Willow Bay Dairy," she said proudly, poking them out more. "Anyway, he'll be graduating in a few months. Don't go getting clit tingles over a guy who's only going to move to Sydney for work or uni by the year's end." She cocked her head, watching him. "Although, if he's dating Renee Aldershot, he's clearly dumber than a bag of hammers, so I suppose that rules out uni."

Jaz had a tendency to nudge the great Aussie tradition of "putting shit on people" well into bitchy territory.

Ash's mates were fist-bumping him, teasing Drew Kendall, who'd managed to miss enough shots to turn him into a HOR.

"Nothing but wax between their ears and sand between their bum cheeks," Jaz muttered, but even she seemed particularly interested in the bum cheeks.

"Wax?"

"Mr. Zog's Sex Wax." Jaz tapped her forehead. "Or Mrs. Palmers. He could have Madame Tussauds' entire waxworks up there, but I bet you ten bucks nothing is going on up top."

My gaze moved to Ash's chiselled jaw, loitered over his lips, and then focussed on his biceps again as he raised his arms and took another shot. *Sex wax?* I had no idea what that was for, but Jaz was wrong; there was plenty going on up top. Time would tell about the brains department, but I couldn't fault his brawn.

He gave a *woot* as the ball sailed through the ring, barely touching the net, and the junior girls on the sidelines clapped and whistled adoringly.

Maybe he has slept with half of Sunshine Shire.

"He's only teaching me to surf," I muttered.

"In one session? Even body-boarding is harder than it looks," Jaz reminded me.

"You didn't exactly make it look easy," I teased. "Ash told me he'd teach me how to 'ride the wave.'" I made air quotes with my fingers.

Jaz waved a hand at me dismissively. "What kind of pervy line is that? He's probably the head member of the V-team, trying to get into your knickers."

I sniffed. "You're just jealous. And who are you to talk about surf wax anyway? If you hadn't dragged me to the beach to fangirl all over Dylan, I wouldn't have met Ash, who, by the way, happens to be Dylan's bestie."

As usual Jaz ignored any suggestion of hypocrisy. "Dylan's not just a surfer. He made heats for Rip Curl Pro. Wait—" She pinched the thin skin of my upper arm. "Ash is Dylan's BFF?"

I tugged my arm away, scowling. "Yep! While you were trying to get yourself drowned out there, I was discovering they've been buddies since they were kids."

"Body-boarding," Jaz sniffed. "It's called body-boarding." Her nails dug into my arm again. "We could double-date—" The peal of the bell cut her off. "If Ash wasn't already dating Renee Aldershot," she added snarkily, tossing the foil wrapper of her sandwich into the nearby rubbish bin with far less skill than we'd been admiring in Ash.

The blonde beach babe from the other day had sidled up to him, her shortened uniform skirt hitched up slim thighs. She wasn't Renee, but it was obvious Ash knew her pretty well.

I bet she has thigh gap. I immediately retracted the thought. Thigh gap was a myth, everyone knew that.

Body confidence, Juls. Body confidence. It was a term I'd pinned onto a cork 'vision board' in my room, along with a photo of Victoria's Secret model Miranda Kerr, when I'd turned fourteen. It was still there, plastered over with study timetables, authors' interviews, and photos of Jaz and me making daggy faces.

Over at the courts, Ash's friend Troy was exploring a girl's throat with his tongue, in direct contravention of Willow Bay High School's "No Kissing" policy. It didn't bode well.

Jaz slid a pale arm around my shoulders. "You got it bad, girl. Don't make me call the Bush Fire Brigade."

"Hardy-har-har."

"I'm serious. Life's not a romance novel, okay? I don't want you to get hurt. And anyway, do you even own a bikini?"

I shook my head. "No. I don't even own a bikini."

She was right, life wasn't a romance novel, but sometimes I wanted it to be.

Jaz's warning returned to me as I sat on the school bus, conscious of Ash's firm, tanned thigh rubbing against mine as the vehicle jolted down the coast road. I wanted to know whether he was dating Renee Aldershot, but it was much too soon to ask. It was only a surfing lesson, after all. My gut told me Jaz was wrong and maybe they'd broken up. But my gut had been wrong on more than one occasion. So had my brain. Even the *mati* wasn't infallible. Maybe he was a member of the V-team. There had been that line about skinny-dipping; kind of risqué coming from a guy I'd talked to for all of five minutes. Did he just want to take advantage of me?

An embarrassed twinge tugged at my nether regions at the thought that Ash Gordon might want to get naked and do wicked things to me. I was sixteen and three quarters, after all. Sweet sixteen and never been... surfing.

Maybe I wouldn't mind an experienced guy being my first anyway, I told myself, watching Ash out of the corner of my eye and pondering his rank in the V-team. It was a secret only Jaz knew, but I hadn't even been properly kissed yet, unless you counted the briefest smack on the lips in grade seven from a boy I didn't even fancy. And I didn't.

"How many other girls have you taught to surf?" I asked him, trying to keep my tone casual.

Ash glanced at me sidelong. "Just one."

"Is she any good at it?"

Behind me, a red-haired girl on the opposite side of the bus hissed, "Nope. Got pounded, didn't she, Ash?"

Ash's nostrils flared. "That's what she says." His tone was flat, and he didn't bother turning around.

I peered over my shoulder at the girl, and then threw Jaz a brief WTF glance, but my bestie looked as blank as I did.

"So what do *you* say, Ash?" the girl threw back.

"I say it's none of your business."

After that, we rode most of the way home in silence.

But even if his jaw was tight and his expression clouded, his hand was large and strong and sturdy as he slid it over mine, clutching me like a life buoy.

CHAPTER 7

"Jazzzzy!" I was sure the entire Wet 'n' Wild swimsuit shop could hear me, including the gaggle of Fantastics near the change rooms. They'd stared at us as we entered, as if we were nuns walking into an adult toy store. But whatever. Even before I saw them talking behind their perfectly manicured hands, I was having serious second thoughts about a bikini.

"What's wrong with this one?" Jaz groaned from the other side of the curtain.

"Nothing much... if I want to look like a Victoria's Secret model. What is up with all this padding?" I prodded the foam underside of the hot-pink cup with my index finger. "I'll drown for sure if I put all of this in the water."

"Victoria's Secret model is totally the look you want," Jaz insisted. "It's hot out there. You wanna look hot? Or you wanna look like you've never been in the surf before in your life?"

"I'm not wearing this one, that's for sure. Get me something black. What about one of those one-pieces with the strip down the middle?"

Jaz's disdain nearly seared right through the curtain. "So *not* going to happen. Here." She flung a skimpy black two-piece through the gap in the curtain, and I contorted myself into it.

Better. But it was still metres less fabric than I was used to wearing.

I pulled a pose in front of the mirror. How did girls who actually had curves stop their bosom from tumbling out of these things? The thought made my guts tighten. *Why am I even doing this?*

"Jaz, you might have to come in and tie up the back. Are you sure I can't wear a one-piece?"

Jaz flung the curtain open immediately, as if she'd been hovering there the whole time, waiting for the go ahead, which she had.

"See!" She grinned. "Apart from that." She waved a hand vaguely in the direction of my bikini line. "It's perfect. I should so be your personal shopper."

She kind of was anyway. That's what came from having a bossy bestie.

"I don't know." I jiggled on the spot. "I'm a bit worried my girls might fall out."

Jaz raised an eyebrow.

"I think you're safe," one of the nearby Fantastics said acidly.

"Hey!" Jaz stuck her head out of the curtain. "Give it a rest, will ya?"

"Saw her talking to Ash Gordon," the girl replied. "Better watch out."

"Watch out for what?" Jaz hissed.

The girl sighed loudly. "You *really* don't have a clue, do you?"

I had a clue that they were determined to sabotage this date with Ash no matter what, but I ignored them. If I could ignore the news and my own weirdness, I figured I could ignore a few snarly Fantastics.

Jaz sniffed loudly and muttered "bitch" under her breath, and then turned to me and pulled the stings so tight I thought they'd carve a groove into my spine.

"Suck it up, princess," she said when I winced. "You'll be fine. Look at you." She gestured to the floor-length mirror. "You look like a proper surfie chick. All you need is a Brazilian and maybe a little eyebrow waxing." She cocked her head, squinting her hazel eyes as she assessed me. "Your mum's salon does bikini waxes, right?"

"No chance!"

With the money left over from the sale of our house, after she'd paid out Dad's debts, Mum had opened her own salon in Willow Bay. Cut 'n' Run wasn't the best name, but I suppose it said something about what Dad had done.

The business had been a great success, but there was no way I was going in there today to get my lady garden horticultured for my first date with Ash Gordon, if you could call it that. Mum would be on that in a flash. It was hard to keep anything secret in Willow Bay, and the Cut 'n' Run was the town's most productive gossip factory.

"So that's a no?" Jaz pushed.

"Definitely no Brazilian."

"Eyebrows?" Jaz licked her finger and slicked down her arched, golden brows.

"Nup." I drew my bushy caterpillars into a frown.

"Fine! The bikini?"

I squinted at my reflection in the mirror. I looked all arms and legs, too thin and not quite tall enough to make the look work. But I had to admit the bikini provided the illusion of curves.

"Okay. The bikini." I pushed Jaz back out through the curtain.

I turned side-on again. Maybe my boobs were starting to come in. I flipped to the other side.

Nope.

Body confidence, Juls.

CHAPTER 8

Freshly showered and shaven, and wearing a pair of denim cut-offs and a yellow tank top with my new bikini underneath, I arrived at the beach with Jaz sashaying along behind me for moral support.

Bronzed bodies stretched out as far as the eye could see, and surfers and body-boarders bobbed on the waves.

"Stinkin' hot." Jaz panted, glancing around to find a towel-free patch of sand somewhere between the flags.

A trickle of sweat licked the back of my neck as I scanned the waves for Ash. He was already in the water, waiting out the back, focussed on the swell. He flicked a flag of wet hair from his face and eased himself down on the board, waiting for the wave.

"Are you bushfire ready?" Jaz smirked, following my gaze.

I watched as he started paddling, then he leapt easily onto his feet, seamlessly manoeuvring the board onto the crest of a wave. Even if he hadn't been the hottest guy in Willow Bay, his fluid movements would have been a beautiful sight. He wasn't the first guy I'd seen with his shirt off; although I hardly ever visited the beach, Willow Bay teemed with handsome surfers and lifesavers most of the year. But he was the first half-naked guy who'd given me full-body flushes in public.

"Christ, you're burning up," Jaz laughed. "Stop, drop, and roll, Juls. I bet he's got quite a fire hose."

I ignored her, watching Ash ride the wave close to the shore. He jumped off his board into the wash, looked up grinning, and waved. A leather cuff ringed one thick wrist, and a silver shell on a black strap around his neck swung when he flicked his hair again.

I lifted my arm to wave back, but my nerves hijacked it, turning it into a strange little palm sweep.

"Nice one, Queen Elizabeth," Jaz snorted. "Come on. Let's go put your fire out." She towed me toward the surf.

Ash was already hitching up his board shorts and striding toward us, bronzed as a statue, moving with the lean, loping grace of an athlete. Years of surfing had given his abs corrugations that would make a tin shed envious. The way he moved so effortlessly, even with a board under one arm, I imagined his bones must be as white and light as driftwood. Despite the day's heat, the strange thought made me shudder—or maybe it was just the sight of him, sending an urgent tremor to my core. I imagined trailing my hand down those ridged abs to the sexy V-shaped hollow that drew my gaze down to his—

Jaz cleared her throat and thrust me forward with a shove to the lower back, forcing me to snap my head up to avoid falling over. I was certain my nipples were saluting him from beneath my tank top, and it made me blush so scarlet that anyone who didn't know better would've thought I was a sunburned Pommy tourist.

"You came!" His grin spread wider as we approached. "Wasn't sure you would." Standing the surfboard up in the sand, he added, "Not after that convo on the bus. Sorry, I kind of..." A shrug of apology followed the trailing words. "Zoned out."

What was that supposed to mean? My paranoid brain flopped around like a stingray thrust unexpectedly up on land. I wanted to ask him what the girl on the bus had meant, but I was worried I'd get the same answer: none of your business.

He was right, of course. It was none of her business, and it was certainly none of mine. What Ash Gordon did was of no concern to me. Absolutely none. Nada. Zip. Zilch. None at all. I was here under duress to learn to surf or to see a dolphin or something.

So why can't I take my eyes off him?

"O-Of course." I gestured to the water. "Who wouldn't want to get close to a sea man... mam... Sea mammal. Dolphin. Learn to surf," I stammered, wondering what the hell had happened to my vocal cords. *Seaman? Was I serious?*

His ocean-coloured eyes trapped mine momentarily, opening wider as they skimmed my outfit. An involuntary nod of approval made his curls flick again, the droplets flung from them onto my T-shirt doing nothing to help hide my high-beam.

"What're you waiting for?" Ash put out his hand for mine and added in a husky voice, "Giddy-up."

"Just like that?"

Jaz nudged me again, as if reminding me to stop narrowing my eyes suspiciously and take his hand. *You heard the man. Giddy-up,* warned her expression.

Ash tucked the board back under his arm and grasped my hand. It was no furtive action this time. Ash Gordon was holding my hand. In public. In broad daylight. And I was naked. Well, semi-naked. It felt naked anyway in this outfit, and I wasn't even in just a bikini yet. My nipples stood to attention again beneath the Lycra.

Stop it! I willed them as I stared at beads of water sliding down his broad back. After a few steps, he turned, catching me totally off guard.

"I'm messin' with ya." He laughed, a deep, throaty, infectious sound. "First we're going to try it on land." He let go my hand to gesture to my shorts and tank top. "You going to surf in that?"

"No." I swallowed. *Der, Juls.* I'd only been here a few minutes, and Ash had already rendered me mute, dumb, and very, very dizzy.

The look on Jaz's face as I dropped my bag on the sand next to where she was setting up her towel suggested she planned to thoroughly enjoy the hilarity to follow.

Facing the dunes, I slipped my shirt up over my head and gave my bikini bra a swift tug. The last thing I needed was a "wardrobe malfunction." I was still trying to live down the first episode on the beach. I did not need nipplegate in the surf. The breeze on my skin made me shiver, or maybe it was Ash's stare burning a hole in my back.

"And the rest." Jaz indicated my shorts.

Oh boy, he better be worth this. The slow fever spreading over my near-naked body suggested parts of me definitely thought he was. When I spun around again, his expression was neutral, but his eyes had darkened and the tip of his tongue wet the corner of his lips.

"Sunscreen?" His gaze swept over every inch of my body so slowly that every blink burned like a laser stroke.

"I… ah… I… forgot it."

"You don't come to the beach real often, do you, Juls?"

I shook my head.

"Explains why I haven't noticed you around much."

To be honest, that was almost how I liked it. If people didn't notice me, they wouldn't notice anything odd about me either. Like how I looked around for danger, scouting for death on every street corner. How I sometimes scrutinised strangers as if I remembered them from someplace. When it got really bad, I was constantly flipping through a catalogue of dreams, searching for a time, a place, a face. Just in case.

"Nice tan anyway." Ash gestured toward my brown torso. "You got a pool at home, or do you just never wear sunscreen?"

"Greek mum." I smiled, glad for the change of subject. "I don't have to work real hard for it."

He jabbed a thumb down the beach to the Fantastics already oiled and turning themselves over, rotisserie-style, on beach towels. "Good genes. You're lucky," he said. "I considered wearing zinc cream. Not hella sexy, but better than skin cancer." Freckles danced across the bridge of his upturned nose when it crinkled.

As if Ash Gordon needed to worry about being sexy!

Fumbling in the pocket of his boardies, he produced a small tube of 50+ sunscreen. "Want me to put some on?"

I nodded, and an uncomfortable pause hung between us as I imagined his hands smoothing slippery white goo over me.

He popped the cap and took my hand again. "You do your noggin. I'll do your back side."

My back side? Or my backside? I shivered, imagining his hands moulding themselves to the curves of my behind, and a flush crept over my chest like an allergic reaction.

Ash laughed at my embarrassment and spun me around, forcing me to curl my toes into the sand, seeking a foothold that might force the giddy out of me. I shot Jaz an accusatory glare. *Why didn't we put sunscreen on at home?*

My body's instinctive reaction to the first generous glob was goose bumps. Then the sensation of warm fingertips stroking my skin made me glad I hadn't bothered to bring sunblock.

Ash smoothed the cream in with firm, gliding waves that made every nerve in my body crawl to the surface, as if he could control them and me like some sexy puppet master. At my lower back, he stopped, clearly not daring to venture below my bikini bottoms, before walking his fingers up to the nape of my neck and tugging cheekily on my earlobe. "Slip, slop, slap," he reminded me.

"Thanks." I stepped away, a mess of grease and goose bumps.

"Right. Let's do it!" His tone was enthusiastic as he slapped his hands together, but something else gleamed in the depths of his eyes, something darker, wetter. Something dangerous even. Something

that made me think it wasn't a mistake he'd phrased it that way—
Let's do it!

Every time Ash Gordon touched me, I was reminded that even if I was cautious, I desperately wanted to "do it." Not learning to surf either. Something darker, wetter. Something dangerous even.

Pull yourself together, Juls.

With his trademark lopsided smile, Ash flipped the tube of sunscreen at me. "Catch!"

I fumbled, but snatched it up before it hit the sand.

"For your face," he said. "And your... backside." He gestured to my bum, winked, and then turned and strode casually to the water's edge as if he hadn't just run his hands over most of my body.

"Let's do it," I mumbled weakly, smearing sunscreen across my face and over my thighs before following him down to the water.

Ash set the board on the sand a few metres back from the waves. "First things first. Surfing is all about balance, timing, and instinct."

The unflinching stare he gave me was definitely all about instinct. I swung my eyes back to the board to hide how rattled I was.

"You have to learn the ocean, feel the wave, respect its power, and then you need to know when to get on top." He patted the board.

Had his eyebrow inched a little higher when he said that, or was it just me?

Ash slid onto the board, his abs flat against the fibreglass, strong brown arms out to the side. Sun-bleached hair kissed his shoulders, and his biceps swelled as he stretched up to bear his weight on his arms.

"Palms here," he instructed. "Up near the chest. Then... up." He jumped easily into a crouch, arms out, like it was the most natural thing in the world. "You try."

"Try that?"

"Yeah, why not?"

It looked impossible, and that was on the sand. I bit my lip, eyeing the board for a long minute.

Please don't let my bikini bottom ride up, I prayed as I slithered over onto it. The fiberglass felt hard and cool beneath me, and my skin tingled when it touched the waxy, wet places Ash's body had been.

He pressed his hands over mine, positioning them on either side. "Hands on the rails. Now, it won't be flat like this out there, but you need to practice how to paddle."

"You want me to paddle on the sand?"

His eyes sparkled with amusement. "Practice makes perfect. You should know that." He took my left hand, dragging it back and forth as he explained. "Long, slow, powerful strokes. Then I'll pop up again."

Pop up. Was that a double entendre too?

"W-What?" I pushed back up, letting my arms bear my bodyweight, and stared at him.

"Popping up—jumping up onto your feet," Ash explained with a laugh. "I'll show you again once you get the paddling right. It takes some practice, but muscle memory will make it easier out there. Push up with your hands, then flick your hips up behind you and tuck your feet underneath your body. You might want to get on your knees first."

Get on your knees! He had to know what he was doing. Biting my lip and concentrating on containing the lava seeping through my veins, I lay back down and attempted paddling.

When it came time to "pop up," my first effort left me sprawled in the sand. The second time, Ash swept me up as I teetered backwards. We did it again and again, popping up time after time until I was sure my knees were too bruised to try the real thing anyway.

Ash never laughed, not once, although his grin was a permanent fixture, almost as permanent as my arse indenting the sand. It was ages before he finally suggested it was time to try it in the water.

"I don't know," I stammered. "Maybe I need more practice."

His tone was low, reassuring, his grip firm as he took my hand and helped me to my feet. "I'm right here," he insisted. "I've got you. I'm a surf lifesaver remember? How bad can it be?"

41

CHAPTER 9

Bad. Worse than bad.

I struggled to stay on the board on my stomach, let alone paddle furiously to catch a wave before the white-water hit, then push up and haul my skimpily clad body upright. Even with Ash holding the board and giving it a big thrust to get me onto a wave, I was hopeless.

"Try moving your hands down a little. And keep them flat while you pop up. He repositioned my left hand, the physical contact between us sizzling like baking sun on bare skin.

Damn. Maybe I'd be better at this if you weren't so distracting.

"When a wave comes, press down on the nose like this, to duck dive." He spun the board, plunging us both beneath a bomb wave that was about to crest, before emerging to a less daunting set. "Again." Ash helped reposition me on the board, and my bikini top suddenly felt too flimsy.

"Don't look down," he cautioned, as I tried to readjust the straps. "Watch the wave. When you're ready to catch it, pop up and stare straight ahead. Trust me." He held the board steady. "I won't stare if your top falls off." He tugged the knot tighter at the back of the bikini. "Every other guy on the beach'll stare," he joked. "Can't blame them. But I won't look. I'm a gentleman. Promise."

After Renee's surgically enhanced rack, I supposed there wasn't much to see when it came to mine.

"I mean it," he murmured, patting my shoulder. "If you're gonna feel it, really feel it, you have to relax a little." His thumb kneaded the base of my neck again.

I flinched. *I'm already feeling it, believe me.*

"Dive." Ash pushed the board under another wave.

I surfaced, spluttering, to find him watching me with his head tilted, a curious smile on his face.

"You don't trust easily, do you?" Something sad lingered in his tone.

I shook my head, sending bright droplets of water sparkling in the air between us. "You could say that."

"Too soon to ask why?"

Unable to answer that question honestly, I shrugged.

Daddy issues.

Because everyone tells me you've slept with every girl this side of Sydney.

Because you've probably got a girlfriend.

Because you're you, and I'm me.

But mostly because if I told you the truth about me, you'd think I was a total nutter.

I certainly wasn't going to get into any of that deep-seated shit today.

Ash swam closer to help me back on the board. His breath was hot in my ear as he whispered, "You flinch every time I touch you, but I think you're deeper than the water is. Deep enough to really sink into, if you'll let me dive in that far."

I especially wasn't going to tell him his touch did something unfathomable to me, or that the intent way he stared at me sent a tsunami straight through my central nervous system.

"I've never surfed before," I muttered. "I don't usually wear a bikini. And I'm not a great swimmer..."

"So you're not a great swimmer." He shrugged, and then laughed and tweaked my bikini strap. "One more reason to stop falling off."

"Right."

"When you pop up, use your quads." He tapped my thigh, the heat of his touch making me clench.

"Relax. Use those pins. Don't just push up with your arms."

Triceps aching, I once more tried to launch myself vertical without my girls tumbling out. I failed. They stayed in, but I didn't get anywhere near vertical. I slipped off the board into the surf as a huge pounder crashed over me. Saltwater filled my nostrils before Ash gripped my wrist and hauled me to the surface, still spluttering.

"I saved your life." He smiled. "And you still don't trust me."

A second unexpected wave swept us both off our feet and made me shriek. Strong hands encircled my waist, pulling me up to bright air, and Ash's streaming, smiling face was just centimetres from my own.

"Juls, trust me. I'm not going to let you get hurt," he murmured, his voice huskier than usual, the tone lower. "Let go a little."

I stared into the gradient blue of his eyes, boundless as the Pacific, but warmer, less cruel, and I wanted to. I wanted to let go—of everything.

His hands tightened on my waist, and his voice grew wistful. "That's the great thing about being out here. You can lose yourself. Forget everything but the swell."

If he only knew how intoxicating that thought was for someone like me: someone who remembered. It was as maddening as his firm abs pressed against my stomach or his hands filling the hollow of my back.

"Surfing makes you stay in the moment." Ash licked saltwater off his lips, his eyes, still fixed on mine, becoming hooded. He bent his head, and for a dizzying moment, I thought he was going to lean in and kiss me. I didn't know what *that* moment looked like in real life, and I certainly didn't know what it felt like. But I knew what I'd read about and seen in movies. And until a third wave slapped against our faces and made us both cough water, I was pretty certain we'd been about to share one of those fabled "first kiss" moments. Maybe.

Ash let me go, laughing, and shoved wet hair off his forehead. "Maybe we shouldn't get so caught up in the moment that we both end up eating ocean." He laughed and gestured to the board. "Wanna try again?"

I wondered if he meant the surfing or the potential kissing, regretting that the moment for my first kiss seemed to have passed as quickly as that rogue wave.

He patted the board. "You got this. Come on, girl. Trust me."

"Did the other girl trust you?" The words slithered out as soon I thought them, and I groaned inwardly. The water was only waist-deep, but it was clear I was hopelessly out of my depth. *She got pounded*, the girl on the bus had said.

Ash's smile dropped. For a moment, he studied me seriously. "Trust is a two-way street. What matters is I trust that you've got this." He tapped the board again, but his nostrils were still flared.

Trust is a two-way street.

Renee hadn't been to school for weeks. Was she the one nursing a broken heart, or was he? And if I trusted Ash, would I be nursing one of my own soon enough?

Suppressing a sigh, I lay on the board and concentrated on an approaching wave. Sunlight spangled the water as I glanced back and began to paddle. The wave surged beneath me and I pushed off and tried to bounce upright. One leg rose faster than the other, jolting me onto my knees, making me overbalance with a lame little scream.

"Easy, tiger," Ash hauled me out by the armpits. "You're getting the hang of it, but you're not exactly Sally Fitzgibbons yet."

"I'm sorry, who?"

"Women's world title holder, youngest ever winner of the ASP Pro Junior, first person to hold the US and Aus Open titles simultaneously. Even won the Fiji Pro with a perforated eardrum." His voice dropped a register. "And gorgeous. Actually, you kind of remind me of her, except your hair's a lot darker." He studied me for a minute, adding with a wink, "And you're better looking. Now try again."

Better looking! My heart unfurled in my chest until I reminded myself who he was—Ash Gordon, popular, lifie, super-stud. Of course he knew how to charm girls into his arms, and straight into his bed. Vowing not to be that girl, I threw my chin up and set off paddling low and deep, chasing a slow wave. Surprisingly, I caught it, but when I glanced triumphantly back at Ash, the look on his face was of alarm, not pride.

"Look out!" an unfamiliar voice yelled above the crash of the surf.

A surfer who'd been chasing waves to our north had dropped in on my wave. In swerving to avoid me, he'd tumbled off his board, which was streaking toward me, its sharp nose splitting the wave, skeg carving up the water underneath.

I screamed, desperately trying to figure out how to turn as a dark shape bloomed in the water below. Ash shot from the body of the wave, brown arms flashing as he freestyled to shove the runaway board away. It veered left, barely missing me, and Ash duck-dived as the wave ate me and my board in a storm of froth.

"Idiot," Ash spluttered when it spat us both out. "Dropping in *and* not wearing a leash. First rule of surfing, Juls, never drop in."

The surfer windmilled through the water after his board, but it had caught the tail end of the wave, and a much larger set was now torpedoing it toward the jumble of rocks at the base of Point Hanrahan.

"It's gonna hit." Ash swivelled to watch. "He'll be lucky if it doesn't crease or smash to smithereens."

Waves folded into themselves off the point, the rocks beneath churning the water like a washing machine.

"God fucking *damn*!" the surfer snarled, snatching for the board again. He missed. The fiberglass shot away and wedged itself between two outcrops, and an almighty *crack* split the air as the next wave slammed it like a bouncer's fist hitting a drunk patron at Swaggers on a Saturday night.

Ash looked at me and shrugged. "He's gonna be aggro now. Serves him right. Sand for brains."

The surfer had already given up. He flipped us the bird, turning the air as blue as the water as he swam back to shore and marched off up the beach.

Ash tweaked the leg rope that kept his board attached to my ankle. "Second rule of surfing: always wear a leggy." He nodded to the splintered board. "Otherwise, what the sea wants, the sea takes."

CHAPTER 10

"Thanks for sticking around and helping me clean it up." Ash finished his foot-long turkey and salad sub, and wiped his mouth with a napkin.

He and I had spent more than an hour on the beach, waiting for the smashed fibreglass board to wash onto the rocks before carrying the pieces up to Ash's Kombi van. It took so long that Jaz had wandered off to the shops, saying she'd meet us on Bloom Street at two for lunch. On the drive to the rubbish tip to ditch the broken board, Ash regaled me with stories of his childhood, tales of his godfather, his parents, the places he'd travelled to, the surf championships he'd competed in, and how he felt about the ocean. He'd seemed so flippant at school, surrounded by sycophants as I watched from afar, but in person he was different: laid-back, funny, loquacious.

Loquacious, Juls. Really? Not just talkative? Chatty? You had to go for loquacious? I pushed the word from my head. Ash didn't need to know about my word weirdness yet, or any of my other weirdnesses.

He chattered away as he sat opposite Jaz and me in the sandwich shop near Dylan's work.

"So many people dump stuff on the beach," he said. "Does my head in. Once I found this turtle heading in to lay eggs. She'd got her head caught in a plastic six-pack holder that'd grown so tight around her throat she could hardly breath, poor old girl."

He held up the ring finger on his right hand to reveal a pink, crescent-shaped scar near the knuckle. "I nearly lost a finger getting it off her. Got her out, though. Did you know they come back to the same beach where they were born to lay their eggs? Travel the seven seas, come all the way home to give birth..." His words trailed off, almost wistfully I thought, and he shook his head. "It's kind of romantic, I guess."

I was immersed in the changing colours of his eyes, the transformation from stormy grey to vivid blue as his mood swung from angry to passionate to melancholy. The truth was, I found this Ash much sexier than the confident basketball player, the hero lifesaver, or the ripped waxhead. When he was passionate, his entire face was illuminated, and his left dimple was a permanent fixture. An adorable horizontal crease appeared on his brow, and the sexy way he occasionally nibbled at his full bottom lip made me barely able to focus on his words.

Romantic! See, who says there's nothing going on up top now? I felt like telling Jaz, not that I could have, even if I'd wanted to. Between Ash and Jaz, I could barely get a word in edgewise, and the thought sent a twinge of annoyance through my brain. Sometimes, I wished I could be more like my best friend: less concerned with what people thought, easy in any company, a talker, not a listener. She was a sunflower to my wallflower, and although I loved her like a sister, her self-confidence and brashness sometimes did my head in, not to mention her lack of respect for my privacy. I wanted to be alone with Ash, not to have to share him, but I pushed the thought away. *Geez how had I let myself get this besotted already?*

"Except the beaches they lay on are getting destroyed," Ash went on. "Plastic bags, drink bottles, camping gear—people leave that stuff lying around, and it all washes right into the sea." He pushed his hair back over his forehead and trapped it with his sunnies. "As if the oceans don't get enough crap in them with all the sewage councils pump in," he continued.

"Sewage. Eww." Jaz pushed her half-eaten sandwich away. "I'm eating here!"

"Yeah, well, so are they," Ash said. "And we're feeding everything in the ocean a diet of shit and plastic." His left foot tapped, making the table jiggle, inching his carton of iced-coffee slowly toward the edge.

"And the occasional surfer," Jaz joked.

The shark dream flashed into my mind, fiercely burned on my retina. I closed my eyes for a second and then snapped them back open, trying to block out the blood in the water. "Not funny, Jaz."

She shrugged. "Ash laughed."

She was right; he was laughing. I wiped clammy hands on my denim shorts. *Don't think about it.*

"You're not afraid of sharks?" Jaz aked him.

"Sure. Surfers are most at risk," Ash told her. "But we try not to whinge about it. It's the food chain, you know. That's life. *C'est la vie. Que sera sera.*" He took a long chug of his iced coffee.

"First rule of surfing: respect the ocean." He went on. "That's why I reckon this stupid new resort thing is a crap idea. We don't need more people mucking up the beach and insisting on shark nets to protect holidaymakers from a coupla sharks. It'll just——"

"Wait." I put up a palm. The dream still screamed inside my skull, its torment mingled with a sudden, gut-churning guilt. Maybe phoning in that shark sighting after the dream had strengthened the council's resolve to put up nets. If they did, surely my shark dream wouldn't come true. But Ash was against the nets. I didn't know how to feel. I did what I always did when a dream threatened to deflate my mood: I tried to change the subject. "I thought the first rule of surfing was not to drop in."

Ash squinted at me. "All right, smarty-pants. You really were listening out there, huh. Okay, second rule then."

"Nope, second rule is to wear a leggy. Else what the sea wants, the sea——"

"We could organise a petition," Jaz interrupted. "Lobby the council to increase lifeguard hours instead, so you guys can warn tourists, and no one gets hurt."

Ash ignored her. "Okay, the *golden rule* of surfing is respect the ocean and everything in it, but all the council gives a shit about is money and publicity. Willow Bay needs tourists. That's what this resort is all about. If lifies keep closing the beach because of shark sightings, the big-wigs at the council worry tourists will stay away. They'll spend their money at the wineries around Figtree or pearl shops down at Anchorage, rather than here on the espy." He hooked a thumb at the esplanade across the road. "Plus, we're all volunteers. The council would have to pay us to work more hours, and they aren't about to do that."

"What we need is publicity of our own." Jaz's hazel eyes burned with enthusiasm, and she slapped the table for emphasis. "What if Dylan agreed to be the face of a campaign! Something like, "No Hope for Rope?" Her dreamy expression suggested she was imagining Dylan in his birthday suit, his wrists ringed with net.

"Nah. Dyl's not real political. Wouldn't want to jeopardise his sponsorship either. Once you get a good sponsor, you want to keep things positive."

"Publicist extraordinaire," I explained, jabbing a finger at her.

Jaz had decided on that career path at the start of the year, after Mum drove us down to Anchorage to get books signed by Colleen Hoover. Out of everyone, the bubbly young publicist was the one having as much fun as the author and fans. Drinking champagne and babysitting authors sounded perfect to Jaz, and pretty good to me too, although I doubted I'd be chatty enough for that gig. I was also sure there was more to the job than Jaz thought there was, but she nevertheless had set her sights on a career in publicity.

I had no idea what I wanted to do once I finished school. Mum thought I should see a guidance counsellor to try to find some direction. Maybe she hoped I'd study business and take over running the salon, but I wanted a life, not just a job. I wanted to do something I loved, something I was passionate about. I figured the right thing would come to me eventually.

I'd considered journalism, like Auntie Penny. The trouble was, in a newsroom I'd be first to see the news. When I was about eleven, and plenty of nightmares had already revealed themselves as true, I'd gone through a phase of vigilantly checking current affairs. Mum had to hide the TV remote to stop me flipping news channels before school. Checking. I was always checking. But the more vivid and terrifying the dreams got, the more I started to avoid the news. I didn't want to see it, not even the sanitised version. I'd seen enough. Imagining having to read from the autocue on a situation I'd already dreamt about pretty much ruled out journalism.

"If you want the world to know, Jaz's your girl," I added. "Mouth on her like a megaphone." I was doing my usual trick, trying to divert everyone, including myself, from the heavy thoughts in my head. "Tell Jaz, and the whole world will know before lunchtime."

"Your Mum, more like." Jaz snorted and flicked a cookie crumb off the table at me. "The salon's the best publicity machine in Willow Bay. I may have a big mouth, but I can keep a secret." She gave me a look that reminded me, *And you know it.*

I did. Jaz did have a big gob, but she had a big heart too, and a big vault with plenty of my secrets stashed in it, especially the one secret I didn't want anyone to know.

"Bitten would be better," Ash interrupted before taking another bite of cookie. When he was thinking, he tilted his head and one eyebrow contorted itself into a wave; it made him look even more adorable.

"What would people think if a dolphin got tangled in the net and drowned, especially one like Bitten who's kind of a celebrity?"

"Good thinking," Jaz said, although her crestfallen look indicated she preferred Dylan in the role of celebrity. "Want me to write a press release about Bitten? We can take some photos and send them to your Auntie Penny, Juls. Doesn't she work for *The Australian?*"

"Sure." I shrugged, annoyed I hadn't thought of it. "I can give her a ring."

"We can set up a petition on change dot org, too," Jaz rambled. "Then maybe your auntie can get it on the news. I'll create a meme of all the things more likely to happen to you than being bitten by a shark, and we can shoot a press release to *The Project* and *A Current Affair.*"

"Exactly!" Ash banged his fist on the table. "You've got more chance of being struck by lightning or winning the lotto than getting munched by a Noah."

"I know which I'd prefer," Jaz said.

I took a sip of orange juice, my gaze fixed on Ash's face. The way his eyes crinkled when he smiled made me feel like I'd been struck by lightning. Or maybe I'd won the lotto.

"Noah?" I queried.

"Yeah, Noah. Noah's ark—shark. It's rhyming slang. Strine," Ash drawled, exaggerating the ocker. "Proper Aussie speak. We won't use it on the placards, though. 'No Noah Nets' is too confusing. I can't believe you've never heard it before."

I shrugged. "My family's mostly Greek. Dad used to say some ocker stuff when I was kid. But he left when I was small."

"You're a Bubble and Squeak." He winked. "Greek."

No one had ever called me a Bubble and Squeak before. But he'd said it affectionately and I knew it wasn't like being called a wog. No one in Willow Bay would've dared call me or Mum that; they'd never get a haircut in this town again, or not a good one, anyway.

Before I could respond, the door opened and a horde of girls from Ash's grade stormed in.

"Oh em gee," one hissed as she strode past us to the counter. "He *can't* be serious."

"Ash." Another girl glided up to our table. "We've been shopping in Anchorage," she purred.

Wow. Conversation starter.

I looked at Jaz, and I swear it was all she could do to stop her eyes from rolling.

"Sweet." Ash's smile was tight. "What'd you buy me?"

The laugh she responded with sounded totally fake. "Actually, we were shopping with Renee ... for makeup. *Concealer* mostly." She slid her hands onto her hips, one manicured fingernail tapping a cute silver chain belt that was only marginally shorter than her skirt.

It seemed a weird word to stress, but maybe Renee had acne or something. Or a hickey. *Please don't let it be a hickey!*

It was completely bitchy of me to wish for the former, but a mean, jealous little part of me hoped she had acne so bad she couldn't leave the house, which would explain her absence at school.

"Renee said to say hi," she said almost acidly and threw him a cute little wave.

"Cool. Tell her I said hi back, won't you, Lacey?" Ash's smile was so stiff I thought it might crack.

Lacey's eyebrows marched up her forehead, and I tried to stop mine from doing the same as I considered what that was supposed to mean.

"Tell her yourself," another girl snarled from the sandwich artistry counter.

"Aren't you going to introduce us?" Lacey's over-shadowed eyes swung from me to Jaz and back, and she jutted out one hip.

"They go to our school." Ash flashed her a look I could have sworn was begging her to play nice. "Jaz, Juls." He waved a hand at us. "Meet Lacey."

I half-rose to extend my hand, and immediately regretted it. She stared at it as if I had Ebola, her closed-mouth smile slipping to reveal sharp teeth behind that saccharine expression. It was the kind of smile a Chihuahua might give you right before you learned it had a tendency to bite.

Smarts and manners, both communicable diseases for a Fantastic, I reminded myself before once again instructing myself not to be bitchy. Ignoring her rebuff, I smoothed my hair and settled back into my chair, pretending to be oblivious to the titters of the others.

"Oh, you must be juniors." Silky blonde hair fanned Lacey's shoulders as she shook her head. "I didn't know you were tutoring, Ash."

Ash's insincere chuckle turned into a cough, and he covered his mouth with his hand. "I'm not," he muttered after a minute. "Surf instructing."

Surf instructing? I gulped a too-big swallow of orange juice to hide my hurt.

It wasn't like I was paying him to teach me! It'd been *his* idea. *It's a date,* he'd said. A red heat crawled up my throat and made the orange juice taste sour. I set the bottle back on the table. I was just a bit of fun to him after all.

Yeah, me. Fun. That's a laugh.

Whatever he'd done to make the Fantastics turn on us today, Lacey left me in no doubt it had something to do with me and Renee.

A shrill laugh from over near the sandwich counter was followed by, "She's flatter than a pancake."

I sourced it to a petite redhead clutching a ham six-inch and clad in hotpants so short her own ham sanga was about to fall right out. I recognised her as the girl from the bus and tried to stop myself from sneering. So she wore short shorts. That wasn't what disgusted me. Her shitty attitude did. And I couldn't argue I wasn't flat-chested. Most people were, compared to Renee and Jaz's pneumatic assets. I glanced at Ash, hoping pancakes were secretly his favourite food.

"Fuck her. Everyone loves pancakes," Jaz said with a sniff, reading my thoughts, as she so often did.

Ash's eyes narrowed, and he chewed on the corner of his bottom lip for a minute. "You girls finished?" He nodded at me and Jaz, but he spoke loud enough to direct the words to the coven currently ordering sandwiches and salads.

"Sure." I smiled just as sweetly as Lacey had. "Thanks for lunch, instructor."

Standing, Ash expertly tossed his trash into the garbage can a few metres away, his jaw clenched. "No problem," he muttered. "Let's roll." He marched out of the store without a backward glance.

Like a true publicist, Jaz plastered an over-bright grin on her face as she rose and shoved her chair back under the table like it was a jousting pole. "Good to meet you, Lacey. I love your belt." She gestured to Lacey's skirt.

Lacey's lips pursed momentarily. "You take care now, *Juz.*"

Two could play at that game.

"Enjoy your lunch, *Lucy.*" I flashed her a grin so wide it made my cheeks hurt.

"Laterz, bitches," Ham Hotpants mumbled as the door closed behind us.

Back at ya.

The heat coming off the street hit me like a slap.

"Fuck, they were particularly ravenous today," Jaz said as soon as we got outside. "I don't think I've ever seen them eat before, let alone devour ham six-inches and two whole word-nerds in one sitting."

"Don't forget the pancakes." I snorted.

Ash was already across the street, waiting on the pavement. A frown furrowed the space between his eyebrows as he fiddled with his phone, texting.

"Anyone would think you'd crapped in their Barbie camper or something," Jaz went on as we crossed over to join him on the esplanade.

"So, surf instructor," I called tartly, reaching in my shorts for my cash. "How much do I owe you for the lesson?"

His head snapped up so quickly that if I'd been closer we'd have enjoyed one hell of a Liverpool Kiss.

"Juls, I'm sorry. Don't be like that." He shoved the phone into the pocket of his boardies. "It's just that..." He looked pained. "You don't know who you're dealing with."

"It appears so." I spun on my heel. "Come on, Jaz. Let's go."

Reaching out, he caught my forearm and gestured to the sandwich shop. "That's not what I meant, and you know it. Those girls—" He gripped my arm so tightly his nails left little half-circles on my skin.

"Mean nothing to me," I finished, drawing on all the rom-com lines I'd heard in my life. "Honestly, I don't care what they think, but it's obvious you do."

"I don't. I'm just trying to protect—" Ash broke off and dropped my arm. "I'm sorry, okay? I shouldn't have said that. You're right. I should have told them it was a date."

It was a date!

I shrugged.

"I had fun, Juls." He chewed his cheek, his eyes imploring forgiveness. "I'd like to do it again."

My mouth could find no words, and my heart was performing a duck dive in my chest.

"The surfing or the sandwiches?" I mumbled, eyeing him warily.

"Both," he said.

Still pissed, I added, "Maybe we could do breakfast sometime. Apparently I know this great pancake place." Then the implication of what I'd just said hit me, and I felt a blush creep right up to the roots of my hair.

He smiled and lowered his voice conspiratorially. "Well, I happen to love pancakes—cooking them and definitely eating them." He quirked one eyebrow and grinned, briefly glancing over my chest. "Maybe we'll, um, do brekkie someday. I make the meanest banana caramel pancakes this side of the black stump. But before then, surfing. Will you surf with me again, Juls?" He pouted and lowered his brow, offering up gorgeous puppy dog eyes of apology. "The only way to get good at it is to do it every day," he coaxed.

"That's the best way to get good at sandwich artistry too." Jaz jabbed a thumb at the sandwich shop. "I worked there for a semester. Sucked."

I was thankful for Jaz's levity, but Ash's snub in the sandwich shop still burned too much for me to crack a smile. I could be a bitch like that. I'd learned how to bear a grudge from my mother, and I wasn't about to let him get away with that just by promising me a future banana pancake fest.

Ash laughed, though, and shook his head. "You're a dag, Jaz. But what happened back in there was rude of me. I should have stuck up for you. It's just that a pack of catty girls is like, well..."

"The scariest thing alive," Jaz helped him, miming pulling hair and baring her teeth. She hissed like a feral cat, and he laughed again.

"Just about. Look, I really am sorry. You still going to help me with that publicity, Jaz?" He put a hand up for high-five. "Don't leave me hangin'."

"If you're game." Jaz slapped his palm.

"I'm always game. What about you, Juls?"

I shrugged, noncommittal.

A buzz sounded from Ash's pocket, and a tone rang out—the overture to OneRepublic's "Secrets." I liked the song, but I wasn't so keen on the secrets. Ash automatically reached for his phone.

"Tell Renee I said hi." I mimicked Lacey's earlier trite wave and turned away, my face burning with the knowledge I was coming off like a jealous little cow.

So there was another girl on the scene. A popular girl with impossibly womanly assets. Big deal. It wasn't like we'd done anything other than surf, even if his touch on my skin was still burning in my mind. It wasn't like we were boyfriend and girlfriend. We were barely even friends. He didn't know me. Who did? And I certainly didn't know him yet, and he *knew* a lot of girls.

"Juls." The warmth of his hand on my arm jolted me back to the present.

Damn muscle memory!

"It's not what you think, okay? Promise."

"It's none of my business." I wet my lips with my tongue. "You're teaching me to surf. We're helping publicise your protest. I was kidding about the breakfast thing. Okay?"

Ash's head jerked back a little, his expression wounded. "Then I guess surf's best at sunset tomorrow. Meet me at Piers?"

"You're the instructor." I shrugged, and Jaz threw me the same withering *play nice* look Ash had given Lacey earlier.

"Juls." He took my hand in his, stroking my palm with his thumb. "I'll make it up to you. I'll bring my GoPro, and we'll take some publicity shots of Bitten."

I sighed. "Okay. But I'm not wearing a bikini."

"Fine." He laughed. "Go nude or wear jeans, but it'll be hard to surf in them. Just say you'll be there."

"She'll be there!" Jaz confirmed, prodding me in the ribs.

CHAPTER 11

Jaz didn't say *she'd* be there too, but as soon as we walked up to the beach and saw Dylan carving up the waves with Ash, I knew Jaz wasn't going anywhere.

Disappointment made my throat constrict, or it could have been the super-tight neoprene of my new wetsuit. I might have folded like a sheet at the thought of another lesson with Ash Gordon, but I was damned if I was going to reward him with a bikini peep-fest, certainly not after all the hoo-ha about Renee Aldershot yesterday.

To tell the truth, I'd tried to discourage Jaz from coming, hoping for time alone with Ash so I could ask him about that. Just the thought of spending time alone with him at sunset made my spidey senses tingle. They were tingling now—or something was—as I watched him cruise in on a wave, his grin bracketed by dimples. He left his board on the sand a few metres up the beach and loped over.

"A wettie, huh? Heaps better than jeans." His unblinking blue gaze roamed appraisingly over me, making me feel even more naked than I had in a bikini.

"Suits you. You look like a pro."

"Ha." I grunted. "I'm total crap, and you know it."

Ash laughed. "I reckon you're kind of a natural."

I glanced down at my flat blue neoprene chest. Was it a play on words from a guy whose girlfriend had fake boobs? Or did he actually think I was getting the hang of surfing?

"Especially for a kook," Ash added.

A what?

He must have noticed my confusion, because his laugh rang out again before he explained. "A grommet. A newbie. A lot of people who try surfing quit quickly, but you're still here, which means you're doing okay. Wait here."

He turned and ran over to the surf lifesaving tower, where a foam board poked up from the sand like a cuttlefish shell dug into the top of a kid's sandcastle.

"Got you a foamie." He jogged back, his rippling abs captivating me like a magic eye puzzle until he thrust the board toward me and forced me to look away. "It's one of my old ones. More lightweight. You can't hurt it, and more importantly, it can't hurt you. Ready for a drubbing?" His eyebrow twitched, and the ghost of a smile crossed his face. "Hope you don't mind it a bit rough."

Brilliant white teeth flashed from his smile, and I once more mentally debated whether he meant to sound dirty.

"Thanks." I took the board and followed him down the sand, knowing I was not ready for rough any more than I was ready for Ash Gordon and his easy innuendo. And I was certainly not ready to admit the crushing, undeniable fact that I wanted him—bad. So bad I already couldn't stay away.

When my toes hit the water, surprisingly cool and dark in the twilight, Ash stopped. "Leash," he said.

"Huh?"

Ash knelt and wrapped both strong hands around my ankle, tethering me there for a moment. "Always wear a leash, remember."

The warmth of his palms, the possessive way they cuffed my ankle, sent a pulse up my body to my crotch. Something about the intimacy of the gesture made me want to skitter away or wrap my legs around him octopus-style and never let go. I couldn't decide which.

He let go one hand to fumble in the water for the board's Velcro strap and fastened it around my ankle. I closed my eyes. Ash Gordon was kneeling at my feet, and the way his tawny head bent to the task, the subtle stroke of his index finger against my Achilles tendon, and the firmness of his hand as he tightened the strap made me want to melt into foam on the sea. Parts of my body were definitely liquefying beneath the wetsuit.

Pressing the strap firmly with his palm, he looked up at me with a panty-melting grin and said, "There. You've got—"

"Ash," I sighed involuntarily.

What the hell? Did I just groan his name out load? I gulped, trying to swallow the word, but my attempt to retract it turned it into an unfortunate hiccup.Stamping my foot in frustration at myself, I accidentally sent a spray of gritty saltwater straight into his face.

Holy Dooley!

I was floundering here, drowning.

"Ticklish," I lied. "Hiccups." He'd reduced me to single words.

I shook my head. I had nothing.

Ash wiped his face with a forearm, rocked back on his heels, and stared up at me. "You okay, Juls? You're not having another turn, are you?"

Great, now he thinks I'm about to pass out.

"Umm. No. Ticklish."

He tugged my big toe. "Good. Because I was just going to say you've got cute feet." Standing, he scrutinized me. "They match the rest of you: cute."

A flush tore across my body, and I let the wettie do its job of keeping me together. If it wasn't so darn snug, I'd be coming apart at the seams even more than I already was.

He thought I was cute. All of me. Not just my feet.

Cuter than Renee Aldershot?

Stop it, Juls. I cursed the shitty little doubting alien in my brain. *Definitely crazier than Renee Aldershot!*

Ash had turned toward the ocean, but I could tell he was still grinning at my gobsmacked response. Slipping the light foam board under my arm, I followed him as meekly as a puppy, the leash slapping sand and sea foam with every step.

"There's one for you," he nodded at an approaching wave, and I set off, feeling it swell beneath me, paddling harder and faster as the power of it coursed up through my arms like a current.

With a rush of pure amazement, I caught it. Remembering what Ash had shown me, I paddled through the ledge and popped up to find myself perched on the wave's inner lip. Arms out, knees bent, I balanced—beautifully, wonderfully immersed in the present. My feet were flat on the board, my face misted with saltwater. And then I took the drop. I coasted down the smooth, glassy slope, shifting my weight against the flow of water, the board swinging beneath me until a wall of green embraced me.

I was flying, or falling, or both.

I was surfing.

Sea and sky glittered from every angle—a green-blue house of mirrors, and the rush of blood in my head sounded like waves pounding out their applause. My limbs relaxed, tension seeping from them as I carved back up the face until I sensed the wave closing and kicked out before I got dumped.

Gasping, I bubbled under, then surfaced, spitting. I was treading water and wiping salt out of my eyes when Ash paddled over and put out his hand. "Come here."

Thinking he meant to help me climb back on my board, I let him draw me close. A gutter between the waves made it nearly shallow enough for me to stand, but the leash attached to my still-floating board prevented it. Ash tugged me to his board, my chest pressing against the rails. Then he leaned down and took my face in his hands. He drew me into a kiss so strong and salty that a warmth spread through me, as if all the world's waves had just rushed to my crotch.

"Ash," I mumbled through his kiss, wanting to stay in it forever—suspended, connected, wanted—hearing nothing but the growl of the surf, smelling nothing but Ash's scent of sea-salt and surfwax, sunscreen, and the faint alkaline sweetness of his breath.

The kiss was perfect, misted in sea spray and feeling so right, so fated, that for a moment I believed every molecule of him was a long-lost part of myself, spray from the same wave. As if all those little particles of him might belong to me, the way they fit me and filled me, and without them, I might dissolve. I might wash away to nothing. By the time Ash pulled away, I was trembling so much I struggled to haul myself back onto the board.

Somehow, Ash Gordon had changed me.

He'd changed everything as soon as his lips brushed mine. And I knew with the clarity and intensity of an epiphany that things would never be the same again.

CHAPTER 12

"Hope I don't wipeout and wreck it, or crease it or something," I mumbled, staring at the brilliant orange fibreglass funboard Ash held against his side, and thinking of the surfer that day at the beach. I'd earned my stripes on Ash's foamie over the past month, but it was time to get myself a real board and the funboard's added width made it a sensible choice.

"You'll have a leggie. You'll be fine. You're ready for this." Ash reassured me while we waited beside racks of swimming togs and wetsuits near the counter. "What are you going to name it?"

"Name what?"

"The board. It's kind of a tradition I have. I name all my boards. And my guitars. Guess what my favourite board is called?"

"Rumplestiltskin."

He shook his head at my bad joke, and a few curls broke free of his sunglasses and tangled on his forehead. "Lame, babe. No. Guess again."

"Lightning?"

He frowned. "Close. It's Firefly," he admitted, his voice dropping to a whisper.

I laughed. "Firefly! Seriously? Does Dylan know? It sounds kind of girly, like something you'd name a unicorn."

"A unicorn," Ash scoffed, waving one hand. "No way. I'd name my unicorn Dreamdancer or Sunshine Sprinkles. Never let it be said I'm not in touch with my feminine side." He bumped my hip with his and one eyebrow shot up his forehead as he muttered, "I also enjoy being in touch with your feminine side." He craned his neck to check out my butt. "All of them."

I ignored his flirting. Ash had no shame. Now that we were something of an item, he pushed the limits of public displays of affection all the time. If it wasn't impossible to resist him, if every touch didn't make my blood surge, I might have been embarrassed by the easy way he took my hand or tucked my hair behind my ear. But after a few weeks, even the scowls of jealous Fantastics couldn't make me tell him to stop.

"Sunshine Sprinkles," I repeated. "I guess that *is* kind of adorable."

"Hey." He put one hand on his heart. "I'm an adorable kind of guy, everyone knows that. Anyway, Firefly is named after my favourite animal."

"Your favourite animal is a firefly?"

"Sure." He looked at me like I was the weird one, and of course I was, so I let it go.

"You couldn't be normal and like dogs?" I nudged him with an elbow.

"Normal is boring. I like dogs, but fireflies are way cool. The way they light up the darkness. The way little kids' eyes sparkle with wonder when they see one. I like that. I was camping when I saw my first lightning bug. I was only five. Still afraid of the dark sometimes back then. Dad tried to explain it." He smiled at the memory. "Maybe the electrician in him felt threatened. But it didn't matter. I didn't care how it did it, I was just in awe that it could. It felt like magic, this little thing buzzing around me, its tiny glow shining on my face. When it landed on my skin, I remember feeling this weird connection, like I understood it somehow, like it understood me. That's why my board's called Firefly." He nudged me back. "So rib me all you like about it. Fireflies are wicked."

The story made his eyes gleam, and for a second I could see the little boy he had been, the look of wonder on his face. "Awww, Ash. That's beautiful."

He put his arm around my shoulder again and nuzzled his nose into my neck. "No. You're beautiful. Besides, you can't keep a dog in an empty Tupperware container until it accidentally runs out of oxygen."

I clamped a hand over my mouth a second, and then murmured. "You killed it! Ash!"

"Maybe. Not sure. I dunno the lifespan of a firefly. Maybe it died of natural causes. But it was my buddy for a while. We should name your board after your favourite animal too. What is it?"

I glanced sidelong at him, hoping I looked flirty and seductive and not just weird. Bumping him with my hip, I answered, "You."

"Ha! Nice one. But you realise you can't keep me in a Tupperware container, right? I require proper care and feeding. And petting. Plenty of petting. Preferably heavy." His hand dropped off my shoulder to skim the curve of my waist and hip. I brushed it away when it headed for my butt.

"I fully intend to keep you on a short leash," I whispered. "Especially in public."

"Once bitten, twice shy, huh? Don't worry, I have absolutely no intention of roaming."

So there's no need to get Renee Aldershot a bitch's box, I thought to myself.

Ash angled his head closer to mine. "Also, I can't lick my private parts like a real dog, so I might require some attention in that department." He waggled his eyebrows at me, his grin so wide that his dimples carved a groove in his cheeks.

"You wish!"

"I do." He nodded. "I totally do. Next time I see a shooting star, I know exactly what to wish for."

Blushing beet-red to my core, I put a finger to his lips to shush him and quickly changed the subject. "I did have a pet once, though."

"What was its name?"

"Nigel."

"*Nigel?* You named a dog Nigel, and you laughed at me for Firefly?" He held the board to the side, away from us both, almost knocking over a stand displaying shell bracelets. "You are so not in charge of naming this board. I won't allow it."

"It wasn't a dog," I explained. "It was a fish. And like you can talk ... Sunshine Sprinkles."

"Nigel the fish!" Ash let out a long sigh and rolled his eyes.

"What? It was alone a lot. It had no friends apart from me."

"Nigel No Friends?" You named your pet Nigel No Friends? That's harsh. You were supposed to be its friend, Juls."

"I was its friend. But it was still a Nigel. All it did was swim around all day looking bored."

"It was a fish! That's what fish do!" He grinned. "Poor Nigel. We are not calling your board Nigel. It's a cool board, and Nigel is just—" He put up a palm. "Not cool. Hella uncool. What sort of fish was it anyway?"

"Goldfish."

Ash turned to the board and swung the tip toward me, dipping it like a tango dancer. "Ladies and gentlemen," he said. "We have a winner. Let me introduce Goldfish."

"Fine." I put a hand on the board's orange nose. "I hope Goldfish won't be too ashamed of my surfing."

Ash patted it too. "The two of you will do fine. In fact, better than fine. You're getting really good, heaps better than average for a beginner." He leaned in for a kiss, the warmth of his lips making my lips tingle, followed by my entire body.

"Whatever." I pushed him away. "I'm average at best. Terrible at worst." I never could take a compliment. It was something I was working on. Ash made me feel special. I just had to believe it myself.

"*Pfft.*" He broke away and added in that sexy, low tone he reserved for flirting, "You're better than average. And you're waaaaay better than average at that."

"You're grading me?" I feigned shock.

"Yeah." Ash tweaked a strand of my hair. "But you're head of the class. In fact, you're the teacher's pet."

The class?

We'd reached the head of the small line in front of the cashier's desk, but it wasn't that which made me pull away; it was remembering how I'd felt that day in the sandwich shop when he'd pretended to be my surf instructor. I still hadn't figured out whether I had competition. The way he looked at me, the way he touched me, the way he flirted, told me I didn't. But there were still times when Ash's eyes glazed over, like his mind was elsewhere. When that ringtone rang out, it reminded me I didn't know his secrets. I didn't know who he rang or texted late at night.

Renee was probably just having a hard time letting go, and who wouldn't? She hadn't returned to school by the time Ash's senior year graduated, and I hadn't seen her around since. Maybe she'd moved to Sydney to find work, like a lot of Willow Bay teenagers did when they finished high school. In any case, whenever I tried to subtly bring her up, Ash's face clouded and his jaw clamped, so I dropped it. I knew what it was like to want to avoid things, painful things, and I didn't want to ruin this. I didn't want to destroy the comfortable way my hand fit in his, or the sexual tension that hung between us, promising something more than just the kissing and petting we had been doing, or the feeling I was his girl.

"Yeah nah, least you're trying, gurl," the cashier, a towering, wild-haired Kiwi whose nametag identified him as Riki interrupted, easily joining our conversation. "If Ash says you're better than average, he oughta know." He winked, and I shoved thoughts of Ash's reputation from my mind, unsure whether Riki was talking about Ash's surfing or his conquests.

"So how'd you want to pay for this today, bru?"

Ash reached in his pocket for his wallet and slid his bankcard across the counter, but I immediately snatched it up and slapped down my own.

"The board's on me, babe." He tucked my card back in my pocket.

"No. I can't let you pay for everything."

"I have a job. You don't."

"I get pocket money."

Riki laughed, and I threw him a warning look.

"Are you for real? Save it for uni. I've got plenty of fun tickets right here." Ash patted his wallet. "Dad'll be working me like a dog all summer, so no more arguing. It's a gift. Accept it. I want you to have it." He pulled me close to kiss my nose, but I tugged myself away. "Besides, it's good karma," Ash insisted.

"Karma?"

"Yeah. Because I've never seen anything as beautiful as you on a board, and I doubt I ever will, so I'm paying that forward." His hand teased the bare skin on my shoulders before coming to rest in the hollow of my back, warm through my thin cheesecloth dress.

"I spend most of my time with my bum in the air, paddling to catch a wave."

Ash grinned and tilted his head toward Riki. "Yep. And *that* is the most beautiful thing I've ever seen on a board."

Riki grinned. "Smooth, bru." He leaned across the counter to high-five, and I slapped Ash's forearm as soon as their little manshake had finished.

"You're totally biased."

"Maybe." Ash held his hands out in mock protest. "But what do you want me to say?" He grinned so wide, it was like he'd just swallowed the Cheshire Cat whole.

"I got no idea what a gurl like you's doing with a dude like Ash." Riki jabbed a thumb toward him. "Punching above your weight aren't you, Gordon?"

I put a stop to Testosterone Appreciation Day with a roll of my eyes.

"Juls, meet Riki," Ash said. "Don't worry, he's married. Me and this sheep-shagger go way back, hey, Rik?"

"If you say so, bru." Riki turned twinkling, wide-set green eyes on me. "By that he means he's snaked me a thousand times."

"Piss off, Rik. If I ever dropped in on you, I was only showing you how to do it. You Long White Clouders, with your clunky long boards. You've got to learn to ride one of these sweet little babies." Ash ran his hand up the side of the board and over the sharp nose.

"Git a look at me, bru. I wouldn't even fit on that thing." Riki jerked his chin toward the board. "I'd be shark shet in no time. He turned to me. "Oops. Shouldn't jinx it, should I? You sure you want this board now?"

I laughed. "*Shark shet?*"

"It's Kiwi for shit-scared," Ash said with a grin. "You'll be fine on Goldfish, and Riki would be fine, too. Sharks don't like the taste of Kiwis. They're too soft."

"They keep spittin' you Aussies out too, bru," Rik quipped. "Didn't you see Fanning the other day? Don't think they like surfers, or maybe they don't like the taste of Vegemite."

"No one does, mate." Ash laughed. "'Cept us. You've got be hard to like Vegemite."

Riki finished up the transaction and printed the receipt. "Hard as a junket sandwich, you are. Firefly," he muttered.

"Where's my discount?" Ash said, checking the receipt.

"Oh, man. I gotta put this through again. You git tin percent, okay?"

"Ten? Come on, big fella, you can do better than that."

"But I heard you're cashed up, bru?" Riki patted Ash's wallet where it sat on the counter.

"Twenty! You heard wrong." Ash smiled at me. "Juls deserves her own board. She's worked really hard for it. And I want to give her something she'll have forever."

Riki's broad nose crinkled in surprise. "Sounds like you need to save up for somethin' dearer than a funboard, bru. Twinty percent, okay? No more." He ran the card back through the machine and grinned like a Tiki as he passed it across the counter. "I'm enjoyin' seein' my bru here happy agin. But you have any trouble with the board, love, or with this clown here, you come see Big Riki, eh?" He pointed to his chest. "I'll sort both out." He put up his fists and gave a mock display of boxing.

"Right," I laughed. "Nice to meet you, Riki."

"Sweet as, gurl. You got a good teacher. You'll be a pro soon, eh?"

"Hear that. A pro!" Ash scooped up the bag containing the leg rope and surf wax, and tucked Goldfish under his arm. "Seeya out there, man." He nodded toward the ocean a few hundred metres from the shop, big, glassy tubes folding themselves into an emerald sea beneath the overcast sky.

CHAPTER 13

"You want to tell me about this guy, *paidi mou?*" Mum stood behind me at the breakfast table, playing with my hair. It was still wet from my post-surf shower, and she stretched out one sun-bleached curl and let it bounce up against the collar of my school blouse.

Hell no! was the first phrase that sprang to mind. But that wasn't going to cut it. Mum was Greek Orthodox, and she didn't like me using the *H* word in the house.

I loved my Mum, but that didn't mean I wanted her up in my business every second of every day, and I knew I couldn't keep the news that I was dating Ash from her, not in Willow Bay. Still, I hadn't been expecting the omnipotent mother routine yet either. Mum's inherited Hellenic talent for melodrama gave her a kind of Cassandra vibe. I may have had the "evil eye," but in Willow Bay, Mum was the eye in the sky. Four foot four at a pinch, for a small woman she'd been blessed with an oversized personality. The Greek islander in her favoured big hair, big earrings, big everything, pretty much—even boobs. And she was a big old gossip, an extrovert to my shut-in little word-nerd. And I knew she'd make a big deal over the news.

Because Mum often worked late at the salon, I'd grown up a latchkey kid, so luckily she hadn't yet noticed I'd been slipping out at dawn. I'd played it safe, leaving a note telling her I was going for a walk and where. It wasn't the whole truth, but it wasn't a lie either. Ash would walk me to and from the beach, or pick me up in his Kombi van, making sure I was safe, and Mum was rarely up by the time I got back. I tossed most of my notes in the bin without Mum being any the wiser.

"Come on, tell me," she pleaded.

I concentrated on pouring milk over my cereal. It splashed over the lip of the bowl, leaving pearly droplets on the blue tablecloth.

"He's a surfer…?" Mum fished. She grabbed a dishcloth off the bench and tossed it at me, nodding for me to wipe it up. "He's older?"

"Who told you?" I asked, like the Cut 'n' Run wouldn't be all over that news already.

"*Ksero*, darling," Mum said. "I know."

Whenever Mum lapsed into Greek, she usually repeated it in English for my benefit. On the rare occasions she'd mutter a complete sentence I couldn't understand, it meant she was swearing at me in her native tongue. Yiayia had done her best to teach me Greek on school holidays, but I could never get the guttural accent right. And where would I use it? There wasn't even a taverna in Willow Bay.

When I was a kid, I'd liked it when she called me "my child" or "my girl" in Greek, until she'd yelled, "Over here, *paidi mou*" out the car window once at school pickup. In English, it sounds like "*pee thee moo.*" When a bully asked whether Mum had called me that because I pissed my pants, I was humiliated. I forbade her from using Greek in public, yelled that I wasn't a child anymore. I still remember her hurt expression. She had the same look on her face again now. It made me sigh, and eventually it made me answer. "Yeah, he surfs."

"*Ksero*," Mum said again, her dark eyes brightly expectant. "Is it Ash Gordon? Was that why you were out so late the other night?"

So she had noticed. One point to Mum.

"It's just that I've heard some… things… about him," she confessed.

I spooned cornflakes into my mouth and chewed. *From one of the Fantastics, I bet.* My mouth was so dry the cereal tasted like sawdust— wet, milky sawdust. "What kind of things?"

Mum shrugged. "He's had a lot of girlfriends." She smoothed down the hair on my crown, then pulled out a chair and sat. "Juliette, it might be time to talk to you about safe se—"

My palm shot up faster than my eyebrows. Then I quickly frowned as I spooned in another mouthful.

"We're just friends," I lied, chewing. "He's teaching me to surf."

Mum's crimson mouth contorted into a surprised *O*-shape. "So the wetsuit and the board behind the door in the garage are yours?"

I nodded. "Yep. Both mine."

She looked relieved, as if before that she'd thought I was inviting surfers over to get naked when she wasn't home. Ash hung out sometimes, but it wasn't like that, not yet. Most times, if things got heavy, he pulled away.

"Yours," Mum repeated. She dabbed at the lipstick at the corner of her mouth with her tongue, and then asked, "And Ash Gordon…?"

"What about him?"

"Is he yours too?" Mum poked me in the ribs with one cherry-tipped acrylic nail, making me spill milk off my spoon onto my school uniform.

She was trying to be jolly, I could tell that much, but her frown belied the humour. I could tell she was worried.

Hell yes! All mine—another answer I couldn't give. Not yet.

"He's nice," I said.

"Rory and Sharon's boy, isn't he?" She stood. "You want to invite him over for dinner? I'll make spanakopita."

Mum's spinach and feta pie in filo was one of my favourites, but I wondered whether Ash would like it. Maybe it would be too "Bubble and Squeak" for his tastes.

The fridge's breath was cool on my back as Mum opened the door and removed a loaf of bread. She popped two slices of wholemeal bread into the toaster.

Hell no.

I shook my head.

"I'd like to meet him if you're spending time with him. Also, there's this…" At the bench, she dug in her bag for a second and slid a packet of condoms across the table toward me.

The toast popped, making me jump, and I nearly choked on my cornflakes.

"Maybe it would be good if we visited Dr Carnegie to talk about you going on birth contr—"

My nervous laugh stopped her. "No need. Honestly, you've probably spent more time with Ash Gordon than I have. I bet you've cut his hair a thousand times."

"These bad boy surfers never cut their hair." She let out a tinny laugh, but she was still frowning.

Bad boy? I felt a strange swell in my belly at the thought of a Fantastic in the salon badmouthing Ash to my mother. It might have only been a month, but Ash was already non-negotiable.

"If I agree to invite him over for dinner, can we change the subject?"

Mum shrugged, not looking any happier. Balancing her breakfast plate, she pulled out the wicker chair next to mine and sat, flipping over the morning's edition of the *Willow Bay Bulletin*.

"*Ai ai ai.* Terrible thing, this bus crash."

Hairs rose on the back of my neck. "What?"

"Jingilly Hill Scouts bus," she explained after swallowing her first bite of toast. "It missed a turn in the road coming down from Carbine Rocks last night."

Gorge rose in my throat, and I could hear my heartbeat drumming in my ears over the screams. *Shut up!* I silently begged my head—and my mum.

Once I'd grown old enough, I made it a habit to not tell Mum about my dreams. Maybe she knew, but if she ever heard me crying out at night, she never asked, not since I'd hit my teens.

I sucked in a deep breath and closed my eyes, ignoring the screaming, tumbling child, the strewn seats, the diesel stink. When I opened them, I pushed my cereal away. The cornflakes were sludgy now anyway, tiny turned-up boats sinking in a milky sea.

"Two little boys killed," Mum went on, "and Gus Linley, the driver. CareFlight flew a couple more kids to Sydney, one critical." Mum sucked air in through her teeth and shook her head. "Gus's wife's a client. Filipino lady. Angelica used to come in for acrylics all the time before the baby was born. Five kids, you know. Don't ask me how. Old Gus was pushing seventy. The baby's just over a month old. The police say Gus might have fallen asleep at the wheel. Poor, poor things."

I had the sudden image of the grey-haired driver up late, rocking an infant as it wailed. If I'd only been able to warn someone, maybe Gus wouldn't have been driving that bus. Maybe he'd have taken time off work to sleep and be with his kid. I closed my eyes again.

"It's awful," I agreed when I opened them.

"I'll put a collection tin in the salon." Mum's eyes were misty. "A year's free haircuts for Angelica and the kids." She slid her hand across the table and patted my arm. "I love you, *paidi mou.* Never forget that. No matter what. You can always talk to me about anything, *entaksi*? Okay? I'm right here."

"Love you too, Mum."

"More than you love Ash Gordon?" She was grinning, but it was fake and never reached her dark, worried eyes. One thing was clear: Ash Gordon had rattled Mum almost as much as he'd rattled me.

CHAPTER 14

"It's not as big as I expected." Ash peered out the windscreen of his battered blue Kombi van as we pulled up at the lookout.

Dawn had just broken near Point Hanrahan, and the sea was a watercolour of aqua and teal beneath a pink sky. Weeks ago, I'd have been far too nervous to attempt to surf the point break. I'd be worried I'd totally wipe out or get laughed at by the boys out the back. But with each day, Ash was helping me see that none of that mattered. Surfing was like a dance with the sea as my partner. I just had to trust that the wave wouldn't drop me.

For a "kook," I was already starting to feel at home, as if I was part of the ecosystem somehow—a piece of something bigger. Sometimes, I'd even manage to catch a wave and stay upright on Goldfish, making a few shallow cutbacks before I kicked out.

Ash pulled on the handbrake and switched off the ignition right as his phone trilled. With a sniff, he threw open the car door and stepped from the van, sliding the phone from his pocket.

"Hi," he said. "How goes it?" His voice was strained, like he was trying his best to sound breezy.

I wondered who'd be calling at this time of day. Dylan, I guessed, or maybe Riki, wanting to hit the waves. But all I could hear was Ash's low murmur and the clatter of boards as he pulled them out of the back of the Kombi. I opened the door and walked to the treated pine barrier of the lookout, stepping up on it to check out the water. The line-up wasn't too crowded, and between sets, the sea was lazy, gentle swells rippling like corduroy in the dawn.

Ash appeared from behind the van and handed me Goldfish. "Come on." His eyes were narrowed, the pupils constricted, turning the blue to brooding.

"Surf's up, and I don't want to be interrupted again," he said, tossing his cell on the seat.

We paddled out together, duck-diving under larger waves, floating there at the start of the line-up, waiting for larger sets that might curl into A-frames—cylindrical tongues of glass that would lap down and encase us in the green room of the ocean. Ash was quiet, which was unlike him, but I couldn't tell if he was pensive or just half-awake. We only had an hour because Ash had to work. He'd taken up an electrical apprenticeship with his dad after graduation.

"Magic day," he said finally, nodding to the horizon. "I just wish I had more time to share it with you. Being out here with you is the best place to be, apart from my special place."

I laughed at the strange phrase. "You have a 'special place?' Childhood cubby house, I bet?"

He shook his head. "Everyone has a special place, don't they? You want to know where mine is?" He paddled closer and our boards bumped as he reached for me and pressed his lips to mine, kissing me long and deep and slow. "There," he murmured. That's my special place."

I bit my lip, already craving another kiss. "My lips are your special place. Sounds like a cheesy line to me, Ash," I said, even though my heart was humming.

"Uh-uh. Just the truth." He wriggled his torso on the surfboard and groaned. "But mentioning your lips and my special place in the same sentence... Let's just say it's embarrassing and uncomfortable what that kiss did to me, let alone thinking about that." He jerked his chin in the direction of his board shorts. "Thank heaven I'm not wearing a wettie today."

"Still wishing on that shooting star, babe?" I giggled.

He laughed. "Absolutely. But I didn't just mean your lips," he explained. "Although they *are* very special." His eyes strayed to my groin. "I just meant you, babe. Your lips, your smile, lying in your arms. You're my special place. It's impossible to be anything but happy when I'm around you, even if—"

"Even if your true special place is *throbbing*?" I cut him off, enunciating that dubious word found so often in romance novels and gesturing to his crotch.

"Especially when my special place is throbbing." He grinned. "But it's true I'd rather be here with you than anywhere, especially work. It's so boring. But someone has to take over the business. The old man can't do it forever."

"What would you do if you had the choice? Surf?"

He sniffed. "Nah. I'm no Dylan. I love surfing, but I'll never be a pro. I guess I'd do the only thing I've ever wanted to do— music. Songwriting. But that would mean applying to the Sydney Conservatorium of Music, leaving Willow Bay. I can't do that with Dad sick. His prostate cancer is in remission for now, but he's wants to retire and travel around Australia with Mum, take the grey nomad route. I'm the only son. So, Ashley Christopher Gordon the First, that's me, taking care of the family dynasty." He let out a long sigh. "All this work and grown-up shit when I just want to surf or chill with you or write songs. Maybe me and being a grown up just don't gel, but I guess it's too late for that now, huh?"

I wanted to tell him that was part of what I loved about him: that he was a boy trapped in a man's body, that it was so easy to imagine him as a kid with a firefly on his face. And I wanted to tell him to chase his dreams, too, to enroll in a music course next year or keep entering surfing competitions, but I knew success in either of those things would tug a guy like Ash away from this tiny town, away from tiny ol' me, too, and I couldn't find the words, so I just nodded, watching him.

"Not all dreams come true, I guess," Ash said eventually, his tone wistful.

The thought made me shudder. My dreams did. And not the ones I wanted. This one, however, this dream of me and Ash together, I wanted it more than ever. Ashley Christopher Gordon the First was my dream too, and I wasn't about to let go of that yet.

"I guess it depends how badly you want them," I murmured.

Ash's head jerked up, and his smile was sad. "Not enough." He reached for my hand. "Not when everything else I want is here. It's hard, though, because deep down I want to matter, really matter. Perhaps everyone wants that, but not everybody does."

"You matter to me, Ash. You'll always matter to me."

He squeezed my hand tighter. "At the start of the year, I was totally ready to try for it. Then, well—" Stopping short, he pulled free and sat up on his board, shrugging. "Shit happens."

It was the closest he'd come to talking about his past, and I didn't want to rush him into clamming up. "What sort of shit?"

He sighed. "Shit that'll ruin your day and mine. And look at this day." He turned his face to the rising sun. "It's going to be a pearler, and I've got to spend it inside, wiring in an oven. So let's not do that to today, babe. Let's just enjoy it while we can."

A promising wave was swelling, and he shoved my board to get me paddling, giving me a helping hand in getting up over the lip. I caught it—a big one for me—and rode it close to shore. I was paddling back out and grinning, loving the wide smile on Ash's face and hoping I didn't have hair plastered across my forehead, when I saw a flash of grey.

A second's panic crested in me. The shark dream was still fresh in my mind, as fresh as any of them. They all lurked there, ready to terrify me. Surfers always kept one eye out for a fin, but that dream made fear play the knots of my spine like a xylophone.

Ash's rippling shoulders glistened as he spun to follow the shadow. "Hey, it's Bitten." He fumbled with the front of his board to detach the GoPro camera he'd affixed there.

The dolphin glided to the surface close to my board, squeaking happily as if to congratulate me on catching the wave. Between sets, the waves had faded to a lull, and the rising pink sun on the horizon turned the whitewash to a lace of fairy floss as the creature stared at me. Then it dipped its head, sank beneath the surface momentarily, and leapt. A single flick of its powerful tail carried it high into the air, its body sleek and graceful, sensuous where it arced up over my board, and I flung my head back, opening my arms wide, breathing through every pore as it flew overhead and splashed back in beside me.

"Incredible! I got that all on camera," Ash waved the GoPro at me. "Catching a wave on a morning like this is a gift in itself, let alone that!"

The dolphin rose again and blew out air before making a tight turn and cruising down the line to a crew of surfers some twenty metres away.

"I wonder why he likes to hang out with surfers so much?" I said.

"Guess he likes our company." Ash splashed me, videotaping my reaction. "You saying surfers aren't great company?"

"Maybe not them." I nodded to where one of them was kicking out as the dolphin approached his board.

"Stupid fucking thing's dropping in on us," he yelled, lashing out with another kick.

Bitten, too nimble for him, shot away, but Ash's eyes narrowed, and he zoomed in on them with the camera. "I don't recognise them. Probably passing through, the wankers. But there's never a good reason to kick a dolphin. I heard they used to help Aboriginal people herd fish. They're clever enough to. They have a brain mass about the same size as a human's."

"I guess that depends on the human." I jerked my head toward the idiots.

"Yeah." He snorted. "Why can't they see they're just visitors here? I don't mean Willow Bay. I mean *here*." He spread his arms. "This is Bitten's home. Be a bit fucking polite."

I smiled, watching the morning light burnish his tanned arms and play over his chest, the muscles honed by surf and polished by salt and sun. He looked like a god risen out of the waves, and the passion in his face made desire trickle through me like a slow, steady runnel. I wanted him, and not just him.

This. His entire world. The ocean ecosystem he belonged to, belonged with. This vast sea he'd introduced me to as if it was an extension of him, of his calm, childlike, uncomplicated happiness. I wanted no past. No dreams, no memories. Just a single, shining, magical present. I wanted to live in the now, every single moment of it. With him. With Ash.

The odd, giddy feeling rose up inside me like a hymn, filling my ears with the sounds of the ocean. The *shhh* of the wind, the squeal of gulls, the thunder of breakers all seemed right, like a song I'd learned by heart.

"Ash," I whispered, so softly I wasn't even sure I'd spoken aloud. "I think I've figured out what I want to do next year, when I leave school."

He was bending down to attach the GoPro to the bottom of his board, to get some underwater shots, and his head was swung the other way. "Swimsuit model?" he murmured in a tone that told me he was only half-joking.

"No." I shook my head. "This."

Ash looked up, and one corner of his mouth quirked into a half smile. "Oh, so Riki says you're gonna be a pro and your first time out back at Point Hanrahan you decide you wanna be a title surfer, huh, champ?"

"No." I laughed at the thought, and then jerked my chin towards Bitten. "Someone has to protect him. This ocean, it's incredible, and no one cares. Someone has to try to save this. Someone has to care. Ash, I think I want to study marine biology."

"Juls! That's perfect." He paddled over to kiss me, and I let the kiss take me, drinking in the immensity of the moment, of the ocean, of him.

What the sea wants, the sea takes.

I knew this dream was real. And I wanted it, like I wanted Ash. The problem was: I wasn't alone.

CHAPTER 15

The sun was sinking over the darkening ocean, throwing barely enough light for me to check my watch. It was past eight. Soon, a waxing moon would dredge the sky of colour, and the stars would emerge. I had to be home before curfew, and since it took Jaz half an hour to drive me there, and another half hour to reach the farm, we didn't have that long left.

Ash had taken the afternoon off to hit the surf with me once I finished school, and my arms were sore from paddling into south-westerlies that whipped up the swell. I sat up straight and rubbed my triceps, smiling as I watched Jaz follow Dylan along the tree line to collect tinder of Casuarina needles and paperbark for the bonfire. Dylan was dragging a pale, trident-shaped log of driftwood, and I smiled even more when he stopped to wait for her, his hand reaching for hers.

It hadn't taken them long to hook up once Ash and I became an item, and the four of us started hanging out more often. For the first few weeks after they'd got together, all Jaz had been able to talk about was Dylan. How his half-Hawaiian skin was tanned like milk chocolate. How his eyes were so black you could see yourself in his irises like they were sunnies. How the tattoo of a gecko on his left forearm was so sexy. How his abs were... you get the drift. She'd starting curling her hair, too, and wearing makeup, even on the beach. I joked she was slowly turning into a Fantastic.

The wind chill made it a cold night for Willow Bay, especially for this time of year. For a few months, from July to September, night frosts turned the beach spinifex to gleaming glass in the mornings, and the stars burned brighter in the sky. But it was early autumn, and the cold was unseasonal.

I rubbed my arms again, resenting Ash's guitar for having his arm around it. He cradled the instrument with the passion he usually reserved for me and tapped the rosewood body to add a beat as he plucked out Tom Curren's "Dandelion."

I loved to watch him play, loved the look of intensity on his face as he plucked the strings; it made my breath catch.

"You still thinking of getting an acoustic, Dyl?" he said without looking up as Jaz set fire to the tinder.

"Not sure." He quit trying to break up the log, cured to a lacquer by the sea air, and instead shoved an end of it into the flames, sending a constellation of sparks into the twilight.

"I'd like to, but I've got my eye on a Les Paul at Beatz in Anchorage. Can't afford it yet. It's a supreme. Maple top. Called Ocean Water. Beautiful axe."

Ash whistled. "Pricey."

"Nah. Secondhand. 'Round three grand. It's something I'm going to keep all my life, though."

"And still not be able to play on the beach." Ash did a double tap on the rosewood before sliding easily back into the chorus, abandoning the lyrics in favour of conversation. "You gotta get a dreadnought guitar, man. Enough electrics."

Dylan shrugged and came to sit closer. "I'll borrow Layla when I need a semi-acoustic."

"No way. Get your filthy hands off her." Ash jerked the guitar away, missing the chord. "Now look what you've done. You made me stuff that up."

"You'll live, Vickie." Dylan laughed.

"Vickie? That your middle name?" Jaz giggled.

"Nope. That's Christopher," I said, as Ash picked up the song from the missed chord.

"Your lover boy here calls me that because he thinks he's a comedian," Ash told Jaz. "He's actually just a dickhead."

Dylan snorted. "It's short for 'convict,'" he explained to me. "His grandmother did this genealogy thing a few years ago and found out some of their relatives got shipped over on the Second Fleet for petty crime."

"It's not a real original nickname, coming from a Seppo," Ash interrupted.

"Seppp? That the best you got, dude?" Dylan slapped his back. "I'm not a Yank. I'm Hawaiian."

"Hah!" Ash stopped strumming and stuck the pick between his lips. "Tell that to the Yanks," he mumbled.

"Half-Islander, half-Dutch, and fully sick—that's what I tell the ladies." Dylan grinned, but Jaz's smile vanished. No doubt she was imagining how many girls Dylan would have to fend off if he made the pro surfing circuit, which was what he'd been practicing so hard for lately. "At least my family migrated here rather than being shipped out in leg irons," he quipped.

"Whatever. I'm proud of it, man," Ash insisted.

"What did your crim relatives do anyway?" I asked. "Axe murder? Serial killer? Anything I should be concerned about?"

"Concerned?" Dylan guffawed. "Wait till you get a load of this."

"You sure you want to know?" Ash said, not waiting for me to reply. "Funny story. One of my great-great-great-granddads flogged a pair of French knickers off some toff's clothesline in Mayfair. Got seven years hard yakka in the colony." He waved the guitar pick toward the beach. "Piss-poor prison it turned out to be, huh? The Poms sent all their crooks to the best place in the world."

Ash finished strumming, slipped the guitar strap over his head, and handed the instrument to Dylan, flicking him the pick.

"You got another one of these?" Dylan pointed to the guitar pick and grimaced. "This one's been in your pie-hole."

Ash shrugged. "My pie-hole's good. I brush my teeth."

"Never put anything in your mouth if it's recently been in the mouth of someone who's descended from perverts." Dylan wiped the pick on his Quicksilver boardies. "That's my motto."

"Maybe your motto should be 'Live a little.' Don't be so vanilla," Ash replied.

"Vanilla? Dude, did you seriously just call me *vanilla*?" Dylan gave a snort of laughter. "You may be pretty fuckin' fly for a white guy, but I'm chocolate. Chocolate aaaalll the way." Dylan ran the pick slowly up one smooth brown forearm. "And you know what they say about that. Once you've had black…"

The tip of Jaz's tongue protruded slightly, wetting her lips as she watched him. I half expected it to slaver right out and roll along the beach like a red carpet. Dylan was right—she was never going back.

"Speaking of perverts," Ash said, pointing to Dylan. "Go easy on Layla. Why are you tuning her down half a step?"

"Scared I'm gonna break her just so you'll finally buy an electric?" Dylan waggled his eyebrows.

"You break her, Seppo, and we're no longer buddies."

The opening riff of a song floated into the air.

"Hey, that's an old one." Ash cocked his head, listening. "Hendrix, right?"

"Yeah, '1983 (A Merman I Should Turn to Be),'" Dylan said. "Dad used to play it when I was a kid. It's way better amplified, though. Just about all Jimi is."

"My godfather's a huge Jimi fan." Ash started to sing, his resonant voice perfect for the song about lovers retreating to the sea after war destroys the Earth.

I didn't know it then, but I'd later download that song, and then, even later, move it to a playlist I promised myself I'd never listen to ever again. Most of the other songs in that playlist were Ash's, and after what happened to him, the lyrics to all of them always felt too sharp in my throat. I knew if I listened to any of them again, I'd go under.

But that night, Ash's voice hovered over the ocean, harmonising with the waves, and when Dylan finally launched into an adlibbed instrumental, Ash slid his arm around my shoulders and nuzzled my neck.

I rested my head against his, breathing in the fragrance of burned bloodwood from the fire, and the faint coconut, lime and surf wax of his hair. I drew the moment into me, held it like a breath, until Ash turned my chin and kissed me, and despite the chill in the air, I felt hot suddenly, and wet too—wetter than I had a right to be. I crossed my legs, trying to suppress the feeling.

"I don't reckon the sea would have survived anyway," Jaz piped up, listening to the lyrics as Dylan moved into the second verse. "The sea would be the first to be ruined. Look at what's happening to the Great Barrier Reef. The ocean's even more vulnerable than the land."

"If sea levels rise, a lot of this beach will go under." Dylan said, the thought sobering us all for a moment.

"Maybe we'll evolve to live there, like Bitten," Ash said. "It'd be kinda cool to live underwater."

Dylan's laughter nearly drowned out the guitar. "You practically do, bro," he joked. "The amount of dirty lickings you took this afternoon."

"You'd've been eating it too, if you hadn't slunk off once the waves got big to pash Jaz. I'm not saying I'd want to live underwater all the time. But the first time I did scuba, man, it was so surreal. I'd take all the time out there I could," Ash insisted. "Even if I spend it getting dumped. You can never spend too much time diving, or too much time on a board."

"Or on a babe." Dylan winked at Jaz. "Muff diving," he chuckled, under his breath, and she slapped his arm, blushing.

But the way she winked back made it certain they were having sex already. She hadn't told me they had, which was unlike her, maybe because she knew Ash and I hadn't gone there yet.

Not because I didn't want to. Whenever things got heated, Ash was the one to pull away, and even though I'd been disappointed, I let it drop. Just another thing to push from my mind. The dark urgency in his eyes when we were making out was enough for me to know he wanted it too, and to be honest, the thought half-frightened me. The force of his kiss, the sensation of his body, his absence like an ache when he drew away, made me feel things I'd never felt before, and I'd spent my whole life trying not to feel anything at all.

"I've got too much work on down at the shop, and the waves are huge this week. I need to get out there if I'm going to make the circuit," Dylan complained, sighing.

"Least you don't have to sit in a classroom and be bored all day," Jaz said.

"Don't complain. One day you'll miss school," Ash told her. "I do already."

"Nuh-uh." She shook her head.

"Nuh-*uh*." I agreed. "You guys make money, you have no homework, no exams, you don't have to wear a uniform…"

"True. But I love the uniform," Ash threw me a pervy sidelong glance. "Not on me. But it's definitely one of the perks of dating a schoolgirl."

"Run if he tells you he's got antique French knickers for you to wear underneath, Juls." Dylan laughed.

"Over two hundred years old and only slightly soiled," Ash added.

"Ewwww." Jaz waved a hand in front of her face as if she could smell them.

"At least you get to choose what you want to do when you finish." The firelight faded from Ash's eyes.

"Maybe you'll get on the pro circuit with me this year, bro," Dylan said, trying to lighten the mood.

"Long shot, unless I up my game. Anyway, Dad'd be gutted if I bailed on him now."

"Look at it this way, you Gordons have come so far from when you used to have to steal panties for a living." Dylan handed Ash back the guitar. "Besides, your dad's a soft touch. He lets you take arvos off if it's quiet or the surf's big, and you're making good dosh."

Ash nodded, but it was clear the mood had turned. He rested the guitar on his knee, flipping the pick over and over between his thumb and index finger, then bent his head to the instrument, fingers firm against the frets as he picked out an arpeggio.

A tune tumbled out, idle at first, folksy, then the melody became darker, deeper, grew roots.

"What's that song, man?" Dylan asked, as Ash started to strum into the bridge.

"Nothin'. Just something I've been writing."

"Any lyrics?"

"Kinda." Ash's smile, under-confident with a touch of melancholy, made me made me want to kiss him, but he'd already started to repeat the arpeggio and to sing in a soulful tenor.

> It is dying, sunk so deep I cannot feel,
> Lost, cut so deep, I cannot heal,
> It was mine—so damn deep it must be real.
> Emptied out, curled inside,
> Taken by the tide.
>
> I hear its gurgling, dying sigh,
> Heartbeat rolling by,
> That surf sound numbing,
> Turn away, eyes closed,
> To the new dawn coming.
>
> My aching brain is humming,
> A dead shell clinging,
> That bitter seaweed smell,
> Sirens lost in singing.
>
> It is gone, so wrecked, no resurrection,
> Lost, so destroyed—we've no connection,
> It was mine, this unquenchable perfection,
> But it's screaming out, 'They lied!'
> Spun around, torn so wide,
> Stolen by their pride.

Ash let the final chord fade before raising his head and glancing at each of us in turn. None of us said anything for a full minute or more after he finished. Something about the song had made us feel uneasy, I guess, sad, or like none of us wanted to lay our words over the top just yet.

"No good?" he said, pocketing the pick. "It's just something I, well..."

"Good!" Jaz said. "*Really* good."

"Amazing," I added.

"What's it called?" Dylan asked.

"'Drowning.'"

Jaz leaped to her feet, clapping her hands. "You've got to record it, Ash. We could put it on YouTube and Facebook. It might even go viral."

He laughed. "Hang on, publicist. It's not that easy to make a song go viral."

"Justin Bieber did it," she insisted.

Dylan groaned. "The Biebs? Come on!"

I elbowed him. "Hey! It might be good exposure."

Ash cocked his head, thinking, but his smile faded. "I dunno. Maybe a different song."

"But a producer could see it!" Jaz babbled. "You could do a whole album. Promote it online. Did you know I play clarinet?"

"Yeah, man. What if you're destined to be a rock god?" Dylan guffawed. "I can play the bongos." He reached over and gently knocked Jaz's head with his knuckles.

"I mean it," she insisted. "You have to do this."

"Can't be a sex god, might as well be a rock god." Dylan said. "Seriously, I say go for it, dude. What's the worst that can happen, apart from becoming the next Bieber?" He laughed, letting out an accidental snort.

"Nah. I can't."

Something about Ash's frown bothered me.

"It's too personal. I just wrote it for me. I don't think I could share my lyrics with a heap of people. It'd feel weird."

"Naaaaaw! He's shy. How cute." Dyl tried to pinch his cheek, but Ash ducked and said, "Piss off, man. I'm not shy. I'm just..."

"An artist." I interrupted, kissing his flushed cheek. If anyone could understand not wanting the whole world to know what went on inside your skull, I could.

"But the sea theme would work great for the protest." Jaz was still agitating over the Dolphin Dayze Resort, which had passed through to the public consultation phase. She'd made a pet project out of it, contacting television shows and papers. Auntie Penny had tentatively agreed to run an article, but more important news kept bumping it down the list.

"Think about it," she told him. "Social media is great for promotion, which reminds me." She pulled her phone from her pocket, checked it, then turned to me and asked, "Hey, is it okay if Ash drops you home tonight? I thought I might stop over at Dyl's before I head home."

Sex. Definitely.

That old Jaz jealousy gripped me, and I pushed it away. I always felt guilty when I got like that. It wasn't Jaz's fault she was normal. It wasn't her fault I chose to live vicariously through her, either. She had a sister and a dog and a horse named Minx and a farm and parents who loved each other. I had none of those things. She also had a hella bosom and a decent night's sleep every night, even if she snored like a freight train. Jaz insisted that all the girls in our dorm who'd shared smuggled vodka cruisers at school camp had snored, even Lisa Rubin. It wasn't true, but Jaz had a knack for generating her own publicity. Of course, that white lie had quickly passed from mythology into truth. All the girls snored. Except me. I hadn't slept a wink. I'd been terrified of having a nightmare. I'd stayed up reading on my phone long after Jaz's freight train pulled out of Land of Nod Station.

Jaz'd had every advantage, so it was no surprise she got to most things before I did. Now, she had the advantage of a boyfriend who no longer lived at home. Mum made me keep the door to my room open if Ash was over, and Ash's mum, Sharon, had a no-sleepover policy. Some time alone with Ash tonight, making out on the beach or in his car, would suit me just fine. I mightn't be able to beat Jaz in the race to lose my V-plates, but I might be able to join her.

I raised my eyebrows at Ash questioningly, and he grinned and nodded. "Sure."

CHAPTER 16

"Let's stay out." Ash kissed the pulse point at the hollow of my throat, the sensation making my limbs loosen beneath the sleeping bag he'd fetched from the back of his Kombi after Jaz and Dylan left. "It's so clear. Perfect for stargazing."

"Ha! You just want to see a shooting star," I joked, but I didn't need any convincing. I was straddling his hips, my hair dangling over him as I leaned forward, letting his kisses pepper my neck.

Ash sat up beneath me, expertly rolling me off him and onto my back in the sand.

"You've convinced me," I murmured as I slid one hand under his T-shirt, appraising the ridges of his abs. Ash grabbed the flimsy fabric of his tee in one fist, shrugged it over his shoulders, and flung it away. His chest was warm, his bare, muscled torso an interplay of light and contrast as he propped himself on one elbow in the moonlight.

The sensation of his fingers trailing down my spine made me shiver, and he pulled me closer, his hand creeping beneath the sleeping bag to rest on my inner thigh like a promise. "Ticklish?"

His fingers teased open the zipper of my jeans and slid beneath the silky fabric of my underpants, finding the gentle, surf-wet curls that sprang up eagerly as he tugged the material aside.

"Yes," I murmured. "Very."

Each small, circular exploration of his fingers sent a star whizzing around my dizzy head, and I sucked in a deep breath and closed my eyes, pressing my hips against his hand.

"Juls," he groaned, the fabric of my panties snapping modestly back into place as he withdrew his fingers.

"What's wrong?" I gripped the thick bones of his wrist, urging his hand back down. "I want to," I whispered.

He swallowed hard and flung the sleeping bag out of the way, and I craned up to kiss him, tugging him to me until he gave in. As I forced my tongue deeper, his fingers resumed their long, shallow stroking, this time above the barrier of my underwear.

"Juls, you have no idea how much I want you."

My body answered him with a warm, wet rush of desire, and his fingers slid beneath the fabric again, making my hips jolt as he brushed the tender button hidden there.

"Pretty sure I do."

"God, you're so wet." His eyes were narrowed, but the dimples returned to his cheeks as he sucked them in, his expression halfway between longing and wonder, and I squirmed beneath him, blushing. "Sorry."

"Shhhh." He quieted me with a kiss. "I'm a surfer. A scuba diver. I fucking love getting wet. Getting you wet is even better. "

He tugged me up so he could expertly snap off my bra and tossed it over with his shirt. Then he leaned over me again and brushed his lips along my collarbone, their heat burning.

Suddenly self-conscious, I put a hand up to cover my small breasts with their too proud, too dark nipples standing out like studs in the moonlight. But he nudged my palm away and took one tenderly between his lips. The tingling sensation set my heartbeat galloping in my ears, and I gripped his head, ruffling my fingers through his hair. His pulse beat fast there, in the blue veins at his temple, and I could feel his girth, hard and thick enough to surprise me where it strained against my soaking, tangled underwear. But his words surprised me more.

"I want you, Juls. I love you." The words slid out as naturally as a kiss, and they made my breath catch.

Did he just say that? Did Ash Gordon just say he loves me?

My hands wandered his body, involuntarily heading for the Velcro fastener of his board shorts as I tried to absorb that wonderful, mumbled phrase.

As if to ratify the words, Ash's lips encircled my other nipple, teasing it to attention. I stared up at the Southern Cross behind his head, lost for words, my grip on him, and on reality, loosening. *He loves me.*

Before I had time to reply, Ash pulled away with a sigh and sat up. "It's true, Juls. I love you."

I jolted up next to him, tugging the sleeping bag over my bare chest. "Ash, I lo—" I started.

"*Shh.*" His fingertip traced my cheekbone, then the outline of my lips, the scent of it more salty than me. Closing my eyes, I opened my mouth and trapped the fingertip that had given me so much pleasure, curling my tongue around its circumference, sunk by how much I wanted more than just his finger inside me.

"That's why I can't do this," he growled, withdrawing his hand.

"What?" My eyes snapped open.

Curling his fingers into a fist, Ash pressed his lips closed and pulled his knees up to his chest. His eyes were steely when he looked at me again. "Juls, I can't do this." He gestured to the two of us.

I felt the disappointment like a rebuke, certain we'd been about to go all the way this time.

"Ash, I want this!" I squeaked, digging my nails into his forearm. "What's wrong?"

"*Hhhh-hmmm!*" a sound issued from the dunes, interrupting.

Jerking his head toward the noise, Ash called, "Hey! Who's there?"

"Sorry, mate." A voice heavily laced with rum drifted out of the darkness, and a man appeared, silhouetted over the sand hill, a bucket swinging from his hand. "Didn't mean to, ah, interrupt. Just goin' for a fish."

"Damn." I muttered, tugging the blue sleeping bag tight around our naked torsos. "I suppose that's a sign."

"It's a sign of sheer stupidity," Ash muttered, leaning into me. "I doubt he'll catch anything other than a cold out here tonight."

"Won't catch a bloody STD either," a second gruff voice said, as another fisherman passed by to join his friend.

"Salt?" Ash straightened.

"The very same." A heavyset man swung a torch over, its ring of light illuminating Ash's bare chest and the shock of grey hair above the man's ruddy, grinning face. I recognised him as one of the regular old guys who loitered at the tables outside Café Conch, down by the harbour.

"That you, Ashley?" he asked, some of the gruffness fading from his tone.

"The very same," Ash repeated, shielding his eyes from the glow. "Bit of privacy, thanks, Salt."

The man gave a low, guttural chuckle as he swung the flashlight's beam down the beach, giving me the opportunity to fumble beneath the polyester for my bra and tug my jeans up. The inner seam felt too rough for my tenderness. It made me wince.

"Hell of a way to introduce your new girlfriend to your oldest cobber, Ash," the man said after a minute.

"Yeah, well"—Ash cleared his throat, obviously embarrassed—"I wasn't exactly planning on introducing you two tonight.

The man's low snort was paternal, with just a touch of condemnation. "Doesn't look like you were, sport," he replied. "Dunno quite what you were introducing her to, and actually I'm not sure I wanta know this time. But after last time..."

After a second's silence, the torchlight swung to us again, and he tossed me an awkward wave, his eyes downcast in the circle of light. "You must be Juls. Sport here's been talkin' you up these last couple of weeks, love. I've been meanin' to invite you both out on the *Sea Change* so I could meet ya. I'm takin' her over to One Tree Island for a spot of diving on Saturday. Why doncha both come along? That way she can meet your oldest buddy, and I can see whether she's gonna be a keeper. And we'll all have our clothes on."

Ash looked more red-faced than I'd ever seen him, as he slid his shirt over his shoulders. There was no mistaking the slight panic in his tone as he replied, "You're on. But I bet you just need a crew for the day, don't you, Salt?"

"You got it." Salt grinned. "Righty-o. I'm off. You kids watch yourselves." He stared at Ash for a moment, his bushy white eyebrows meeting over the bridge of his nose before adding, "Be good. And if you can't be good, be careful." He followed his mate down the path to the beach, whistling.

"Nice," I said, now more pissed off than frustrated. "Am I right in thinking your godfather just implied I could have a sexually transmitted disease?"

Ash grinned sheepishly, and I nestled closer to his warmth.

"Crabs in the intertidal zone, hey?" He elbowed me in the ribs, but his smile quickly faded to a frown. "Honestly, he was probably talking about me. He's a funny old bastard, is Salt. Bit embarrassing, though."

"You think *you're* embarrassed," I grumbled, pulling my shirt back on.

"Sorry. But it's curfew time anyway, I guess." Taking my jaw in his hands, he tilted my chin up to his and kissed me tenderly. "I wasn't just saying it, though. I wanted to tell you how I really felt before we—"

"Maybe it's for the best." I cut him off, annoyed by the sudden disruption to the night's plan. "There's a lot of sand in my jeans. Imagine if we'd…" I paused and ran a hand through my hair, shaking out the sand. "I really wanted to, Ash. And I'm glad you said it, even if we didn't…"

In that moment, I realised I hadn't actually said it back. Still half aroused, my head swimming with his words, I silently cursed Salt and his friend.

"Ash, I love you too. I was just shocked…" I rested my head on his shoulder. "I've never said I love you to anyone before, apart from family or Jaz."

He rested his head on mine, and his breath was warm in my ear as he whispered, "Me neither."

How was it possible that Ash Gordon, with all the girls who fawned over him, with Renee Aldershot and half of the shire on his list of ex-lovers, had never been in love?

"Really? You've never said it?" I pulled away to stare at him.

He must have heard the scepticism in my voice, because his answer was halting and soft, laced with some emotion I struggled to determine with his downcast eyes in shadow. "Well, I've never meant it. I guess I only wanted to mean it," he explained. "But I didn't. Not really."

"But you've…?" I shuffled my position in the sand, confused, putting space between us. Maybe Renee had broken his heart after all. Maybe that's what this denial was all about.

"Juls." He smoothed a strand of hair off my cheek, tucking it behind my ear. "I've done things before," he admitted. "Lots of things. Plenty of times with plenty of girls. I've done rash things and senseless things and fun things and crazy things, but that doesn't mean I never cared about people. I've just never felt like this. *It's* never felt like this. Not with any of them. I didn't even know what love was supposed to feel like back then. Not until I fell in love." He said the last sentence like it hurt him, then craned his neck to set a string of small kisses along my cheekbone.

"I know I love you because I need you, Juls. I need you like you're a part of me. I thought I just needed to feel alive again, someone new. But I was wrong. So wrong. I needed someone to care. I needed someone to love. And if I lost you now, it'd feel like not being able to surf, or to sing. It'd feel like not being able to breathe."

He caught my jaw between his fingers and tilted my face up to his. "That's love. You're essential to me, Juls. You're like air, you're like water."

CHAPTER 17

"It's your first time, isn't it?" Salt peered at me from under drawn eyebrows as he inspected my oxygen tank and equipment again.

I nodded and gulped, already feeling the weight of it, already afraid of losing the lightness in my lungs, but Ash had convinced me I'd love scuba, and I'd love Salt too, and he had coerced me into coming out to One Tree Reef early in the morning to dive.

I nodded again. "First time," I confirmed.

For a brief moment, I thought my answer brought a look of pity to Salt's watery blue eyes, and I wondered whether he'd even been asking about scuba at all.

"You'll be all right. Ash'll take good care of you. And I'll be up here, watching out for you both." He patted my shoulder, and Ash appeared in his wetsuit, the neoprene clinging to the hard planes of his body, accentuating his fitness as he bent over to check my gear again.

We spent half an hour down there, clasping hands, our flippers cleaving the water as we slowly swam after sea turtles and among schools of angel fish and brilliant, colourful fairy damsels. I only wished I could talk to Ash instead of signalling, wide-eyed at gorgonians and coral, wrasses and anemone-fish and enormous groupers. By the time we emerged, I knew what Ash meant about living underwater, and although my cheeks hurt from the mouthpiece, Ash couldn't miss my smile.

"That's my kingdom," Ash told me, gesturing to the reef as soon as we climbed out. "Amazing, huh? I've been diving since I turned ten." He pulled me into his arms. "You want to be my queen?"

"Depends. Do I get my own throne?"

"Totally. Made of pearls and jasper, inlaid with coral. You get a coral crown too." His dimples deepened as he added. "And if I ever see a shooting star, I might throw in a pearl necklace." He winked, and I was glad Salt was out of earshot, putting our gear back in the hold.

It hadn't taken me long to recognise a kindred spirit in Salt, even if his expression was inscrutable most of the time. I saw the way his eyes darted around, cataloguing our surroundings. The way he cocked his head at an angle, listening but rarely speaking unless he had something important to say.

Ash hadn't bothered to tell me his real name, but the nickname suited him. Like every true sailor, Salt was covered in the stuff. His greying hair was wiry from the wind and waves, his lips were cracked and chaffed, and his eyelashes and eyebrows were bleached pale as driftwood.

"Salt of the earth," Ash had explained to me as we'd driven out to the harbour. "That's where the nickname comes from. It's true too. Salt's the best guy I know. Dad went to school with him, but he said he didn't make Salt my godfather for that reason, or because of his religion. He reckoned Salt was the only other man on earth who'd put his life on the line for me if he had to. Dad's always warned me that if you piss Salt off, he turns into the scariest son of a bitch you've ever met. I've only done it once. Not so long ago really, and that was enough. I guess he learned some tricks in Vietnam."

"He's a veteran?"

"Sure is. When he came back, he bought the *Sea Change* and spent years sailing around the world. Couldn't stand the sight of people for a while, he told me. He wasn't around much until I turned seven, when he came back to the bay for good. He used to send me the coolest presents. Layla was a gift from him. He's got some ripper yarns to tell, too, if you can ever manage to drag any out of him."

In the half hour before we dived and the half hour on deck with him since, I'd discovered Salt's reluctance to share information about himself. Luckily, he wasn't as reluctant to share information about Ash.

"Where were you posted in Vietnam?" I asked, once Ash had disappeared into the yacht's cabin shortly after we'd come aboard the *Sea Change*, insisting I should keep Salt company on deck.

I'd asked about his deployment to break the awkward silence, the question slipping out to fill the space before I could process how taboo a topic it was.

"If I told you that, I'd have to kill you," Salt said with a sad grin. "Truth be told, to this day I don't know whether to love the place or hate it. A bit of both, most vets'd probably say. Don't like to talk about it, love. This place, though." He looked at the reef and the small coral cay with its lone mangrove tree and then back in the direction of Willow Bay. "This place I love. Ash loves it too, you know. So many kids just pack up and piss off once they quit school. But not our Ashley. He's a bay boy, that one. Head, heart, and soul. How about you, love? You in it for the long haul?"

So that's what this was: Salt was Ash's version of a matchmaking consultant.

I smiled my best "sweet girl" smile and crossed my legs beneath the sun-damaged old table on deck, feeling like I was at a job interview all of a sudden. "Hopefully."

"Not goin' away to study next year?" Salt pinned me with a scrutinising stare.

"Maybe, if I can't get into the Uni of Western Sydney course. There's an online component, and I can do the tutorials on campus at Anchorage."

"Good luck to ya then, love. What is it you want to be?"

"A marine biologist."

Salt's expression opened, interested, and a smile tugged at one corner of his mouth. "A scientist, huh? Clever. Don't know a man alive who doesn't like that in a sheila. Plenty of scuba in your future now, I'm guessing, love."

I smiled and nodded, and the old man watched me carefully for a moment before leaning in and folding his arms across the table.

"Here's the thing, Juls. You seem like a nice kid and more sensible than most. But in case you hadn't noticed, Ash here's kind of special to me. I'm every bit as biased as his old man, maybe more so. Pete knows Ashley ain't never been perfect. He talks more'n is healthy, and he's put it about some, but a man with half a head of sense'll sow his wild oats while he's young. Doesn't mean to say he bears no responsibility, but what I'm suggesting is..." Salt paused for a moment and bit at a flake of skin on his lower lip. "What I mean to say is that it ain't easy for Ash to care right now, not any longer. Not after Renee."

"Renee?" My throat constricted.

Salt nodded. "Don't get me wrong. Anyone worth a pinch of poop has had their heart hammered at some stage. Ash ain't no different. It's a rite of passage. But the manner of it is the thing. She took him down real brutal like. Then you come along, and the two of you haven't been on this old boat as much as an hour, and I see the way he's lookin' at you. Well..."

He sat back in his folding chair, crossing his legs at the ankle, staring at me. "I gotta admit it's got me fearin' for him again already. Not just him either, seeing the way you look right back at him like he's the most wonderful thing since fairy bread."

He raised an index finger and waggled it at me. "But it's not kid's stuff now with Ash. More likely it won't be again. Maybe he's better for it, too. Wiser. But once a man gets that shape hole in his heart, it always leaves him this close to falling through again. So, love, if you're gonna skin out or find someone better, or you got considerations other than loving our boy good and proper, despite his past, you might want to think about steppin' off now while the water's still shallow enough to swim to shore."

I tried to stop my eyes from widening. First trip out on the *Sea Change,* and I was already getting Salt's version of "You hurt him, you die."

Wow. And was that a "behave or walk the plank" threat?

It was confronting, to say the least. The first time he met me, he'd implied I had an STD, and now this! Yet as I stared back into his level, steel-blue eyes, I couldn't dislike him. Part of me respected him for giving it to me straight. No funny business. Renee had broken Ash's heart, whatever Ash told me or his machismo told him; Salt had made that pretty clear. He'd also suggested I was at risk of being his rebound girl, which made my heart bungee-jump in my chest. *Was I?* Did Salt have the wrong idea, or was Ash kidding himself he'd never loved Renee.

"Salt, I... She broke his heart?" I managed eventually.

The wind ruffled Salt's white hair as he nodded. "And then some. I'd have thought he'd have learned his lesson after that, which was why I was so surly the other night in the dunes. Apologies for that, love." Leaning forward again, he patted my hand with his arthritis-gnarled one. "I'm not really tryin' to scare you away, you know. Not the way Ash looks at you. I'm just tryin' to make sure you're gonna stay."

Footsteps sounded below, and we both turned toward the ladder as Ash emerged from the cabin, balancing two plates.

"Oh, here we go." Salt winked at me. "Romeo is really out to impress this time." He rubbed his palms together, grinning innocently as if we'd just been talking about the weather.

A grin split Ash's face too, as he carried two plates to the table.

"Breakfast fit for a queen," he said, setting a plate piled high with pancakes in front of me and the other in front of Salt. Slices of banana swam in a river of dark, sweet caramel, the ice cream on top already melting in the morning's heat.

"I told you pancakes were my favourite," Ash murmured, bending to kiss the top of my head.

CHAPTER 18

I put my fingers to my lips and smiled, searching for Ash out on the ocean. It was a big surf day, off the hook and completely crowded out, so I'd decided to read instead. After each chapter of the latest Amy Harmon novel, I looked up to watch the swirls of rips and runnels from my little nook under my propped-up board, or to admire Ash out there, poised on the cliff of a wave, the sea a sheer drop of glass at his feet. The board was invisible beneath him as he wove and turned and danced, and for the moment that he rode a wave before it crashed, he always looked so calm, as if he was about to step off and fall into the ocean's embrace.

Maybe, all along, he had been.

When the wind dropped, and the waves subsided a little, he came to find me. Saltwater streamed down his lean body as he jogged over.

"Hey." He stood his surfboard up beside mine, and lay down next to me, the weight of his body on one elbow, making his bicep bulge. "Did you see me get air out there, babe?" He stroked my cheekbone.

"Yep. Impressive. As always."

"Not as impressive as this though, right?" Sand sprinkled me as he rolled on top of me, lacing his fingers through mine. His stubble scratched my cheek, and I felt him stiffen through his board shorts, his erection hard against my thigh until he pulled away and rested his head on my stomach. "Maybe you need to go back to wearing jeans on the beach," he said, readjusting the waistband of his shorts. "It's a tease, seeing you in a bikini again."

"A tease?" I picked up the tablet propped on my bag and shook it at him. "I'm innocent. I'm a little bookworm minding my own business."

"Yeah. Innocent." The word sounded less so on his lips, and he slicked them with his tongue.

"Do I have to wear one of those sonar wrist thingies too? Keep the predators at bay?" I grinned.

"You better," Ash growled. "But don't count on it working." His teeth grazed my ribcage, the tender nip sending an electric tingle down my obliques, as if I'd just brushed against bluebottle tentacles.

"Guys, spare me the PDAs!" Jaz crouched next to us on the sand. "Really, get a room already. I'm trying to eat here."

She held up three ice cream cones. "I bought some for you lovebirds. Reckon you can stop dry humping long enough to eat them and hear the news?"

I sat up and straightened my bikini, flushing, and Ash immediately rolled on his stomach, looking equally as pained.

"Here." Jaz passed me a macadamia nut cone.

"What news?"

"That I'm a publicist extraordinaire."

Ash grimaced as he took the mango ice cream she passed to him and licked at a drip threatening to make its way down the waffle cone.

"The petition is doing great," Jaz told us through a mouthful of boysenberry. "Stacks of signatures. And I've got better news, big news."

"Auntie Penny's finally agreed to run a piece?" I chimed in. "She told me on the phone this morning. That terrorist attack kind of bumped everything else out of the news for weeks, but she's got space in the Saturday paper."

"Way to kill my buzz, bestie." Jaz frowned. "I wanted to tell him." She pouted. "But not just your auntie. *The Project.* They want to cover the protest against the developers." She clapped her hands and gave a high-pitched *squee* of pleasure.

"*The Project.* Is that the news show?"

"*News delivered differently*," she proudly quoted the show's tagline, beaming. "I've told them we'll have hundreds of protesters for them to film. But I need something more."

"What did you have in mind, publicist extraordinaire?" I asked. "Male surfwear modelling show?"

"That's a great idea," Jaz bubbled. "But no. I was thinking more that we need some performers. Like, I know this guy who writes these amazing songs, and he's an awesome singer." She jutted her chin at Ash. "If only that guy'd perform for us live." She gave a faux sigh of longing. "But maybe Dylan could model some speedos too. Where is Dyl, by the way?"

Ash laughed and nodded out beyond the breakers. "Still carving."

"So what do you think?" Jaz asked as Dylan did a bottom turn and came back up to smack the lip. "Will you play a gig at the protest, Ash?"

"I dunno." He frowned. "Thanks for believing in the fantasy of my Bieber-like world domination, Jaz, but the reality's not that simple."

"Nothing good is ever simple," Jaz said, doing her best life-coach impersonation. "I know, because I tried body-boarding."

Ash laughed, but he looked sceptical as he licked the ice cream.

"The truth is I don't even know if I can do it," he admitted. "When I wrote that song, it was just for me, just what I was feeling. But playing if for a whole heap of people? Something would feel really weird about that, like I'm sharing my private thoughts with all these strangers. What if they don't get it? Some of them might even hate it."

I made a *pssstth* sound.

"As if they'll hate it," Jaz said.

Ash shook his head. "I mean it. Putting stuff out there is part of why I didn't end up applying for the course at the conservatorium of music, too. I love writing songs. But I do it for me, not for anyone else. I'm just not sure I've got it in me to ever record one of them. Mum and Dad always treated guitar like a hobby that was never going to go anywhere. I mean, how many people make a living out of music, right? It's like being a pro surfer. You got this tiny percentage of people who can do it and an even tinier number who actually make it doing that?"

"Dylan will," Jaz said. "One day he will. I know it."

"See? You still believe," Ash said, crunching on his cone. "Maybe I don't." He chewed, watching Dylan surf.

"Maybe my old man's right. Maybe songwriting's just a fantasy, and some things are better off staying that way. I don't want to try this and kill the dream. I've already kind of given up on it."

"Coping with fame—all part of being a superstar." Jaz waggled her finger at him, speaking as if she'd already gone platinum twice over. I once again admired her confidence. I always had. Jaz didn't have confidence in spades; she had it in tip-trucks. Well, it was either confidence or a whole load of horse manure. She definitely didn't suffer from the self-doubt Ash was telling her about.

"Look." Jaz pressed on, determined as ever. "Everyone's going to love it. Love it! Trust me. And if you don't trust me, trust yourself. Let me record the song on my mobile and put it up on YouTube first." She held up her index finger. "We won't promote it," Jaz promised. "We won't tell anyone." She mimed zipping her lip, then crossed her heart and threw away the key. "But if it gets some hits, maybe even some comments, you'll see this dream isn't as difficult as you think it is. And then maybe you won't be such a pussy, and you'll be able to play your first gig at the rally." Her tone was persuasive, wheedling. It was a tone I knew well. There was no way he was getting out of it.

"A pussy!" Ash laughed. "Gee, thanks, Jaz."

"Maybe she's right," I said, licking a stream of melting ice cream off my wrist. I knew better than most how hard it was to tell fantasy from reality, and even if I was pretty sure it was a song about his heartbreak over Renee, Ash's talent was real. Anyone who'd heard him play would have said the same.

"Sure that song's a part of you," I told him, "but when other people hear it, it becomes a part of them too. Even if you don't trust yourself or Jaz"—I poked my tongue out at her—"maybe you have to trust the song, trust it'll have the power to touch other people, too. Remember that conversation we had about doing something that mattered?"

Ash nodded.

"Maybe that song matters. Maybe it has the power to make someone who listens to it matter too," I said. "Make them remember someone they love, or remember you."

He rubbed his square jaw, and I could tell he was considering what we'd said. "Maybe that's what I'm afraid of," he muttered.

"You're afraid of success," Jaz chimed in. She tapped her temple with one finger. "But emotion, that's what it's all about. That's what makes a song great. Then it's not just the songwriter's song, it's everyone's. The people's song. Maybe if you let me put it on YouTube, you'd see that. Also, you have a publicist extraordinaire to help you make this go viral, so what are you afraid of, pussy?" She stood up and stretched. "Anyhow, I gotta go pee. Back soon," she said and wandered off up the beach.

I finished my cone and balled up the paper wrapper, stuffing it back into my bag to go in the bin later. "She's right," I told him. "Maybe you'd get your dream back."

Ash stuffed the rest of his cone in his mouth and then kissed me with frozen lips.

"You two crazy kids!" he said, ruffling my hair. "The things you believe could happen." He tilted his head, studying me, then said, "That's what makes you different from other girls I've been with, you know. There's this thing, this recognition when you look at people. Like you're really seeing them, like they matter. Not just me or Jaz or Dyl, but strangers, too. Just people you pass in the streets. I can't explain it. Maybe it's empathy or something, but you look at them like they matter to you, really matter. That day you helped me clean up the smashed board, and in the sandwich shop when I was talking about the ocean, I could tell you cared—really cared. It's like everything matters to you, Juls."

He wrapped his arms around me, and I relaxed into his chest, feeling the weight of his head laid on top of mine, his curls tickling my cheek. Strangers' faces, dead and alive flipped through my mind like a shuffling deck of cards, and I closed my eyes.

"You're real—real in a way some girls can't even fathom," he muttered. "And when I'm with you, I can't help but feel more real too. I can't help but care more. I can't help but matter." Craning his neck a little, he kissed my forehead. "You don't even realise it, but you make everything matter more."

A chime from Ash's mobile phone interrupted him, and he sighed and straightened to pick it up from where it lay on his towel, to check the message. A *schwooop* soon indicated he'd sent a reply.

Suddenly frowning, he said, "I'll think about YouTube. Maybe you're right about this mattering too. But right now, this pussy's gotta bail. Enjoy your book, babe." He didn't say where he had to go, and I didn't ask as he lifted his board under one arm and strode off up the sand.

When Renee and a gaggle of Fantastics arrived on the beach five minutes later, I was alone.

CHAPTER 19

"Maybe you can work here once you finish uni." Mum's red-lacquered nail tapped the *Willow Bay Bulletin's* second page.

"I'm not studying journalism, Mum. I've decided I want to do marine biology."

"*Ksero*, darling," Mum replied. "I didn't mean at the paper. I meant here." The newspaper crackled as she folded it and passed it to me. "This dolphin business Allen Aldershot wants to set up. It sounds perfect for a marine biologist."

MAYOR'S ECO-TOURISM RESORT TO PUT BAY ON MAP the headline blared.

"You could be a dolphin trainer," she added.

"I'm not going to be a dolphin trainer," I muttered.

"But you could be."

"I could be an astronaut, but I'm not going to," I said snippily.

"Juliette." Mum's tone rose at the end in warning. It was a tone she usually got just before she started swearing in Greek.

"What?" I feigned innocence, levelling out my attitude as I pushed the paper back over to her. "It'll never pass environmental planning. Where's the 'eco' in it? Unless he means *eco*nomy. Fish-feeding's bad for dolphins. It makes them trust people. Then they get hit by boat propellers or follow fishing trawlers. That's if they're not tangled up in Mayor Aldershot's stupid shark nets."

Mum huffed. "Just because Ash has gotten into your head and—"

"So that's what this is about? You don't like Ash? Because he cares about the environment?"

"It's not that. It's that he's... Well, he's older. And not everyone's a good influe—"

"You think he's a bad influence because he gives a shit about stuff? Important stuff—like climate change and marine conservation." I snorted. "Last I heard, caring wasn't a crime."

"I'm just saying, *koritsi mou.*" Mum widened her eyes, trying to look innocent. "Mayor Aldershot was in the salon. He mentioned that Ash was..." She fluffed her fingers through her hair, clearly considering how best to frame her argument.

The mayor of Sunshine Shire was also Renee's dad, regrettably. He got his hair done at Cut 'n' Run like everyone else, not that there was much of it to snip. His comb-over was often embarrassingly harassed by sea breezes, but Mum couldn't convince him it'd be better to go with a buzz cut; Allen Aldershot was that kind of guy.

"I don't like all this activism. It's too political."

That was really saying something, coming from a Greek. I'd been subjected to countless political arguments at my grandparents' place. Most of them ended with one party or the other storming off in a huff.

"This resort might bring jobs, *paidi mou,*" Mum suggested. "Where will you work here in Willow Bay as a marine biologist without this? You'd have to leave to find work, maybe even go overseas. Besides, all these new tourists." She tapped the paper again. "It's good for business."

"Good for business" had been Aldershot's campaign slogan.

"*Good for business!*" I spat. "What bullshit. He's selling us out, buttering up all the local businesses with dreams of extra profit. You really think 'ecotourists'"—I made quote marks for emphasis—"are going to visit the salon?"

She shrugged. "They go to the beach, they feed the dolphins. It's windy. Their hair goes everywhere. Then they need a blow-dry, or they get a massage. They have sandy feet from the beach—they need a pedicure. They have sunburn—they need after-sun body treatment, *koritsi mou.*"

"You do massages and body treatments now?"

"Of course. Massage. Pedicure. Manicure. Seaweed Wrap. Milk Bath. Botox. Facial..." She ticked off the list on her fingers until I put up a hand to stop her.

"And the salon is opposite Windmills. *All* the tourists stay at Windmills," she insisted.

I didn't burst her bubble by telling her that was because there was literally nowhere else outside of Willow Bay Caravan Park, or that "all the tourists" consisted of the occasional campervan-load of British backpackers passing through on their way to Bluff Bridge National Park.

"You could work at Dolphin Dayze. I'm busy at the salon. No one leaves Willow Bay." She shrugged, palms up, and stretched a bright smile over her dazzling teeth. "Everybody's happy."

"Except the dolphins."

"Oh, *paidi mou*, the dolphins have fish. Fish! What else you think a dolphin wants?"

"Maybe to not have to worry about drowning in shark nets."

Mum picked up the paper again and squished her lips together, making a *pish* sound. "Mayor Aldershot says here that they'll check the nets for other sea life and set it free."

"Mayor Aldershot," I said, "is a moron. Everything gets caught—dolphins, rays, even baby whales. As if they're going to be able to save them all. Nets just give people a false sense of security anyway."

"Juliette. He is the mayor."

"And he is a moron." *Just like his daughter,* I added mentally. "What happens if Bitten gets caught in a net, Mum?"

Mum stood and tipped the rest of her coffee down the sink. "Dolphins are smart, darling."

"Unlike mayors," I growled.

CHAPTER 20

"It's supposed to be a blood moon tonight," Ash told me, hugging me tight against him as we lay on his bed. We'd spent the Saturday chilling, surfing in the morning before watching all *The Hunger Games* movies at Ash's in the afternoon. Like my mum when Ash was over, Ash's mum, Sharon, prowled around outside his room like an over-protective lioness: hoovering, cleaning and calling out occasionally to offer us food. Whatever she was doing, it was only marginally more annoying than Ash's phone beeping with a new text every few minutes. Even though he ignored it, it was successfully throwing me off my game, and by early evening Ash must have noticed my frustration enough to suggest heading out.

"If we leave now, we'll have time to grab some Chinese for dinner and then go down to Point Hanrahan to watch the moonrise. It's meant to be spectacular. There won't be another one like it for years."

"Perfect. But promise me there won't be any fisherman this time," I insisted.

He laughed and extricated himself from my hug. "I can't promise that." At the dresser, he slid his wallet and keys into his worn jeans pockets, and checked his phone. A tone indicated another text.

I moved behind him and slid my hands around his waist, resting my chin on his shoulder. It was sneaky, half hoping to see who it was on screen, but I was curious.

"So, what *can* you promise?" I murmured, kissing his neck.

"More privacy than we've got here with Mum buzzing around outside like a blue-arsed fly."

"Anything else?" I aimed a second kiss at his earlobe.

"Delicious food, fine wine, good conversation, that kind of tinkly awful Chinese music."

I pouted. "Is that all?"

105

"And this." He spun me around until my back was against the dresser and kissed me deeply. "Lots of this." His hands slid up and over my breasts, despite Sharon's humming and dusting in the living room next door. "And astronomical wonders. And starlight. And the music of the ocean."

"I'm sold." I told him, snatching my handbag from the dresser and marching him out the door.

The Sun Hing was the fanciest restaurant in Willow Bay if you discounted Windmills, and most people did. Although Windmills was Willow Bay's highest-rated accommodation, its out-dated décor, stale modern Australian menu, and Sydney prices kept it out of favour with the locals.

But the food at the Sun Hing was always wonderful, and most nights of the week it was busy. The mood was cheery, the restaurant bright with crimson feature walls and fountains and waving golden cats. Beribboned happy bamboo plants twisted from scarlet pots on the tables.

"I suppose we should have dressed up a bit more for the occasion," Ash said, gesturing to his jeans and Foo Fighter's T-shirt, his thong-clad foot nudging my sandals under the table. "But I hate wearing collared shirts. It makes me feel like my dad."

"It's not exactly Milan here tonight anyway." I jerked my head toward the diners at other tables, all dressed in casual, holiday get-up. "But I hear you. I hate wearing heels. Let's pass on the wine, too," I suggested, running a finger down the laminated drinks menu.

I wasn't yet eighteen, and Cheryl Hing knew it because I'd done a stint there as a waitress last Christmas. Plus I didn't really like the stuff, or hadn't found my vintage yet.

"Done," Ash agreed, opting for a Corona when the waiter came to take our drinks order. "You know another thing I love about you?" he asked, watching me with a lopsided grin as I thumbed through the rest of the menu.

"My sparkling wit?" I said, without looking up.

Ash chuckled. "Actually, Juls, about that..."

I closed the menu with a snap and gave a faux sniff of outrage. "What are you saying? Should I cancel the stand-up tour?"

"Seriously, I love that you're the first girl I've dated for more than a few weeks who's never demanded a posh dinner date at some fancy restaurant in Anchorage," he explained.

I frowned. "That's a good thing? Fair enough. Let's talk about what else you love about me over special fried rice and beef satay."

"Let's." He closed his menu with a snap too, and then relayed our choices to the water, who'd dropped off our drinks. "That's a *great* thing," he continued once the server was gone. "I'd much rather eat here than sit in some trendy minimalist restaurant named Twee or Air or Zone or something, feeling cold and bored and struggling to make *appropriate* conversation while the waiter drops in on us all the time to look at us like we're vermin." He put on an affected British accent. 'Sir, would you like to taste the Sémillon? Everything okay, sir and madame? Madame, I trust you enjoyed your entrée of devilled frog thigh poached in a cider broth with a claptrap *jus* and Turkmenistan truffle mash and a sprig of imported rhinoceros grass as garnish.' Even then, you have to go to Macca's after to fill up because the portions are miniscule. Nah. Give me good old sweet and sour pork any day. And thongs, and no dinner dates, only surfing dates."

I grinned. "I never even knew there was such a thing as a surfing date until I met you. But given your, ahem, extensive knowledge of fine-dining ingredients, I'm kind of glad you made me breakfast instead of dinner. Just so you know, in romance novels it's *always* about dinner or movies or picnics. But I'll take pancakes."

"Hey!" Ash put his hands in the air and frowned with mock offense. "I don't just do pancakes, by the way. I cook a mean steak too, with or without a claptrap jus and Turkmenistan truffle mash. Movie dates are okay, too, except you can't talk."

I giggled. "Well, that wouldn't suit you."

"Picnics—now they're a dating concept I can get behind," Ash went on. He raised his beer glass. "To picnics and surf dates and camping. Boo to the other crap."

I clinked my glass against his, confessing as I did so, "Actually, I've never been camping."

Ash's head jerked back, and he took a long sip of beer and licked the froth from his lip. "Never been camping! We'll have to fix that. As soon as you're off school for summer, we're going bush."

"Doe school camp count? I've been on school camp."

"School camp in a bungalow at Bluff Bridge, doing ropes courses and rappelling and having pillow fights and drinking smuggled butterscotch schnapps, is definitely not camping," he insisted. "At best it is glamping. At worst, it's soul destroying."

He leaned forward, eyes shining. "No, Juls. Camping is about freedom. Camping is the wind in your hair and sand in your jocks, and wiping your bum with gum leaves. It's pitting yourself against the elements, being at one with the wilderness, cooking on an open fire, making love beneath the stars." His eyes gleamed, and he held my gaze, two of those words crackling in the air between us.

"Wiping your bum with gum leaves, huh? Wow. You make it sound so tempting," I joked, feeling that curious tingling sensation the mere thought of sleeping with Ash always stoked in me. "Although I guess I am kind of intrigued about that *last* activity."

There was no denying his comment about making love under the stars had set off firecrackers in my crotch. The way he'd stared at me, it was like he wanted to be clear he wasn't talking about past occurrences either. I wanted to make love to Ash more than just about anything. If camping was the catalyst Ash needed, I was absolutely ready for him to pitch a tent.

Ash laughed. "I still haven't seen that shooting star, remember. But seriously, it's the realness I like most about it. It's naked ape stuff. Cave people business, except with tents instead of huts. When you camp, it reminds you we're not meant to wall ourselves off from nature. It's about getting amongst it, appreciating your animal side and living off your wits, like how our ancestors would have lived."

"Clubbing a woman and dragging her back to the man cave for some romance." I jutted out my jaw and beat my chest with one fist. "Captain Caveman."

Ash's eyes darkened momentarily, and his forehead crinkled. "No," he said in a clipped tone. "No matter what you hear about me, there's never any reason to go full Neanderthal. Anyway"—he brightened again—"I'm an alpha male with hunting and fire-lighting skills. Cave women are putty in my hands. Once they see my enviable skills and my enormous weapon, it's me who has to run away from them, although I guess I could tolerate a small harem if I had to."

"Ha." I laughed. "Just you try it, mister."

Ash took another swig of Corona and snaked a hand across the table to clutch mine.

"I know all the good spots," he went on. "My old man used to camp with me heaps when I was a kid. Mum wasn't a fan. She was always bitching about sand in the swag, but Dad went through this prepper stage, and he and Salt taught me all this 'guy stuff,' like how to navigate by the stars or light a fire with a flint chip. I even learned how to pulp the storage roots of casuarina trees to get water. Real Bear Grylls stuff. It's hard to do now, because there's not many bush camps left, but back then, Dad refused to camp anywhere with amenities, so we had to swim in lakes or the sea, or 'moss it' and rub ourselves down with baby wipes instead of showering."

"So romantic." I crinkled my nose but couldn't stop myself from imagining him attending to his naked body with moist towelettes.

"It doesn't sound particularly hygienic if you're planning certain activities under the stars, though." I ran my tongue over my lips, tasting the vanilla of my gloss and hoping I looked seductive.

"I even had this British SAS handbook, and I wrote tips and tricks in the back. It was my go-to survival guide—that, and a book by the Bush Tucker Man." He grinned and lowered his voice to a whisper. "Incidentally, bush is still my favourite tucker. Unfortunately, it wasn't on the menu tonight, but maybe it will be for dessert." He licked his lips, one of his eyebrows forming a crooked inverted V on his forehead.

I groaned. "You're in form tonight. Stop with the suggestive lines. You're killing me here."

"It's my sparkling wit," he replied.

"You know, when I first met you, with some of the things you said, I didn't know whether you were trying it on or not."

Ash chuckled and put both of his palms up. "I plead no contest. I'm a hot-blooded bloke, and you're a beautiful woman. What're the chances every single thing I said wasn't some version of, 'My God, you're so incredibly, amazingly, dick-hardeningly hot. Please let me live and die inside you. Thank you.'"

I shook my head. "Again, not so romantic, Prince Charming. *Kiiind* of compelling, but let's hope I never have to explain anything like that to a coroner."

"At least I'd die happy," he replied flippantly. "Like a redback spider or a phascogale."

"A what now?"

"Tiny little Aussie marsupial," he explained, holding up his thumb and forefinger. "The males shag themselves to death. Literally. Well, not themselves, but the females. They root till they can't even... Honestly, they keep on fucking until they die of exhaustion. Exhaustion!" He enunciated it. "You can thank the Bush Tucker Man for that knowledge too."

"Who said romance is dead?"

The waiter cleared his throat as he approached and set our dishes on the table. "Sweet and sour pork, special friend rice, Sun Hing house special satay, honey king prawns." He identified them all for us, trying to stifle a laugh, which made it obvious he'd heard at least some of our inappropriate dinner conversation.

"And no rhinoceros grass in any of them." I smirked.

Ash's lips curled up into his trademark lopsided smile, and he picked up his chopsticks and gestured for me to dig in.

"Mock me all you like, babe, but something tells me you'd enjoy camping a lot more than you'd like being shut up in a five-star hotel. You might even get to see a phascogale, or at least a pademelon. That's like this adorable little wallaby critter, in case you're wondering."

I was. "I've never stayed in a five-star hotel either," I admitted, piling my bowl high. "Mum was always busy with the salon, so most of our holidays were in Melbourne with Yiayia and Pappous. She always spoke about taking me back to Tinos for a visit, because you know Tinos is the most *gorrrgeous* place in the world, according to her, but it's hard being a single mum, running her own business. When she had the money, she never had the time."

"Maybe we'll have to try camping *and* a luxury hotel, and see which one you prefer," Ash said, picking up a piece of pork with his chopsticks. "But camping first. So I can show off my mad bush skillz." He stopped, the chunk of pork halfway to his lips. "Hey! We could camp tonight, if you like! My tent's one of those thirty-second ones that fold down nice and small, so I keep it in the Kombi with a yoga mat to sleep on, just in case."

He finally popped the deep-fried morsel in his mouth and chewed. When he'd finished, he added, "There's a free camp down at Figtree that's right on the water. It'll be a great place to watch the moonrise. Text your Mum and let her know."

I cocked my head, considering it as I swallowed another bite of satay. "Tonight?" *Making love beneath the stars.*

"Why not, babe? It'll be awesome. A bit bright, but all the better to see you with." Ash put his chopsticks down and made a prayer motion with his hands, his eyes enormous as he tilted his forehead toward me. "Come on, gorgeous," he pleaded. "It's only a half-hour drive away. If you get scared, we can always sleep in the back of the Kombi."

I had to stop myself from laughing. It wasn't sleeping in a tent I was scared of, or even having sex for the first time. The *mati* had given me so much more to fear than that. It was sleeping beside Ash all night long. It was waking up in a cold sweat, screaming and having to explain to him what a weirdo I was.

"I'm not scared. I trust you, Bear Grylls, and your mad alpha ape skillz."

I rested my chopsticks on my bowl and pushed my chair back. "Now excuse me. I need to use the lady's room one last time before I abandon civilization for gum leaves and baby wipes."

I grabbed my handbag off the chair next to me and made my way to the toilet to text Mum as a flock of brightly dressed, stiletto-wearing Fantastics clip-clopped in through the Sun Hing's sliding glass doors.

When I emerged again, freshly lip-glossed and with Mum's reluctant approval to go and get my camping on with Ash, the complete cohort of Fantastics was seated at a large banquet table near us—all but one of them, anyway.

Renee Aldershot was sitting at our table, perched in my chair, across from a forlorn-looking Ash.

She was crying.

She'd dressed for the occasion in a metallic blue dress a size too small, matched with towering stiletto heels and a silver handbag. The dress hugged her curves, which seemed even more impressive now that she had put on a bit of weight. She wasn't heavy, only less emaciated than the other Fantastics. Thick eyeliner made her green eyes look slitted and catlike, and a trail of mascara snaked down her cheeks with her tears. She dabbed at it with the table napkin from the spare place setting and sniffed.

Just my luck. What is she doing here?

I watched as Ash moved a plate of honey king prawns aside to reach across the table and pat her hand, and it was all I could do to stop my nostrils flaring. The hot, dry feeling in my throat had nothing to do with the spice of the satay, and an evil thought flitted into my head. *For a table that big, the Fantastics had to have booked in advance.* Maybe the question I should have asked myself was: *what are we doing here?*

Ash had been the one who had suggested the Sun Hing. Was that what all those texts today had been about? Had Ash known Renee was going to be here? Had he been invited to come? And if he had, why? An icy numbness gripped my brain.

What if he wanted to run into her? What if Salt's right? What if she did break his heart, but he's still in love with her? What if she wants him back?

Ash chewed on his cheek, looking uncomfortable, and then muttered something that made Renee withdraw her hand and wave it angrily in his face.

"Like you care!" I thought I heard her wail.

He folded his arms across his chest. They were both upset now, their pitch higher. Ash's toe was tapping at an alarming rate under the table.

"You think it was any easier for me?" he muttered, rubbing a hand over his jaw. "You think I wanted things to go this way? Jesus, Renee."

"You're the one seeing *her*?" Renee spat. "Like you're Mister Perfect."

Her?

I realised they were talking about *me*, and right at that moment, I also realised I was standing like a statue in the middle of the restaurant, flushed crimson with humiliation, my mouth open in shock while my boyfriend had a very public fight with his ex. In the reflection of the window behind them, I could make out the gloating expressions on the faces of the other Fantastics and the whiteness of my face, the wideness of my eyes under the paper-lantern lights.

"What about *her*?" Ash said, his eyes fixed on Renee's, his jaw tight. He still hadn't noticed I'd returned from the bathroom.

My heart sank to the bottom of my stomach. *What about me? Was he ready to dismiss me, just like that?*

Renee flicked her blonde hair back from her face and threw the napkin down. The chair screeched as she pushed it back and stumbled to her feet. She teetered more than the stilettos alone could account for, and I realised she was half-drunk. Leaning close to him, her face right up to his, she hissed a threat I couldn't hear properly, although it sounded something like, "You'll pay."

"I already did," Ash muttered in reply, his gaze briefly skimming Renee's curvaceous figure as she stood there, trembling and wobbling. "You got your pound of flesh, Nay," he said calmly. "And then some. What more do you want?"

Renee tugged at the hem of her short dress and put one hand on the table to steady herself. She slurred, "You *know* that, Ash. You were the only one who ever did."

That was when Ash looked over and saw me. I clamped my lips together, and he stared at me for a long moment, swallowing hard, looking miserable.

That was also when I found my feet again. And my voice.

I strode to the front counter and paid the bill before marching over and grabbing his hand. Ignoring Renee entirely, I said to him, "We're all paid up. Let's go."

CHAPTER 21

The moon was rising, large and orange as a jack-o'-lantern, and the trees Figtree beach was named after sent dark, spidery branches across its Halloween face. Ash was setting up the tent away from them, in a nearby clearing, in case there was a storm in the night.

As soon as we left the Sun Hing, I'd whispered that we needed to talk, but I was still shocked by what I'd seen, and Ash had been silent and distant in the car on the way over. Part of me was surprised I'd still agreed to come, but he had driven here without asking if I'd changed my mind.

"Sorry about that," Ash had muttered as he turned the key in the ignition and the Kombi spluttered to life.

"What do you have to apologise for?" I crossed my arms, feeling cold despite the mild weather. It was an actual question, not rhetorical. I wasn't letting him get out of it that easily.

He turned to stare at me, his lips opening and closing like a fish's, as if he desperately wanted to say something but didn't quite know how. Eventually, he closed them again, set his jaw, and shrugged.

After five more kilometres of silence, he said, "What have I got to apologise for? Nothing to you, Juls. I'd never hurt you. You should know that. But everyone has their skeletons, their regrets."

Ash flicked on the indicator and pulled into a drive-through bottle shop on the outskirts of Figtree, ordering a six-pack of Tooheys and another of premixed Jack Daniels and Coke.

"Did you know she was going to be there? Is that why we went there tonight?"

He handed his key card to the attendant. "Of course not. You really think I'd have taken you there if I'd known?"

I didn't know how to take that. Did he mean he wanted to protect me from the Fantastics or just hide me from Renee? I let out a long sigh and dropped my hands to my lap.

"Juls, I know how humiliating that must have been for you." He reached over the gearstick to rub my knee. "That's why they act like that, I guess, to humiliate us. How much did you hear?"

"Everything," I lied.

And that's all we'd said about it in the car. Ash had been quiet the rest of the way, biting his cheek, clearly mulling over the incident. And I'd been doing some stewing of my own.

After a few minutes, he came and sat beside me on the sand, throwing me a crooked grin that was weaker than usual, more fragile. "See? That was quick," he said, gesturing to the tent. "Want a beer? Or a can?"

I shook my head. "Neither."

Ash popped the top of his can of JD and set it in the sand, then he leaned over and cupped my chin in his hand. Turning my face up to his, he said soberly, "Juls, I'm not going to tell you that was nothing. Renee and I have a past. It's not easy knowing her like I do, feeling what I... feel for her. I'm not proud of what went down, but I'm trying to be better than I was. Not just for you, for everyone. For me, too."

He leaned in, and I let him kiss me. His lips were more tender than usual, brushing my face, my cheeks, and trailing kisses up to my eyelids.

"Why won't you share it with me?" I asked in a small voice. "You don't talk about her, Ash. It scares me. Does it still hurt that bad?"

He pulled back. "I want to tell you. I want to share everything with you, Juls. But I can't. I made promises. Promises I'm not sure I can keep anymore. We agreed not to talk about why we broke up, not to anyone. And I haven't really. But it hurts not to. I try to pretend it doesn't, but it does." His Adam's apple bobbed as he swallowed.

"Is that why you told me you'd never loved anyone? Because it hurt too bad to admit it?"

Ash sighed deeply again and shook his head. "It's not like that. It just hurts that you'd think less of me if you knew what happened."

"Were you dating her when we met? Is that it? You dumped her for me?"

"No." He shook his head. "But maybe I would have, before."

He took a long swig from his can and then another. "I just want to hold you tonight. Is that okay? I just want to watch the moon rise. I don't want to think about that guy anymore."

"What guy?"

"That guy I was. Fun, flippant, fatuous. All the f-words I've been. Mostly a frivolous fucker who didn't care enough about anything but having a good time—until he wasn't actually having one. I don't want to be him. I want to be *this* me, the one who's happy being here with you, emjoying the universe."

We watched the moon come up in silence, holding hands, my head on his shoulder, and before it climbed too high overhead, and after the cans had run out, Ash took my hand and led me into the tent.

The mattress was thin, and the sleeping bag rustled as he spread it over us. I lay next to him on my side in my thin summer dress with his strong arms around me, one leg thrown up over his hip. He was still wearing his T-shirt over his briefs. His sadness troubled me.

My jealousy had flown, but Ash still seemed pensive, and his kisses, though deep, felt melancholy and filled with an impossible longing that made me want to cry.

"The moon's too bright," I complained after a while, rolling onto my back to stare up through the mesh canopy. "It's blocking out the starlight. Maybe we won't see a meteor tonight after all."

He smiled. "I suppose that's my fault. Another promise I can't keep. Starlight."

He pulled me back, and I arched against him, more desperate than ever for him to prove his love for me. Perhaps only that could make him happy tonight: letting go. Release. Returning to me, living in the now and not the past.

"Yes, you've been very bad," I scolded him, waggling my index finger at him. "Egging me on all night with all that sparkling wit and innuendo, and now you're so distant." I slid a hand up under his shirt and tugged it off.

"Maybe I'll let you off the hook," I whispered, running a finger down his abdominals. "Maybe you won't even need a meteor. You delivered on the food, and the tinkly Chinese music, and this..." I kissed him, pressing closer, feeling him respond immediately.

"Juls," he murmured, rough hands sliding up under my dress, over my thighs, and slipping the cotton up and over my head before slithering back down my body, under my panties.

"Make love to me, Ash," I whispered. "I need you."

He swallowed hard and brushed the hollow of my throat with his lips as I tugged at his briefs.

He was ready. Thick and firm, gleaming and slippery at the tip, standing boldly as I clenched my hand around him, making steady, insistent movements, encouraging him to make this real.

His kiss turned cavernous, his lips and tongue devouring mine. His fingers were rigid and penetrating where they probed deep beneath my underwear. Then, with a groan, he cursed loudly and sat up.

I'm sorry, Juls. I thought I could do this. I wanted to do this tonight so bad ... before she..." He rubbed his temple. "But I can't. Not now. Not tonight."

"Please," I begged, crawling into his lap. I straddled him, pressing my aching heat to his bare erection.

"You have to understand." Ash encircled me with his arms, his words almost lost as he snuggled his face into my chest. "I want to make love to you, Juls." He kissed the hollow of my throat again, where my pulse hammered. "God. I want that so bad. But this"—he gestured to our bodies—"wanting you... it hurts. It's like an ache. An instinct." He let his hands rest on my hips, as if at any second, he might pick me up, fit me to him, force me down on him.

I wrapped my hands around his back, stroking the bare skin of his shoulders, folding my legs around him.

"Goddamn it, Juls. I want you more than I've ever wanted anything. I want to take you right here, this moment. I want to carry you away, let myself get carried away." His hips moved involuntarily, uncomfortably, his erection springing up awkwardly until there was nothing between us but his resolve, and desire sharp enough to bite lurked in the depths of his oceanic eyes. I shifted my hips again, twisting them, circling him, but he gripped them and easily lifted me off, setting me back onto the thin mattress.

"Stop," he moaned, turning away. "I want to make love to you, Juls. Hell, I want to make love to you, and then I want to shag you, and then I want to fuck you, and then make love to you again and then flip you over and do the whole thing over and over again forever like a horny phascogale. I want to do it even if kills me. That's how I know I can't." The moonlight gleamed off his broad, naked back, and once more my vulva ached with the heavy, wringing weight of disappointment.

"Damn you and your stupid antiquated notions, Mr Darcy," I said with a huff. "Last time I looked, it was the twenty-first century, and you were threatening to go all Captain Caveman on me, and now you're worried about chivalry." I lowered my tone to a seductive wheedle. "I know you want to. You keep telling me so. So just do it. Make love to me. Fuck me. Whatever you want to call it, Ash. I'm all yours."

I wasn't trying to be sexy. I really meant it. So what if it hurt? So what if it ruined my perfect little hymen. I wanted him, and he wanted me too. Even if he had some complex madonna/whore thing going on, we were both adults, and I was done with waiting. D.O.N.E. Plus Jaz had already told me it didn't hurt all that much anyway, even though Dylan was supposedly hung like a Mallee bull—at least that's what she called it. I had no idea what that even was, but it sounded big and kind of filthy.

Ash turned to me and smiled apologetically. "Juls, it's not about that. It's..." He faced the moon again, watching it through the open tent door, and I wriggled forward to wrap my arms around him from behind.

"You know that moment when a perfect A-frame is building and you're itching to own it?" he asked, the longing in his expression unmistakeable. "To go before it peaks, before anyone else can ride it?"

I nodded.

"But if you go too soon, you'll miss it," he said gruffly. "It'll just roll right on by, and then that perfect thing will vanish. Someone else will claim it. Or it'll wash away. And once that moment's gone, you can't ever get it back. And you know the next wave won't be the same, nor the next. But if you're patient, if you wait for the right moment, once you make it, it's yours, and no one can ever take it away from you."

I knew the moment he meant: it was that moment on the brink of change, that pivot where things could go either way, could be different. I knew it not only from being on a surfboard, but from every time I closed my eyes, every time I dreamed. If only...

"I thought that moment was tonight, but I was wrong. And I won't let you get away from me. I won't risk that. Doesn't that mean anything to you?"

"It means everything," I whispered, my eyes brimming.

"I won't let you go too soon, Juls," he promised. "I can't. I need you to be mine. Forever."

"I need you too, Ash," I whispered, meaning it in more ways than one. I kissed the firm line of his jaw, the pale stubble ticklish on my lips. "I love you."

The moonlight made dark mirrors of his eyes as he turned to stare at me. "I believe you. But for how long?" He sounded so sad it was almost bitter, and it threw me off balance.

"What's that supposed to mean?"

"It means for how long?" Sighing, he pulled me down beside him, his obliques grazing my side. "You think I'm some hero, some perfect guy. But how long will that last, really?" Pointing to the heavens through the mesh roof of the tent, he added, "Look. There's still a few stars out tonight, Juls. See them?"

I followed his gaze, up to where the Milky Way was a fat seam of smoke in the sky. "Yes. They're magical, even if it's too bright to see that many."

"They're dead." He corrected me. "Or some of them are. Light years ago. Now they're nothing. Nothing but light."

It was true, of course—sad but true—and I shivered, suddenly feeling the night's chill.

"It doesn't matter how much we love their shine, or how much we need their heat," he went on. "They're not what you think they are. And one day they'll all wink out. They'll all be forgotten." He slid his large, square hand over mine and squeezed hard.

"Maybe our sun will have stopped shining by then, too. Maybe it'll be cold, and we'll be gone, and there'll be no one left to remember them—no one left to remember us." His dark brows were drawn together, his words laced with pain. "But some things get remembered—that's what I believe."

Turning my hand palm up, he began to trace the constellation of whorls and grooves there. Lifeline, headline, heartline, mount of Venus, all while watching the stars, the moonlight illuminating his face.

"Is that why you write songs?" I asked. "To be remembered?"

"No. I write them to remember. Love gets remembered, that's what I think." He brought my hand to his mouth, kissing each fingertip with gentle lips.

"Ash." I tried to cup his firm, square jaw and tug him in for another kiss, but he pulled free and turned his gaze skyward again.

"Maybe that's all they are, the stars," he said. "Maybe their light's just the shine of souls someone still loves too much to forget."

The sorrow in his tone made me blink back tears. He sounded so lost, so empty, and I thought about Salt's comment about heart-shaped holes and squeezed my lips shut tight against the hot, queasy feeling of jealousy.

I'd never had an ex; I had no way of knowing how that felt, but in all the rom-coms, exes were either hated or loved. It seemed like there was no in-between for two people who'd once been intimate.

Ash swiped at his left eye with his thumb. "Maybe I've had too much to drink. It's making me maudlin, but what I'm trying to say is I don't ever want to forget you." His gaze finally swung back to mine, but darkness had drawn all the shine from his eyes. "I want this love to be remembered always, even after all the stars wink out."

"Of course it'll be remembered," I scoffed, tugging my hand from his and hugging him. "I'll always love you. That's why I want you to be my first, silly."

"What?"

"No girl ever forgets her first," I told him. 'You're my first kiss, first boyfriend. And you always will be. When we make love, you'll be my fir—"

His eyes narrowed suspiciously. "You're telling me you never even kissed a dude before me?"

I swallowed hard, nodding. "You couldn't tell?"

"Geez, Juls." He looked uncomfortable and sat up, drawing his knees up to his chest. "Why not? I mean, you're seventeen, right?" He ruffled a hand through his hair.

The truth was, I didn't just want Ash to be my first; I wanted him to be my only. My always. And the other truth was no one else had ever wanted to, or not that I knew of. Insecurities started to swell in my chest like indigestion bubbling to the surface.

I sat up too, sliding my arm around his waist, but he caught it fast at the wrist and wriggled free. "Geez, Juls. If I'd known you'd never even kissed a bloke before, I'd have—" He broke off.

My face began to heat up as I realised how lame I must sound to him, how immature and shallow compared to his depth and experience.

"I-I'm sorry." I stammered. "No one else..." My tongue felt fat in my mouth. I couldn't tell him I was damaged goods. I couldn't say, *No one else ever wanted me.*

I was no seasoned flirt like Jaz. I was no Ash Gordon, who'd shagged half of Sunshine Shire without giving a shit about any of them. I was just me—the shy, skinny, flat-chested, curly-haired loner whose Mum yelled at her out the car window in Greek at school pickup. The girl who'd never had a boyfriend who existed outside a romance novel. The swept-away little girl who foolishly believed that someone like Ash Gordon could ever be her first, let alone her only. And at that moment, I realised I was also a colossal sucker.

Ash Gordon didn't love *me*. He loved the *thought* of me. The girl I pretended to be around him. The girl who surfed and wore bikinis and liked hot guys who played guitar and joked so casually about sex. The girl who read on the beach instead of holed up in her bedroom. The girl who cared about marine conservation and scuba diving and was no longer afraid of sharks. The girl who wasn't afraid to dream. The girl who lusted after him. The girl who mattered. *That* girl had experience. Confidence.

Like Renee Aldershot.

And maybe Ash liked girls like that. He'd certainly loved Renee— the kind of girl who'd open her legs far more easily than her heart. I'd never wished more in my life that I'd kept my heart locked up with barbed-wire and thrown away the key to my cardiovascular chastity belt. Sure, I'd read about love and sex plenty of times—way more than Mum ever would have let me if she'd known—but for me, the real me, fooling around was like surfing: most of the time I still had no idea what I was doing. From what I'd heard of Renee, she knew, and plenty of guys *knew* her too, in the biblical sense. I'd spent years closing myself off to people. Renee Aldershot, with her long legs and her big boobs, was as open as a 7-Eleven.

Which is probably why he writes songs about her. Probably why he still wants to fuck her, not me.

I'd once heard one of the Fantastics joke that the best way to get over someone was to get under someone new. Had that been Ash's plan too? Choose someone as unlike Renee as possible for a rebound fling? If so, it had backfired as badly as the Kombi did sometimes.

I shook my head. *No. Ash was the one who turned away from sex. It didn't make sense. What good was a rebound relationship with a virgin, after all?* A sudden terrible thought seized my mind: *Whenever things get heavy, he remembers you're not her. He remembers you're not the one he wants.* The poisonous realisation brought on an immediate headache, and I snapped my mouth shut and folded my arms over my chest.

It seemed an age before Ash spoke; when he did, it was in a gruff whisper. "I'm worried I'm not the right guy for that."

What was that supposed to mean, coming from someone who'd slept with more girls than I'd had Greek salads?

"I thought you knew!" I couldn't stop the hurt from creeping into my voice, manifesting as the quaver that comes right before you dissolve into a sobbing, snivelling mess. Ash had told me he loved me, but what if he only loved the better, cooler version of me we'd concocted together?

"You don't understand." Curls bounced over Ash's forehead as he shook his head. "There are things I did, and I should have known better. Things that hurt me, hurt others—"

"Renee? I know." I tried to keep her name neutral on my lips, but it came out snarly nonetheless. "I know she broke your heart. I know you still love her! You think I didn't see the way you looked at her body? You think I don't realise you still want to fuck her?"

Ash's forehead crumped into waves of WTF. "You cannot be serious!" he snarled.

"I'm not stupid, Ash. Those song lyrics were about her, weren't they?" I plunged on, unable to reign in the heady, snorting wild horses of my jealousy.

"I don't want to talk about it, okay?" he said sharply. "That's why I write songs—because I don't want to talk about it. I didn't want to talk about it with *her* tonight, and I especially don't want to talk about it with *you.*"

I pulled my knees up to my chest like a barrier, folding my arms over them, convinced I'd already got the answer I expected. "You're still hung up on her."

Ash exhaled deeply and waved a hand in resignation. "Juls, look, I can't do this. It's over. Drop it, okay?" He turned away from me to face the ocean.

"It's over," I whispered, the final word hitting my heart like a tiny hammer. *It's over? Or we're over? Over before we've even begun.*

"Did you... did you make love to her?" I asked in a strangled voice.

"I had sex with her. Of course I did. That's what this is all about— sex." He whirled on me with indignation. "Not that it's any of your business," he ground out between clenched teeth.

"Then why not with me? It's because I'm not her, isn't it?" I was surprised he even heard me, I'd said it so quietly, but a puff of exasperation escaped his flaring nostrils.

"Renee wasn't a virgin."

"So, what, you make it a rule to only sleep with *sluts*?"

Once again, I immediately regretted not keeping my mouth shut. I was being stupid, judgmental, childish. I knew it, but my anger was driven by something else, something that swirled in my guts and ate into my brain. Fear.

Fear that I wasn't doing this right—any of it. The kissing. The dating. The surfing. The lovemaking. Even the fighting. And most of all, fear that the past wonderful months had been nothing but a mirage, a dream. Fear the reality I'd dreaded was tapping me on the shoulder. *Wakey, wakey, Juls.*

"Don't call her a slut!" Ash snapped. "Renee..." Her name sounded bitter on his tongue, and he dropped his head and muttered, "She might've been—" He broke off, pinching the bridge of his nose. "Look, she wasn't perfect, and I never said she was—far from it actually—but she doesn't deserve that. No woman deserves what happened to her, okay?"

My sour laugh barely concealed my humiliation. I was just a little girl to him, compared to Renee's womanliness.

"How could you not have noticed I'd never done this before?" I muttered. "It couldn't have been more obvious if I had a giant V tattooed on my forehead and V-plates hanging off my arse. I guess you're not a card-carrying member of the V-team after all."

Ash threw his hands in the air. "The V-team? Dickheads trying to score with underage girls. Is that who you think I am? Really, Juls? Someone like those guys?"

"I'm just trying to apologise for sucking extra hard at being sexy," I said, choking back a sob.

"What?" Ash growled, his expression fixed somewhere between exasperation and hopelessness. "You're perfect. You've always been perfect. Except now you've gone straight-up crazy."

Crazy!

The word snapped in my skull like a trigger.

Maybe I am. You think I'm so simple. You say I'm so perfect. But maybe I've always been crazy. Crazy and complicated and fucked up.

I gulped down the ache in my throat like I was swallowing a burning coal, and let the little alien in my brain take over.

"I'm sorry," I spat. "That's just how I am. I'm inexperienced. Immature. *Crazy!*" I raised my voice, and the word echoed back to us. "*Especially crazy!* Now I'm going home before I get any *crazier!*"

Ash spread his palms. "What'd I say, Juls? I don't get it. Just because I don't want to fuck you, you lose the frigging plot."

Fuck me?

I snorted my disgust. "No chance of that happening now. Or *ever*! No chance of fucking or making love, or whatever you want to call it. This was a bad idea. This whole night has been a bad idea. I just want to go home, Ash. Now." I scooted forward to grab his car keys from the little mesh bag that hung near the door of the tent and marched up the beach to his Kombi. The stars seemed to shimmer with laughter the entire way, as he pleaded with me to stay.

"You stay," I told him. "You're drunk. You can get Dyl to pick you up tomorrow and come get the keys off Mum."

"Maybe you're right. Maybe this whole thing was a bad idea," he said, eyes hardening.

I yanked open the door, climbed into the driver's seat, and wiped a bitter, burning tear from my eyes.

To avoid having to think, I plugged my iPhone into the USB connector, and a song came on: "Starry Night," by Patrick Park. As I drove off, I wasn't listening to it, not really. Ash's words and lyrics were already playing on an endless loop in my brain.

She wasn't perfect, but no woman deserves that... It was mine, this unquenchable perfection... You're perfect. Simple perfection....

I clearly wasn't the first perfect idiot to have fallen for Ash Gordon's lines.

CHAPTER 22

Wind sucks the dress in and draws it tight around my legs, and I twist to straighten it so I can carry on down the sand.

They're all there, all of them, but at the front sits Mum, snivelling into a white embroidered handkerchief Yiayia sent. She sent one for me too. Na zisete ke kalus apogonus, *carefully stitched in Greek letters, decorates one corner. "We wish you to live many years together."*

That one is tucked into the bodice of my dress, warm between the ivory corset and the silk.

My feet are bare, the sand not so hot at sunset. I slowly make my way toward a heart-shaped henge of surfboards on the beach. The sun hangs heavy and red behind them, like a movie backdrop, turning the groomsmen to silhouettes.

I want to see them, to see him, and I put a hand up to shield my eyes. For a moment, I long for sunglasses, even knowing they'll destroy my false eyelashes. But the sun is too lurid, too bright. I pad on, feet sinking into the sand.

Strains of music float out into the air from somewhere off to my left, the slow croon of Jack Johnson, and the guests swivel on their white deckchairs and smile. Someone catcalls. My cheeks feel flushed, my heart frothy in my chest, rising above my ribs like a bubble. I grip the arm that steadies me and keep walking.

Beyond the beach, out of the black backlit waves, a fin rises.

I wake with a gasp, feeling like my oxygen tank has just run out, longing for Ash.

CHAPTER 23

Sunset stained the sand, throwing a lurid orange cast over Ash's face as I focussed on his expression. The two days of ignoring each other after our fight had been brutal, and the dream about the beach wedding hadn't helped. Our whole time apart, I'd berated myself, hated myself, and wondered who I even was anymore. I cried so much I couldn't read through my slitty little fucked-up alien eyes, and I certainly couldn't surf.

When he came to get the keys, I put a note on the door that they were in the mailbox and sulked in the toilet, pretending not to be home, trying not to think about how deliriously happy the Fantastics would be once they learned about our bust-up.

But when I arrived home from school the next day to find an enormous bunch of sunflowers and a gilt-edged card that read, "The sun doesn't shine as bright without you, Juls. Stars, babe. Love forever, Ash xxox," and my very own love song he'd recorded onto a CD for me, I'd burst into tears and forgiven him—even if I hadn't yet forgiven myself for the scene I'd made.

Within fifteen minutes of my apologetic text, he'd dropped around to pick me up for a surf. Ignoring the web of questions still hanging between us, we focussed on letting the waves wash away our hurt and then retreated to the beach to eat fish and chips and talk it out as the sun sank.

"We've known each other since primary school, me and Renee," Ash explained, awkwardly twisting the brown-leather cuff around his right wrist. "More buddies than anything. But when we were, like, fourteen or something, drunk at this party..." He waved a hand in front of his face, as if to dismiss the memory. "I guess you could say we were each other's first. I think so anyway. Pretty sure. I didn't ask her, but there was blood and stuff. She cried. Anyway, it was nothin' serious. We were both pretty blotto. We didn't mention it again, and I doubt it was anything special for her either." He bit one corner of his lip and looked at me sheepishly. "Maybe this is TMI, but word is that everyone's first time is a bit of a disappointment."

"Is that what you're so afraid of? You don't want to disappoint me?"

"Maybe. A little." He tucked a curl behind my ear. "That would suck. But give me a bit of credit for knowing my way around a vagina better than I did as a grommet." He winked, but I could tell he was still wary. His innuendo was more forced today. "I think most young guys think those things should come with an owner's manual, though."

I was glad he'd said "owner's manual," not "user's manual." The thought of being owned by Ash Gordon was a lot more appealing than the thought of being used by him, which was one of the things I'd figured out since our fight the other night. I might not have known who I was, but I was once again certain I was his.

"Well, mine's only ever had one owner," I said drily. "In case you hadn't noticed, it's in mint condition. Hardly used. If someone doesn't take this baby for a spin soon, it'll practically be vintage. And it definitely needs a service."

Ash laughed at my bad puns. "So I've been warned." He looped one arm around my shoulders and drew me closer, kissing the tip of my nose. "But that's what I'm afraid of—banging up something so priceless."

"Banging!" I laughed and slapped his knee. "Wow. You really do have a way of making it sound uber romantic."

"Yeah, well, it's not just romantic. Not really. Dangerous, more like." Ash was serious again. "My thing with Renee was a total car wreck. I never even saw it coming. It seemed really easy, a bit of fun, so we hooked up again late last year, both drunk again, another party. But things got... serious. For her, mostly."

His arm tensed around my shoulders, his index finger absently winding and unwinding one of my curls.

"Shit got weird," he added. "Really weird. And that's what you saw at the Sun Hing. Shit's still weird between us. Maybe it always will be."

A little gutter of concern separated his brows, and he pressed his lips together. "There are some things I promised I wouldn't tell anyone. But she just won't stop texting, calling. I had to block her on Facebook and Snapchat. That's when the abuse started again."

He removed his arm and twisted the wrist cuff again, scratching at the paler skin beneath that rarely saw the sun. "I felt sorry for her at first. But she's gone nuts, completely nuts."

As if to agree with him, a beach stone-curlew let out its eerie, wailing call from the dunes.

"I wish we'd never—" Ash got to his feet and put a hand down to help me up. "Juls, sex changes things. I want to be careful this time, do things right. I don't want to ruin this." I could have sworn I heard him mutter, "Or you," under his breath, but by the time I'd gotten up, he was biting his bottom lip and staring out at the sea.

A stiff breeze tugged my hair away from my face, and Ash pulled me close and nuzzled my neck. "I'm sorry about what I said." His words were muffled, and I craned my neck, giving him access to my ear.

"I'm sorry about calling you crazy," he whispered. "I didn't mean to upset you. I didn't mean it literally." His lips moved from my ear to my temple, then fluttered tenderly around the hollow of my eye and along my cheekbone to settle on my mouth. "You're the least nuts person I know. And believe me, I know *kerrrazy*."

Mid-kiss, I failed to stifle my disbelieving laugh.

"What?" Ash pulled back, squinting, and I shrugged.

"Don't apologise. Maybe I was being crazy. I mean, maybe we're all a little crazy."

"Not you, Juls." He held me tighter. "You're a lot of things—gorgeous, honest, kind, caring, sexy, smart—but you're not crazy. Somehow, though, you've managed to make me completely and utterly batshit about you."

"You sure about that?" I asked breathlessly, pulling away.

"Absolutely."

That's when I did it. I sat him down with me on the sand, drew in a deep breath, and told him. *"There's something about me you need to know—something I'm not sure I can tell you."*

And after I told him everything, Ash Gordon never said I was nuts or ridiculous or that I was a liar or a fruitcake.

He hugged me for a while, thinking, and then said with a tender smile, "So, Madame Fortune Teller, care to tell me how I'm gonna go?"

I smiled back, feeling freer than I ever had without a surfboard beneath me, and shook my head. "It's not like that. It's pretty random."

Shutting my eyes for a second, I willed away the images, all the terrible images. Then, to lighten the mood, opened them again in a squint. Peering at him, my hands hovering over an invisible crystal ball, I answered, "But my best guess is it'll be as an old man, worn out in your bed after a long night of this." I pressed my lips to his, kissing him as if I had just seen him die, as if I might lose him. As if neither of us needed to breathe, so long as we just kept on kissing.

"You're planning to suffocate me to death with kisses." Ash laughed when he finally drew away. "You must be a demon after all."

A pod of dolphins rode the shallow waves offshore as, laughing, he lay back on the damp sand and pulled me on top of him, my salt-streaked body feeling him beneath me like a wave I hadn't been good enough to catch yet.

"It's either that or choke to death on a sprig of rhinoceros grass over dinner at Zone with a girl in stilettos you don't really like anyway," I said with a shrug.

"Never!" He tickled my side. "It's all picnics and sweet and sour pork from now on."

He bent his head to me, his eyes filled with warmth and love again, and we kissed the moon up into the sky.

CHAPTER 24

Sheet lightning from a late storm illuminated Ash's profile as we made out on my bed, my jeans already curled like a sleeping cat on the bedroom floor. We'd gone for a late lunch at Café Conch once we finished up another day diving off the *Sea Change*, until a late afternoon storm rolled in over the bay and Ash had driven me home. Mum was still at work, and Ash's shirt had already joined my clothes on the floor.

The sensation of his body against mine made my every muscle feel tight, wound up, like a spring waiting for someone to touch it and send it flying. I hitched up on one elbow. "Ash, I don't think I can stand it if we keep doing this."

He laughed and kissed me again, and by the time he pulled away, the rain on the roof was so heavy it nearly drowned out my words. "Are we ready to catch that wave yet? Because I am wet, wet, wet. Wetter than it is out there." I made an *ugh* sound and slapped his arm. "Start paddling, buddy. Long, slow, powerful strokes."

Ash shut me up with another peck on the lips. "Shh, you minx. The prohibition on penis in vagina stands."

The look of longing in his eyes was turning me into a liquid hot mess. If he didn't give in, I imagined myself dissolving fanny first, before seeping all over the doona. I groaned and flung a pillow over my head.

"I meant what I said about wanting it to be special," Ash said, lifting the pillow and peering underneath.

Lightning flashed again through the half-open window. "Look, nature's fireworks. Tell me what's not special about this moment?"

"Juls," he warned, waiting for a peal of thunder to fade before adding, "You know I want this to really mean something to both of us. Not just *something* either—everything, I guess. I get that it's not the done thing anymore, but how would you feel if I told you I want us to wait a long time, like potentially a really long time?"

"I'd feel like you're a total hypocrite," I huffed. "How long? Please don't tell me until all the stars wink out!"

He took my hand, unconsciously stroking my ring finger. "Until you're mine."

"I'm already yours," I insisted. Thoughts of the heart-shaped henge of surfboards flashed through my mind. Was that what he meant? He wanted to wait *that* long? Kill me now!

Tugging my hand away, I trailed it down his body, only to be stopped at his crotch. "I've been yours since the first moment you kissed me."

Lightning flashed again, and his lopsided grin lit up his face as he let go my hand and tilted my jaw up. "You don't get it, do you, babe?"

My bedsprings squeaked as he eased me back, and his weight on top of me was promising. "When I'm with you, it's like I need to protect you from anything that could ever hurt you. Right now, I'm protecting you from myself."

"Okay, caveman." I rolled my eyes as I slid open the drawer in my bedside table and pulled a condom from the pack Mum had tried to give me. She'd left them on the breakfast table after our talk. I waggled one at him, along with my eyebrows.

"Protection," I admonished him. "We'll be totally tarped up. Now I do remember someone bragging about an enormous weapon...?" I went for his groin again.

He snatched the condom from me and tossed it back in the drawer. Then he cuffed my wrists and threw me on the bed.

"You're incorrigible," he said, "and damn persistent, and definitely part demon."

I grinned, loving the sensation. "Maybe. Want me to show you which part?" I pressed myself against him.

Ash laughed and let go one wrist, moving his lips down over my chest. "Could be any place. Every inch of you is hotter than hell."

"So exorcise me," I pleaded. "Lord knows I'm gonna need to sweat this evil out of me."

He gripped my wrist tighter, and ran his other hand over the contours of my body. Letting me go, he slid both hands under my panties and peeled them down my thighs.

I wriggled my hips to help him, surprised he was capitulating so easily, and started to reach for the condom again, but he shook his head and ran his tongue in circles around my belly-button, making me wriggle. "Get thee away, Satan," he said, jerking his chin to the condoms. "Every happy camper knows that a true bushmaster always has a backup plan."

He jerked his chin to my raised hips, my parted legs, and his eyes gleamed as they focussed on the cleft between them. Lightning made the wetness of his lips gleam.

"Stay like that," he instructed, as my offending underpants joined the rest of our wardrobe on the floor.

Ash brushed his fingertips over me, and I shuddered, crying out when their firmness was followed by the wonderful, tender wetness of his tongue.

Oh! My! God!

"Ash." I knotted my hand in his hair as his mouth played over me, winding me tight with anticipation, the way I'd seen him tune a guitar, twisting the pegs until the thrumming strings were taut to breaking point. I groaned his name again, hips bucking wildly, as if I really was possessed. And each subtle strum of his tongue felt like a slow unravelling. His tongue moved like his fingers, thrusting inside me, slowly at first, and then faster, until the movement became an unrelenting drumming, a steady syncopated rhythm that made my senses hum along, seeking the high notes. The pitch of my moans rose too—higher, higher, higher, higher, until...

I took the drop.

My hips collapsed, jerked up, and then surfed the intoxicating, convulsive movements of his mouth. The room crumbled and flashed, the rain coming harder as I did, and all the while I clutched his curls tight in my fist, trapped his head between my thighs.

His movements stilled, and it was several minutes before my whimpering subsided enough to let me rasp out, "Holy fucking God, Ash."

He laughed, looking up at me with the smuggest, most self-satisfied grin I'd ever seen on his face. "Do you renounce Satan and all his works, demon?"

"Yes. Oh God, Ash. Yes." I muttered, still trembling.

"That's better, Angel," he soothed, walking his fingers up my stomach. "And I'm pleased to report there are definitely no crabs in the intertidal zone."

He ducked as I threw a cushion in his direction.

"However..." Ash wriggled up the bed to lie beside me, licking his lips, one eyebrow cocked. His palm slid down over my stomach again, his fingers feather-light as they teased my tender skin, dabbling in the slick mess he'd made of me. "You're right about this weather. It's wet all right! I think it must be a king tide."

When he circled my soaking clit again, I slapped him away, too sensitive now, and shy.

"Should I start building an ark?" He winked.

I shut him up with a *thwack* of the pillow, and threw the condom at him. "Hey, I offered you wet weather gear, remember."

CHAPTER 25

A sea of blue-painted dolphin placards leaped over the head of the crowd as I searched for Ash.

I'd already texted him twice and called, but his phone was off. "He's got to still be here somewhere." I towed Jaz along behind me, past families setting up picnic blankets.

"Probably celebrating," Jaz said. "The gig's made him the star of the show. Can you believe this crowd? I knew they'd love his song. Maybe this is his break. Maybe I can be his manager!"

I laughed at her enthusiasm, but I had to hand it to her: she'd done her job of getting publicity for the protest. In many ways, that had been easier than convincing Ash to play his song. When she'd shown him the positive comments and shares and subscribers he'd picked up on YouTube, he'd reluctantly agreed.

Seeing him up there on stage, I'd felt like my heart was going to explode with pride, showering a confetti of post-nerves butterflies everywhere. *Poof!*

Ash Gordon. My boyfriend. The songwriter.

The crowd had loved him, and the speakers that followed him, all from non-profit environmental charities, had received plenty of applause too. Granted, only a few hundred people had packed themselves onto the rectangle of beach near the harbour, most of them kids or hippy backpackers who were passing through, but it was something for the local news networks to televise.

"I saw Drew and Troy with Salt over at Cafe Conch earlier," Jaz said. "He's probably over there, getting something to eat. You know what guys are like—walking stomachs."

She pushed past me and then stopped dead in her tracks, sucking in breath. "Don't look now, but he's there." She gestured. "Surrounded by Fantastics."

"Where?"

Great. I supposed I wasn't the only one fangirling over Ash's performance. Now there'd be even more girls willing to bat their eyelashes at him, girls who probably weren't virgins, either.

Jaz craned her neck past a rainbow-haired woman wearing a tie-dyed kaftan and pointed. "Thataway."

I stepped in front of the woman and stopped. Ash's face was crimson, and he was waving his hands in front of him, his shoulders taut with anger. Troy and Drew were with him, and they were ringed by six or seven Fantastics, including Lacey and Ham Hotpants, the snippy little red-headed girl who'd made comments on the bus and in the sandwich store.

"All I'm saying," I overheard, above the applause of the crowd, "is that she set me up. I'm not the bad guy here. This is bullshit. It's slander. I kept her secrets, and this is how she repays me!"

"Like that song wasn't payback!" someone sniffed, and I identified it as coming from Ham Hotpants, sneering, hands on her hips. She wasn't wearing much more than tiny denim shorts today either, but she had Kylie Minogue's arse, so who was I to judge?

"Don't act like you're perfect. You were screwing that nerdy little bookworm, 'teaching her to surf.'" She made disbelieving quote marks with her fingers. "While Renee was in hospital because of you!" she hissed at him.

Bitch. I judged, but I couldn't deny her words had piqued my interest. Renee was in hospital when he'd asked me on that date? He'd never mentioned that. Suspicion rose in me like a hackle.

"*It wasn't because of me!*" Ash glared at her. "And I wasn't with—"

"Mate, give it up." Drew Kendall clapped Ash's shoulder. "You can't talk sense into them right now. They're like a pack of dingoes when they're all together. It'll all come out in the wash."

"What do you even know about it?" Lacey screamed at Drew. "Renee told us what he did to her!"

"Drew doesn't know anything about it!" Ash shouted, hands clenched into fists at his sides. "None of my mates do, and nor do you! I did what she asked—and this is how she repaid me, bad-mouthing me all over town. None of you know the truth."

The crowd of girls parted, and Renee Aldershot was thrust forth. She looked shocking, far less put together than the last time I'd seen her. She was bloated and puffy-eyed, and it was obvious she'd been bawling. "You fucking liar," she screamed.

Ash gave a disbelieving snort. "Fuck off, Renee. Do you even know the truth anymore? Shall I tell them?" His words were as vicious as the scowls on the faces of the baying mob.

"You've been drip-feeding everyone lies for months, haven't you? Playing the perfect little victim."

Lacey waggled her head from side to side. "Save it, Ash. You cheated on her, you screwed that little mole, and worst of all, you beat her up. You deserve everything that comes your way."

"This has nothing to do with you," Ash growled at her. "It has nothing to do with anyone else. It's between me and Renee, okay? So why don't you all just piss off. Let us deal with this."

Us.

I'd never seen him so angry, but he wasn't the only one. He'd cheated on her, with me? All the furtive phone calls, the texts, the Fantastics' bullshit reeled through my mind.

Was that why he wouldn't sleep with me? He'd been trying not to cheat? I'd been such an idiot. To think that five minutes ago I was so proud, so in love that my heart was fluttering around in my chest like a butterfly.

Butterflies! I'd read this book before. I had the signed bookmark to prove it. Ash Gordon was a player, and the sneering faces all around resembled the cast from a deck of cards, with me as the joker. But this game was over. I was tossing in my hand. Fuck them. Fuck *us.*

The crowd thinned as I marched toward them, poker-faced. "What's between you and Renee?" I demanded, feeling all the colour drain from my lips.

"Yeah, spill it." Jaz jutted her chin at him too. "What's all this crap?"

"T-This..." Ash paled as he indicated Renee and then the rest of the Fantastics, who were now glowering at us both. "Discussion..."

"A discussion about *me*. Again. And once again *I'm* not invited." My hands were on my hips as I looked back and forth between them.

"Juls, this isn't about you," Ash mumbled, all the rage faded from his voice. His irate expression was gone too, replaced by what looked to me suspiciously like desperation.

"Really? There's some other nerdy little bookworm you've been 'teaching to surf,' or some other 'little mole' she thinks you're screwing?" Jaz stood up for me. "Which is it, Ash?"

"Yeah, and while Renee was in hospital because *he beat her up!*" Ham Hotpants upped the ante, bobbing her fiery head in Ash's face.

"For Christ's sake! *Get your fucking facts straight!*" he bellowed. He took a step towards her, his jaw clenching and unclenching.

"After all you've put her through, you can't even tell the truth," Ham Hotpants spat, standing her ground.

"*I've* put *her* through? Puhlease. And I wasn't screwing any little mol—" He stopped abruptly, obviously realising how it must have sounded to me.

"You're right," I said, doing my best to keep calm. "We're not screwing. Not now. Not ever."

All this time, I'd thought he loved me, or at least cared about me, but suddenly the scales fell from my eyes, the sensation every bit the way it felt when a nightmare came to life. It was clear he'd been playing both Renee and me for fools.

Of course he's been sleeping with her. Why else would she be carrying on like this? Why else the tears in the restaurant when she saw us together? Why else had he reached for her hand that night?

I'd just been too naïve to notice it, or too gullible to believe it. I spun on my heel, feeling dizzy.

You're so stupid, Juls, sneered the little voice in my head. *No wonder he thinks you're just a bookish little nerd to toy with.*

"Juls, this is bullshit. I didn't mean it like that," Ash started, his voice pitched high with exasperation. "I'd never call you a mole or a nerd. You know that."

I flung a hand up to cut him off. "Spare me more lies about stars and love and waiting for the perfect wave and all that Zen bullshit, Ash." I pointed to Renee. "You want a girl with experience, you've got her. Knock yourself out."

"Juls!" He gripped my shoulder and spun me around. The muddle of anger and hurt and fear on his handsome face would have made just about any girl pity him, but I was my mother's daughter, and I'd watched too many rom-coms, read too many romances. Plus, Ash Gordon had just torn my heart from my chest and tossed it to a bloodthirsty pack of Fantastics as casually as he could a basketball.

"Don't touch me." I tugged my arm away. "I can't believe this."

"*Don't* believe this!" He seized my waist instead, but I wriggled away.

"Goddammit, Juls!" he roared, knuckles white as he clenched his hands. Everyone around us who wasn't already enjoying the spectacle turned and stared. Jaz visibly blanched.

"This isn't what you think it is," he added, dropping his voice. "Juls, I promise you."

"It never is." Jaz sniffed.

But it was. In the books and the movies and the real life heartbreak, it always was. Jaz had warned me: life's not a romance novel. So why had I expected any different? Salt had tried to warn me too, and Mum, but I'd been so foolishly in love, I couldn't see that Ash Gordon was hot as Hades and his big swinging dick had been burning his personal brand of playboy on half the girls in Sunshine Shire for years, the flippant, fatuous little fucker.

Right now, I'm protecting you from myself.

Hell, Ash had even warned me off! Why had I thought he'd be any different? And how had I turned into the kind of daft little instalove ninny I always scoffed at in the pages of a novel? How had I been idiotic enough to let him in, to thoroughly let him in—into my body and my heart, into my head? I'd told him everything, even about the *mati*, while he'd clearly been feeding me glib lines and innuendo and lies the whole time. The thought made me even more determined to stay strong now, especially in front of the rabid Fantastics, all waiting to sink their fangs in.

"It's not true! She's a liar. She's a pathetic little liar. She's the cheat." He flung an arm toward Renee. "She's a miserable, bitter little bitch who can't let go. Who pretends to be everything she's not, just like her arsehole father, and he's right, she's nothing but a—"

"Slut?" I interrupted him. "Come on, Ash. No woman deserves to be called that, although *you've* certainly been one, haven't you? Looks like you can't handle a harem after all, you fucking Neanderthal."

"Juliette, stop!" he growled, as Renee started to laugh.

Her laugh was tinny and fake and as sour as old milk, and Ash's eyes flashed with hatred when he turned on her. I'd never seen that in him before, and it frightened me. Spite pinched his face and made him look suddenly ugly, contorting his beauty into something so twisted he was almost unrecognisable. For a brief, dark second, I believed maybe he had hit her. After all, how well did I really know Ash Gordon? Hardly at all, I was discovering.

Everyone has their skeletons, their regrets. His words from the night at Figtree ran through my mind, and I shuddered.

Was that why the girl on the bus had said he'd "pounded" her? Was that why Lacey had said they'd been shopping for *concealer*?

Holy fuck! I guess it was true you never really knew a person.

"She's been stalking me," Ash hissed, full of vitriol. "I wasn't even the one who knocked—"

"Break it up! Break it up!" an officious voice bellowed from behind the Fantastics. Mayor Aldershot broke through, his face as awful and red and twisted as Ash's. A burly security guard was flexing his muscles at his side.

"Young man, the conditions of your restraining order insist you are to remain at least four hundred metres from my daughter at all times."

Restraining order!

Major Aldershot's comb-over flapped in the wind, and his nostrils flared as he stabbed Ash's chest with his index finger.

"I should have you arrested. Or shot. Things have gotten out of hand." He stabbed Ash's chest again. "Out. Of. Hand. *You hear?* I'm not in the least surprised to find you and your waxhead friends behind this fracas." His piggy eyes narrowed, his jaw set tight.

Ash moved back several metres before bellowing, "None of this is my fault, and you know it! Why are you ruining my life?" He wheeled on Renee, snarling. "Why are you and your psychopath father ruining *my* fucking life?"

"That's it!" Aldershot nodded to the security guard, who made a lunge for Ash but missed. "How *dare* you absolve yourself of responsibility?" Aldershot thundered, spittle foaming in the corner of his mouth. "You are SCUM—that is what you are and what you've proved yourself to be here today. That is what you druggie, surfer, activist types who plague this town will always be. *Scum!*" Allen Aldershot slapped his comb-over back over his head and grabbed his daughter's shoulder, harshly shoving her forward, as if to rub her in Ash's face.

"*You ruined her,*" Aldershot hissed. "*You and your ilk!*"

He pointed a trembling finger at me. "Any sensible young lady who wishes to retain her virtue is well advised to stay as far from this low-rent Lothario and his ignoramus friends as possible. Not that it'll be hard, once he's in prison for breaching a restraining order."

"You ruined her, you fucking arse—" Ash choked out before Drew pulled him away.

"Mate, it's not worth it. Come on, shoot through before he calls the cops."

"Too late!" Mayor Aldershot snapped as Ash and Drew pushed past the onlookers and passed me.

"Juls." Ash's voice was scratchy and low, and the hate in his eyes was gone. "You've got to believe me. Even if no one else will. You know me. I didn't do any of the things they're saying. Any of them. I love you, Juls. Trust me."

All I could think about was that restraining order, and all of the other things I didn't know about him.

"Famous last words," I said, so calmly I shocked myself. Then I turned my back on him.

Yeah. Exactly!

Famous last words.

The last words I said to Ash Gordon, the day before everything changed forever, weren't "I love you, Ash. I've loved you ever since you first kissed me. I've loved you since the day you decided to teach me to surf, to make me laugh, to make me yours. And I'll love you forever... until all the stars wink out."

No. I said, "Famous last words" to a man I didn't know, a cheater, an abuser, if the restraining order was anything to go by. I didn't know then how wrong I was. I didn't know that once again I'd jinxed something. I'd predicted something.

I didn't know that the nightmare I hadn't seen coming was already making itself true.

PART II

After

The sea is full of dead men; their spittle is the spray,
Their cold breath is the vapour that blows silently away.
Their laughter is the frenzy of the surf upon the sand.
But their sadness is in parting so, without a waving hand.
ANONYMOUS

CHAPTER 26

They called off the search on a Wednesday. I'd always hated Wednesdays, sandwiched in the middle of the week, too far from the weekends to do anything but long for a lie-in. Even the sound of the word annoyed me. The way our history teacher always enunciated the syllables. Wed-nes-day.

Dad had left on a Wednesday too.

When the State Emergency Service abandoned the search for Ash that Wednesday, the sea whipped itself into an indignant frenzy, matching the turmoil of the crowd gathered with me at the boat ramp.

Ash's mum was absent from the beach. She was at home in their sprawled old Queenslander on Bitou Street, manning the control centre in case a call came in. When one did, it wasn't the one she wanted. It wasn't the one she had prayed for every second of the past three days. Instead, it was the SES ringing to tell her they were calling off the search for her only son and my only boyfriend. It was to tell her that Troy Pearson and Drew Kendall, whom Ash had taken out with him in his boat, had been found. Drowned.

"Sorry." The Search and Rescue diver's hand on my bare arm felt heavy and scratched like sandpaper. His words were heavier. "It's rough as buggery out there, love, and growing dark." He squeezed my shoulder.

Bluey Marone, his name was. I recognised him vaguely because he was the captain of the local footy club, and his shock of red hair was hard to miss.

"All going well, we might resume things tomorrow." His voice grew softer. "But don't get your hopes up, kiddo. It's been three days of this." He gestured toward the whitecaps; relentless waves carving up a bruised sea, beneath a sky as dark as my thoughts.

Ash had started Nippers in first grade. As a Nipper and later a lifie, he'd practically been raised by the ocean. He could swim like a fish. But I stared out at that roiling ocean, thinking even a fish would struggle to stay afloat. I slumped down onto the sand and pulled my knees up to my chest, wondering what I was even doing here. The past few days had been a nightmare.

The night of our breakup, in between ignoring Ash's texts that it wasn't true, that Renee had set him up, and his countless, almost stalkerish calls, I thought I'd done enough crying to last a lifetime. But the real tears hadn't started until the following night, when the alert went round that a boat hadn't returned from a fishing trip. When Sharon Gordon rushed over in a blind panic to see if Ash was at our place, I realised whose boat it was.

Who it was.

Ash Gordon. The guy I loved. Still loved, even if I didn't know him, even despite Renee.

He wasn't even supposed to have been out there. Last week, we'd planned a movie marathon: back-to-back *X-Men* at Willow Bay Cineplex. But after the scene with Renee at the protest, I'd ignored his texts and pulled a no-show. I'd treated him like one of the mutant monsters onscreen, and maybe he was. I never got to hear his side of the story, not really.

Ash had played it cool, as if I hadn't just publicly dumped his lying arse. As if I hadn't been deleting his texts and ignoring his phone calls. As if I hadn't left a box of letters and cards and the CD with the song he'd written for me on his doorstep.

No worries, babe. He'd texted once I'd ignored his umpteenth effort to contact me. *It's a perfect arvo for fishing anyway. We can do the X-Men thing some other time, if you like. Got most of them on DVD anyway.*

Still fuming, I'd deleted the message without responding and consoled myself by crying some more. Screw him. As if there'd be "some other time."

He'd texted again about half an hour later.

I'll come around tomorrow night & we'll talk. It's not what you think. Promise. You know what they're like. They've been out to get me ever since I met you. Trust me. Stars, babe. xox Ash.

Ever since our conversation about the heavens, "Stars, babe," had been Ash's favourite way of saying I love you. It had almost been enough to make me cave in, before I reminded myself what a laughing stock I'd been for half the shire and deleted that text too.

Now all I wanted to do was bury my face in the faint lime and brine scent of his neck and take it all back. Go back to a time when I didn't know about Renee or the restraining order. When Ash was here and perfect and mine—only mine.

As if there'd be some other time.

Because there was no more time. It couldn't ever be like that again.

I just didn't yet know how far from perfect it could get.

CHAPTER 27

I didn't know whether it hurt more or less that Ash's body was the only one among them that hadn't been "retrieved." That's the word Bluey Marone used when he'd phoned back to search and rescue services in Sydney. "We've retrieved two bodies. Both jacketed."

He meant that Troy and Drew had both been wearing life vests when the chopper found them. The fluorescent orange jackets had been spotted bobbing in the seas below. It had been too rough to take the lifeguard boats out to bring the bodies in, so an SES worker was lowered down on a rope and winched them up. Another fierce squall had then sent the helicopters scuttling inland, rotors clacking like crab claws.

"The third?" Bluey rolled a cigarette as he spoke, the satellite phone pressed into the crook of his neck, one booted foot propped against the boat ramp.

I fixed my eyes on his hands. They were shaking badly, the way my entire body was trembling, as if a little earthquake was forcing its way through all the searing cracks inside me.

"No sign. Scoured the area from the air, but it's too rough to take 'em out again." He nodded in response to whatever he'd heard down the line, and said, "Call it in."

He listened again.

"Yeah, the Gordon kid. Presumed drowned."

The Gordon kid. His words made me furious, reducing Ash to some stupid kid who got himself drowned, rather than a nineteen-year-old lifeguard with a history of surfing, boating, and understanding the ocean. The words stung, and they sent a red-hot prong of terror and anger right through me. Was I the only one who thought Ash was still worth looking for?

"You can't stop looking!" I screamed. The wind peeling off the ocean tore the words from my mouth and flung them back over the sand dunes with a furious vehemence. In that moment, I hated the ocean and everything in it. The sea had swallowed everything, had taken everything—everything I'd ever wanted.

CHAPTER 28

The coastguard chopper eventually found what was left of the boat, up near the Archway Bar. The fibreglass hull was split, the wreckage strewn about. Ash's bright orange Esky was lolling in the waves along with the other life vest, which had a bite taken out of it.

Once the weather calmed, Rory Gordon took his boat out, and Salt and an armada of weekend fisherman and lifies searched the area around where the *Daydream* had been smashed to smithereens. They found nothing.

I was too scared to go out with them. Too afraid of not finding him, and even more afraid of finding him, if I was honest. He would have been days in the water. I was under no illusion as to what that might look like. Not even Salt could coax me out.

The day they'd called off the search, Salt was the only one who'd been like me. Something more than just fear and hope had flickered in Salt's eyes—anger. Like me, he was angry at the world, or at the ocean, or both, for all the things they'd taken away from him over the years, despite what they might have given him back. It was just a flash, but I saw it. I felt it too: that white-hot rage.

Not even Jaz could really understand, and she spent most of her time with Dylan now anyway. Rory and Sharon Gordon were bundled up together in their grief. They seemed faded: a pair of moths trapped in a grey web of memories.

Ash as a baby.

Ash as a toddler.

Ash's first steps.

Ash's first surfing win.

Ash's graduation.

Sharon called to check up on me those first few months, and even invited me over for dinner, but I declined. It didn't seem right for me to grieve around them. I'd had him for less than a year, after all; they'd had nineteen years of Ashley Christopher Gordon.

Sharon, of course, was taking it particularly hard. Even though she'd come to accept he was gone, she kept his room exactly as it was. I couldn't bear to see the lines in her face, the grey in her hair. But most of all I couldn't bear to think of Ash as dead.

Part of me hated all of them for that, for quitting on him.

Because in my heart, Ash wasn't gone. He couldn't be. Because I was the girl with the *mati*, the girl who saw things coming. Terrible things. And I hadn't seen this. Sometimes I woke with a start, convinced I'd felt his lips on my forehead or his fingers stroking my check. Then I'd realise that, wherever he was, Ash wasn't here. Not now. Yet that was as close as I wanted to come to admitting he was actually gone.

Some days I pretended it was a bad dream I was going to wake up from, jolting up to find him stretched out in my bed, one tanned arm behind his head, his eyelashes throwing shadows on his cheeks, his chest a ripple of sun-kissed muscle rising and falling with each breath. I imagined his eyes opening lazily, the spark of recognition when he saw me, his crimson lips parting to reveal that dazzling, crooked smile as he reached for me.

But I'd seen the end of too many dreams.

Following Ash's accident, I couldn't bear to surf. It was too lonely out there without him. And I was too angry. Even surfing couldn't fill the empty places inside me or take away the pain of the final parting words I'd thrown at him.

But after a few weeks, I knew I couldn't shut myself up in my room either. Books were no solace; romance novels used to make me happy, but now they made me sob uncontrollably. Eventually, I wandered back down to the beach, stood swearing at the sea with my ankles deep in the foam.

And that day, I discovered another reason to come back.

I shaded my eyes and stared out to sea, scanning the horizon for the glint of sunlight on wet grey skin.

The dolphin usually came around the same time each day, either early morning or late afternoon. I couldn't see Bitten yet, but out behind the break, a lone surfer lay on his board, paddling half-heartedly for a wave. He missed it, disappearing into the gutter for a moment and then rising, legs dangling into the blue as he sat up, arms up to push long wet hair from his eyes. I put a hand up to shield from the sun and saw a fin rise, short and sharp.

My breath caught in my throat.

My eyes darted to the surfer before the dorsal fin arced from the water a little more and I saw the characteristic chunk out of it.

Bitten. Got me every time.

Calm descended on me, and out on the water, a wave swelled to breaking. The surfer paddled furiously and caught it as it peaked, pulling a floater and surfing its wash all the way into shore. He stepped off the board into the shallows as if he was walking off an escalator, hefted his board up under his arm, and picked his way over the hot sand to the parking lot.

Bitten swam closer, leaping to let me know he was still there. But I knew it anyway. I sensed it somehow. Some connection, something that pulled me out of myself, something that had dragged me down there, with the tides and the slowly tumbling sand.

He lives.

CHAPTER 29

A scale settled on Salt's bottom lip, which was sunburned and scabbed, and jutted out as he concentrated. He didn't flinch as another flicked up, just kept on scaling fish.

"How's school?" he asked, not looking up. "You crook today?"

I nodded, but the truth was I'd blown off school, preferring the beach, and I was sure Salt knew it, too.

I hadn't meant to bump into Salt today on the jetty, although I should have anticipated it. The wind made it too rough for him to take the *Sea Change* out, and this was one of Salt's usual hangouts aside from Cafe Conch. He was scaling two trevally and a flathead at the aluminium cleaning station at the end of the pier. Scales kicked up into the air like small silver sprites. They caught in the grizzle of his beard—salt 'n' pepper, just like his hair. Just like him.

Salt was mostly calm around me, but although I'd never seen the pepper, aside from that flash of anger the day they quit the search, Ash had warned me Salt had a fiery temper if pushed. He could flay the skin off you with a tone if you did something to really piss him off. Ash said he'd only done that once, although he wouldn't say what it had been about.

Salt looked up, still scaling. "You making good grades?"

I shrugged.

"Juls, love, one thing I've learned is you can't let life get you down, can't let the bad shit beat you. You let it get to you, you're as good as dead or courting death anyway. And you're a long time dead and only a short time livin'."

He didn't mention Ash, but I knew what he meant. *Time to move on, Juls. Time to start living again, in the now, not in the past.*

I drew in a breath. "It's just that since Ash... I can't concentrate. I don't want to think about the future."

He cut me off. "No one does. Not really. Because no one can see the future, Juls. No one knows what's ahead. I don't reckon anyone appreciates that feeling. Way I see it, the future's kind of like faith, almost like heaven, you know. You can't see it, you just have to trust it's there, and it's going to be better than today."

But I couldn't trust that. Whenever I saw the future in those damn dreams, it was never better. It was worse. Much worse. And without Ash, how could anything ever be good again, let alone better?

A scale skittered onto my arm.

"I didn't pick you as a religious man, Salt," I said eventually.

"Well, I don't pretend to be the pope or anything, but a man has to find something he believes in." He cleared his throat. "Don't rightly know whether what I believe is in the pages of a Bible or at the bottom of a bottle, but I know I have to believe in somethin', so I'll take the lesser of two evils. Already learned my lesson with the other."

I didn't say anything for a while after that. Ash had once made a throwaway comment about not being able to go out on the *Sea Change* with Salt on a Sunday. I wondered whether it was because Salt had been in church.

"Not suggesting you should try church," Salt spoke up, finally wiping away the scales with his brawny forearm. "Or that any of the answers are there, either. I didn't believe in anything meself for a long time. And I'm still not sure anything believes in me. Thought there was nothin' except the inevitability of death and taxes. Anything else, well, you've gotta decide for yourself. But how I see it"—he swept a hand toward the ocean—"there's more here than we can understand. More'n we can see or feel or explore with the senses we got." He considered the dead fish on the board before going on.

"Yep. It's like the ocean. You can't see it all from here, barely see a fraction of it, but we know it's there, all around the world. Even if it's shallow in parts, it's much deeper than we can imagine. My guess is life's a little bit like when you're out there." He nodded to the waves.

It was peeling off sets that would have made Ash's eyes shine the way the blade of Salt's filleting knife gleamed in the sun.

"When everything's tossin' and turnin' and your guts are churning and you're not sure whether to head back or press on, first thing you need to do is find somethin' to cling to, or you'll go overboard." He fixed his gaze on mine, direct eyes as penetrating as an osprey's, nested in wrinkles.

151

Overboard. My mind seized on the word.

Had Ash gone overboard? Was that what had happened to him?

Salt cleared his throat, and his rosy cheeks grew ruddier. "Probably a bad analogy," he said gruffly, rubbing one snowy eyebrow. "'Cause I'm not saying you're going overboard with this grief." He returned his attention to the filleting knife, testing its sharpness with a finger. "Not saying that at all, love." His voice caught, and the words that followed came out in a rasp. "We all loved Ash. But me, I lose a mate, I try to keep busy."

It was Salt's way of saying I should keep making an effort at school. Saying things without directly saying them had always been Salt's specialty. I wished I could ask him whether he ever cried himself to sleep, whether he wanted to turn back the clock. I wanted to ask him how he'd coped with losing mates in the war, whether he thought Ash was capable of hitting a woman, even if she had hurt him. But I knew I couldn't. He wouldn't have wanted Salt to know that, and I doubt he'd have told him. I doubted Salt would talk to me about it, or not directly. He was a closed book with a battered cover. If I found the dog-eared page where he'd scrawled his feelings in the margin, I knew Salt would just want to turn to a new one anyway. The end.

After the first time I'd met Salt, as we'd driven home, Ash had told me that all the years he'd known Salt, after he'd returned to Willow Bay from wherever the wind and water had taken him, the old sailor had told him only three things about Vietnam.

It was bloody humid.

The Viet Cong were clever little shits.

And that he was no war hero, and he didn't want anyone suggesting he was.

That was it. No amount of discussion could drag any more out of him.

Snap. Book closed.

Salt's peaceful existence in Willow Bay was his epilogue, and he wasn't about to let me or anyone else skip him right back to the start, sad story or not. I'd come to respect that about him. He was an introvert like me. A listener. One who whistled with faux nonchalance while he watched. And whistling, I knew, was Salt's favourite way to change the subject.

He was doing it now. "Sitting on the Dock of the Bay."

After a few bars, the subject sufficiently changed, he stopped, laid the blade against another trevally's tail, and began to shear off the fillet.

Conversation over.

I watched in silence, thinking about his words.

Maybe he was right. Mum had tried to raise me Greek Orthodox, but other than at Easter, her efforts were half-hearted. Once Dad was out of the picture, Mum's attempts waned even further. Maybe she'd lost some of her faith after Dad left, although I sometimes caught her talking to the wooden effigy of Christ that hung in the hallway near the coatrack.

I thought about what Salt had said about hanging on, finding something to keep me busy, about there being more to life than our senses could pick up. It was a blustery day, and the wooden slats of the jetty were pale and warm beneath my bare feet. I sat down to the left of the cleaning station, ignoring the salty, fish gut-scented air, and peered out at the sea, still thinking.

Bitten's curved fin rose from the waves like a beckoning finger, as if he'd come to check on me.

The dolphin swam closer, his sleek body rising lazily from the surface, his large, dark eye studying me. Tears welled in my eyes as I remembered the day I'd first seen Bitten up close and Ash's face as he'd videotaped my joy when the dolphin leaped overhead.

You miss him too, don't you? I asked him without words. *You trusted him too.*

"Likes the fish," Salt said.

I jumped, so absorbed in my memories I'd forgotten Salt was there.

He held up a carcass, shaking it in my direction, and then tipped his head to the dolphin. "He's been coming in for a couple of weeks now at about this time."

"Are people feeding him?"

"Yep." Salt threw the fish hulk off the jetty, and the dolphin torpedoed from the water to snatch it.

"All part of Allen Aldershot's plan for the region," Salt said.

Within seconds, the mammal reappeared, trilling and clicking, its beak convincingly resembling a smile.

I grimaced. "But it's bad for them."

"I know. But there's no one else here this morning, and I haven't caught that much meself."

"He'll stop hunting."

"This guy looks pretty healthy to me. I've seen a few more come in, but none as regular as this one. The kids've apparently got a name for this guy. Chomp, or something."

"Bitten," I said.

"Chomp suits 'im better. Look at the way he's getting into those fishheads. He can probably catch his own fish just fine. Just lazy." He tossed another hulk to Bitten, who snapped it up. "Besides, there's hardly anything left on these. The commercial fishos won't give him too many. But I agree we don't need a bunch of bloody yuppies here throwing fish into the water like berley and attracting sharks, then suing the council when one of 'em gets involved in a feeding frenzy. Nah, I'm pretty happy with Willow Bay staying sleepy, lack of tourists or not." He leaned down and swished the blade of his knife in the bucket.

"So you're not going to be running fishing charters anytime soon?"

"Can't see meself doing it."

Understatement—Salt was a master at that, too.

"You want to throw him this one, love?" He waggled the last fish frame at me.

I shook my head.

"Aw, c'mon." Salt wiggled it again. "You can be an eco-warrior tomorrow, Juls."

Bitten chirruped and clucked his agreement as Salt leaned over and let the fish dangle. I heard a splash and barely saw the mammal leap, its body brushing against my feet as it dove. It clicked that same short, long, short combination, and that awkward, fierce electrical tug sent my thoughts into a sudden, inexplicable spiral.

A body lies on the beach facedown; emaciated, spindle-thin, its legs a lattice of scars and coral cuts, back flayed with sunburn. It is naked, arms twisted to the sides, but I recognise the broad back, the shoulders, even withered as they are. I recognise the tousle of brown-blond hair, the length of the shin, the heel. I know it all.

I've known it all.

Waves suck at the toes, and a small crab scuttles beneath the bridge of one ankle. Foamy wash pushes a small blue sea star onto the beach and digs a channel around the angles of the prone body, the water pooling and then dispersing, anchoring the limbs with ropes of seaweed.

For an instant, my heart leaps. I think I see a twitch, a toe shuddering against the niggling crustacean and the outstretched arms of the sea star, but it could be the movement of the tide. It's rising so quickly now that it will soon lift him up, spirit him away like an undertaker. Further out, a fin rises, pushing a spangled school of fish before it on the water.

Then the dream's colours ebb like the tide, and the heat starts to fade, the seaweed-stung air masking the pungency of decay, becoming fainter.

"Ash," I bellow. "No! Ash!"

But the hiss of the sea is the only reply.

"Ash. No! Ash!"

"Juliette!" Salt shook me, his gruff voice panicked.

My eyes fluttered open, and I wondered at my own voice; it sounded far away, muffled, not mine. "Salt?"

"Jeez, love, you look like you've seen a ghost." He ran one hand over his jaw.

Please. Listen.

I sat up, wobbly and fuzzy-headed. That voice again. Dammit if I wasn't hearing things. *Listen to what?* I thought. I swallowed and my throat tasted like brine, as Salt turned to his blue cooler to fill me a cup of cold water.

"I gotta admit, Juls. I'm worried about you. Bunking off school, now this. You sure you're all right?"

"I'm fine. Just a bit sick." I rubbed my eyes. "I'm... confused. Tired."

"Hm." Salt looked sceptical. "You were out to it, eyes rolling and everything. Yelling for Ash. Love, maybe you better get yourself off to the doc. Have yourself checked out. What if it's epilepsy or something?"

I waved him away. "It's not. I'm just tired. A twenty-four-hour bug." I attempted my best Arnold Schwarzenegger voice. "It's not a tumour." It did nothing to erase the worried expression from Salt's face.

He patted my shoulder with one large, calloused paw, and I almost flinched, half expecting that strange jolt again.

"Well, if you reckon it might be worth getting a second opinion..." He dug a battered leather wallet from the pocket of his shorts. Flipping through, he eventually slid out a business card and pressed the rectangle of white cardboard into my palm.

155

"You and me, we're not great at talking out our troubles. Ash could talk the hind legs off a donkey—underwater, with a mouth full of marbles. Half of it rubbish. Spent more time listenin' to that kid over the years than to anyone, I reckon." He coughed again. "I miss it. His chatter's probably the only thing that got me through my own… well, my own troubles at a certain time… you understand? Except—" He tapped the card I held between my fingers. "Except this lady. I'm happy to listen to you if you want to talk, but she was a real help for me."

He gazed at the horizon and squeezed my hand again. "Have a think about it, love. It's not a crime to ask for help."

I nodded. Maybe Salt was right. Maybe I did need help. I glanced at the rectangle of white card. Dr Birgit Jorssen, it read. Melody House Holistic Healing Centre, Figtree.

"It's got her private mobile on it, too." Salt said. "If you get too down, think about givin' her a call."

"Thanks," I said and slid it into my pocket.

Then I reached into Salt's bucket and drew out a fish frame. *To hell with it.* Bitten curved in to snatch the Trevally hulk, giving me three grateful clicks in return as he surfaced.

I cocked my head, listening. Three clicks short, three long, three short. If I didn't know better, I'd have thought I could understand them, as if they were in Morse code.

SOS.

CHAPTER 30

I focussed on Dylan's back as he paddled out ahead of me. Around thirty surfers formed a circle far behind the break, their bodies gleaming copper in the burning light, boards bobbing beneath them on the waves like cuttlefish shells. Two wreaths already floated in the circle they'd made, the flowers studded with candles that burned white in the sunset. The one on the front of my board was the biggest, the one for Ash. Jaz had organised them all, organised the whole thing with Sharon's help, and the fragrance of white lilies and frangipani mingled with surf wax and salt, and filled my throat, my mind, with Ash.

No one said anything as I paddled closer. What was there to say? At least Drew and Troy had been buried. Ash was still out there somewhere. With no body, there was no way to do anything but wait for the coroner's report. This memorial service was all we had.

We were all silent, sad.

I looked down at my board, hiding dry eyes as I pushed the wreath out to nudge the others. I hadn't cried in the weeks before this stupid service. And I'd barely slept. Whenever I did, I saw him face down on a beach, still as a corpse. His back burned red and lacerated, his ankle lapped by swell.

The sun sank on our silence, and the waves tugged the wreaths away. The sea was lulling, sympathetic, pulsing out small wrinkles of waves. It was no good for surfing, even if I'd wanted to. And I didn't.

A few of the guys and girls turned to paddle back to shore, back to where friends and family stood among a maze of burning candles on the beach, spelling out the boys' names, and hearts, and R.I.P.

The sun dipped below the horizon, and the water grew shadowed and sharky. Bull sharks ventured out at dusk; we all knew they were some of the worst. Chilled flesh rose on my dangling shins at the thought. The shark dream still lurked in a corner of my mind. As if

I'd channelled him, Bitten's malformed crescent fin rose above the waves. He chittered and then turned back to the vanishing wreaths, circling them.

He's alive.

I shook my head. The thought had been too clear, as if someone had spoken it aloud, but when I glanced around at Dylan and Jaz, they were both silent, heads bowed.

He's alive.

I glanced around again. It wasn't in my head, was it? It hadn't seemed angry enough. I stopped, head tilted, listening.

Nothing. My head was as empty as an abandoned shell.

Emptied out, curled inside,
Taken by the tide.

The lyrics of Ash's song inserted themselves into my mind momentarily.

Stop it, I instructed my brain. *Just stop. He's gone. In truth, he never really was anyway, or at least not what you thought he was.*

Now his songs just angered me. That one about Renee had been all over the radio in the days following Ash's accident. After the rally, The Project had broadcast a short clip of Ash playing it live, and 5GB at Figtree had later picked the song up and played it repeatedly over the airwaves as a tribute. It hadn't changed anything anyway. The paper had published photos of Ash's life vest with a bite out of it—the perfect propaganda for the council to insist on shark nets. The nets went up. Everyone forgot about the protest, and about the song, and about Ash.

Everyone except me.

Every time the lyrics sprang into my mind, they made me want to scream. They made me want to cry. Sometimes, they made me want to die.

It was mine, so damn deep it must be real,
Now it's gone, cut and dried,
Emptied out, curled inside,
Taken by the tide.

I wondered how it was possible for me to love and mourn and hate Ash simultaneously. I was angry too, angry that he'd gone off and left me still trying to puzzle out his secrets and unravel his lies. But most of all, I missed him. The him I'd thought he was. I missed his arms around me. His lopsided grin. His scent. His kiss. His laugh.

Help.

I spun around, but everyone was silent, lost in their own thoughts and unaware of my turmoil.

Something cruised past my shin, and then Bitten was there, dark eyes and beaked snout rising beside my board, nuzzling my knee. That odd electric sensation struck me, and I wasn't there anymore. Suddenly, nothing was real. Or everything was.

Humming intensifies in my head like altitude sickness, and I'm floating, peering down at a pale strip below that contrasts with the sapphire of the ocean. Waves kiss the shoreline, and I'm tipped beachward, bright lights sweeping the break and picking out the beach and the palm-fringed island, little more than a coral cay, beyond.

I'm wheeling again, spotlights seizing on whiteness in the night. Vegetation matted together with sand. Beach spinifex. Milky pools of brackish water. Pearls of shallow reef braceletting the beach. And then, there on the sand, something that makes my heart heave into my throat. Something that catches my breath and holds it fast.

A word.

Not even a word. An abbreviation.

SOS.

CHAPTER 31

"Quick, get her back on the board."

I came to in the water, limbs floppy, as Dylan dragged me back onto Goldfish.

Jaz's worried face peered down at me. "Juls." She patted my hand as I squinted at her, focussing on the flag of wet hair plastered to her wrinkled forehead.

"Are you okay? What in the flippin' heck was that?"

"W-What?" I tried to sit up. *What the hell was that?* Even I wasn't sure.

"Just lie down, okay?" Jaz pushed me back. "We're towing you to shore."

"Has she got epilepsy?" Riki yelled from somewhere behind us.

Epilepsy? I shook my head feebly. "No. I don't think so."

There was no way I was going to explain the *mati* to these guys; in fact, I wasn't even sure that's what it was. It had happened so quickly, as if Bitten's touch had knocked me out cold. But the thing my brain couldn't comprehend most was that tiny abbreviation—SOS.

Maybe Salt's right. Maybe I am losing my shit. Maybe I do need help.

"Get back to shore and call an ambo," Dylan instructed Riki, who set off paddling.

The dolphin reappeared about a metre away, as if worried about me, and all the blood drained from my face as I realised what it might mean. What if Bitten *was* worried about me? And not just me. What if...?

He lives.

"Geez, she's white. Something's really spooked her," Dyl muttered.

I sat bolt upright on my board, the voice loud in my head again. On the beach, everyone was thronging around, their grief turned to worry.

"Is it a shark?" someone bellowed from the beach. "Nah," Jaz called back. "It's just Juls."

"I'm fine," I said, but my voice sounded overloud, overbright. "It's just... it's been a tough day. I'm okay." The words stuck in my throat and thudded in my temples like the lie they were. Dylan tugged my board up onto the beach and helped me off.

Tear-stained faces crowded us—Mum, Sharon, Salt, and Lisa Rubin, ugly crying as if Ash had been her boyfriend. It made me feel claustrophobic.

"Step aside, folks," Sergeant Kendall instructed, clearing his throat as he pushed his way through the crowd. "We've... ah... got an ambulance coming."

I wondered how he managed to stay so calm, how he managed at all. His youngest son, Drew, had been out on the boat with Ash that day. Sarge Kendall was already middle-aged when the youngest of his three boys was born, and he was practically grandfatherly by the time Drew died. A kind man with a habit of clearing his throat all the time, he was Willow Bay's highest-ranking and only police officer. The rest of the force was based out of Anchorage. Before Drew died, Sarge used to coach the football team. He even dressed up as Santa each year for the Lion's Club Christmas Carols in Beechwood Park. He'd been known to ring the publican too, whenever a booze bust was set up out of town by the coppers from Anchorage. Ash once told me he'd been in the bar of the Sailor's Maid with Salt when Saul Rogers, the publican, had put Sarge on speakerphone.

"You tell any boys who've... uh... had a few, they need to call a taxi from Figtree tonight, Saul. I hate to... err... have to charge one of our own for something as idiotic as driving with a brew too many under the... uh... belt. Looks bad on the books, Saul. You know what they say, if you drink and drive, you're a bloody idiot."

But now Sarge Kendall looked old—old and sad and officious in his immaculately pressed dark-blue uniform, his police hat hiding grey hair that ringed a shiny bald spot. He might have been managing better than me, but it was true he'd never been the same since Drew died.

Died. I swallowed the word, but despite the stinging salt and wind, I couldn't force out another tear. Drew Kendall was dead. And yet...

He lives.

Sarge and Dylan walked me up the beach to the ambulance, my arms over their shoulders like an invalid.

"I know this is... er... hard," Sarge said, his arm tight around my waist. "But they'll always be with us. They all will. Drew and Troy and Ash."

Dylan thumped one fist against his heart. "Right here. You just gotta believe that. Right, Sarge?"

Sarge nodded.

But I couldn't believe it.

Because a little voice in my mind told me otherwise. I just didn't know whether to listen. I didn't know whose voice it was, whether it was mine, or Bitten's, or whether it came directly from Planet Fucked-Up. I had no idea what was real and what wasn't, what was a dream and what was a nightmare. And I guess you could say I never had.

CHAPTER 32

The sea spread flat and empty before me, and most of the surfers had already packed up and left. Everyone else was at work or school. I'd wagged school to be alone, the way I liked it. Remembering. Trying to shake last night's dream from my mind, I picked over the detail. It was the beach wedding again, the silk handkerchief tucked into my bodice, and I was desperate to see who was waiting near the ring of boards, knowing it could only be one person, and also that it couldn't be that person. Because that person was gone. And not just *gone*. The coroner had just this week finished his report. He'd given Rory and Sharon the certificate to prove it. According to the coroner, Ash wasn't just gone. He was...

I couldn't bring myself to say the word.

It made me shiver, and I wondered how I would ever believe it. How I would ever be able to say it. I couldn't imagine not being acutely aware of the hollow in my back where Ash's hand would have rested, the crook of my neck missing his kisses. I couldn't imagine a single day without him, yet how many had it been already? Years stretched out ahead of me like sets, each rolling into the next, and all of them—if I believed Mum and Jaz and Salt and Rory and Sharon and everyone, including the coroner—without Ash. But if I believed Renee, maybe I'd dodged a bullet.

I replayed all the dreams over and over again in my mind, squinting into the sun.

"Maybe it wasn't the *mati*, Juls," I told myself out loud, sounding even crazier in my solitude. "Just wishful thinking." Thrusting my hair back from my face, I gripped my skull tight for a second and closed my eyes. "It wasn't real. It was just a dream. None of this is real."

Real.

But the voice sounded real. Muffled again. Not mine. Slipping my sunnies off, I scanned the ocean. It was featureless, changing only minimally as each shallow wave slid in.

"Bitten?"

Listen.

My heart grew buoyant, bubbled up. "I'm listening."

Come.

"Into the water?" Something suspicious in me, some paranoia or cynicism, made me hesitate. Was that what this was? Voices telling me to do something harmful, to wade farther in, farther out?

A chitter made me swing to the right in time to see the whorl left by Bitten's vanishing fin.

Help.

"I want to follow you. I do. But how do I know this is real?"

The fin rose again, beckoning from behind a larger wave.

I projected my voice over the crash of waves on the shore. "I can't do this alone. I need help."

Help.

"From who? If I tell them Ash is alive, if I tell them I can hear you, they'll all think I'm mad. Crazy." Before I knew it, I was in the water, wading in after the dolphin. "Maybe I am mad," I muttered.

"Who are you talking to?"

I spun, jumping out of my skin. "Shit, Jaz!"

Her hazel eyes narrowed as she splashed toward me through the shallows. "You all right?"

"Yeah. I was just thinking. I don't want to talk about it, okay?"

"Figures." Jaz slipped her sunnies up to squint at me and then put her hand on my forearm. "I know I've been hanging with Dyl a lot lately. But"—she waved a hand to the beach and eyed me warily—"if you want to talk to someone, you know. A friend. An actual person. We used to be able to tell each other anything."

My throat felt scratchy, and the rising wind stung my eyes. "I know."

"Dyl's bringing his board down from the car. You want to hang with us for a while? Maybe you should go for a surf with him some day."

I shook my head. The dolphin had vanished, the sea was glassy and unbroken, as if he had never been there. Had he been there?

"Not much surf anyway." I motioned to the pathetic break.

"Nah. But some days it's just about being out there. Dylan, well, he misses Ash too, you know."

I swallowed again. "Yep."

I did know. The surf called to me every day. I felt each ripple like a pulse. But it reminded me of Ash, and every wave threatened to overwhelm me.

"You know Dyl never believed any of that palaver with Renee and the Fantastics," Jaz said, squinting. "He said there's no way Ash would ever do that. No way. You know what they're like."

I swallowed.

"Hey, you wanna blow off the beach and come for a coffee instead?" Jaz jabbed a thumb over her shoulder toward the esplanade. "It's not like Dylan doesn't get enough of an audience anyway. He's a bloody show-off." She smiled, an effort to hide the concern that cratered her forehead.

It bothered me. I didn't reply.

Jaz must have decided it wasn't worth the effort to pretend, because she said more abruptly, "Try not to push people away, okay? We're all worried about you."

I exhaled, my toes puddling in the wet sand and sea foam. "Don't be. I'm fine."

I didn't want Jaz's pity. I didn't want anyone's pity. I wanted... I wanted things to be normal again. But they couldn't be. Not now. Not ever. And what was normal anyway?

"Hey, Juls." Dylan waved with one arm, the other wrapped around a board.

I waved back, but it felt clumsy, half-hearted, like I was swatting him away. Was I pushing people away? Maybe Jaz was right to be concerned about me. After all, I'd just been busted standing in the surf having a telepathic conversation with a dolphin—or perhaps with the voices in my head. I wasn't sure.

"Nah. I have to..." I gestured vaguely to the parking lot. "Mum's going to need the car later on. I'll catch up with you later, sometime soon."

"Okay." Her frown deepened. "Say hi to your mum. How is she anyway? Feels like I haven't seen her in ages. Also, you didn't RSVP to Zara's twenty-first on the weekend. You're coming, aren't you?" She pinned me with a stare. "I won't take no for an answer. I'll pick you up at ten on Saturday morning, and we'll go to Anchorage to buy something new."

I smiled. "Fine. Mum's fine too. Still gossiping."

I didn't tell her Mum was worried about me as well, and she'd just this morning suggested I visit the salon for a massage and a makeover.

"A change, honey," she'd said, tucking a lock of hair behind my ear. "To cheer you up, *paidi mou*. My heart is breaking to never see my baby smile anymore." She set a cup of freshly brewed coffee on the table before me. "We could go red," she said, eyeing my hair. "Or short? You've lost so much weight. All this hair is making you look too skinny." One palm snapped up decisively, cutting off my refusal. "I know Ash loved your long hair, but a pixie cut would give you zip. The girls from the salon are raving about some DJ who's playing an all ages gig at Swaggers this weekend, after Zara's party. Some hit song about Ibiza." She pronounced it Eye-beee-zah. "You could go out, maybe meet someone." Mum waggled her eyebrows.

"Eee-beetha." I said. "It's pronounced Eee-beetha. And I hate Swaggers."

"Juliette." Mum hugged me tight and then pulled away and held me at arm's length, her brow lowered. "This new you, she hates *everything*. Where did my baby go, who loved to read, eat, watch movies with me?" Her tone gentled. "Don't you think it's time to start living again, *paidi mou*?"

"I'm living." I tried to tug away from her, but one manicured hand still gripped my shoulder.

"So you'll have a makeover?"

"Nope."

Her hands flew to her hips, elbows jutting out in exclamation.

"No thanks, Mum." I corrected myself. Then I drained my coffee, rinsed the cup, and left the house for the beach.

No, Jaz wasn't the only one worried about me today, and she likely wouldn't be the only one worried about me tomorrow, either. I sighed as I set off for the car.

I was halfway there when Jaz yelled from the beach. "Juls?"

I turned, the wind catching my curls, their tips sun-bleached and frizzy with split ends. "Yeah?"

"All your back freckles'll turn into melanomas if you keep sitting on the beach all day without anyone around to rub sunscreen on for you." She poked her tongue out.

I laughed, but it made me think of Ash, of the way I'd shivered that first day as he'd smoothed sunblock over my shoulders.

"Thanks for the tip," I yelled back, "but tell that to the Fantastics. I'm not the one slathering myself in coconut oil."

"Cancer kills, yanno," she bellowed after me. "And so can besties gone bad. If you even think about piking on Saturday, I'll throttle you. You'll be dead to me. Dead. Got it, princess?" She made a throat slitting motion and crossed her eyes.

I laughed and saluted. "Gotcha." Turning, I waved over the back of my head. "Bye, Jazzy."

"Bye, bestie."

But my word-nerd mind had already seized on the words: *Dead to me.*

Who cares? I thought. *Without Ash, who cares if I die?*

CHAPTER 33

The sauce bottle squelched out a burp as I squirted it too vigorously over my chips. I didn't really feel like them, but Salt had insisted I eat something. He'd called to me as I walked past the harbour, headed for the beach, looking for Bitten. I hadn't heard him at first. My thoughts were too loud.

Every step echoed a question: *what's going on?* For a moment, I considered telling Salt about the voice, about the dreams.

"You give that doc a call yet?" Salt asked as I set the sauce bottle back on the table.

I sighed. He already thought I was destined for the funny farm. "Not yet." I concentrated on dabbing a chip in sauce.

Salt studied me intently for a moment, then nudged me with one freckled elbow. "Eat up. You're getting scrawny. I oughta order you a milkshake as well. God knows the Conch could use the business. Everyone's tightening their belts. From the looks of ya, you've had to tighten yours a few notches. There's nothing left of you."

"Thanks." I smirked as the waitress arrived with Salt's steak sandwich. "But I'm guessing that's not a compliment, coming from you."

"Everyone knows the way to a guy's heart." Salt jerked his chin to his lunch and grinned. "Bit of meat."

"Well, I'm not interested in anyone's heart. And with lines like that, it's no wonder you're a bachelor."

"Maybe I should go on that telly show," he said with a laugh. "*The Bachelor.*"

"You're bound to be the next star of *Sailor Wants a Wife.*"

He laughed. "Just get those chips into you. After that we'll order dessert and work on putting some meat back on your bones."

I half-heartedly bit the tip off another chip. It was too hot.

"Do you believe in soul mates, Salt?" I asked eventually. "That two people are fated to be together, to get married?"

He brooded on it a minute in silence, chewing.

"How come you never married anyway?"

"Who says I never?" He picked his sandwich up with both hands and took an over-generous bite. Beetroot dripped out the bottom, staining the plate. "Besides, if I was married, the Conch would go under. I'm supporting local business, eating here all the time."

"You've never said anything about a wife or kids. So I'm guessing you weren't."

"Some things don't bear repeating." He chewed for a minute. "Course, that doesn't stop us repeating them." He put the sandwich down, and I thought I saw the faintest of frowns run over his forehead.

"Repeating? Are you saying you have been married?" I pointed a chip at him. "Twice?"

Salt scratched his head and focussed on his plate again. "Not saying."

"Aw, come on, Salt."

"I've never been married." He followed that tidbit with a long slug of beer. "And I'm not sure how I feel about 'soul mates.'"

"Engaged?"

"None of your business." We sat in silence for a minute as he munched another bite of his sandwich. His eyes had clouded over, and I wondered if I'd pushed him too far.

"You ever heard of a dockside guarantee, love?" he asked, taking up his beer again.

I frowned. "A what?" It wasn't like Salt to volunteer information.

He took a long swig. "Guess that answers that question." Licking the froth off his lips, he put the schooner down again and mumbled, more to himself than me. "I wonder how many of them broke their word? Used to be the thing to do—tell a beau you'd wait for him. I wonder how many poor sappers paid for a ring that ended up going to the United States."

A gull frittered around our feet, demanding a chip, but Salt ignored it.

I did my best to keep surprise from registering on my face. So Salt had once had a fiancée, but she'd left him for an American GI, I guessed.

"What was her name?"

He shook his head and took another wolfish bite of sandwich. Eventually, he swallowed hard and said, "Told meself I'd never say it again."

"Not once."

"Never. But you know these things… Probably for the best in the long run. Wouldn't have worked out. Not once I got back. Neither of us were the same person."

"You never thought of going after her?"

Salt shook his head. "When a bird chooses to fly away, you'd best let it go, lest you get shat on. Confucius says."

"Or you could get on a plane and fly after it."

"A plane? Why do you think I've got a boat?" Salt said. "I'm no bloody fan of flying. Not anymore." Wrinkles carved lines around his mouth as he smiled, but it didn't reach the hollows of his eyes. "That old yacht's still the sweetest girl I ever met. Present company aside.

"Because she doesn't yabber on, and she kept her figure even after all these years," I joked. It was a joke I'd heard before, the *Sea Change* being his great lady love.

"Of course! I take good care of her." He jogged my elbow with his again. "Don't think I appreciate you mocking my prowess with the ladies, though, Juls. I may be nothin' but an old sailor now, but I did all right back in my heyday." He hid his half-smile behind what remained of the sandwich. "Not everyone's made for marriage."

"I had a dream I'd marry Ash. It seemed so real, like I could pinch myself and wake up, and it would still be true." I pushed my plate away.

Salt reached across the table and squeezed my fingers. "First love. You're just kids," he said. "Maybe you would've married him. Maybe you wouldn't've. Can't speculate, and there's no point dwellin' on it. Truth is, there aren't any guarantees, love, dockside or otherwise. Not all dreams come true."

Then why did mine, but not the ones I wanted? I wiped a smear of sauce off my lip with a serviette, wondering what Salt would say if I told him about the *mati*, about Dad, the Jingilly Hill bus crash and the shark attack, the fire, and all of the other dreams. Most people wouldn't believe me, but Salt wasn't most people, was he?

"What if it was like a… premonition?" I asked.

"A what?"

"What if some people can tell the future?" I sucked in my cheeks.

"Then I pity the poor bastard who can. If I'd ever known what was more than ten minutes into my future, I reckon I'd have packed up my bat and ball years ago. Not knowing's the only thing that got me through. Knowing will make a mess of you."

I couldn't argue with that.

Salt put an imaginary gun to his right carotid artery. "Back in 'Nam, the moment you took time out to wonder what was going to happen next was the exact moment you were most likely to cop it in the neck. Let someone else anticipate. I'll react once I see what's coming."

"But that's my point. What if? What if someone can see what's coming for them? I mean, you believe in God. Why not things like prophetic dreams, telepathy, ghosts? That day on the pier, you told me I looked like I'd seen a ghost."

"Oh, we've all got ghosts; some more than others. But I'm not gonna say it's okay to let some charlatan swirl your tealeaves and tell you it's Tuesday. That's just supernatural nonsense."

"It's not Tuesday. It's Thursday," I reminded him. "And what if some of that supernatural nonsense isn't nonsense?" I shook my head, knowing I didn't have it in me to convince a sceptic.

Salt tapped his weather-lined forehead. "Take it from a man who's got more regrets than you've had hot dinners: the only ghosts you gotta fear are the ones you won't let go of. They're the ones that scare the bejesus out of you." He nicked a chip off my plate.

"I can't forget Ash," I muttered. "I won't. I'd have known, I'd have seen him if he'd di—" The word died on my lips. Was I afraid that admitting Ash was dead might make it real, might make his death more than a figment of my imagination? The island, the SOS scratched in the sand, flashed into my mind.

"Not saying you should forget Ash," Salt's tone was gruff. "But one day, you will. You'll forget the bad stuff, focus on the happy memories. I heard about how it ended between you two, and I guess that doesn't help, but I reckon he loved you, Juls. Reckon I knew him well enough to know that."

He squinted and then gave a small nod. "Remember him the way you two were when you were happy. You hang on to all that hurt forever, it'll erode all the things you ever thought about him, Juls. All the dreams you had."

Erode all the dreams. I wished I could. All of them, good and bad.

I sighed. I couldn't tell him. "You know, Salt, not everyone's as tough as you."

He put both elbows on the table and leaned forward. "You're right. They're not." He winked. "But I reckon you'd be surprised how tough people can be when they gotta. Right now"—his tongue swiped across his beetroot-stained lips—"right now, well we gotta be tough, you and me. Only way to get through something like this, other than go see a quack and let it all out."

The waitress interrupted with another schooner, on the house.

Salt lovingly wiped a bead of moisture off the side with his thumb and then licked it dry. "Truth is, I wasn't always so tough, either. I did my share of running away. Maybe you need to take a breather, girl. Find your peace again." He picked up the glass and sipped it like an afterthought, watching me over the rim.

"Is that why you came to Willow Bay, to find your peace?"

"Reckon it is, love. That and the Gordons."

The seagull stopped casing the tables for food and flapped off, disappointed. The cafe was quiet.

"And I liked the stillness." He motioned to the calm ocean, the sleeping streetscape.

"It can't get much stiller than this."

"You say that like it's a bad thing." He glanced at me sideways. "Too quiet for you, love?"

I shook my head. "Too empty."

Salt put his beer down and reached over to clap my shoulder. "You'll get there." He rubbed a hand over his grizzled jaw. "Ash told me this quote from some kid's movie once. Remember that lifesaving accident about five years back now? The year the Schyler's lad drowned when the boat capsized?"

I nodded. I'd dreamed about it. The weather had been too rough. Organisers said the competition should have been cancelled.

"Really thumping surf," Salt went on. "Waves over a couple of metres high. Ash and a couple of the other lads went under too. Ash said it was like being in a washing machine, told me everything rushed to his head, like that cinematic moment when life flashes before your eyes, but the only words in his head were this silly fish voice, telling him to keep on swimming." He looked down at the table, but not quickly enough to stop a tear leaking down his leathery cheek.

I swallowed. *Just keep swimming.* That was what Ash would do, too. Ash, the lifesaver. Ash the surfer. Maybe that was what Ash had done. Maybe he'd swum to safety somewhere.

SOS.

I pressed a finger to my temple as Salt took another swig of beer.

"Just keep going," Salt said, patting my hand. "Don't you quit on life."

The waitress passed again, and he slipped her his credit card, insisting, "I got this."

"Salt?" I asked once she'd returned with the receipt.

"Ye-ah." He looked up from flipping his wallet closed, sliding it back into the pocket of his khakis.

"The woman, your fiancée, She Who Must Not Be Named. Do you ever think about her, ever wonder whether…?"

Salt drew in a deep breath and downed the rest of his beer. When he looked up at me, his blue eyes were still watery. "Every day, Juls. Every. Single. Day."

CHAPTER 34

"Are you sure, Jaz? I mean, it's a little—"

"I'm sure." Jaz moved closer to the mirror and smoothed down her hair. "It's fun. We both need a little fun."

I held the short orange dress she'd ordered me to try on up to the mirror and sighed. "Honestly, Jaz, I don't even know what fun looks like anymore."

"It certainly isn't that." She gestured to my jeans and khaki tank top, and winked.

"Thanks."

Silence.

"Look." Jaz took a seat on the wooden bench in the Target fitting room. "Tonight is supposed to be a laugh, okay? Ever since Ash di—"

"I don't want to talk about it." I wriggled out of my shorts.

"You never want to talk about it. But what if you have to?" She pulled a MAC lip-gloss out of her purse and retouched her pout in the mirror.

"I don't have to." The mirror reflected my wan, glossless smile, the bags under my eyes. Another dream had kept me awake the night before. A factory fire somewhere. Crowded. Unidentifiable. All I could smell today was charred flesh.

"Look, Mum says it helps to talk about it. I mean, what if you really need help, Juls? Even that crap with Renee would be enough, let alone what happened to Ash."

The way she said it, the look in her eyes, chilled my soul. I pulled my shirt up over my head to hide my face.

What if I did? It was none of her business. And what did Jaz know about it? Her boyfriend was alive. And he wasn't a cheating scumbag who hit women.

"Fun!" I said, as I straightened the hem of the dress, ignoring her question. "That's our mission."

We were silent for a while as I stared at myself in the mirror, wondering who that person was anymore. Finally, I asked, "You sure I look okay?"

Jaz eyed me for a minute. "You look incredible. As always." For the first time, I thought her tone contained a trace of envy. "I wish I was skinny enough to wear it."

I bit my lip, still unsure about it, not feeling the fun. But it was Jaz's sister's twenty-first, a beach party. If I decided I didn't want to be there, I could always stay for a while and go looking for Bitten down the beach.

Jaz appeared in the mirror next to me, standing on one foot and then the other to determine whether the heels she'd decided to buy matched the miniskirt she had on. She looked over at me and smiled. "Hey, I'm sorry."

"For what? For diagnosing fun?"

"No. For suggesting you might really need help." She hugged me. "I wish I could make you happy again since Ash—"

I hugged her so fiercely I thought her bones might snap. *Don't say it. Don't say the word 'died'.*

"Quick. Stamp it out." Lisa Rubin tossed her head back so dramatically I thought I heard the bones in her neck crunch.

Embers floated on air currents, fizzing as they sank down onto wet sand.

"It's just a spark," the tow-headed boy next to her scoffed. I couldn't make out his features from the other side of the fire, and his face was obscured by a hoodie, but he was probably just like all of the guys here: a bronzed, slim, half-cut surfer, likely with an ego bigger than his board. He carried a bottle of something in one hand—Jim Beam, I thought. In his other hand, he twirled a glowing stick from the bonfire.

"Stop flinging it around, or you're going to set someone's hair on fire," a black guy with dreads complained. He tossed the burning stick into the flames and then swung an arm over Lisa's shoulders and leaned in to kiss her. She pulled away and stood, with a little stumble of her own, to fetch another vodka cruiser from a nearby Esky cooler.

I glanced over at Jaz.

Yep, still getting it on. She and Dylan had been going at it for a while now. I glanced at my phone. It wasn't yet past ten o'clock, and I was already considering ditching Zara's party.

Earlier, things between Jaz and I had been almost back to normal. We'd laughed and gossiped as we dolled ourselves up in front of her bathroom mirror, and I realised how much I'd missed her. Since then, though, even the three vodka lime-and-sodas I'd consumed had done nothing to bring back that easy camaraderie.

"Shove over a little," Lisa said and sat down heavily.

She hadn't been at school much lately either, but I remembered her face at Ash's memorial service, her tears. I drew in a breath and shifted in the sand, curling my legs beneath me, biting back the bile-taste of that day's pain.

Her blonde hair hung in loose waves that owed something to a curling wand, and she squinted overly made-up eyes at the guy opposite us. She looked older, I thought, but then we all did. We all were. In a few months we'd be graduates, ready for jobs or college.

"How are things?" she asked.

I smiled and shovelled a hole in the sand with my toes. "Okay, I guess." It was a better answer than the truth.

Did I look so sad that she felt compelled to come and cheer me up, or was she as bored as I was?

"Here." She nudged a UDL can of vodka and raspberry into my hand. "I didn't want it. I just needed to get away from him." Her eyes narrowed as she watched the guy with dreadlocks. His shirt was off, and a feather tattooed on his pecs rippled as he stoked the fire, sending up a *whoosh* of flames.

"I thought he was your boyfriend."

"He is." She shrugged. "Man trouble."

"Oh." I dug my toes deeper into the sand.

"Wow, those two don't quit, hey." She tipped her chin toward Jaz and Dylan.

I popped the top of the can. "They've got to come up for air sometime," I said as a waft of sweet liquor escaped with the fizz. "She'll get major pash rash otherwise."

The drink was too bubbly. It made me hiccup. I wasn't yet eighteen, so there were plenty of good reasons for me not to drink whatever it was she had handed me—the taste was just one of them. It was like creaming soda mixed with methylated spirits. Still, it gave me something to do with my hands, and I was bored.

"Hey, you'll probably know." Lisa bumped my arm with her elbow. "You know Renee Aldershot, right?" She flipped a lock of golden hair off her face.

"Not really." I felt the familiar prickle of jealousy. "Why?"

"No reason. It's just..." Her eyes were still on the dark-skinned guy stoking the fire. "Well, I'm... I heard a rumour about something I thought you might know about."

"You'd have to ask Mum. I don't go into the gossip factory much anymore. You can probably tell." I ran a hand through my hair; it was long and frayed, and I'd worn it loose aside from a messy braid at each temple.

Lisa gave a half laugh and cocked her head. "Oh, I don't think your Mum knows. She'd say so if she did. Didn't she tell you I've quit school and started a hairdressing apprenticeship at the salon?"

Had Mum told me? Possibly. I couldn't remember. Was that why Lisa had come to talk to me, because Mum had put her up to it? It was the kind of "check-up" Mum would orchestrate.

"Oh, that's right. Mum did say something about that," I lied.

"I really love the work," Lisa gushed. "It's, like, now my job is just chatting all day and sweeping. Sometimes it's really gross, all that hair, but mostly, it's like, just sweeping and talking and making tea. I have to work early tomorrow, which is why I shouldn't drink any more of those tonight." She gestured to the can gripped in my hand.

"As far as I know, Mum doesn't run any breathalysers in the morning, not even on the weekends. Could result in some interesting hair-dos, though."

She laughed. "Your mum's cool. But I don't think I could stomach sweeping up all that hair hung over."

"Fair play." I took another chug of the drink. I had never been a fan of small talk, and the vodka couldn't change that.

She lowered her voice. "But some people, wow, they just never stop yammering. Personal stuff too. Gossip. Affairs. You get to know people *really* well when you're a hairdresser. It's like you're a trainee shrink, listening to people's problems all day." She giggled.

I stared at her pretty face with its pert, upturned nose.

Had there been any malice in that last comment about the shrink? I thought of the white business card I'd stashed in my underwear drawer. Had Mum found it? I made a mental note to bin it as soon as I got home.

Lisa smiled back blankly as I took another swig, each sip washing away some of my animosity. Maybe she was nicer than I'd thought, just a bit clueless. Maybe I was being paranoid.

"Anyway, I wondered if you knew whether… Well, if Ash ever said anything about Renee and Darius?"

"Darius? No. Look, Renee and I weren't close at all." Understatement. "I've never even met Darius before tonight."

"I heard about your fight," she added. "It was all around town. Ash wasn't seeing her, you know, not by then." She lowered her voice. "Someone told me a few juicy deets. But I've promised to keep my lips sealed."

"What details?"

"About Renee and Ash, silly. You know?" She nudged me again.

"What about them?" I muttered. Clearly, I didn't *know*. Not at all. Had I ever?

"Oh." Lisa's mouth snapped shut. "I thought you knew." She sat back and scrutinised my expression, then leaned in and whispered, "Lacey told me about the pregnancy ages ago, but—"

"Pregnancy!" This time I totally couldn't keep the shock from my voice.

"Yeah, but look, you, like, totally have to keep this secret, okay? One hundred per cent." She mimed zipping her lip.

I nodded, still trying to process the idea of a love child.

"This Indigenous lady came into the salon the other week for a pamper pack. She's totally not a fan of the Dolphin Dayze resort thing. And she kept going on and on about politics. You know, like how someone sprayed 'Mayor Aldershot is a dickhead' on the council chambers?"

I nodded. I didn't know that had happened, but it was an insult I could get on board with.

"Well, she said she could guess who it was. Allen Aldershot's a good client at the salon. He tips well, too. I did his hair and makeup for that TV appearance he did about the protest, trying to make out it was all a storm in a teacup, so I asked this woman why she hated Aldershot so much. She said he was a liar and a racist, so I asked her how she knew that." Lisa gripped my arm. "It turns out she's a midwife, and she was on duty the night Renee went into labour. She could get into huge trouble for breaking client confidentiality, so I can't tell you her name, and don't tell anyone, but, like, apparently the baby was premature, and it died just after it was born."

"That's awful." My guts churned. More information Ash hadn't shared with me, more secrets he'd hidden from me. I didn't think I could take much more. He wasn't even here anymore, and he was still messing me up.

"Anyway, after Ash hooked up with you, there was all this chatter about it. Most people hadn't realised she was even pregnant, because she'd moved to Anchorage to be home-schooled by her aunt, but Lacey told me. Then word started going around she was pregnant, and the story was that when she found about you and Ash, she dumped him and told him he'd have nothing to do with the kid. Lacey told me he punched her in fit of rage, and that's what sent her into labour."

She paused for a moment, and I tried to mentally digest that. I couldn't; it clogged up my brain like concrete.

"I was shocked by that," Lisa admitted, "but honestly, it never seemed like something Ash would do. I've known the Gordons since I was in kindergarten. I've known Renee for years too. Ash has always been a sweetheart, a bit goofy and highly sexed but never violent. Lacey insisted Renee told her that herself, and that Renee had a black eye for nearly two weeks afterward."

I swallowed hard and smoothed my dry lips with my tongue. Ash hitting a girl wasn't the kind of thing I wanted to imagine either. Yet I'd seen him that day, swearing and yelling at Renee. It hurt that I even had to wonder whether it was possible.

Firelight made Lisa's eyes shine, as if she was enjoying herself. Maybe hairdressing was the right career for her. Then she glanced across at Darius again, and her pupils shrunk.

"So I kind of said something about how disgusting it was that any guy would beat up his girlfriend, let alone when she was pregnant. And get this... this midwife's a big, half-Aboriginal woman, right? I was halfway through waxing her bikini line when she leaps straight up off the table, fully nude except for her knickers. Hands on hips, she scowls at me and goes, 'Sista, where'd you hear that steaming pile of cowshit? Is that what that dickhead's sayin' now?'

"I'm like totally freaking out I'm going to lose my job for upsetting her, because she's a good client too," Lisa said, "so I go, 'Ash? No. Lacey told me Renee told her....' and I swear she sort of huffs and says, 'Rotten apples don't fall far from the tree, do they? Don't you listen to any crap that girl tells you. That poor Ash fella was right there while that girl was in labour, rubbing her back, helping her through it. I've never seen a young fella be such a good natural birth partner, and I've seen a lotta pregnant teens. But that father of hers, he's a snake of a thing. The moment he got there, he started banging on about adoption, gettin' on everyone's tits. And when the kid died... you've never seen a devil more thrilled to discover his own granddaughter was stillborn. That boy, on the other hand—that Ash fella—even after he realised that baby girl wasn't his, he still cuddled that poor precious little thing. He still cried for it. He was the only bloody one who cried for that dead baby, except me and the other midwives once we left the room.'"

Lisa paused for a minute to absorb my reaction.

"Wait... what? It wasn't his?"

A terrible dread gripped me, and I thought of Ash's sadness as he'd looked up at those stars. Had that heart-shaped hole Salt talked about been baby-booty sized? It would explain why he'd grown so melancholy. Had Ash been mourning something that hadn't been his to lose in the first place?

I couldn't bear the thought, knowing what it meant. I'd believed her. I'd taken her side. He'd needed me, and I'd shovelled dirt right into the hole in his heart.

"Nope. Wasn't his." Lisa said again, shaking her head. "I was shocked by that too, because I'd never heard any different. Lots of us believed it was Ash's. So I asked her how she knew it wasn't Ash's kid. She climbed right back onto the massage table, lay down, and said, 'Well, honey, you don't see many mixed-race baby girls from a white mum *and* a white dad. As soon as that racist Aldershot saw the baby, he started calling Renee every swear word under the sun, no regard that she'd just lost her bub. Dirty whore, disgusting slut, pathetic little bitch who'd sleep with anyone..." Lisa lowered her voice. "Well, I'm not going to repeat any more of the racist crap she told me he said, but it was all that kind of colonial bullshit." Lisa scowled. "She told me Mayor Aldershot gave Renee that black eye. He slapped her right upside the head once all the other doctors and midwives left the room."

It was much easier for me to believe it of Aldershot than of Ash.

"The midwife, she's a Koori woman, you know, and she told me she was super pissed off by that. She told him to knock it off, or she'd call the cops and have him charged with racial vilification and assault. And what does Aldershot do?'"

She waited, and I shook my head.

"Threatens to sue the hospital for negligence if anyone breathes a word about the baby not being white or not being Ash's. She said Aldershot forced Ash to sign the birth certificate. Threatened that if Ash didn't, he'd lodge a restraining order against him, make his life a living hell with the coppers. He practically admitted he had the Anchorage cops in his pocket. So this midwife has had enough, right? She says to Aldershot, 'Trouble is, he's got witnesses, and you haven't." And you know what he told her?"

I shook my head, guessing it would be something particularly repugnant.

"'Who's going to believe a gin over a Shire mayor who used to be a defence lawyer?' Can you believe that?" Lisa *tsk*ed. "Poor Ash."

"Poor Renee too, I guess," I murmured, thinking of how she'd gone to pieces in the restaurant. "She kept ringing him all the time. That's why I thought... when we had that fight... I didn't know."

By that point, I felt so wrung out I wished Lisa would just disappear. The thought that I'd been as bad as the Fantastics and the Aldershots, believing the worst of him... I wanted to cry, but I swallowed instead.

Lisa sniffed. "Renee's been in love with Ash for years. That's why she told him it was his. But I'm guessing her dad put her up to everything else. Can't smear the family reputation, you know. She's not real stable, though. She's taken it really bad. I thought Ash would have told you. You two seemed so in love, so close. I thought you'd have told each other everything."

Me too. Unable to speak around the lump in my throat, I just shook my head.

"It kind of got me thinking, though"—Lisa's voice tightened— "about who the father really was. Darius and Renee used to be friends. I even found some texts on his phone from her ages back, signing off with kisses. He insisted it was nothing. But..." She pursed her lips. "If that arsehole cheated on me and knocked up Renee, I want to know about it."

"Look, Lisa." I set down the can, feeling nauseous. "I don't know anything about all this. I never knew Renee was even preg—"

"Shh," she cautioned. "Hardly anyone did. She's trying to pretend like it never happened."

"You two playin'?" Darius interrupted from the other side of the fire.

"Playing what?" Lisa yelled back.

"Truth or dare. We were gonna play spin the bottle, but Benny here won't let go of it." He pointed to the guy with the Jim Beam, who brandished his bottle with a cheer.

"Lemme finish it first, then you can spin it as much as you like." He put it to his lips and chugged it so hard that liquid streamed down the side of his mouth and soaked his shirt.

"Eww," Lisa muttered.

"I guess this is your chance to ask Darius the truth," I said, standing up. "Thanks for—well, I gotta go."

"Hey." She rose and hugged me. "I'm sorry about Ash," she whispered. "I really am. He was a good guy. They all were, him and Drew and Troy. I shouldn't have listened to what they said about him. Imagine going through all that for a baby that wasn't even yours."

"I know. It's fine. I just need to..." I gestured to the beach. "I need to go walk it off."

I stumbled off down to the beach, Lisa's words ringing in the echo chamber of my booze-addled mind.

Imagine going through all that for a baby that wasn't even yours.

I remembered what Ash had yelled at Renee at the protest. *Why are you ruining my fucking life?*

He was right. The Aldershots had, and I'd helped them. I'd taken their side over his. And it was far too late to apologise.

It was cold down by the water with my feet in the wash. Moonlight silvered the waves into scales, and further out, beyond the bommies, the sea was a green dream of phosphorescence. I hugged myself, crying, letting the cold water crash up to my knees while I searched the waves with bleary eyes for Bitten. It was late, far later than I usually visited the beach, and the dolphin was nowhere to be seen. *Maybe he's abandoned me too.*

The thought came that I could just step in and in and in, as if descending into a Roman bath, the gutters beneath my feet forming into sandy steps leading down, down, down. *And then what?* I wondered, cocking my head. Drift away like Bitten? Or drown like Ash?

Ash. Grief and regret twisted my stomach into knots. If only I'd listened, really listened. If only I'd trusted him, like he'd told me to so many times.

You're like that to me. Like air. Like water.

Tears sprang to my eyes. *If he... di*—left *thinking I hated him...*

"I loved you, Ash," I whispered. "I still love you. I always will."

Something cut through the mess of words and emotions in my head, something loud and clear and calm—a series of clicks that could only be one thing.

SOS.

Help.

The dragon scales parted. The buoys demarcating the nets bobbed fiercely on the water's surface, spreading ripples toward me on the beach.

Help.

My mind was half embalmed in booze, but the word still buzzed with a chattering frequency.

HELP!

It thrashed in my brain, and a sudden coldness that had nothing to do with the waves, crept up my spine as I realised where it had come from.

CHAPTER 35

This was real. This was not a dream. Bitten was out there, thrashing in the deadly shark nets Ash had hated so much. I rushed forward, gasping as the icy water hit my torso. It was too far to swim. How long could dolphins survive underwater anyway? Minutes, hours? I wasn't sure.

A boat—the thought formed itself out of the ocean, as if it was Bitten's idea.

Salt's boat. I turned and ran to the pier that pointed to the horizon like a white, bony finger.

The runabout Salt routinely used to ferry to and from the *Sea Change* bobbed against its ropes, held captive alongside the pier on a bollard. Salt must've been in town. Once in a blue moon, he was known to visit the Sailor's Maid for the evening. Booze didn't agree with him (let's face it, it probably didn't agree with me either), but after one of those nights—which usually turned into a dawn walk off a long pier, followed by a short boat ride to severely hung over—the *Sea Change* would disappear for a few days, Salt taking to the waves until the sun and sea stripped away the evidence of his excess. The dinghy looked as solitary as I felt, and it rocked drunkenly as I clambered in.

Chikkkk-chikkk-gnnnr. My first attempt to start the motor failed. I searched for a starter button to press, or a choke or something, hoping it wasn't one of those boats that required arm work to fire up. Finding a key, I turned it, and then tried again.

GNNNNRR! The thing blared to life and took off in a crazy circle, hammering back against the pier just as I realised I'd forgotten to untie the rope.

Crap. Crap. Crappity-crap.

The orange nylon rope frayed and then snapped, and I shoved the rudder to the left and gave it full throttle. Spray flicked up over the hull, droplets wetting my lips like a salty kiss.

The speed was like a cocktail shaker to the alcohol in my system, and if the thing had been able to go any faster, I would have made it do so. My emotions accelerated: grief, regret, and a pinpoint-accurate rage at Renee and her father, with his stupid killer nets.

Out beyond the wave, the tide tugged at the buoys that secured the shark nets, each float regular as vertebrae beneath the ocean's blue skin. Here and there, the surface puckered above the web of netting. Somewhere down there Bitten was thrashing and bucking in its grip.

I frantically dug around the bottom of the boat for something sharp enough to slice the net. It was filthy—a jumble of buckets, a terry-towelling hat, mosquito repellent, hand lines, and a grimy snorkel mask that might be useful. I kicked a faded tackle box out of the way, loosing a handful of sinkers, which rumbled around like a nautical game of Mousetrap.

An oar stashed along one side of the dinghy was too blunt. A gaff, bent at the tip, too curved. Then I saw the knife. It was one of those old cane cutters, curved as deeply as Bitten's fin, and sharp, even if rusty. Heaven knows what Salt used it for. Maybe in case he ran into something piratical out there. But it was perfect. It wasn't long enough to slice down from the surface—the shark nets floated more than a metre deep, so I'd have to get wet if I wanted to use it—but nor was it so long it would be hard to wield underwater.

I picked it up and slashed the air.

Help.

"I'm coming, Bitten." Setting the motor to idle, I scrabbled around the front of the boat for the anchor. The chain was mud-covered, and the rope showed signs of too much sun exposure, but I hurled it over the side anyway, away from the net. It better hold; Salt'd kill me if I lost his dinghy.

I peeled off my dress, washed the facemask in the salty water, and snapped it on, and then, holding the knife high above my head, I stepped off the side into darkness.

CHAPTER 36

I surfaced immediately in a gush of bubbles, the cutlass still clasped in my hand. The water was freezing, and as dark and thick as wine. The rusty gleam of the knife, and the whiteness of my underwear-clad body, provided the only contrast. Treading water for a moment, I put my face in the water and searched the gloom for Bitten.

I still wasn't a great swimmer, but the months of surfing with Ash had made me a lot better than I used to be. I swam down, noticing something jittering in the net below, but it was too dark to see it properly. The last thing I wanted was to accidentally hack at Bitten, and I definitely didn't want to get wound up in the net myself.

Help.

I rose to the surface again for another deep breath, and leading with the knife again, I dove. About a metre down, my ears filling with the heaviness of water, I felt the resistance of fibre against the blade. The webbing had the springiness of a safety net, immediately shoving me back. I grasped it and pulled myself closer. The rope was thicker than I thought, and twisted and gnarled in places. Here and there down the line, I could make out the shapes of creatures, some living, others corpses, bloated and half-consumed by submarine scavengers. Sensing Bitten's clicks to my left, I turned and swam towards the sound, but all I saw was a slow flapping of submerged wings. A ray.

Careful not to touch its barbed tail, and sawing through sections of rope as I passed, I hacked away until it freed itself, net trailing out behind it as it soared away.

Here.

I kept hacking down the net, kicking frantically when wisps of net drifted past me. Rope and floats bobbed to the surface as they were released. I'd have to haul it all into the boat later. Loose rope could be just as dangerous to sea creatures as the net itself, but first I had to save Bitten.

I shot back to the surface, sucking in air.

Help. Floats thrashed wildly a few metres away, and I dove again, following the voice in my head until the dolphin's pale, tangled body was visible, his flipper caught and mashed in the meshing.

Easy, Bitten.

Sensing my approach, the dolphin stopped thrashing. Like a bad seamstress unpicking poor work, I used the point of the knife to nick apart the strained net. It was easier to cut when it wasn't floating freely, but the darkness made it difficult. Nearby, a leatherback turtle writhed, its beak opening and closing incredulously.

Dammit, I have to breathe.

I shot to the surface again, gulping another mouthful of oxygen before diving to resume my task of unravelling Bitten's flipper.

The last strand sliced away, and Bitten clicked and shot to the surface, with me following in his wake. A fountain of stale water burst from the dolphin's blowhole as Bitten sucked in oxygen as readily as I did.

The dolphin's dark eye pinned me with a stare. *Help.*

I was pretty sure a marine turtle could stay under longer than a dolphin, but I knew Bitten was right. The leatherback would drown down there if I did nothing.

I ran a hand over the dolphin's slippery back, feeling that strange, electrifying kismet. This time, it gave the sensation of comfort, of thanks.

"Okay. I'm going back in." I pulled the facemask on again.

The leatherback was caught by its stout neck and one stubby limb. I put a tentative hand out to feel the flesh, hoping the reptile didn't have the freedom of movement to snap. Rope ringed its flipper so tightly I doubted I could cut it loose with a scalpel. The limb would be probably be lost unless I could somehow heft the turtle into the boat, but the creature weighed more than I did. I remembered Ash, smiling as he showed me the scar on his finger, and decided the best I could do was to cut its head free and try to remove any excess rope. I sliced each little tic-tac-toe box of netting until only a small square dangled from the leatherback's damaged flipper. It closed its beak with a snap and lumbered off through the dark water.

Strands of net wisped away half connected as I hurtled back to the surface. It was only once the night air hit that I noticed the sting of salt and the smell of blood.

I held my left arm out of the water and winced. Moonlight revealed a streak of black cascading down my forearm. *Crap.* Somehow, in cutting the turtle free, I'd sliced my wrist too. *Dammit, Juls!*

The cut was clean but deep, shearing diagonally across my wrist. It stung, but that was the least of my worries. Blood in the water was never a good thing, and especially not at night. Dead things caught in the net were a smorgasbord for passing sharks. If I wasn't careful, I'd end up like the surfer in my dream.

"Come on," I said as the dolphin rose nearby and sent a fountain of droplets and air through its blowhole. "Let's blow this joint."

CHAPTER 37

Help. The word drifted into my head again as I hauled my shivering body up over the side of the runabout.

"I did help," I said aloud. "You're free. Is it your fin?"

I examined my arm again. Blood snaked down my forearm, and I dug in my handbag for a tube of hand sanitiser. The blade was less than sanitary, and I couldn't remember the last time I'd had a tetanus shot. After squeezing out my sopping bra, I wrapped it around the cut before pulling my dress back on over wet knickers. "I'm kind of having my own limb issues right now." I admitted aloud. "And I'm not sure the local vet has much experience with dolphins."

Bitten appeared near the back of the boat.

"You'll have to follow me," I told him.

The dolphin rose in and out of the water, shaking its head.

Follow. Help.

My breath caught in my throat. *Don't go nuts out here, Juls.*

I closed my eyes for a second, trying to make sure I wasn't just giddy from blood loss. No. It felt real. I could understand Bitten, and he could understand me.

"What did you say?" I asked.

He lives.

"Ash?" His name was little more than a whisper, but as soon as I said it, the dolphin's mouth stretched into a beaky grin.

This isn't a dream.

"Where. Where is he?" I babbled, clutching the bra bandage to stem the bleeding.

Follow.

The waves were bigger than I expected out beyond the sheltered waters of the bay; each one smacked against the small boat like a fist, and I was soaked long before the shore faded from view. Shivering, I eased off the throttle a little. Bitten was fast, despite his injured flipper, and I kept one eye on the ring of water he vanished and appeared from, out alongside the hull. The moon was high now, the ocean endless and enveloping beneath the Milky Way. I'd been following Bitten for more than an hour when the motor caught a little, coughed, and seized.

I twisted the throttle, trying to wring it back to life, but it hacked and spat out the sour smell of four-stroke. The motor revved again, momentarily propelling the boat forward, and then died with a splutter.

Crap.

Out of fuel, I guessed. I'd been in this dinghy plenty of times with Salt and Ash, but I'd never driven the damn thing. Maybe I should have paid more attention.

Bitten popped his head out of the water and stared at the motor.

"Maybe there's a jerry can or something in here," I told him. "Let me look." I dug through my bag for my iPhone, but it was nearly out of charge and using the torch would only run it down. I switched it off and unlocked the dry-safe under the boat's seat instead, poking around for a torch.

Bingo!

Dolphin, read the brand on the side, which made me grin. It threw a cats-eye of pale amber light over the dinghy.

"Don't worry. I'll get it started again." I reassured Bitten, totally unsure how as I began to pick through the remaining storage lockers for anything of use, cataloguing as I went.

A tin of sardines destined to be used as bait. An out-of-date box of Barbecue Pizza Shapes in a cavity near the front anchor well. An opaque plastic water container—drinkable, no matter how warm and funky. An old towel bearing a snarling tiger and a myriad ferocious stains that smelt of fish guts. Tackle boxes. Waders. A cast net. A compass. A tobacco tin filled with a fuzz of dried leaves. I sniffed it. Tea? No! Weed. *Salt, you old dog!* I supposed it was a relic from Vietnam days.

There was no spare fuel. No flare either. I supposed Salt's flares would be on the *Sea Change*, not on the dinghy. "Geez, Salt, what a mess," I said aloud, setting the tin down on the seat. A mess stranded about ten kilometres off the coast of Willow Bay. I peered back the way I'd come. Stars stretched to the edge of the earth and fell away into the water. I couldn't even see the land, which ruled out trying to swim for it. I'd have to row.

I leaned forward to pull one oar from its position down the side of the boat. A ring and pin gripped it midway along its length, sliding into a small hole on the gunwale. Once fastened, I let it dangle in the water while I hunted for the other.

There was no second oar.

"Salt, you stoner! What on earth is the point of one fucking oar?"

The dolphin dipped its head out of the water and cocked it, wondering.

"You don't know what an oar is, do you?"

The dolphin just looked at me.

Follow.

"I can't swim like you can."

Follow, Bitten insisted.

"I can't," I said, pointing to the gunwale. "No oars."

The dolphin lapped the boat in increasing rings, coming up to blow and then leap, anxious to keep moving.

"I'd only go around in circles with one."

Go back. Bitten's voice in my brain had the tone of disappointment.

"I don't know that I can go anywhere with one oar and no petrol." As soon as the words left my lips, I realised the seriousness of them. I was stuck on the open ocean at night with nothing but a container of fusty water, a bag of Pizza Shapes, a tin of weed, and a friendly dolphin.

Shit. Shit. Shit!

Panic threatened to overwhelm me. *Think, Juls.*

I clutched my handbag. "I'll ring emergency services and..."

Great plan, Juls. I admonished myself. *You've stolen a boat, destroyed shark nets, slashed your own wrist, and you're in possession of illicit drugs.*

I considered chucking the tin overboard, but I'd already stranded Salt's boat so I figured he'd probably be even more pissed if I ditched his stash. I set it down on the seat instead, and snapped my fingers.

"My phone has GPS. I'll figure out where I am, phone Salt the coordinates, he'll come get me in the *Sea Change*, and we'll go get Ash. It's possibly the worst time ever to call him, but I know Salt. He'll do it."

Bitten clicked and nodded. My phone beeped ominously when I switched it on. Dismissing the notice informing me the battery was low, I swiped straight to my contacts screen and dialled.

Come on, Salt. Pick up!

It rang out. No message bank. *Dammit, Salt!* I dialled again. Same. *Double dammit.*

Plan B: Mum. I'd barely dialled her mobile before I heard the dulcet beep of my phone's dying battery, and the iPhone's glowing screen went blank.

Well, that's just awesome.

I pinched the bridge of my nose, unable to meet Bitten's questioning eyes and not wanting him to see the tears that pricked mine. After a minute or so, I flicked the torch off too. No point wasting it. I might need to signal an SOS later. I needed to think. I put my head in my hands, craving sleep. Ash would have known what to do. The only interruption was the breathy sound released from Bitten's blowhole as he surfaced occasionally.

"Where is he?" I asked. "Why didn't they find him?"

Island.

The vision of the island, of the crab scuttling around that familiar foot, flashed into my mind. "And he's definitely alive?"

The dolphin rose and then sank again, a motion I took to be a yes.

He lives.

"I know Ash. He'd know what to do. He'd have made a bonfire or swam for it or something."

The dolphin's tail fin slapped the water like an exclamation mark, as if to chide me.

Sharks.

I exhaled slowly. Bitten did the same. "And you came to tell me so I could help him. Didn't you? That's why you were always there, on the beach?"

The dolphin leaped, so suddenly and so spritely it scared me.

Help.

I dipped the single oar in the water again and pulled it through, but the nose of the boat shifted only a little.

"Well, we both need help now."

A hearty slap caught the side, throwing water up over me and making the boat rock. Losing my balance, I squealed and slid back on the aluminium seat.

"I suppose I better throw the anchor back in," I said, not sure why I bothered speaking aloud, except that it made the darkness feel safer. "We'll wait the night out until Salt notices his boat's missing.

He'll probably put two and two together once he sees my missed call."

But I knew it was a long shot. It would likely be the wee hours before he finished drowning his sorrows, and then he'd probably think his shitty rope had snapped. But he'd still go looking for his runabout, wouldn't he? I eyed the tin on the seat. After all, he had incentive. Of course, if he did, whether he'd believe I'd followed a dolphin to find his supposedly dead godson was another matter.

A surging wave slapped against the boat, tearing at the taut anchor line, and the dinghy sprang away from the wave as the anchor slipped. The water was too deep; the anchor wasn't touching the seabed.

I sighed. "I suppose we'll go wherever the sea wants us to," I told Bitten as I hauled the anchor back up.

I hoped that might be closer to Ash, rather than out to sea.

What the sea wants, the sea takes.

But I want you back. I need you back.

A wave of tiredness hit me like a blast, and I sat back on the seat and cried. When I was done, with the grotty towel folded up as my pillow, I slept.

I dreamed of fish—fish with razor-sharp, bloodstained teeth.

Nudge. Nudge. Nudge. The boat's thudding woke me, the dinghy's bottom striking sand and tipping the vessel up a little. I cracked one eyelid to the smear of dawn and immediately searched for the dolphin. Bitten was nowhere to be seen, even if I was sure he'd stayed close during the night.

My mouth felt gritty, my back ached, and my head was a hum of hangover. Waves frothy with a lace of sea foam lapped at my outstretched arm where it dangled in the water. Sitting up, I rubbed the sleep from my eyes and winced at the blood staining my makeshift bra bandage. After carefully unwinding it, I examined the cut. It would heal okay, even if it looked like I had a death wish. I washed the wound in saltwater, wincing at the pain, scrubbed the bra clean with saltwater and sand, and hung it over the prow of the boat. Then I stepped out of the dinghy and looked around.

"Bitten?" I called. No answer. If it hadn't been for the gash on my wrist, and the dinghy, I might have believed it had all been a dream.

The shoreline curved in and around to a headland. Lefthanders were peeling off the arrow-headed break to my right. To my left, the sea was waking up, a swell rippling like silk all the way to an unrecognizable southern point, or was it?

I put a hand to my brow and squinted, then turned to find an army of she-oak trees approaching the dunes. *Bluff Bridge National Park*, I decided. I'd been on a school excursion there for the day when I was younger. Only about forty-two clicks from home. I wondered how many kilometres I could walk in an hour.

Salt's boat bobbed against me again, and I hauled it up past the waterline, where the tide couldn't claim it. The canister of weed was still on the seat, and I snatched it up and slipped it into the pocket of my dress. Salt might be pissed about the dinghy, so maybe that would soften the blow a little.

The sun was barely up, but heat already made the sand sizzle where it clung to my wet feet. By the time I'd managed to drag the boat up the beach, walking home seemed impossible. I was considering whether or not the situation called for breaking Mum's golden rule never to hitchhike when the whine of a car engine made me jerk my head up.

A police car approached from around the headland.

Crap!

At least I wouldn't have to walk home.

CHAPTER 38

"And that's where the police found you?" the doctor asked.

I stared at the wall. The clock ticked, annoying me, each second making me feel more like a bomb waiting to explode.

"Yep," I conceded.

Mum had leapt out of the car and run down the beach even before Sarge Kendall turned the motor off.

"How did you find me?" I croaked.

"Find my iPhone app," Mum admitted, waving her phone as I started to complain. "I only installed it because I've been worried."

"Whatever. We have to find Ash," I insisted, tiredness and dehydration making it impossible for me to think straight.

"Bitten was taking me to him. He's alive. Ash is alive, Mum. Bitten told me. He's on an island somewhere. We have to go and find him." I flung my arm towards the ocean, watching two sets of startled eyes flick to the bloody gash up my forearm.

Sarge's brows crumpled with concern, and Mum put a hand over her mouth as she stared back at him. A look of mutual understanding I didn't like passed between them.

"I know you're... er... keen to look for Ash Gordon." Sarge patted my shoulder and his eyes were watery. "Honey, I understand. I do. But we're taking you straight to hospital. It's been an ... uh... er... shit of a night, to be honest." He cleared his throat. "One of your, ah, mates from the party has been hurt pretty bad. Real bad, actually. We're hoping he'll going to pull through, but you're not in... er..."

He stopped and gestured to my wrist. "Well, ah, it looks like you're not in great shape yourself. Jaz Piper was beside herself, not to mention your poor mum here." He coughed. "I'm... ah... worried about you too. We all are. That's why I'm taking you in for an EEO."

"An EEO. What's that? Some kind of brain scan? I told you, there's nothing wrong with my brain. I don't have epilepsy. Mum, tell him."

"Emergency Examination Order," he explained. "It's more of an... er... a little chat. Folks at the hospital will have a little... ah... well, a conversation with you Juliette. See whether or not you're... um... okay. Then we'll see what we need to do about the damage you've done to these nets. I doubt Con McGuire will want to press charges, but given what happened to Dylan, it might be that the council wants to take the matter of the... ah... nets further."

"Con! Salt's real name is Con?"

"Connor," Sarge admitted, glancing at me sidelong.

And then my addled brain seized on the other name that had been in Sarge's sentence: Dylan.

"What happened to Dylan?" I asked. I gripped Mum's arm, feeling suddenly dizzy. "Mum, what happened to Dyl?" As the words left my mouth, I already knew. I'd seen it. Blood in the water.

"Oh my God," I said. "Oh my God, not Dyl."

I let them lead me to the police car as quietly as a lamb.

Dylan! How had I not known it was Dylan? The long hair. The dark skin. The short, squat board he preferred. Dylan! Oh no. No, no, no.

Dylan's dark skin was nearly as wan as Jaz's, and he was out of it, an oxygen mask over his face as they rolled his bloodstained hospital trolley down the hallway past us, into another round of surgery.

I'd found out the rest from what Jaz yelled at me as I sat in A&E, waiting to be evaluated, my wrist bandaged all the way up to the elbow.

You could say I'd left the party at the right time, before things totally went to shit. I couldn't remember a game of Truth or Dare that hadn't ended badly, but this one had ended worse than most. That drunken idiot Benny had dared Dylan to go for a night surf. None of the other guys had their boards in the back of their car, so Dylan been alone out there when...

"What the hell happened to you?" Jaz gestured to my arm, but I knew she meant more than that. It was obvious she'd been up all night. She looked exhausted under the fluorescent lights of

Anchorage Base Hospital's waiting room, her face contorted with worry and, once she saw me, with rage.

"I cut myself," I mumbled, taking in my best friend's red-rimmed eyes and tangled hair. Guilt made me look away.

"I suppose that's only as stupid as some of the other things you've done lately," she said acidly, her voice hoarse from crying.

"You were gone," she said, throwing her hands in the air, "and Dylan was..." She rubbed her eyes. "He barely made it back to shore, Juls! There was so much blood, and I couldn't remember what to do. I couldn't remember my first aid. Everyone else was drunk. Dyl was screaming and screaming—" She broke off into fresh sobs, and I jumped up and threw my arms around her, but she pushed me away.

"Don't." She stumbled back against the vending machine. "You did this. You ruined those nets. Didn't you, Juls?" She gestured to my bandaged arm. "There was net washed up all over the beach. You cut them."

"It was Bitten," I mumbled. "I didn't mean to—"

"Those nets were there to protect people, to save surfers like Dyl. You think a dolphin is more important than your friends!"

She was right. This was my fault. I should have anticipated what would happen. But I couldn't let Bitten drown. I couldn't just let him die, like I'd let Ash...

I swallowed my guilt and followed it with a chaser of shame. "Jaz, we were all against the nets. You helped organise the protest."

She snorted. "Ash was against the nets. But after what happened to him, you'd think you of all people would want them. But you don't give a shit about anyone anymore. You don't surf. You don't hang out. All you think about is yourself. Losing your shit, talking to a dolphin, getting drunk and running off and slashing your wrists. Do you think that's what Ash would have wanted, to see you so pathetic, so off the rails? Destroying shit? Destroying yourself? Refusing to get help?"

I slumped in the plastic chair, reeling from her words. Her accusations hurt much worse than my wrist or my hangover. I knew she was in shock, but did everyone think that? Did everyone think a shark had eaten Ash? Did everyone think I was pathetic, off the rails, insane?

Jaz put one hand to her forehead and turned away. "I'm sorry," she said in a low whisper. "Ash was my friend too, you know, and Dyl's best friend, but just because he died—"

"Don't." I muttered. "Don't, Jaz. He's not dead. Don't say that."

"Don't you fucking dare tell me what I can say to you!" She whirled on me again, one finger in my face. Her eyes burned topaz under the fluoro light. "You cost Dylan his arm last night. You nearly cost him his life! And Ash *is* dead. He's been dead for more than six months. Everyone knows it. Everyone but you."

"And Bitten," I whispered.

"I swear, that fucking dolphin," Jaz started.

"It isn't Bitten's fault," I shouted. "Surfing cost Dylan his arm. Being out in the ocean at night cost him his arm."

"Oh, so you're going to blame this on *surfing* now? On Dylan? For fuck's sake. You used to love surfing. You're being ridiculous."

"You're right," I said, flatly. "It was reckless of me."

I'd been worried about Bitten and Ash, and not really thinking about anything else. How was I to know someone was going to dare Dylan to surf at night?

"I'm sorry. I'm sorry, Jaz. I'm sorry for leaving you alone. I'm sorry for everything." But even to me, my words sounded robbed of emotion. The night had been too big for me, and the day too strange. I looked down at my hands, twisting them in my lap.

"You're my best friend, Juls," Jaz said, her voice thick with sobs. "But some days I don't even know who the hell you are anymore."

I sighed. "I guess that makes two of us."

"The last thing Dyl needs right now is to have a Debbie Downer around. He's going to need a lot of physio, a lot of therapy. Maybe it's best if you stay away from us. From both of us."

By that point, I was already so dead inside that her words felt like little more than a pinprick.

"Jaz, I'm sorry. Don't hate me."

My best friend's face was so blank and cold I stopping talking.

"Get help, Juls," she said, storming off down the hall. "Get help or get lost."

I glanced around the room, snapping back to the present and trying to push Jaz's words way down deep, beyond the dreams and the fears. Ambivalent, pale-green walls. Jade vinyl chairs. Jarrah-wood desk with a glass paperweight. Bookshelf. Anatomical model of the human brain. Hacky Sack on the desk. The room was functional but muted, kind of like my brain on whatever it was they'd force-fed me in the emergency room after Jaz left, when my first meltdown started.

"Sergeant Kendall wrote on the paperwork for admissions that you appeared to be suffering from delusions and hearing voices. Would you say that was correct?"

I stared back at Dr Riva Vikram's broad, cafe au lait Pakistani face, gold nose ring, and brown curls, which tumbled over the collar of a benign hospital uniform the same pale green as the walls, as if she might camouflage herself in here sometimes to enjoy a coffee in-between the mayhem. She took a sip of water from a bottle and set it back on a coaster printed with the enigmatic face of the Mona Lisa. "The immediate concern is that you tried to hurt yourself.

"I'm not a suicide risk." I snapped. Maybe I should be, given all that's happened, given what happened to Ash, and now to Dylan, but I'm not."

I waved my wrist in her face. "This wasn't deliberate."

"I understand this has been a distressing day for you, Juliette, but I'd like to understand why you feel so anxious. Would you care to tell me?"

Would I! And be labelled a lunatic? No thanks.

"Not really."

"Okay, that's fine." She was clearly trying to be as reassuring as possible, but it was having the opposite effect on me.

"Right." Scooting forward in her seat, she glanced down at the papers on her desk. "You've been brought to the hospital because others are concerned for your safety." She glanced at my wrist. "Would you like to tell me what happened?"

Would I!

"I cut it," I said, bluntly.

She leaned back in her chair again, her expression unruffled by my hostility. "Right. You cut it, you say. How?"

"With a pirate's knife."

"Hmmm." Her nostrils flared ever so slightly at the unlikelihood. "Would you care to share the reason you did that?"

I crossed my arms over my chest. "It's called an accident."

"Okay. Has there been any other time when you thought of cutting yourself, or perhaps hurting yourself some other way, maybe during a past relationship break-up or during a time of grief?"

I uncrossed my arms and tapped my fingernails on the desk, staring at the clean white bandage that wrapped my right arm. "Nope."

"Did you hurt yourself in any other way over the past twenty-four hours, deliberately or accidentally? Like, maybe you hit your head or something?"

"I got sunburned." I patted one shoulder. "Also an accident."

"But no head injuries?"

"Absolutely nothing wrong with my head at all," I said, shaking it over-enthusiastically.

She read from the admissions paperwork again. "You told Sergeant Kendall you could hear a dolphin talking to you. That must have been frightening for you, hearing voices."

I shrugged. "Only if you consider dolphins frightening."

"Was that the first time you heard voices?"

I glowered at her.

"You've never heard any other voices. Not God's or anyone else's?"

"God's!" I laughed. "What is this, Sunday school?"

"So that's a no?"

I nodded. "Only Bitten's." It was a half lie. I didn't tell her about feeling like an alien from Planet Fucked Up. I didn't tell her about my brain's constant guilty, overworked monologue, or the *mati*. I certainly didn't tell her about the flashbacks or flash-forwards or whatever they were. But I didn't need her approval anyway. The crab, the circle of surfboards—they'd all been trying to tell me something, but I hadn't listened, not until Bitten. Since there was no way of explaining the feeling of just *knowing* to someone who didn't have premonitions, I figured telling her any of that would be a huge mistake.

Riva said nothing for a minute or two, just scribbled on her notepad.

"The police noted there was trouble at the party even before the incident involving Dylan Hoffstede. A noise complaint and reports of underage drinking. Was that why you left?"

"No. It was boring, so I bailed."

"You had marijuana on your person. Would you say you're a regular user?"

I didn't respond.

"What about any other some sort of substance?" She had a half-hopeful look on her face, as though she was desperate to discover I'd been kite-high on pingas. As though I wasn't already a shrink's wet dream.

"Drinking," I said.

"How did that make you feel?"

"Drunk." I was being smug, and I knew it.

"Anything else?"

"Just the weed." I lied.

One of her eyebrows tweaked almost imperceptibly. "Okay, and how did that make you feel?"

"Stoned." Another lie. Actually, I wished I had chucked the tin in the ocean. They'd made me strip out of my dress and put on a hospital gown while they cleaned up my wrist, and the canister of dope had fallen out right in front of Sarge. I'd felt too guilty about nicking Salt's boat to let him get busted for it. Plus, I figured I was a minor, and I was already in enough trouble. In for a penny, in for a pound. In some sun-scrambled part of my brain, I'd even considered that it might make my situation better: diminished responsibility and all that. I was regretting it now, though.

She looked at her notes. "Can we talk about the vandalism, then? What made you want to destroy the nets?"

Something about her gentle tone made me want to explode. I was tired and thirsty, and whatever the nurse had given me had made me feel nauseous and woolly-headed. Most of all, I just wanted to get out of here and go and save Ash. I wanted to save him and hold him and tell him I was sorry. I wanted so badly to tell him I'd never doubt him again, not even after all the stars winked out. And that I loved him, and that I knew he'd never hit me or anyone. But I couldn't, because Dr Vikram was sitting here quizzing me and looking at me like I was mental, and Mum and Sarge and Jaz were sitting beyond the door in Outpatients, and all of them were wasting my time, and Ash's.

"The nets were vandalism—environmental vandalism," I insisted. "They were drowning Bitten."

"Did you have anything to do with any other vandalism, like the graffiti on the council chamber?"

"Of course not," I snarled. "I didn't even know about that until Lisa told me, or about the midwife, or about Renee and the baby, or Aldershot and the corrupt cops. And anyway, Aldershot deserved that. He *is* a dickhead. A racist dickhead. And a liar! And you think *I'm* the crazy one. You think *I'm* the one who should be locked up."

I was babbling, partly delirious I think, and even as I let it all out, I knew it was a massive mistake.

The satisfied expression on Riva's face as I spewed the truth over her made me want to scream even louder.

"Aldershot was out to get Ash," I bellowed, ignoring the screech of my chair against the linoleum as I rose. It toppled over, and I hammered one fist on the desk.

"Renee lied." *Thump.* "He didn't cheat on me. Allen Aldershot lied." *Thump.* "They lied about Ash hitting Renee." *Thump.* They lied about it being his baby." *Thump.*

I stopped, and my fingers curled into themselves. Holding her gaze levelly, even if I could no longer keep the quaver from my voice, I said, "Ash would never hit anyone. He'd never hurt anyone. He never meant to hurt me."

Dr Vikram scribbled on the notepad again, and my anger died away to hopelessness, my voice to a whisper. "And he's not dead. Not to me. You don't even care that you're letting him die."

"Juliette." Riva stood and righted my chair, gently guiding me back into it. "I do care, and so do your loved ones."

I shook my head. "Jaz doesn't. You didn't hear what she said." I gestured to the door. "She'll never forgive me. Never."

"She was angry, Juliette, and very worried. People say things they don't mean when they're angry and upset."

I shook my head. "I know Jaz. I know her better than anyone. She meant every word. And she was right. I ruined the nets, I should have known that would happen."

"Juliette, no one is blaming you for what happened to Dylan Hoffstede."

I snorted. "Jaz is. Dylan is." I swallowed the lump in my throat, remembering the moment I'd encountered Jaz in the hospital hallway, how pale she'd been, her eyes like hazel saucers, even wider than mine after a nightmare.

My vision started to swim with blood and my ears with screams. Screams I could now identify as Dylan's and Jaz's.

"No one has any control over events like that, Juliette."

But I did. I'd known it would happen, and I'd destroyed the nets anyway. I took a deep breath, and squeezed my eyes shut, seeing again the gunmetal grey body, the pale eyes and bloody teeth.

Great wracking sobs came out of nowhere. They made my head hurt and streamed snot from my nose. "All of this is my fault."

Dr Vikram clucked as she handed me a tissue. "Given everything that has happened, I think it would be best for you to stay in a facility where we can help you. A place where you can calm down a little and rest. Would you like that?"

"Calm down. A facility like…?" My mouth tasted like iodine. I wiped my eyes on the white bandage, realising what she was saying. "You think I'm insane!" I said. "You think I'm delusional, don't you?"

"I'm not saying that." She put up one palm, her bovine eyes on mine. "Deep breaths please… breathe deeply, Juliette."

I scowled at her, wanting to pick up the Hacky Sack and hurl it through the window.

"The police feel, and I certainly feel, that you're not in the best frame of mind to give a statement about some of the criminal matters they want to talk to you about. I'd like to recommend the police delay taking any statement or pressing charges for the time being. But in order for me to make that recommendation, you have to agree to cooperate with medical professionals."

"You're saying I won't be arrested if I talk to a doctor some more?" I snapped my arms across my chest.

"Well, yes, to a degree," Dr Vikram replied. "Unfortunately, we don't have psychiatric facilities here at Anchorage Base Hospital, but in Sydney there is a public psychiatric clinic—"

Psychiatric! "Wait! You think I need to see a shrink?"

Riva smiled sadly, as if to say *Oh, sweetheart, you already are.*

CHAPTER 39

"This is the kind of thing—exactly the kind of thing—we've all been worried about, Juliette," Mum started scolding me even before I slid the seatbelt into the buckle with a dull click.

By the time I made it through Accident and Emergency, and Dr Vikram had finished the EEO, it was afternoon, too late to start the three-hour drive to Sydney for admission to the public psychiatric care unit. Instead, it was decided they would release me with medication into Mum's care overnight, with the paperwork for my admittance the next day. It was either that or stay in hospital overnight under a supervision order, and because Anchorage Base Hospital dated from colonial days, with linoleum floors and cramped wards and no room or need for a specialist psychiatric ward, that would have meant ending up in a bed in post-op, with a nurse assigned to keep me in her sight at all times to ensure I didn't neck myself.

Dylan had made it through his second surgery, which meant he would be on the same ward, and the last thing I needed was another dressing down from Jaz, let alone imagining what Dyl would have to say when he woke up and realised they'd taken his arm off just below the shoulder. I'd take my chances with Mum, thanks, even if she was spitting mad.

Her hands were white, her bony knuckles clutching the steering wheel in a death grip as she muttered a string of Greek curses under her breath.

"You won't talk to me. You won't talk to Jaz." She raised one hand and swept it wildly in the air. " And now this." For a second, she turned to face me, and I saw the worry in her brown eyes, the bags under them, before she returned her gaze to the road. "Stealing things. Wrecking things? Marijuana! What were you thinking?" she continued. "What *are* you thinking?"

I shrugged.

Mum glanced at me again, and I wished she'd just focus on the road. I'd seen enough car accidents to not want to actually be in one, especially when my entire life was already a mangled wreck.

"You used to talk to me. Before, *paidi mou*, you used to come down to the salon sometimes... but now..."

A tear trickled down her cheek, and she immediately shot a hand up to swipe it away. I sensed the swell of her inherited talent for Greek theatre.

"I'm fine, Mum," I began. "I don't need all this." I waved my hand in the air. The movement felt erratic, drawn out and sketchy, like the way the cursor clones itself and stutters when a computer mouse needs new batteries, and I wondered whether it was the drugs Dr Vikram had prescribed for my "psychotic episode," as she'd called it, or whether I just felt amped, charged, alive now that I was out of the hospital—as if I could actually make a difference again. I was already thinking of how I could escape Mum tonight and go and save Ash.

"I don't need psychiatric help," I insisted, lowering my hand again. "I was just drunk."

"You had pot, Juliette. Marijuana! It's illegal, you know. So's underage drinking and stealing and vandalism." She sighed and briefly let go of the steering wheel to make a desperate, overblown shrug. "I knew this would happen. What did I expect? Pappous warned me when I moved to Willow Bay. As soon as I told him about Ash, he told me to watch out for you."

I stopped her with a snort. "So this is all Ash's fault?"

"Before you met him, you were a good gir—"

"And I'm not a 'good girl' now?" I shrieked. "Now I'm Satan incarnate? Because my boyfriend had an accident, I'm such a great shame to you?"

I had long ago learned it took more than one character to make a good melodrama. But the truth was that I felt terrible about everything that had happened in the past twenty-four hours: stealing Salt's boat, getting busted with his weed, Dylan and the shark.

But most of all, I felt terrible I'd stuffed up Ash's rescue mission. There was no way Mum was going to believe me now. Dr Vikram had told her she wanted to monitor me for schizophrenia. Schizophrenia!

Which meant there was no way anyone would let me waltz out of mental hospital and go look for Ash. The worried way she looked at me made it clear Mum was as convinced I was nutso as the rest of them, and something about that hurt deep inside. I moved my hand to the car door, close to the handle, fighting the urge to fling it open, to roll out commando style and run, like they did in the movies. But my escapade was up, and deep down, I knew it.

"*Paidi mou*, I know you're a good girl. I know you're my same old Juliette in there somewhere." Mum snaked one a thin brown hand across to squeeze my knee. "You just need help, especially if you won't talk to me or to Jaz." Her hand moved from my knee up to smooth the lines on her forehead. "I'm just trying to get you that help."

She checked her blind spot before indicating and moving into the right-hand lane. "I miss you, Juls. I miss how it used to be, with you and Jaz over all the time, eating baklava in the kitchen and talking about books you'd read and funny movies and her horses. Then you met Ash, and it felt like you were growing up too fast all of sudden, and I wondered where my baby girl went so quickly. And when you lost him, I lost you. And Jaz too, it seems." She wiped at the corner of her eye with her acrylic nail. "So my two little cuckoos have flown the nest." She sighed. "Even when you're home now, you're not there. You're alone. I'm alone."

For the first time in years, I noticed Mum was lonely, maybe even as lonely as I was. I'd always thought she preferred to be at the salon, that she enjoyed working so hard, but in that moment I saw the salon for what it was, and possibly for what it had always been. The salon was her "beach," the only refuge she had to get her mind off Dad, the place she went to try to forget she was in love with a man she couldn't be with. It made me feel terrible that I'd neglected her. And it made me feel even worse to think I was my father's daughter.

I'd been a shit daughter. A shit friend. And a particularly shit girlfriend who couldn't even manage to pull off a crucial rescue mission.

Maybe she'd believe me about Ash if I just tried again. After all, she knew about at least one of the dreams, even if she and I never talked about the *mati* or about the night I'd driven Dad away.

I studied my mother's face: the sharp lines of her aquiline nose in profile, her expertly plucked eyebrows, her full, crimson lips. Fine lines were only now starting to spread around her eyes. She was getting old. The thought made me sadder. Old and lonely.

Her bulbous gold bracelet slid down her wrist as she leaned over and flipped open the glove box.

"This came from the school on Friday." She waved a slip of paper in the air. "You've been skipping class. I thought you wanted to go to university, Juls? Where do you go all day? What do you do? Is it pot? Ice? Is that what's making you like this? Are you a drug addict?"

I sniffed. "No, Mum. A drug addict? Ice? Honestly, the weed was Salt's."

She bit her lip a moment, and then tipped her head to the side, as she considered it might be true.

"*Paidi mou,* I need to know what is going on with you. Lisa said—"

"Hairdressers," I stopped her, snatching the paper from her hand and shoving it in the glove box before closing it with a snap. "You don't need to talk to me. You can talk to anyone in town and find out *exactly* what's going on. Ask Lisa. That's how things work in this town, for Chrissake."

"*Ai ai ai,* Juliette Evangelina Papavasilou Brewer." My full name slithered out like a curse, which let me know I was now officially a Bad Girl. "Do *not* take the saviour's name in vain in *my* car." She threw me the look she reserved for occasions that warranted eternal damnation.

I took a deep breath. *To hell with it, I thought. If she won't believe me now, she never will.*

"Mum, do you remember when Dad left?"

Her dark hair whipped around her face as she turned to stare at me, her gaze snapping back to the car in front just as quickly.

"Sweetheart, is that what this is all about?" she asked, sounding as miserable as I felt. "Growing up without him? I know you've always blamed me, but you don't—"

"Blamed you? No. I don't blame you, Mum. If anything, I blame myself." I sucked in a big breath. "I'm not going crazy, Mum. I'm not. It's just the *mati.* I dreamed about the shark getting Dylan, just like I dreamed about Dad that time, and I've dreamed about Ash. He's alive. That's why I took Salt's boat. You've got to believe me, Mum." *Even if no one else will.*

Her breath hissed over her teeth, and she wet her lips with her tongue. "I wish Yiayia had never started you on those silly Greek superstitions." She accelerated past the blue Honda Civic that had been speeding up and slowing down erratically in front.

"Juliette," she started to say, and then sighed loudly. "You know I wasn't always such a good girl either." She sighed again and then clamped her lips shut and switched on the radio.

"You like this song?" she asked after a while.

It was an over-bright, manufactured pop song by the DJ Mum had told me about weeks ago; one that had climbed the charts and stayed there for weeks until everyone was so sick of it and every dub step beat was like a bullet to the brain. *Doof. Doof. Blam!*

"S'okay." I shrugged.

She tapped along on the steering wheel. "We play it in the salon. Lisa loves it."

I watched the blank beach rush by out the window. A stiff breeze was curling the dark waves into a tight perm, barrel upon crashing barrel gleaming white for a moment in the darkness. Mum tried to sing along, but she kept saying Ibiza wrong, and her natural soprano was a bit too high.

"That's where I go," I said, staring out the window.

"Ibiza?" Mum stopped singing to ask.

It took all of my strength not to answer sarcastically, *Yeah, Eye-bee-za.*

"No, the beach."

"All day?"

"Sometimes." I nodded. "Is that what the Find my iPhone app told you?"

Mum sucked air through her teeth but continued tapping the steering wheel. "You wear sunscreen?"

I rolled my eyes.

After several minutes of silence, she turned right at the three ways, heading towards Figtree. I wasn't expecting that.

"Where are we going?"

"*Paidi mou*, I know how hard Ash's death has been for you." She completely ignored my question. "It's been a terrible thing, a tragedy. But do you think your great-grandmother didn't have to pick herself up and carry on when grandfather Vasili was killed during the war? Or Yiayia and Pappous didn't want to quit after Christos died? You think I didn't want to jump ship back to Tinos when your father left?"

I sniffed. "You mean when I scared him away."

She swung to me again, mouth open like an amusement park clown. "No," she said, quietly. "You didn't. He loved you, Juliette." Her voice sounded strangled as she added, "He just didn't love me. He never did. Not really."

I'd never asked why it hadn't worked out that second time around. I'd been too small, and I supposed I'd assumed it was still the debt. Or still me—the freaky kid with the stupid dreams.

"When I fell pregnant, your father did the honourable thing and stayed. And then you were born. And he loved you, Juliette. It was me." She put a hand up to touch her collarbone. "I lost him. He wasn't perfect, far from it, but how I loved him."

There were unrestrained tears in her voice as she added, "*Paidi mou*, I couldn't bear it if I lost you too. That's why I have to do this, to help you."

My mind was still somersaulting over Mum's revelation that Dad had been the Ash to Mum's Renee—the guy who'd stayed with a woman he didn't love, because he'd knocked her up.

"He had a funny way of showing he loved me," I said drily, thinking of all the Christmases that had come and gone without him. "Not bothering to call your kid on her tenth birthday, let alone her sixteenth, doesn't exactly scream doting daddy."

"Juliette." Mum's voice was even more strained. "He did love you. He didn't call because..." She cleared her throat. "He died, *paidi mou*. Not long after he left."

"He what?" I snapped my head up and eyeballed her, but she was staring at the car in front. "Why didn't you tell me?"

The blue veins in her throat moved as she swallowed hard. "How do you tell a nine-year-old that? You're more like him than you know, Juls." Mum rubbed at the crease on her forehead. "That's why I need to make sure you get help. I couldn't bear it if you..." Her breath hitched, and a chill came over me and I felt my neck constrict as if a noose had tightened around it.

"He killed himself, didn't he, Mum? You didn't tell me because he ... hung himself."

Mum bit her lip, tears gleaming in her eyes. "I meant to tell you. I just didn't know how, and I thought it would only hurt more, so I told myself I'd wait until you were older, old enough to understand. Then you turned sixteen, and then Ash died, and..."

The Hanged Man. It hurt like a knife to the ribs, and I was surprised, surprised that with everything that had happened, with Dylan and Ash and Jaz, and all the medication Dr Vikram had given me, I could feel anything at all. I hadn't seen my father in over a decade, but it hurt knowing he had loved me, and that he had killed himself anyway.

I glanced at Mum. She was gripping the steering wheel tight again, her face taut with the effort of not crying.

Imagine how she feels. She has a hanged asshole ex and a crazy, suicidal daughter.

My seatbelt felt too tight all of sudden. I yanked it away from my chest, but it snapped right back. "Mum, I'm really sorry. I wish you'd told me."

She choked back a sob. "Oh, Juls." She squeezed my hand again. "*Ksero.* I know. So do I."

We drove in silence until Mum finally said, "So you see why I worried about you and Ash? Getting pregnant, making bad choices. I wasn't always such a good girl myself."

"You just made a mistake, Mum."

She shook her head. "You were never that. You were never a mistake. Not to me. You were a miracle. Your dad wasn't a religious man. I guess he couldn't see what a miracle you were. But I did, *paidi mou.* I always have."

She flicked the blinker on, and its steady clicking bothered me like an itch.

"Where are we going, Mum?"

"I was packing your things for the hospital when I found this card in your sock drawer." She plucked a business card from the centre console. "Dr Jorssen. You kept this card, Juliette. Even you must realise you need help. It's a private centre, but at least it's nearby in Figtree, not in Sydney. And I don't care what it costs. You need help."

"It was Salt's," I said. "He used to see her."

"It has her cell on it," Mum said. "I explained what happened at the hospital, and she agreed to an immediate admission. It's for the best, Juls."

"It's not," I insisted. "Mum, what I said about Ash is true. You can't do this. I won't let you!" I snapped off my seat belt.

The muscles in Mum's throat tightened again, and I heard the *clack* of the child safety switch, locking the doors. She slowed the car and turned right onto a tree-lined avenue with a street sign cautioning her to go slow, twenty kilometers an hour.

Avoid running over lunatics, it'll only make them madder.

Mum pulled into a circular drive edged with low hedges. A cheery, multi-coloured sign read "Melody House Holistic Healing Centre," and a single light burned in the courtyard out front.

After switching off the ignition, she reached over and took both of my hands in hers. "Juls, the therapist will listen. That's what they're for. It's what they're good at. She's going to help you, *entaksi*? Okay? We're going to help you. I won't lose you too, *paidi mou*. I can't."

I nodded, throat dry as Mum snapped the electric button on the key-ring and the child-proofing switched off. She swung her door open.

"I'll come with you."

"Thanks."

I'd been going to leg it if she didn't.

"Tell her everything." Mum helped me out of the car and led me toward the entrance. "Let her in."

I sighed, remembering the endless, probing questions of Dr Vikram.

"I'll try."

CHAPTER 40

"You mean I can't even pee in private? This is ridiculous."

Sister Abernathy peered at me owlishly around frames so gargantuan they took up a third of her crumpled face. It was past midnight my first day, and I was already sick of Melody House.

"Not for the moment," she said in an ex-pat British accent as I shoved shut the opaque door that divided my single bed from the ensuite.

"We need to be able to see into the lavatory for precautionary reasons, dear."

"What am I going to do? Strangle myself with this?" I tugged a single square of toilet paper out of the dispenser and threw it in the toilet. The room and ensuite resembled something out of a minimalist gallery or a sterile IKEA without the Norwegian wood or chrome cabinet handles, towel racks and coat hooks. It was all blank, flat spaces that you couldn't hang a picture frame from, let alone yourself. There were definitely no sharp edges. I wondered whether Dad might have lived if he'd found a place like this. The image of the swinging body loomed large for a moment in my head. There was no danger of that here; everything was flatter than I was. It was like living in one dimension.

"I can't even be trusted with a roll of dunny paper?" I complained.

The sister's sigh was only half-suppressed. "It won't be forever, dear. Just until the doctor determines you're well enough to go home. It doesn't take long for most of our guests to get used to the open plan or the cameras or the pop-ins from the staff."

Guests. Open plan. Nice euphemisms, Mrs Doubtfire.

I flushed the toilet, slammed down the lid, and turned the faucet on full bore to wash my face. "I don't need to get well. I already feel very well, thank you." I pushed the glass door open again and brushed past her. To her credit, she didn't look shocked that I was wearing nothing but my knickers.

"Well, that's good, dearie." It was not an attempt at sarcasm. "Now, if you don't have any more questions about your room, I'll be on my way." She patted the enormous matronly French twist pinned around her head. "Catering drops a menu around in the morning for the day's meals. It'll be on your tray." She gestured to a wheeled table close to the bed. "We have gluten-free, lactose-free, halal, vegan... whatever you like.

"Activities in the common room are decided on Mondays, and you'll find a timetable for those pegged to the noticeboard in the corridor." She padded to the door. "Try to relax and enjoy your stay, dear."

Said like it was a five-star luxury hotel.

I wondered what she'd do if I called her back to complain there was no turn-down service or chocolate on my pillow.

As soon as her footsteps faded, I plopped on the bed facedown, head resting on my arms.

"And, dearie." Her head appeared around the doorframe again. "Just one more thing." She pushed her spectacles back into place on her squat nose and pointed to the ceiling. "Any attempt to tamper with the cameras results in an immediate upgrade to the high-security wing."

Upgrade. Hardly.

I turned my head to the side and glowered at the flat, blue-black eyes that stared down from each corner of the box they called a room. "Got it." I yawned.

They'd fed me another dose of something earlier. The nurse insisted it was only a temporary calmative to help me relax and get some sleep, but whatever it was, it did little to dull the feeling of being contained. Trapped. And knowing I couldn't do a damn thing about Ash from in here filled me with futility.

Sister Abernathy smiled, revealing uneven yellow teeth courtesy of some British dentist, or lack thereof.

"You've an appointment booked for tomorrow"—she glanced at her watch, one of those naff ones designed to look like a bangle— "oops, it's after twelve. I mean *this* afternoon, with Dr Jorssen. I'll send Colin, our wardie, to escort you, unless you'd prefer me to do it."

"Colin will be fine," I mumbled, the words smothered by the pillow as I pressed my face into it again. It smelled of laundry detergent and sick people. "Sister Abernathy?"

"Yes."

"May I have visitors?"

"Of course, dear, on Wednesdays and Fridays."

What a shithole. How on earth was I going to make it to Wednesday, let alone get out of here? I sat up, the over-starched sheets scratching my crossed thighs. Mum had brought an overnight bag for me, but the pyjamas she'd packed were too large now. I hadn't realised how much weight I'd lost until today. I folded them over at the waist and threw a plain white tee on over the top.

I felt shrivelled, desiccated. The night spent in the boat, followed by the dry air spat out by air-conditioning all day, had sucked the life out of me.

I glanced around the room again. The windows were sealed and unable to be opened. What would they do if the air-conditioning stopped working? I wondered. Maybe they had backup fans or a generator in case of electrical outages. No point trying to get out that way, I decided. And it wasn't as if I could nick an access card either. My stage-managed exit from Anchorage Base Hospital was one thing, but it was clear there wasn't going to be any of that here, even if I pinched Nurse Abernathy's specs.

Staff keyed in a code, I'd noticed, carefully concealing it from the inmates at every locked door—and there'd been a lot of them. And the way some of the folk had been zombieing their way around the hallways when Sister Abernathy brought me in, I guessed they updated the codes daily.

Melody House was far from melodic. "Shambolic" suited it much better. Only the hardiest of patients were awake at this hour, but most of the "guests" we'd passed earlier had been either screwy enough or medicated enough to not know their elbows from their arseholes. I doubted any of them had ever attempted to escape.

Even if I somehow managed to escape to ground level undetected by the cameras in the lift, the twenty-four-hour ground-floor security would grant me an immediate upgrade to "high security."

Fire?

They'd have to evacuate us then.

I shook my head. The room had no drapes and there was nothing to light them with anyway. If there had been, I simply wasn't that fruity anyhow. People could die. I'd be charged with arson at best and manslaughter or murder at worst. Those kinds of measures were too desperate and dangerous for me.

I'd have to accept I was going to have to talk to another shrink. *Dammit!*

CHAPTER 41

Dr Birgit Jorssen, PsyD, PhD, MD, was the anti-Riva. Fair to Dr Vikram's café au lait, she hit a button on the automatic transcription program on a laptop on the desk, leaned back in her chair, and pinned me with a Nordic stare that made me want to squirm like a bug on a board. The letters after her name made it clear she was no hospital-based evaluator designed to placate me and pass me on for diagnosis, but a proper headshrinker—a psychiatrist who could put me on all sorts of mind-altering drugs if she really wanted to.

And who was to say she wouldn't want to?

Once she found out I'd been having premonitions most of my life, hearing voices, seeing things, I figured she'd definitely want to.

The first thing she said to me was, "Shall we begin?"

She meant business, but I wasn't ready to drop my pissy little rebel act yet, even if she was already seeing right through it.

I shrugged. "You're the skull-cruncher."

She gave me a sardonic smile that had all the warmth of a glacier and sat up straight as a spear. "I am."

Sharp features and silver frames made her look older than she was. I pegged her for about forty-three.

"Where would you like to start, Juliette?"

Staring at the pendant around her neck, a pearl enclosed by some diamond wave type thing, I replied. "Actually, I'd prefer to finish."

She didn't even blink. "The best way to finish things is to first start them," she said matter-of-factly. "Juliette, you have every right not to speak to me if you don't wish to, but you should know these sessions cost $180 an hour, and they'll be of little help to you if you refuse to address your issues head-on."

The clock ticked. I had another forty-five minutes of this shit left. I did the calculations in my brain—$3 a minute. I stared around the office. Surprisingly, despite Dr Jorssen's robotic demeanour, it was an office designed for good feng shui. A green potted plant sat in the corner, a water fountain on a side table, and there were liberal strokes of red.

"Why don't we talk about you, *Brigit*?" I said after a long silence. "I mean, I feel like I barely know you."

She didn't even flinch when I mispronounced her name. "You want to talk about me?"

"Sure, Brigit." I said it again, just to rile her. Birgit seemed a funny name to me anyway. What was it with shrinks and funny names? "How am I meant to know whether I want to talk to you?" I added. "Or whether I even like you?"

"Okay," she agreed, which surprised me. "We're not all gregarious, are we? Some of us are introverts. Tell me, who do you regularly talk to about your emotions? Is there anyone you feel comfortable talking to about your boyfriend's deat—"

I cut her off, palm up. "Not this."

She scrawled something on the notepad that sat next to my file. It was a large promotional pad for some kind of drug. "Zopiclone" was printed in a squarish font across the top.

Dr Jorssen leaned back in her red leather chair, which croaked when she moved. She moved again, making a second creaking fart to ensure I knew the noise hadn't come from her. "Fine. What would you like to know about me?" she said calmly.

"Have you ever lost someone close to you?"

The barest of lines appeared in her smooth forehead.

"You haven't." I pre-empted her answer.

Dr Jorssen cleared her throat. "My ex-husband," she said. "Cancer. And a nephew. Be that as it may, this isn't about me. It's about how you feel. It's about finding ways to help you deal with your grief."

I crossed my arms, staring at her. "How would you know how I deal with it?"

"I don't. And I won't if you won't trust me. " She shrugged, and then placed one hand back on the mahogany desk and picked up the fountain pen again. "I won't pretend to know how you feel. But I will tell you that discussing emotions can help people work through them, particularly anger."

"Who says I'm angry?"

"Your behaviour is hostile." She said it without any kind of judgment, as if it was a perfectly natural thing to call someone hostile. She tapped the stainless steel fountain pen on the binder file open before her. "According to the police EEO and Dr Vikram's assessment, you stole a boat, cut your wrist, and deliberately destroyed council property. Dr Vikram described your mood as 'volatile, potentially psychotic.' Your mother is worried about you, worried enough to call me on my personal cell to facilitate a late admission. Now, I'm sure that some of this behaviour isn't like you—"

"How would you know? You don't know me." I bit the inside of my cheek. "Maybe it's hereditary."

Dr Jorssen paused and ran her tongue over her teeth. "You seem an intelligent young woman, and you have no history of youth offending." Again, no judgment, but this time she hesitated, as though I might respond.

Setting my lips in a tight line was my only reply.

"You also have no history of suicidal ideation, according to your medical files from"—she delved into the notes again—"Dr William Carnegie."

"I didn't try to kill myself." I said, glowering at her, forcing back images of the swinging body I called Dad.

"Good." Dr Jorssen gave a short, sharp nod. "However, from my understanding of your case, you presented at Anchorage Base with a slashed wrist and episodic psychosis, possibly marijuana-induced, which required you to be medicated." She glanced back at the file. "Risperidone, I believe. Given your wrist, and your distress over what happened to your friend, you've been moved to the head of my consultation list—precisely because Dr Vikram felt you represented a danger to yourself or to others. It's my job to determine whether that's the case."

I nodded.

"Tell me, Juliette, did Riva Vikram tell you why she thought you might be feeling this way?"

"What way?"

"You tell me," she replied, spreading her hands before her. "How are you feeling?"

Nice try, Birgit.

She stared across at me again and then changed tack. "She believed you might be suffering from a mental illness known as schizophrenia."

I rolled my eyes.

"It's a serious condition," Dr Jorssen admonished me. "Difficult to diagnose. Your behaviour over the past few days suggests you exhibit at least some of the markers for it: lack of interaction, apathy, delusions, hallucinations, paranoia. But the best and only way for us to confirm a diagnosis or rule it out, is to monitor you. That can sometimes take months. "

Months! I didn't have months. It had already been months, and Ash was alone out there, probably starving to death.

"At $3 a minute," I added, straightening in my seat. "That's convenient for you. I'm sure you'll make a killing. But to save you the time, I don't have epilepsy or schizophrenia or any other condition, and I'm not a danger to myself or anyone else, so I guess you'll be able to let me out of here today."

"So you can't communicate with dolphins? You don't have hallucinations?" She pushed a bowl of mints on the table closer to me. "Have one, if you like."

"I don't want one." I felt like face-palming. Why had I told anyone about talking to Bitten?

Dr Jorssen took a mint herself and chewed it slowly, watching me. Her eyes looked huge, icy and exacting behind her frames. "Grandiose delusions are not uncommon for schizophrenics. Nor is paranoia. You insisted your boyfriend was alive and that only you could save him, that the police were all corrupt, that Shire officials were liars who had it in for you, and there was something about a baby that wasn't yours. Care to elaborate?"

I shook my head.

"So you don't believe the authorities in Sunshine Shire are corrupt?"

I sniffed. "No more than any other place."

"The voice in your head, is it coming from inside your brain, like a thought, or from outside, like an audible voice?"

I swallowed, unwilling to keep up my tough girl act on Mum's dime but knowing my answer would result in a frenzy of note-taking and probably some mind-altering drugs. "At first it seemed like just a thought, until I realised it was Bitten's way of talking to me." I said.

I was right. Birgit scrawled something down. "Can you still hear the dolphin?" she asked eventually. "Even in here?"

It was a warm day, so warm that even with the arctic Melody House air-conditioning, I could feel a trickle of sweat working its way down my back, and the woman was wearing a cardigan. *Yeah, I'm the whackjob here.*

"Of course not. We're nowhere near the beach." I nodded to a long, soft white hair that curled up her sleeve. "You have a cat, don't you, Birgit? A chinchilla, I'm guessing."

"A Persian."

"Ever talk to it?"

She sat back, brushing at her sleeve. "Yes. But I don't expect it to talk back to me."

CHAPTER 42

"I know this is painful for you." Birgit stood and walked to the water cooler, returning with a paper cup. She set it in front of me, and then sat and cradled her red coffee mug in her palms. "And expensive. But even the most painful things can be made less so by sharing them."

It sounded like something she'd ripped straight out of a Harry Potter novel.

"I'm an only child. I've never been a fan of sharing."

"We can start with your childhood, if you like. It's usually a good place to begin. How did you feel about being an only child? Were you lonely?"

I chewed on my top lip. "No." I lied. "Just a loner."

She'd cut my session short yesterday after the cat comment, as if to see whether I'd be bothered by her dismissal. I wasn't. She might be a hard-arse with no tolerance for my hostile witness crap, but if she thought I was going to slip up and let her into the vault, she was dead wrong.

Birgit leaned back in her chair and pursed her lips. "So I've noticed."

"What's that supposed to mean?"

"You've been here a week, and you've mostly stayed in your room, reading. You've made no effort to engage with anyone, including me."

"Just because you've decided I'm screwy doesn't mean I want to hang out with the other screw-loosers," I snapped, picking at a hangnail on my middle finger. I really wanted to flip her the bird. *Screw you, too, Birgit.*

She was right, though. Mum had brought in a stack of paperbacks, and I spent my first week at Melody House lying on my bed, losing myself in literature. It had almost felt like the old days, except the lustre had worn off some of the heroes. They all paled in comparison to Ash.

"Maybe I just like to read. You should try it. You might learn something."

I thought I detected the faintest narrowing of her eyes at that—and no wonder. The shelves behind me were crammed with tomes on everything from psychology to philosophy to hypnotherapy and phrenology.

"You know"—her tone was more philosophical—"sometimes the best way to learn is by watching."

She picked up the red coffee mug and sipped again, even though I was sure any coffee in it was long cold. Maybe it was water. Or booze. The kind of person she was, she was probably drinking straight Jose Cuervo out of a coffee mug without a grimace, just to mess with me.

"I'm not a lab rat," I muttered. "Don't you think it's an invasion of privacy to watch people all day and all night? It's like the fucking *Truman Show* in here."

Dr Jorssen set the cup down, eyes glistening, and I inwardly cursed myself. "Interesting reference. Except that this is real. You know that don't you, Juliette? Would you say it is easy for you to tell the difference between fantasy and reality?"

I nodded, even if it wasn't true. "Yes. The fantasy is that you'll realise you're wrong about me and let me out of here, and the reality is that you're still wrong about me but you're too arrogant to admit it."

The corners of her mouth crept into a tight smile, red lipstick bleeding into the trellis of lines around her lips. "We do keep our patients under tight surveillance, mostly for their own safety. But you should know I met with your mother yesterday morning. I thought it might help to get her perspective on your situation. She told me you spend a lot of time on the beach, watching the ocean, and that you wish to study marine biology. Do you think that by watching the ocean you get a feel for it? Understand it even, through a kind of osmosis?"

I'd always hated people who used that word. "I don't think it's that simple."

"Well, it's rare that anything is simple," Birgit replied, "yet most people strive for simplicity. Over-complicating things only makes them more difficult, which leads to anxiety or frustration. Do you think you have a tendency to over-think, to over-complicate?"

I chewed my cheek. "I think life is over-complicated."

"Is that why you surf, to simplify life?"

Damn, Mum! What was the point of maintaining a stubborn silence if Mum was blabbing all sorts of stuff in her ear. "I sur*fed*," I said. "And it was never simple."

"Surfed. So not anymore?"

"No."

"Why not?"

I shrugged theatrically. "In here?"

"Before you were admitted, why not?"

"Didn't feel right."

"What does feel right?"

"Nothing." The word slipped out, and I realised right away I'd given her something to pin her psychiatric hopes on. I swallowed and glanced at her from beneath my brows.

"Not even destroying those nets?"

It was another small victory for her, and we both knew it.

"It must have felt good, cutting them," she continued. "Cathartic."

I wondered whether she was only talking about the nets.

She peered at her notes again. "Do you think you directed your anger at the nets because you were unable to direct it at those who'd called off the search for Ashley Gordon, or perhaps at the coroner who'd determined he was dead?"

I shook my head.

"When you think of him, what do you feel?"

"Pain," I said.

"Interesting."

"Why is that interesting?" I snorted. "It might be fucking fascinating to you, but it's real to me, as real as he is, and painful."

Dr Jorssen wet her lips. "It suggests you're more grounded in reality than Dr Vikram believed," she replied. "It suggests that on some level you understand that Ashley Gordon is dead."

CHAPTER 43

The noise slices into my brain—first the needling, mosquito whine of it, then the inconstant, disabled whup-whup-whup *of the rotors. The machine flings itself toward the ground, its tail whipping it into a spin. All around, metal strikes metal with a knife-edged ping, followed by a wet shearing through bone and flesh.*

Curses punctuate the white noise between each heartbeat of the rotors. Somewhere in the background, a radio crackles and a barely discernible American drawl says, "Ranger Seven, cover fire. We got a dust-off Huey hit. Bird's coming down."

"We're going in. Fuck, fuck, fuck!"

The voice sounds strangely familiar, gruffer than Bluey Marone's and with a hint of an accent. It rambles loud and fast over the din. "Righto boys, we're hit. I'm gonna try to land this baby, but… Copper, I know you're a religious man, so I suggest you pray. Wheeze, you cover fire if you can. If you can't, you might want to put your head between your legs and kiss your arse goodbye. Going down in three, two, one…"

Jungle looms up below me like a net, a canopy of camouflage colours. Then I feel the thud, so fierce, so total it stops my heart.

I jolted up in bed, clutching my sheets. My fear of helicopters was another reason I hadn't gone on the initial search for Ash, before the storm made it too rough for a chopper to go out. The fragility of them, as they zipped over the ocean like metal dragonflies, made me nervous. In a small town like Willow Bay, it was also the portent of them. Out west, past the undulating hills of Bannockbrae to the vast, dry cattle stations, choppers frequently buzzed above scraggly gums and wattle. Jackaroos at the gears shoved the nose down to meet the rolling eyes of cleanskin cattle and muster them into a sorting yard to truck them across the country to market. But here on the coast, only big news drew them in, like blowflies come to feast on a corpse.

Sometimes they'd be branded with news stations: Channel Seven, Channel 9, WIN. But most of the time, they were Search & Rescue or Medevac choppers, scanning the seas for someone who hadn't come home, or flying the lucky to hospital in Anchorage or Sydney. In Willow Bay, it was instinctual to mistrust them and be grateful for them in equal measure.

Since Ash's disappearance, I'd added them to the list of things not to think about, which was fine when I was awake. When I was asleep, well, anything could happen.

I rubbed the gooseflesh on my arms and stood to make my way through the darkness to the kitchen for a glass of water, which was when I remembered I wasn't at home. I was here, in Melody House. The funny farm. The blue eye of the security camera gave the room an eerie cast as I shuffled to the bathroom and washed my face.

There'd been no identifying marks on the chopper, but it was clear to me it was military.

Afghanistan? No.

I considered the swathe of jungle. Somewhere else.

Maybe it was some other war yet to come. A lurking death, just waiting for space in the papers.

I flipped down the lid of the toilet and sat, not needing to go, only wanting to feel something solid.

A light flickered on in the hallway.

Tap, tap, tap. "Juliette?" Nurse Abernathy's voice floated in from the hall. "Are you okay? I heard a scream."

"I'm..." My voice wavered. "I'm fine. Just a nightmare."

She craned her neck around the door. "Okay. I'll wait here until you come out."

I could see her rotund shape, blurred by the opaque glass. I flushed without needing to, ran the tap in the sink again, and then slid the door open. "It's fine. Go back to bed."

"Get some rest, dear."

As I crawled back under the covers, I cursed the *mati* and the infernal air-conditioning that hummed like a grounded chopper.

No more. No more dreams, okay? I don't think I can take anymore.

CHAPTER 44

"Care to tell me about the nightmares?"

Birgit caught me off guard, until I remembered they had video cameras on me twenty-four/seven.

"It was just a bad dream," I said, arms folded, defiant.

"I saw the tapes from last night," Birgit said, folding her own arms. "You were terrified."

I shrugged. "It's nothing new."

"Your mother told me about the thing you call the *mati*."

Mum! Why had she blabbed her mouth off about that to someone who could lock me up for life if she chose to? I wished I could end the stupid *mati* and its horrible precognitions. Just thinking about it made the *whup-whup-whup* of helicopter rotors start up again in my head, followed by screams and the smell of burning hair.

Snap out of it, Juls! I rubbed my temple and shut my eyes for a second, but it didn't help. The dreams all came flooding back, staining the back of my eyelids with blood, sending shrieks ricocheting through my brain.

"I don't want to talk about them."

"You typically avoid thinking about things that upset you?"

"Doesn't everyone? Except I can't avoid thinking about them," I snapped. "I can't make them go away. I wish I could, but I can't. Every time, I'm right there, like it's happening to me, even if it isn't. And there's nothing I can do. No way I can stop it. Not even waking up—" I jerked my head up, snapped my mouth shut, and glowered at her, knowing I'd probably just handed her my ticket to a month-long bout of intensive therapy. "And even if I got started, you'd never believe me anyway."

"Try me." She rubbed her chin between her thumb and forefinger.

"You're scientific. You're a psychiatrist, for goodness sake. There's no way."

"It might surprise you to learn, Juliette, that being a shrink doesn't mean I think I know everything about the brain or about life in general. There are plenty of things no one understands about the human mind—not neurosurgeons, not psychiatrists, nor gurus or what have you. And there are plenty of things we don't understand about life. That's why I'm a consulting member of the AIPR."

"The what?"

"The Australian Institute of Parapsychological Research. Of course some clinicians insist the entire field of parapsychology is nothing but pseudoscience, which is why the AIPR only publishes studies that are evidence-based."

I stared at her, wondering whether to trust her.

"What are your nightmares typically about, Juliette?"

Words pushed against my teeth, wanting to break out even as I determined not to tell her. *What the hell. If it'll help me get out of here.*

I sucked in a big breath and then said, "Death. Disaster. People who are going to die or are dying or being hurt. Pain, mostly. So much pain." I heard my heartbeat in my ears as I remembered, and I put a hand to my temple. "Pain I can only watch and never stop." A tear streaked down my face, but I swiped it away angrily. "I've tried to stop them. I've rung the police. The papers. The council. No one ever believes me. I don't know when. I don't know where, and I don't know who. So I just sound crazy, like I do right now."

Birgit's lips were pursed, her eyes intensely blue as she listened.

"I didn't know it would be Dylan," I rambled. "I didn't know it was the Jingilly Hill Scouts bus. If I'd seen a badge on one of the kids, or the scout logo, I might have been able to do something." The vision of the bus wreck twisted my brain, and I rubbed my eyes furiously, as if that could expunge the memory as well as the tears. It did neither.

When I looked up, her face was white and her dark brows were knit together high on her forehead.

Her bottom lip trembled as she asked, "Jingilly Hill Bus crash. You were there?"

"No. I wasn't *there*. That's just it! I've never been there. If I had, I might have stopped it. I saw them. I saw them all. Dreamed them all. I dreamed them all before they happened."

Birgit straightened. Unblinking, she drifted out of her chair and stood, pushing her glasses back up her nose. "Tell me about the scout bus."

I shook my head. "I can't. It's awful. One of the worst. I don't want to think about the bus crash." I rubbed my eyes again, with my palms this time. "There was this little blond kid with a Lightning McQueen backpack on. He was tumbling, tumbling and tumbling. His screams..." I trailed off and pressed my fingers to my forehead.

Birgit looked exhausted suddenly. Human. One hand clasped the pearl pendant at her neck. "His name was Henry Jorssen," she whispered. "He was my nephew. The one I lost."

"I'm sorry." Guilt burned in my throat, and I tried desperately to kill the visions erupting in my brain.

"If the bus's name had been clearer," I stammered. "I'd have known who to call. It was so dark. I'm... I'm so sorry." Even the apology ached. "I should have done something. They were just kids."

Birgit closed her eyes and corrected her posture, stiff as a birch. "Driver error, the police report said." She composed herself with a deep inhalation. "An accident, Juliette. A terrible accident. None of this was your fault."

I nodded, but it didn't erase the feeling of culpability. Fear. Guilt. Shame. Emotions buzzed around me like vultures.

Birgit composed herself. "I don't know what Connor McGuire told you about me, Juliette, but Melody House is a holistic mental health and well-being centre, incorporating many techniques, some rather experimental. I'm not ruling out parapsychology or precognition, but the kind of research we do in those areas must be rigorously tested, you understand?"

I nodded. "You want me to prove I'm not lying."

"It's not a matter of whether you're lying. It's possible you saw this in a newspaper or on the television, that you identified with it somehow and empathized."

I shook my head. "You don't get it, do you? I don't read the papers. I don't watch the news anymore." I tapped the centre of my forehead with my index finger, a little harder than I meant to. "I see enough disaster, right up here."

"You avoid current affairs because you're afraid of witnessing particular events?"

"Since I was about ten. Right about the time that Dad... Did Mum tell you about Dad, too?"

She nodded.

"Well, it was about then, I guess. I'd been having recurring dreams, the Hanged Man and a few others. Mum reduced our Internet data package so we didn't have enough gig for me to click on every news link. I was obsessed with finding out where things were happening or who they happened to. It was driving me crazy."

"You know that's not a word we like to use here at Melody House." Birgit placed her palms flat on the desk. "When you say the dreams are recurrent, are they different scenarios or a repetition of the most recent one?"

"Mostly the latest. New ones never push the others from my mind. Sometimes they appear out of nowhere. The littlest thing can remind me, and then they're real all of a sudden. I get this bizarre sensation, like a curtain's been pulled aside at a magic show, and the air feels more real, and then everything's shown to be true, realer than I ever imagined." I stopped and swallowed again. "Can we stop? I can't do this. I don't want to do this!"

Birgit shook her head, and the human was gone; the robot returned. "We're making progress. I know it's painful, but I need you to face this for a little longer in this session. I want to be sure I know what this is."

"Schizophrenia," I whispered, for the first time acknowledging I was scared of the word. "Did my Mum tell you whether Dad had a mental illness?"

She stared at me for a moment and then shook her head. "Not according to his medical records. But depression is remarkably common, Juliette, particularly following marriage breakdowns or the loss of a loved one. I'm not discounting or confirming anything at this stage. It's too soon for that. Still, I wonder if you've heard of Post-Traumatic Stress Disorder?"

I sniffed and rubbed my wet palms on the side of my shorts. "A little bit. Soldiers get it. Is that what Salt was seeing you for?"

"Confidentiality necessitates I don't answer that question," she said coolly. "But I've worked with numerous veterans suffering from PTSD. Not only veterans either. Anyone can suffer from Post-Traumatic Stresses. Anyone who's experienced disturbing events."

I bit my lip. *How many would you like?*

"Subsequent actions or events operate as a trigger for the original trauma. In a case such as yours..." She rubbed her chin and took her glasses off, cleaning them on the hem of her crisp cotton shirt. "It's not something that's been considered before in detail, but with persistent precognition such as you've described, it might be that you being asleep when you witness the traumatic incident is irrelevant, especially when your reality is so fragmented."

Birgit picked up her silver pen and scribbled something on the notepad. "How long have you been having these dreams?"

"Since I was four."

Her eyes flicked to her notes. "Since your father left?"

"Just before."

"And you're now nearly eighteen, is that correct?"

I nodded.

"You've been seeing graphic, disturbing visions for"—she took a moment to do the math—"fourteen years, and you never thought to seek professional help?"

"Who'd believe me? They'd put me on drugs, or lock me up."

Her frown suggested she agreed. "Have you been hearing voices since you were four as well?"

"No. Never. Not until after Ash. Not until Bitten."

"And you didn't think it was strange to suddenly hear voices? You didn't think about seeking help?"

"I did. But they only happened when Bitten was there, and then I had the flashbacks, and I was sure it wasn't just me. It *isn't* just me. It's like they were linked somehow, like I could hear Bitten *because* I have the dreams. Not because I was going mad, but because Bitten was trying to tell me something or show me something that was going to happen or that was happening, just like the dreams." I looked up at her, pleading. "Birgit, I'm not lying. It's real. All of it. "

She cleared her throat, and her hand returned to the pearl at her neck. "Your mother told me something similar, independent of what I've seen on your room tapes. Juliette, you should know that my nephew's name was never released in the newspapers, nor was it on the television. I read the articles. I watched the reportage. I used to pick him up from school on Tuesday and Thursday afternoons, I knew his backpack well. It was never shown." She crossed her hands on the desk, her eyes glassy, narrowing as she considered my expression. "Paramedics were first on the scene. One of the older kids with a mobile phone called Triple 0. Single vehicle accident. No witnesses. Which leads me to believe that what you're telling me may indeed be true. It's an interesting proposition."

My trauma, an *interesting proposition.*

Lines creased her forehead, reminding me this was her trauma too. The kid's blond hair was the same colour as hers as she bent over her notepad.

"At the very least, one could make a case that the trauma of losing Ash in tragic circumstances could precipitate the kind of emotional disturbances you're experiencing with Bitten and possibly result in a diagnosis of PTSD. As for schizophrenia, you've been in Melody House for two weeks under constant supervision, yet I've seen no evidence of psychosis or hallucination. PTSD, however..."

Birgit splayed her hands on the desk, counting off on her slender fingers. "Flashbacks, avoidance, withdrawal, a lack of interest in the present and in activities you used to enjoy, hyper-vigilance, anger, frustration." She fixed her eyes on mine. "Some PTSD sufferers even experience psychosis, which can cause them to hear voices."

I sighed. "It doesn't change anything. You still think I need to be here."

Birgit leaned both elbows on the table. "It could change everything, Juliette. A drug named prazosin has shown some success in preventing night terrors in clinical studies, and a technique known as Image Rehearsal Therapy could help reprocess some of your recurrent flashbacks. The medication Dr Vikram prescribed for you included calmatives and anti-psychotics designed to treat what she considered a drug-induced psychosis or the potentially more serious diagnosis of schizophrenia. But the standard treatment for resolving PTSD is different. It's cognitive behavioural therapy, which can help you understand the effects your thoughts have on your emotions and actions." She paused, and a half smile spread over her lips. "It might be that prazosin and a course of antidepressants, perhaps combined with CBT, IRT or hypnotherapy, will have a great outcome for a patient such as you."

She was staring at me the way a small child might watch a chrysalis about to split open, and I realised she was excited. All of a sudden, I knew why she did this. She wasn't a sadist who wanted to crack open my skull and scoop out my brains or wear me down and take me apart bit by bit. It wasn't the delving that excited her—it was straight-up diagnosis.

In truth, she wasn't all that different from me. With a diagnosis, she could fix people, or at least try to. She could take broken individuals and put them back together, bit by fractured bit, to stop them doing what Dad had done, or worse. Unlike me, she could prevent things from happening.

I gestured to the bookshelves behind her, to the diplomas. "What makes you think any of these methods, or anything in any of these books, can stop a single one of my dreams coming true? You can't shut my dreams down any more than I've ever been able to."

Birgit's glacial eyes gleamed as she slid the papers from my file back into their folder, preparing to end the session.

"Perhaps not," she answered honestly. "But I might be able to stop them from shutting *you* down."

CHAPTER 45

"Thanks, but you didn't have to."

"I know I didn't have to. I wanted to." Jaz set the bunch of frangipani flowers and the hot pink, glitter-skinned dolphin toy on top of my low, handle-less chest of drawers. "I wanted to say sorry for that night in the hospital."

"Nothing to apologise for." I waved her away. "I'm sorry, too."

I couldn't stop looking at Dylan's arm, or at the blank space where it used to be. But I didn't want him to see that.

It wasn't your fault. It was an accident. Birgit's words inserted themselves into the little slot in my skull that guilt usually filled. My brain was working overtime to turn things around, both in and out of our sessions.

"I wasn't sure they'd let me bring a dolphin in here," Jaz said with a giggle. "I thought that after what happened, it might be a dolphin-friend free zone. But your doctor told me you're doing really well, and she doesn't think you'll let it lead you astray this time."

I smiled. "Very funny, Jaz."

"Who said I was joking?" Her nose crinkled, and she slapped my forearm. "Seriously, though. You doin' okay, bestie?"

I nodded, forcing an errant tear from my eyes with a blink. I'd missed her, and Mum, and everyone else these past few weeks. None of the people in the constant stream of paperbacks I'd read had managed to be quite real enough for me.

"I'm doing good. As good as can be, under the circumstances," I said, believing it myself for once. "I'm okay."

I'm actually going to be okay.

"How are you doing?" I turned to Dylan to change the subject.

"Me? I'm a total one-armed bandit. Every time I visit the bottom bar at Swaggers, old blokes keep coming up and trying to put coins into me." He mimed pulling a lever on a slot machine and laughed too loudly. The pain beneath his humour was obvious. "You know, Juls," he said more honestly. "It takes some adjusting. I have to let Jaz put my hair up for me."

"I refuse to let him cut it," Jaz told me. "It's too gorgeous." She kissed him on the cheek, and he put his arm around her.

"When he gets his prosthetic, he'll be able to do it himself again anyway."

"Any news on when they're going to let you out of here?" Dylan asked.

"When I'm normal I guess, or better."

"*Pffft.* Better. You're already the best." Jaz nudged me. "Please don't ever be normal."

I smiled in return.

"It's nice to see you smile again," she said. "But I'm gonna need you to get a wriggle on. We've got final exams to sit in a month, before you and I blow Willow Bay High for ever, and I'm organising a fundraiser for Dyl's medical bills, so I'm gonna need a roadie. Guess who I managed to line up to come play in Willow Bay?"

"Who?"

"You'll never guess."

"Five SoS," I joked.

"Hardy-har-har. No! Seriously, guess!"

I rattled off a couple of local pub bands, but she shook her head, grinning.

"Hurry up and tell me already."

"Angus and Julia Stone and Jagwar Ma. And then, for the oldies, Jimmy Barnes is going to make a guest appearance."

"Who?" I cocked my head and looked confused.

"Oh, shut up!" Jaz whacked me. "Classic Aussie pub rock will draw in all the jackaroos and jillaroos from the stations."

"How are you going to pay all these bands?"

"We used some of Dyl's TPD insurance, but most of them have been awesome. Since it's for charity, they've agreed to do it for a cut of the takings. Barnesy used to camp down at Bluff Bridge when he was a kid. He loves the place! So he's doing it *gratis* as long as I pay his accommodation, and Windmills has stumped up for that. And I've got a whole heap of people raising money for us, too. It's going to be awesome." She was grinning from ear to ear.

"The surf lifesaving club's got extra lifies on to patrol the beach, and they're going to run some charity events in the afternoon. The gig will start at five. Twenty bucks entry, all ages. Saul's running a booze tent, but you need an over-eighteen bracelet to drink." She winked. "Don't worry, I think I can wangle you one, assuming you're out of here."

"Jaz, that's amazing."

Dylan pinched her cheek. "She's a pocket rocket, isn't she? I don't know where I'd be without her."

"Hands Up To Help," Jaz said. "That's what we're calling it. It's all come together well. If I can pull this off, Jazz it Up Promotions will be off to a good start."

"Jazz it Up Promotions?"

Jaz shrugged. "Why not? The protest was good practice for event planning, and I've been doing some online promo for authors while Dylan was in hospital. Work kind of took my mind off it, so I started my business a little early."

"So when's the big day for this concert?"

"Next Friday. It's going to be enormous. Half of Sunshine Shire's coming. We even had to organise more security. Aldershot's not happy."

I snorted. "He's never happy. But Jimmy Barnes... you realise Barnsey will be total bogan bait for the Bachelor & Spinster Ball crew out west. All those horny country folks flocking to the local watering hole."

Jaz nodded sagely. "Hang on to your Akubras! I plan to reel 'em in and chuck 'em back, make a truckload of cash, and get Dyl a state-of-the-art prosthetic. So you'll come?"

I nodded and glanced around the bare room suddenly brightened by flowers. "If I'm out of this place."

Jaz leaned close to me and whispered conspiratorially, "Want me to bust you out? I've got a sexy nurse's costume at home."

"I bet you do." I threw a pillow at her before Sister Abernathy came and kicked them both out.

CHAPTER 46

"I want you to tell me about your most recent dream."

I felt hazy, dizzy, a sensation not unlike the weird feeling I got when a nightmare turned into reality, although this was almost the opposite and my reality was just about to descend into a hypnotic nightmare. I'd never been hypnotized before, though the sensation was familiar.

"It was a strange one," I answered. "A helicopter crash. I didn't see anyone die. That's unusual for me. It seemed..." I could hear my breath, my heartbeat, and the hum of the video camera recording the session. "Military. But I couldn't say where. Not Afghanistan. There was jungle. It was old, kind of. "

"Old?"

"Like it had already happened."

"Is that unusual?"

"Very."

"And you woke up when?"

"Right as it crashed."

"Do you usually wake up on impact?"

"No. I mostly get to see the full monty." I felt my eyelids flutter rapidly, as if trying to blink away a string of bodies, and then Birgit's voice came again, calm in my ear. Her hand was cool on my upper arm.

"We're going a little deeper now, Juliette. I want you to think about the dream, and, if you can, enter it. I'm going to count you in, but this time, focus on your breathing and on acceptance. Nice, slow, steady breaths. And as you breathe, I want you to keep telling yourself it's just a dream. You're in a dream. Don't try to find ways to prevent what's happening. Accept it. Know that you'll be okay because it's not really happening to you. Ready?"

I mumbled, "Okay."
"And in three, two, one..."
Operation: No More Guilt had begun.
Whup-whup-whup.

We'd been doing this for days now, going over the dreams one by one in excruciating detail. It was physically exhausting, emotionally draining, and I hadn't even got to the flashbacks yet. And the one that troubled me most wasn't a flashback. It was the one I hoped beyond hope was a flash-forward. The one with the heart-shaped ring of boards. The only dream I'd ever really wanted to come true.

"I have something else I want to discuss with you today." Birgit said as we finished up a harrowing session of Image Rehearsal Therapy. "I'm still speaking to other clinicians from the Society for Mental Health Research about a possible diagnosis of PTSD in your case, but given the lack of suicidal ideation, hallucinations, or paranoia in our sessions, and the success we've had with the prazosin and CBT, I'm considering discharging you from Melody House."

I must have perked up at that, because Birgit lowered her head, eyed me over her frames, and added, "It will still take several months to rule out a diagnosis of schizophrenia. You'll still be an outpatient for once-weekly cognitive behavioural therapy sessions and fortnightly IRT. For the time being, you'd also still be unfit to stand trial if charges were to be brought against you. The good news is you'd be allowed to return home, provided you keep your appointments and contact me immediately if you start hearing voices or having suicidal thoughts. Does that sound like something you'd be interested in?"

I straightened in my chair. "I can go home?"

She nodded. "Thursday. I'll write you a script for antidepressants too, if you want them."

"Do I have to take them?"

"No. But they'll elevate your mood, which could be a good thing."

I sniffed. "My mood." Something rose in me, something buoyant, lighter than hope. I knew what would elevate my mood. And it wasn't antidepressants. It was getting out of here.

I was going home.

I was going to find Ash.

CHAPTER 47

The minute I got home late Thursday afternoon, I ditched my overnight bag, pulled my swimmers on under a dress, slid my feet into thongs, and headed straight for the beach.

"Do you think it's a good idea to go out so soon?" Mum drew me into a hug in the hallway.

"Are you kidding? I've been locked up for weeks. I need to get out."

I returned her hug, inhaling her perfume. It was woody and oriental, but it smelled right on her skin, like home. The wooden effigy of Christ on the wall behind her seemed to eyeball me. If it could speak, I was sure it would quote Ephesians: "Honour your father and your mother."

But I had no father anymore, and as for my mother... I closed my eyes, feeling bad about lying to her. *She'll forgive me for this, if I'm right.*

"It's nice to have you home, *koritsi mou*." Mum pushed me away by the shoulders and peered into my eyes. "You want me to give you a lift? We can get ice cream?"

"Nope. I'd rather walk. Feels like I've been cooped up for months."

Her mouth turned down at one corner, but she nodded and smoothed a curl away from my cheek. "Okay. Be home for dinner. I'm making prawn saganaki. Your favourite."

"Yum."

Mum's face lit up. Food wasn't just the way to a man's heart; it was also the way to a Greek's heart.

"And kataifi for dessert," she added.

"Are you trying to fatten me up?" I grinned.

Mum laughed. It was too bad that if Bitten was down the beach, I had no intention of being back in time.

"Seeya." I waved over my shoulder and opened the door, catching Mum's reflection in the hall mirror.

238

She was making the sign of the cross.

I waited for hours past sunset, until panic began to well up inside me. *He's gone. Something's happened to him.*

No, you're just anxious. The nets are gone. He'll be back.

I waited another hour, and when it grew too dark to tell whether there was a fin out there or not, I remembered the way Mum's lips had moved in a silent prayer as I left the house, and I turned and made it home in time for dinner.

For once, I ate more than I should have, finishing up with the walnut-crunched pastry drenched in syrupy lemon and declaring it Mum's best ever.

"Thanks." I kissed her goodnight as soon as I'd stacked the dishes, and stifled a melodramatic yawn with my hand. "I'm going to hit the hay. I've been thinking about taking my board out early tomorrow."

"Surfing?" Mum turned down the volume of the telly and swivelled around from her position on the couch.

"Maybe. It's been awhile."

She set the remote on the grey suede ottoman and considered me for a long moment. "Well, you should, I think. But I don't like the idea of you surfing alone. Maybe you should ring Jaz."

I smiled and waved her off. "A body-boarder! I'll be fine, thanks. I might not even surf. I don't know. Maybe I'll jog instead."

Mum stood and kissed my right cheek and then the left. "Just remember you don't have to do everything all at once. If it's still too painful, after Ash and after Dylan's... well, one step at a time, okay? *Entaksi?*"

"One wave at a time," I replied, wrapping her in a hug. "Mum, I'm sorry. Things are going to be better. I'm going to be better. Everything's going to be all right."

She relaxed and closed her eyes for an instant, breathing in a deep breath. It reminded me how much I'd scared her. Standing there, with Mum's arms around me, for once I believed my own narrative.

Everything was going to be all right.

CHAPTER 48

A body lay on the beach face down, emaciated, spindle-thin, its legs a lattice of scars and coral cuts, back flayed with sunburn. It was naked, arms twisted to the sides, but I recognised the broad back, the shoulders, even withered as they were. I recognised the tousle of brown-blond hair, the length of the shin, the heel. I knew it all.

I'd known it all.

It's him. But this is just a dream you'll wake up from.

Waves sucked at the toes, and a small crab scuttled beneath the bridge of one ankle. Foamy wash pushed a blue sea star onto the beach and dug a channel around the angles of the prone body, the water pooling and then dispersing, anchoring the limbs with ropes of seaweed.

It's just a dream. This isn't real.

For an instant, my heart leapt. I thought I saw a twitch—a toe shuddering against the niggling crustacean and the outstretched arms of the sea star, but it could have been the movement of the tide. It was rising so quickly now that it would soon lift him up, spirit him away like an undertaker.

You'll be okay. All you have to do is wake up. Just wake up.

Further out, a fin rose, pushing a spangled school of fish before it on the water.

Wake up, Juls.

Then the dream's colours ebbed like the tide, and the heat started to fade, the seaweed-stung air masking the sweeter pungency of decay, becoming fainter.

"Ash," I bellowed. "No! Ash!"

But the hiss of the sea was the only reply.

"Juliette?" The hall fluoro flickered on, light crawling under the doorframe like a thin strip of hope. "You okay, sweetie? You've been crying out."

My mouth felt glued shut, and I reached for the bottle of water on my nightstand and kicked off my doona. It was too hot for it anyway, although I preferred something over me.

Yeah," I muttered after taking a sip. "Just a dream. I'll be fine."

The light blinked off again, and I drew a pillow into my embrace, my knees bent up to my stomach.

He can't be dead. He can't be. Ashley Gordon cannot be dead.

He had to be out there somewhere, but where? Where to start looking in the thousands of kilometres of ocean and coastline, the hundreds of small islands that sat like green jewels in the azure waters off the continent's coast. I might never find him, I realised. Not without Bitten. My heart hung its hopes on the dolphin being at the beach tomorrow, and on two small words: *He lives.*

CHAPTER 49

A ray of sun warming my face woke me, and I rolled over to the brightness of open curtains and the havoc that was Jaz rummaging through my closet.

"Who let you in?" I grumbled.

"I came down the chimney. Ho ho ho." She laughed when I groaned at her bad joke. "Now get out of bed. It's nearly midday. I've been extremely patient."

Realising I'd overslept and likely missed my best shot at catching Bitten, I pulled the pillow back over my head.

"Does any of this stuff even fit you anymore, skinny minnie?" Jaz threw a pair of denim shorts and a black halterneck top over the back of my desk chair.

"Dunno." I yawned and sat up.

"Well, we've got to find something for you to wear. It's the big day, remember? Hands Up To Help. The lifesaving events are kicking off already. What about this?" She held up a blue jumpsuit I'd grown out of more than two years ago.

"Possibly."

"Up! Up! Up!" She tossed the jumpsuit at my head, and I shoved it and the pillow off me and sat up. "Try it on." Without waiting for me, Jaz rummaged about some more. "And this." A summery pink top and skirt followed.

"Your mum told me you'd planned on surfing." She eyeballed me for a minute. "That right?"

I yawned again. "Well, I wasn't planning on sleeping in."

"I wasn't planning on either." She bounced to the bed and hauled on my arm. "Come on. I need a lovely assistant if I'm going to pull this off perfectly for Dyl tonight. You're Jazz It Up Promotion's newest executive assistant. Reckon you can handle it?"

I stretched after I vacated the bed and picked up the jumpsuit. "Do I get my own office?"

"No. But you get a backstage pass to Jimmy Barnes."

"Woo-hoo." I threw the blue jumpsuit up in the air, and it fell down on my head. "What's the pay like?"

"Non-existent."

"Company car?"

"Toyota Corolla. New gearbox. Comes with free NRMA roadside assistance." She dropped her voice to a mutter. "Because you're going to need it."

"I happen to know a very good mechanic."

She angled her chin and said seductively. "Not as well as I do."

I grinned. "Well, gee, it sounds like an awesome opportunity, but—"

"Today, junior!" Jaz clapped her hands together and marched me toward the shower.

CHAPTER 50

"Jaz?" I pushed my way through the crowd, holding the press pass she'd given me straight up in the air, struggling to forge a way through as Angus and Julia Stone eased into their set. The protest had been one thing, but this event was incredible. Jaz hadn't been kidding when she said most of the Shire was coming. Tweens lolled on picnic blankets on the grass, and a wedge of dancers surged up the inverted V security corridor to the mosh pit. Over by the beer tent, parents, farmers, and button-down-shirt-clad, booted-up farm folks—Jaz's parents among them—exercised their elbows at the bar, waiting for the pub rock to start and clearly perplexed by the surfie, hipster and emo crew from Anchorage and Figtree.

I glanced at the fluorescent orange ID bracelet Jaz had insisted I wear and considered joining them. At least I could tell them to let Jaz know I was leaving, if nothing else.

The bracelet provided immunity from the burly security guards who ringed the bar area to stop tweens getting in, but Jaz's folks had known me since I was in primary school. Her mum knew my birthday was next month. And after weeks of solitude at Melody House, it felt strange enough walking among the living again, let alone conversing with Jaz's mum, who'd be worried about me after hearing about my stint in therapy. Remembering the last time I'd engaged in underage drinking had landed me in Melody House, I changed my mind and turned back to the mosh pit.

Come on, Jaz, where are you?

I wasn't heading home right away. I wanted to slip down to the beach and see if Bitten was there. I just didn't want Jaz to worry—not after last time.

Mumbling apologies, I contorted past a group of older surfers who were entertaining a coven of Fantastics.

"Hey!" A hand gripped my shoulder, and I turned, thinking it was Jaz, only to be yanked straight onto the crotch of some grinding guy who immediately groped my arse and swayed in for a drunken kiss.

"Hands off!" I pushed off his chest, reeling from his beer breath, and recognised him as the idiot who'd been downing Jim Beam the night of Zara's twenty-first.

"Come on, baby." He danced toward me again. Badly. "Don't be so uptight. Dance with me."

"Fuck off." I spun on my heel, but he grabbed hold of the spaghetti strap of my jumpsuit and tried to reel me back toward him. It snapped and I swore, then I dove forward into the crowd, holding the fabric up over my bra.

"You frigid or something?" he called after me.

Ignoring him, I elbowed my way forward. A broken strap would give me another good excuse to leave.

"You're so flat I could iron my shirt on your tits!" he bellowed, and a burble of inebriated laughter from the Fantastics followed the insult.

A security guard pushed past me, heading in the guy's direction, as someone else grabbed me.

"Juliette, hi!" Lisa Rubin pulled me toward her. She'd cut her blonde hair short, an asymmetric bob that swished around her face as she danced.

"Hey. Seen Jaz anywhere?" I asked.

"She was down the beach with Dyl last I saw her, about half an hour ago, sucking face." The spiky-haired, muscular guy she was dancing with twirled her around, and she squealed as he pulled her to his chest and placed a series of lingering kisses up her neck.

"This's Jono," she told me with a grin when they'd finished pashing.

It told me all I needed to know about how the game of Truth and Dare had gone down with Darius that night. I wondered whether Darius had known the truth about the baby any more than Ash had.

"Good for you." I grinned.

"He's a *darliiing*," she cooed, patting his cheek. "A firie," she whispered. "You should see him in uniform."

"Cool. If you see Jaz, can you tell her I've gone home?" I pointed to the broken strap of my jumpsuit. "Wardrobe malfunction."

"Sure thing." Lisa let go of Jono and hugged me. "I'm so glad you're well again, Juls," she said before Jono dragged her back to him. The two immediately locked lips.

I felt a pang of something: envy or longing or... joy. Joy! I laughed aloud. A real laugh. I was happy for her. When was the last time I'd done joy? Back before Ash...

The crowd was pumping even harder as Angus and Julia riffed the intro to "Big Jet Plane." I made it through the crush and headed for the beach, hoping Jaz was still there.

Overflow from the gig on the esplanade had already made its way to the sand, and I let the crowd pull me along. Down by the pier, dark shapes crowded around the empty deckchairs, and the dunes glowed with cigarettes being hastily sucked down. A group of jackaroo types lolled against the wooden water sports hut, clutching beers from a slab they'd carried from the back of someone's car.

Jet skis were lashed to the pier railings with bicycle locks, and a folded sign near them read: Get up close and personal with Willow Bay's amazing aquatic mammals. One-hour jet ski tours $55.

Water sports had been another of Mayor Aldershot's initiatives for Piers Beach, because it was clearly a great idea to put jet skis, shark nets, and dolphins together. What could possibly go wrong?

Between the jet skis, paddleboards, and banana boats that had been buzzing off the beach all afternoon, it was no wonder Bitten was nowhere to be seen.

The thought of another day without Bitten, another day without being able to save Ash, hurt like a brick to the face. I walked along the water's edge, cursing that Bitten wasn't here to lead me to him. I could hire a boat, steal one if I had to; if only I knew where he was. The swell was small, serrated waves like rows of tiny teeth, and I turned back to the silhouettes on the beach. I was listening for Jaz's loud laugh when I heard my name.

"Jazzy?" I called.

"No." A figure rose from a driftwood log near the dunes. "Dylan."

I could make out the whiteness of his teeth, his hair like a black wing around his face.

"Oh, sorry." I walked closer. "Amazing turnout." I gestured to the people spewing out of the meshed off stage area, and he nodded. "Do you know where Jaz is?" I asked.

"Last I saw she was dancing with Zara."

A spark flickered from the darkness, and I realised he was smoking. It seemed weird for him. Dylan's pro surfer dream usually made him a total health nut.

"You okay?" he asked.

"Yeah. I'm tired. Ready for bed."

"Me too." He sucked on the cigarette again, and the pungent scent of it floated out into the night. It smelled musty and aromatic, and I recognised it as weed.

"I didn't know you smoked."

"Used to," he said, blowing out rings. "Took it up again lately, since the accident." He brushed sand off the log and sat, patting the spot next to him. "Too much. But it dulls the pain."

The dry sand squeaked under my bare feet as I followed him, my gaze on his single hand clutching the bent little cigarette.

"I don't think Jaz is happy about it. Has she said anything?" He put the joint back in his mouth, puffing.

"No." I stared at his profile. "But we haven't really talked all that much since—"

"Have some." He nudged my elbow and held the spliff out to me, pinching it between his thumb and forefingers.

I shook my head. "Can't."

"It's just that, well, you seem a bit—"

"Uptight?" I said. "Tell me about it. Some idiot up there told me that earlier." I pointed toward the gig. "I guess being in a mental institution will do that to you."

Dylan laughed, then threw his head back and blew a wisp up toward the moon. "I was going to say 'lost.'"

He gestured to where a group of teens were starting a bonfire on the sand. "It seems a million years ago we were like that." He held the joint out again. "Come on. It'll make you giggle. Can't think of anyone who deserves a laugh more than you do, not since Ash..." He trailed off, and his smoke formed a pale question mark in the darkness when he exhaled. "You ever smoked before?"

I shook my head.

"Never? I heard the cops found you with—"

I snorted. "Bloody gossip. That was Salt's."

"Salt?" Dylan laughed. "Cheeky old bugger. I thought you and Ash might have. He and I sometimes used to, back when we were groms."

I didn't reply. That small word, Ash, was always able to empty my mind of everything else.

Used to.

I licked my lips and watched the joint burn. Half of me thought, *what could it hurt?* But the rest recoiled as if Lucifer had just nudged me and offered up hell's hookah. Remembering Dr Vikram's initial diagnosis of drug-induced psychosis, I said, "Nah. Not tonight."

Dyl flicked ash from the burned end onto a bed of beach morning glory. "Sorry," he muttered. "I miss Ash too, you know. A lot."

"I know."

"You've never really been one for talkin', have you?" He glanced at me sidelong, and I stared down the beach and shook my head. "Since this happened"—he wiggled the stump under his shirt sleeve—"I know how you feel. Most of the time I just want to be alone. Jaz's heart's in the right place, but all these people, all this fanfare." He rolled his eyes heavenwards and punched the air in mock revelry. "Hands Up To Help. Woo. Hands—plural. And here's me with this." He dropped his arm to his lap and jerked his chin toward his stump. "It's hard enough for me to look at it. Imagine how gross it is for everyone else." Smoke curled from his mouth up to his nostrils as he took another draw on the spliff. "Especially Jaz."

"Jaz isn't like that," I said. "She wouldn't care."

He put his hand up to stop me, pinching the butt between strong brown fingers. "Everyone is like that. Everyone cares." He nodded back toward the gig. "I used to walk through a group of girls like that and have them all flirting. Now, all I see is pity… or disgust."

"But you've got Jaz now. You don't have to hang around people who make you feel like that."

"Doesn't matter where I go. Most people make me feel like that. They don't even realise they're doing it."

We watched the waves in silence for a minute, Dylan breathing out another plume of smoke. The passive smoking was getting to me. I felt the top of the world spin a little, and it made me cough.

"Here." Dylan reached down and handed me a bottle of beer. "I don't want it."

I took a gulp; it was warm, but its sourness was effervescent in my throat.

We both went quiet for a moment, letting the world turn, just watching.

"I shouldn't have taken that idiot's dare," Dyl said eventually. "I'm a fucking surfer. I know better than that. But he was being such a cocky little fuck."

"You weren't to know. No one was."

Squeezing my eyes shut, I remembered what Birgit had taught me. I focussed on my breathing, resisting the urge to tell him I had known, resisting the urge to tell myself I'd known and done nothing.

Out beyond the breakers, the tide sewed sequins of moonlight into the water. Small waves sloughed over the rocks near the point, and Dylan's gaze was out there, too, where mine was, searching for the gleam of light off a slippery fin. I sat up straighter and strained my eyes, but there was nothing there.

"I miss it," Dylan said, so quietly I could barely hear him. "I miss the waves. But I'm a coward. Even if I can surf again, I don't know if I ever will." He dropped the roach and screwed it into the sand with his foot.

"You will."

But I wondered whether he actually would. Surfing was a lot like life. All about timing, balance, and power. The way he was sucking down joints, the balance part seemed a lot harder for him now.

Dylan shook his head so firmly that his long hair tickled my shoulder. "Jaz says I should see a counsellor." He picked up a shell and turned it over and over in his fingers. "That's what part of the money from this gig is for, not just prosthetics."

"Maybe you should," I murmured.

"I don't know. All of this talking about feelings. It doesn't feel right to talk like that to a stranger."

I nudged his knee. "You're talking to me."

"You're not a stranger." He laughed. "Just strange."

"Thanks. That's why I saw a shrink."

My mind returned to the dream. The blood in the water. The screams. Exactly as it had played out in reality.

Deep breaths, Juls.

Dylan flipped the shell over again, and the mother of pearl gleamed in the dark before he set it down on the log and threw his arm around my shoulders. "You remember that bonfire we had on the beach that night?" he muttered. "I played a Hendrix song, 'Merman'."

How could I forget? It was the night I'd first heard Ash's song too. The night I'd almost lost my virginity. It seemed so long ago. It reminded of me of a quote I'd read as a kid, back when Mum still used to send me to Bible study.

"'When I was a child, I spoke as a child, I understood as a child, I thought as a child; but when I became a man, I put away childish things,'" I murmured, feeling old all of a sudden, and wise but tired, so, so tired. Maybe it was the smoke getting to me, or maybe this was just what it felt like to be a grown up.

Dylan sighed. "You mean like guitars?" he muttered, alerting me to the fact that I'd said it aloud.

"I can't play guitar anymore," he said. "Can't surf."

"Not being able to surf isn't a disability. You've seen me. I can't surf."

"You can. You just have to keep at it," he said, seriously. "And to me it is. I've been strumming and surfing since I could walk."

"You could learn the drums," I suggested.

"Like the drummer from Def Leppard?" He laughed, but it lacked humour.

"I'm sorry. I didn't mean to make it sound like a joke. I meant that if you want to surf, when you want to surf again, you will. Maybe you'll even play guitar too, with a good prosthetic."

His stump moved in a half-shrug, and he frowned. "It hurts, thinking I might never play Hendrix again."

Slipping a tobacco packet out of his pocket, he opened it and stuck a paper on his lip. "If it's impossible for a man to breathe underwater, like that song says, why do I feel that's what I've been doing the past few weeks?" He began to roll the joint on his knee.

"If you can manage to do that one-handed"—I gestured to the spliff on his knee—"you can probably do anything."

Dylan turned his ink-black eyes on me momentarily. "You're right. I should be grateful I survived. Plenty of surfers don't. I survived, and it wasn't even the arm I write with, and I have Jaz and all those people up there helping me out. Yet…" He gave a snort of frustration. "I sometimes wish I'd fucking died. A gun surfer who's too afraid to go into the water. It's pathetic. None of the greats would have done that. Look at Fanning. My Uncle Mike was a top surfer, too. A pro. He'd never have let a shark stop him. Remember how I had that gecko tattooed on my forearm?"

I nodded. Jaz had loved it. She used to go on and on about how cool it was.

"It's how I used to remember him. He died when I was a kid." Dylan gave a bitter little chuckle. "Now even my tatt's gone. Uncle Mike's gone, Ash's gone, and I'm still here, and most days I don't want to be."

He licked the joint closed and put it in his mouth. "Most days I wish I was dead." The vowels came out strange around the spliff, slack between his lips.

The sea blurred through the film of my tears. "Dylan," I cautioned. "Don't."

"I don't know what the fuck is wrong with me. It's like I've lost myself."

"Nothing's wrong with you. You just need help. Maybe stop smoking so much for a start. But you'll get past this. I know you will. I know you can." I didn't add, *because I know I can. And if I can do it...* although I thought it.

He curled his hand into a fist and stared at it like he wanted to punch something. Then he sighed and stubbed the joint out.

"Thank you, Juls," Dylan muttered.

"For what."

"For getting it. I feel like Jaz doesn't. Not always. She's trying so hard to help me get strong again. All this physio. Therapy. She's trying to get me back to the old me. But I'm not the old me. Sometimes I think I'll never be the old me again."

His Adam's apple bobbed as he swallowed hard, and I put my arm around his waist and hugged him, wondering what the old Juls would have told him. The pre-Ash Juls. The pre-Melody House Juls. The Juls that hadn't yet figured out we were all different versions of ourselves, all the time.

The two of us sat there like stones in the silence, letting our rough edges be smoothed by the same ocean.

"No one stays the same," I said eventually. "Things change us. Life changes us. But you'll always be you, Dyl, no matter what happens. No matter who you become, you'll still be the one and only Dylan Hoffstede. Half-islander, half-Dutch, and fully sick."

He snorted. "That fucking special snowflake. Can't I be Wolverine or the Incredible Hulk or someone?"

I smiled. "Only if I can be a unicorn Pegasus."

Dyl laughed and fist bumped me. "Deal."

When he spoke again, his tone was serious. "I don't know whether I'm more pissed off at the old me for being stupid enough to accept that dare, or the council for the dolphin-feeding drawing in sharks, or the idiot who ruined those nets. Or pissed off I was so unlucky. I mean, why me?" He leaned back, sliding off the log to collapse onto a mat of pigface. Turning his face to the sky, he added, "I don't go to church or anything. I'm not religious, but I'm a good guy. I never hurt anybody. So why the fuck me?"

I set the beer down, digging the base into the sand, and followed him.

It was clear Jaz hadn't told him it was me who cut the nets. Dyl had been out of it with blood loss, then in surgery, and then so sick in intensive care on an IV drip to prevent infection, so I supposed he wasn't in the right place to hear it anyway. But although Jaz had blamed me, she'd still protected me.

My shoulders hit the sand with a *thud,* and the shell grit felt hard and real and grounding beneath me, infused with the scent of dead bonfires and brine.

"I think that nearly every day. Why Ash? Why you? Why me?"

Above us, a star twinkled, red and irregular. *Planet Fucked Up. Maybe there's a lot more Fuckedupians down here than I'd thought.*

I pointed to the Milky Way. "Look at all those stars and try to convince me life's not all just totally random, Dyl. Bad things happen to good people every day. And sometimes good things happen to bad people, too. It's just probability. Maybe some things are meant to happen, and they'll happen no matter what you do. Maybe it's all preordained, like the Bible says. Or maybe anything can happen, and it just depends on your choices—a bit like one of those Choose Your Own Adventure stories. Or perhaps things happen no matter what you choose, not even in this universe but in one of them. In a different universe, another version of you might be Wolverine."

As I said it, I laughed, thinking that some of Dyl's smoke had definitely affected me. Then I remembered that stargazing always made me feel like this: smaller, less important, little more than a single idea in a whole starry sky full of them. That was what I loved about it.

Stars, babe. My chest constricted with pain at the memory.

I didn't think I'd ever missed Ashley Christopher Gordon the First more than I did right at that moment.

Swallowing back tears, I shook my head. *Crunch time.*

"My guess is there was nothing you could have done to stop it, Dyl. Just like there was nothing I could have done either, even if I hadn't cut those nets."

Dylan jerked his gaze away from the stars and stared at me. "What are you talking about?"

"I didn't slash my wrist, Dyl," I told him, swallowing hard. "I accidentally sliced it when I cut the shark nets. Bitten was trapped in them. He was drowning. And even if I'd known it was you, I don't know if I could have let Bitten drown."

"What do you mean 'even if you'd known it was me'?"

I clambered back up onto the log, facing away from him, taking a long slug of warm beer for Dutch courage.

Dylan would understand this, wouldn't he?

"I saw it, Dyl," I said eventually. "Your shark attack. I dreamed about it. I knew it was going to happen, I just didn't know it was going to happen to you."

He sat up, and I turned around and put out a hand to help him stand.

"You dreamed it?" He sat down next to me on the log. "Jaz told me you used to have night terrors."

"Course she did," I said with a sniff. "Ol' big gob Jaz."

I felt a momentary wash of anger. But of course she'd tell Dylan everything, just like I'd told Ash everything. Between best friends and lovers, there were no secrets. Or there shouldn't be—I knew that now.

"She was probably meant to keep mum about it," he said.

I shook my head. "No more secrets. I cut those nets to save Bitten because he's my friend. But I knew he was out there drowning because I can hear his voice in my head."

Dylan glanced at me sidelong, obviously trying to determine whether I needed to be readmitted. "There was nothing you could have done," he said eventually, putting his arm over my shoulders again. "There was nothing anyone could have done to save my arm. I was in the wrong place at the wrong time. Like Ash."

I took another gulp of beer, feeling as flat as it was. *He still doesn't believe me. And there's no way he's going to.*

"It sounds crazy. Maybe it *is* crazy." I started to doubt myself. "But when I stole that boat to find Ash, I was following Bitten." I searched the ocean for a fin again.

Dylan cleared his throat and let his arm drop away, and the torn strap from my jumpsuit caught in his wristwatch before flapping down onto my chest. I flicked it back over my shoulder and snared it under a bra strap.

"Sorry. I think I broke your dress." Dylan gestured to it, changing the subject.

"It's a jumpsuit, and it wasn't you. Some idiot in the crowd tried to grab me earlier. It's all right."

He stared at me intently. "Are you all right, Juls? I know Ash. If he'd known he wasn't going to be around to do it, he'd have told me to look out for you. So, I'm asking for Ash. Are you okay, Juls?"

Was I?

"Yeah." I smiled, feeling as though I believed it, even if no else did. "I'm okay. Are you okay, Dyl?"

"No." Leaning forward, he butted his head gently against mine, foreheads bumping in a gesture of friendship. "But I'm glad you are."

CHAPTER 51

"Get it on." The drunken catcall was followed by the *zzzzt* of a zipper coming down and then a stream of piss pattered into the sand just metres away.

Dylan cleared his throat. "Reckon you could have gone somewhere more private to take a leak, mate?" He faced the idiot who'd strolled down from the dunes behind us.

"Reckon you could have gone somewhere more private to try to slip one into Little Miss Uptight there?"

I heard the zipper again, and then that idiot Benny said, "Tell me, is she as tight as she is uptight? I barely copped a feel off that frigid bitch, but from what I did grab, she ain't got no boobies anyway."

Dylan leaped to his feet.

"I heard even Ash Gordon couldn't get his knob wet with her." Benny laughed.

I followed Dylan up, sending the empty beer bottle flying. Part of me wanted Dylan to shake the shit out of him for insulting me and daring to mention Ash's name, and Dylan's flared nostrils suggested he felt the same way. But I didn't want anyone to get hurt either.

"Just rack off," I told Benny.

Dylan swung around to me. "Did this little douche grope you? Is that what happened to your top?"

"Dyl, it's fine." I put my hand on his arm, but he shrugged me off.

"It's not fine." He took a step toward Benny.

"What're you gonna do?" A cigarette dangled from Benny's mouth, and his words slurred around it. Dropping the fag in the sand, he drew his dukes up to his chin. "Ya gonna throw a two-punch combo at me, big guy?" He jabbed his left arm forward, followed by his right.

"Oh that's right." He pointed to Dylan's stump and laughed. "You're that idiot I dared to become shark shit."

Dylan moved so fast over the sand that Benny's laugh was cut off before he saw Dyl's fist coming. The single jab dropped the shorter man to his knees in the sand instantly.

"Fucking hell!" Benny stumbled up, clutching his jaw. "You hit me. You fucker."

Dylan grabbed him by the T-shirt and swung him around to face me. "Did you touch her?"

"Dylan, don't. I'm fine."

"Frigid bitch," Benny groaned.

And it wasn't fine. I groped for the flapping string of my jumpsuit. What if I hadn't defended myself from Benny? What then? What if I'd been a younger girl? Even I could see that Benny had it coming.

Crack. Dylan swung him around by the collar and then let him go, ploughing him into the log.

"Yeah, you hit pretty hard for a one-armed man." Benny said as soon as he stumbled to his feet again. "But try this on for size." He swung and landed a punch on Dylan's jaw, and they scuffled.

Then Benny was up again, though hunched over, clutching my empty beer bottle. "Fucking freak." He spat. "You wanna go, huh, champ? Have a go at this." Holding the bottle by the neck, he smashed the end against the log. Its new teeth gleamed shard-sharp in the moonlight. "I'll take your other arm off as well," Benny threatened, stumbling forward.

"Stop it!" I yelled. This had gone far enough already. "Stop! Dylan!" I screamed. "Benny, put the bottle down."

Dylan's single hand clenched and unclenched at his side, but he took a few steps back.

"Thatta boy, yellow." Benny smirked as Dylan and I backed off down the beach, moving toward the clubhouse. "Let your little bitch put you back on your leash."

"What's goin' on here?" A voice rumbled out of the darkness as shadows descended toward us from down the beach.

"This little prick's been roughing up chicks," Dylan said as the shadows turned into a group of brawny country lads.

"Has he now?" A big, curly-haired cowboy stepped forward, knuckles at the ready.

"Don't worry, I got this." Benny used the smashed bottle to gesture to Dylan. "He's armless." He guffawed at his own joke.

"Let it go," I said to anyone who might still listen. "He's an idiot. It's not worth it."

They stood there, staring each other down as I began to walk backwards, nearly bumping into a bunch of half-drunk Anchorage boys who were coming up the beach.

"The fuck you doing, Benny?" one of them called, and I recognised Darius as the bunch swung and started across the sand toward Dylan and the cowboys.

Benny kept his beady eyes fixed on Dylan. "Not even gonna follow her, are you?" He jerked his chin toward me. "It's not worth getting glassed for a chick with no tits, is it? What happened to that blonde that was with you that night? What? She doesn't like her men half-eaten? Not like this one here." Benny jabbed the bottle in my direction. "This bitch creams her panties over dudes who've got a bite taken out. That's what happened to her first boyfriend." He started humming the theme song to *Jaws*—der-dum, der-dum—and suddenly I didn't give a shit if Dylan pounded him.

"I bet she's hot for that ugly stump you got there, bad boy," he said.

"Fuck you." Dylan's foot shot a spray of sand into Benny's eyes, then he lowered his head and charged.

"Dyl," I screamed, as the two groups came together like front rowers at a bush footy match.

All I could hear was Dylan's roar, and then swearing and grunting as the mass moved like a rugby scrum down the beach.

"Dylan!" I screamed over the melee, unable to see him beneath the crush. Eventually someone hauled Benny out of the ruckus and hurled him down the beach.

"Not so tough without a glass in your hand, are you?" A well-built redneck threw him against the wall of the water sports hut, and he landed with a *thud* that shattered the window above, sending its glass raining down around him.

He staggered up again, his hand was squirting blood, before Dylan broke out of the mass of bodies and charged once more. He hammered into Benny, pushing him up against the wall of the shack, his fist a piston of guaranteed pain.

"Dylan!" I screamed, following it up with, "Jaz!"

She'd know what to do. She'd know how to stop him. Angus and Julia Stone were finishing up, and the scream of the crowd as they left the stage drowned out my yell. Assorted other voices provided commentary.

"Christ, he's going to pulp the little shit."

"Pull him off then."

"You pull him off! He's totally lost his shit."

"Let him go. This little dick's been molesting every sheila in the mosh pit for hours. Serve the little coward right if he's beaten up by a dude with one arm."

"Knock it off," someone else started yelling, tugging Dylan off Benny.

Dyl was heaving for breath, pushing dark hair and blood off his forehead.

"Bros!" A silhouette appeared on the dunes, a grommet kid I recognised as one of Ash's surfing acquaintances. He chucked his can of rum and Coke into the bushes and waved both arms above his head. "Security's comin'. They've called the cops. Skin out if you're underage."

"Or don't want an assault charge," one of the Anchorage boys said.

I pointed at Benny. "He's the one trying to glass someone."

"Yeah, well, who do you think they're going to believe?" Darius snarled, pointing to the blood pouring from Benny's gashed fingers. "Benny's the one with the munted hand."

Benny laughed, spitting blood, then pointed to the dangling sleeve of Dylan's shirt. "I'd argue that point."

Jagwar Ma had taken to the stage, the heavy percussion kicking out the intro to "Come Save Me."

Dylan stood his ground, glowering, molars grinding like continental plates. Then he turned to me. "I'm sorry, Juls. I didn't mean to go all—"

"Incredible Hulk?" I finished for him. "Hey, it's cool. Time to go now, big guy." The wail of a police siren cut me off, and I gestured to the red and blue lights strobing out from the parking lot beyond the dunes. Somewhere nearby, a dog barked.

Anchorage coppers. The dog squad.

"You better get out of here," I told him. "Everyone better."

Remembering I was already in enough trouble, and I'd been drinking underage and probably passively smoking weed too, it occurred to me I better leave too.

That's when I heard it, louder than the sirens and clearer than the drum beat or the song's lyrics rebuking me in the background.

Come.

I spun. Out beyond the breakers, ripples formed a ring of shining water around a damaged crescent fin. *Save Me.*

"*Bitten!*"

Forgetting everything else, I set off at a sprint down the beach, hurdling over the folding sign that advertised the jet skis.

Come Save Me. The thought hit me like a fist, coming into my head louder than the barking of dogs, and I spun in place and raced back to the jet skis roped together like mechanical horses on the sand. I spent several seconds tugging at one before remembering it was locked.

Keys. Keys. Keys. The word hammered in my brain with each *thud* of my feet as I pelted toward the smashed-up water sports hut.

I was about to launch myself through the broken window when I realised Dylan was already bent under the counter inside. Straightening, he tossed me a key-ring. Five sets of keys *clinked* as they tumbled through the air towards me, all hooked to a Marvin the Martian figurine.

I caught them, laughing at the irony. *Thanks, Marvin.*

"Juls," Dylan called as I turned to go. "You know a sane guy would stop you doing this, right?"

I grinned back at him. "I know."

"And you know I can't come with you? Not out there." He looked down at his stump. "You're on your own."

"I know that too."

But if life was one of those Choose Your Own Adventure stories, I didn't need any other hero in mine than Ashley Gordon.

"Dyl, I have to do this. I have to find him. If I don't—"

"You'll lose yourself," he finished for me. "I know. Here." He dug in his pocket and tossed something through the air. "Take this."

I deftly caught his iPhone.

"Just in case."

The barking was coming closer, and the band had stopped. Cops and security guards had already begun streaming onto the beach. I didn't care. Nothing mattered anymore as I sprinted towards the jet skis. Nothing but Ash.

It was time to exit Planet Fucked-Up.

Three, two, one, blast-off.

CHAPTER 52

They're noisy. The dolphin's shining black eye rose above the water, and then it dove again.

"I know. It was the best I could do at a moment's notice."

Not having had time to uncouple all of the jet skis, I'd taken off on one with the second still roped behind it, figuring I didn't want to run out of fuel this time either. I'd already swapped over. If this one ran out of fuel, I was screwed.

It felt like I'd been driving for hours—if you could call it driving. Wave after wave battered me, soaking me to the skin and making me contemplate osmosis for the second time that month. Salt speckled my face and burnt my eyes, and if this kept up I was sure I'd resemble Lot's wife by the time I found Ash. If I found him.

I had no idea where Bitten was taking me. Sometimes, I'd lose sight of him for long minutes and be forced to slow, the machine skidding on the waves, its wake combining with the swell to threaten to tip me off or make me puke. My butt was sore, my wrists and fingers stiff from gripping the handlebars, and my hair had whipped itself into a medusa of briny dreadlocks. But none of that meant anything if I could find Ash.

"Bitten?" I rasped, scanning the blank sea. "How much longer?"

A wave shoved me forward, and the stationary jet ski behind me nudged the back of my ride. The wind was picking up again, stoking the waves into an orgy of chop. Out this deep, there were no breakers, but the big waves still tried to unseat me.

Just keep swimming.

The *shirr* of the motor starting up again drowned out my laugh. Had that been me or Bitten? Or someone else? Someone nearby? How I wanted it to be Ash. How I hoped it had been his lips, his thoughts that had sent those words into my head: *Just keep swimming.*

The pleasure craft kicked up over a wave and landed with a *thwack* in a trough, and my stomach muscles clenched like my hands on the throttle. I gripped the seat with aching thighs. I was exhausted. We had to get there soon. We had to be close.

Squinting to protect my eyes from the wind and salt, I focussed on picking out the dolphin's grey body beneath the dark water as I tried to manoeuvre the craft over the lip of another giant wave and avoid the inevitable crash into the gully. In doing so, I slowed down too quickly. It was a rookie mistake. The jet propulsion slowed too, preventing me from steering, and the powerful wall of water slapped against me side-on.

Thwack. I guttered out with a crash that sent the second jet ski rocketing into the first vessel, throwing me right off.

The force of the hit plunged me under, and I was surrounded by sudden darkness and an entourage of bubbles. I squeezed my eyes shut and struck out for the surface, emerging with a gasp to my second rookie mistake of the day.

Earlier, when I'd run out of fuel and swapped onto the second jet ski, I'd forgotten to attach the kill cable from the second key to my wrist. After I'd fallen off, the engine kept running, spiriting both of them away, the first towing the second like a captive of some war I had definitely lost. The blunt *gnnnnnrrr* of them escaping sounded like a long, wet raspberry.

Fuck!

I wanted to scream, but the swell was dunking bucket-loads of water over my head, and even if I'd had the energy to swim after them—which I didn't, not after hours of gripping the damn things—they stopped too far away and there was no way I'd catch them now in this swell.

"That's why you always need to wear a leggie. Otherwise, what the sea wants…" Ash's words returned to me.

The damn sea. What about what I wanted for once?

At least I'd retrieved a life vest from the hold-all under the seat of the second when I'd swapped jet skis. I began a fierce eggbeater kick, trying to poke my head far enough above the swell to search for Bitten, but I couldn't see him anywhere.

"Screw you," I whispered to the waves that faced off against me. "What the fuck do you want with me anyway?"

A wave slapped me in the face.

Goddammit!

CHAPTER 53

Stars. There were stars, pinpoints of light that pricked my swollen eyes like needles.

Five hours. I'd have said it aloud, if for no other reason than to keep myself awake, except that my tongue was coiled in my mouth like a fat snake hibernating with thirst.

Bitten?

He'd been here earlier, even nudging me onto his back for a while. I'd swum, clutching the familiar, handled shape of his fin, soothed by the smooth skin, his sonorous *clicks* and *coos*. He'd towed me along for ages, until I felt him tiring.

After that, he'd been here and gone and here again intermittently.

I was too tired now to hang on anyway. I was drifting again, floating on my back. My mind wandered through dreams and snippets of thoughts and conversations that could have Bitten's or mine or the voices of dead sailors. They all seemed so near, like mermen. Drew and Troy, hair streaming out like tentacles. I closed my eyes before a seaweed-scented slap perked me up again like a dose of smelling salts. Bitten was back. And then gone. Back.

Help.

Was that where he kept going? To get help?

My eyes were slitted like a reptile's, and I could hear my heartbeat ticking like a clock, and beyond it a distant, repetitive gnawing that reminded me of a snore, as if I'd just fallen into a deep sleep. A final sleep with no dreams, nothing. Then Bitten nudged me, and the *thunks* became clearer, more defined.

Whup-whup-whup.

Only when the needling stars turned into a searing chamber of light did I realise it was a chopper. I lifted my arms above my head, but they were too waterlogged to wave. A voice beyond Bitten's squeaking sonar rang out. It sounded worried, familiar, auto-tuned somehow by the cadence of the rotors.

"Juliette. Hang on, love, we're going to winch you up," it blared.

And in that exact moment, I knew whose voice it had been in that dream.

Righto boys, we're hit. I'm gonna try to land this baby, but…

My throat was so thick with relief that I could barely squeeze out the word. "Salt."

CHAPTER 54

"Get an emergency blanket around her," Salt commanded Bluey Marone, who was holding a water bottle to my mouth. I shivered and sucked at it weakly before pushing it away.

I was trembling all over, or was it just the motion of the chopper? It had taken a while to haul me in, and the whole time I'd been trying to warn them.

"It's going to crash." The words chattered along with my teeth. "The chopper. I saw it. It's going to crash."

Salt's jaw was so square and pale I thought it would shatter like glass if this bird got any jumpier.

"If you say that again, I'll throw you off myself." He swore. "Thought I'd put my flying casket days behind me, till tonight."

For a second I wondered if I wasn't still dreaming. Salt McGuire, the man who hated flying, the man who sailed everywhere he needed to go, was flying a chopper!

"CareFlight chopper was out," he explained. "Some kid got himself gored by a bull down past Conalbin, had to be flown out to Sydney. This bird's the mustering chopper off Len Hardy's property out near Roebuck, but the only joker who knew how to fly it was off on R&R in town and wouldn't answer his friggin' phone. Mobiles! Waste of time if you ask me. Although we wouldn't have found you at all without that Find My iPhone App on Dylan's cell. Found the jet skis first. Out of fuel. That's when we saw Chomp down there."

"You're... Salt, you're flying!"

Salt wrenched an imaginary zipper across his lip to indicate I should be quiet and pulled the headset closer to his mouth. "Yep. Too rough and too dark to get the boats out to look for you, so guess who volunteered for this job?" He pointed to his chest. "I haven't flown a midge for more'n thirty years, but you'll never meet a gladder man than me to discover this wasn't another dust-off mission, Juls. Back in the day, I got all but one of these bloody buzzers home in one piece, even if some of the cargo was in pieces—if you know what I mean. I might be out of practice, but don't you worry. I'll get you back safely if it's the last thing I do. God knows I got one other flight to atone for."

"B-But I s-saw..." I managed between my chattering teeth.

"Sit there and get some fluids into you," Salt commanded, "and I won't even ask what in the blue blazes you were doing out here, let alone call you a bloody idiot for doing it."

"S-Salt."

He pulled on the joystick and the nose of the chopper dipped and then rose as he prepared to wheel it about.

"D-Don't t-take me home," I said, leaning forward.

"I'm not. Anchorage Base Hospital," he said resolutely. "You need some fluids. Geez, Juls! What were you thinkin'? Doin' something like this the day after they discharge you. You want to go straight back to Melody House?

"N-No," I stammered. "N-Not back. W-We're so close."

"Here, love," Bluey soothed. "You're confused. Have some of this." He held a silver capful of tea from a flask to my lips, trying to keep his hands steady over the movement of the machine.

"No!" I pushed aside Bluey's mug. "Where's Bitten?"

The chopper lurched up again, lights blazing. "Oh, you mean Chomp. He's down there." Salt pointed.

"Y-Yes. I was following him. He was taking me to Ash."

Salt scratched his head with a thick index finger. "Juls"—he exhaled loud and long—"it's been a big day."

"No!" I forced myself not to stammer. "A big year. Salt, Ash is alive. It's true. I've dreamt it."

Let it be true. Please let it be true.

"Dreamt it?" Bluey Marone said and looked at Salt wearily, the wrinkles around his eyes deepening.

"The shark attack on Dylan—I knew it was going to happen. I foresaw it, Salt."

"Foresaw it?" He frowned.

"Remember when you told me there was more to life than what we can understand, more than what we can see or feel or explore with our senses?"

Salt nodded.

"You said the future was kind of like faith, like heaven. You can't see it, you just have to trust it's there. But I can see it, Salt. I've always been able to, and you just have to trust that I can."

"And Ash?" Salt scratched at his chin. "Did you see him too?"

"No." I shook my head so hard it made my dehydrated skull ache. "I never saw him. Because Ash is alive."

Salt considered it for a moment. "I know you believe that, love. I know you want it to be true, and so do I, but when you got in this chopper, you were certain this bird was going to crash. Juls, I've crashed a chopper before. Got the scars to prove it. It's not an experience I'm about to repeat." He turned to face the windshield. "Maybe you're wrong on this one, too.

"That's what I mean, Salt,' I babbled. "I saw that crash, too. I didn't know it had already happened until you mentioned it, because most of my dreams are of the future, not the past, and I didn't know who Copper and Wheeze were."

Salt's head snapped back around.

"When you crash-landed that chopper, you told Wheeze to kiss his arse goodbye, didn't you?"

Salt's eyes widened with disbelief. "Well, shit. You got me there, love."

I stared back, not giving up. "I dreamed it. I know it's true. Trust me, Salt."

"Where the hell is he then, kiddo?"

Close.

"Watch Bitten." I pointed, and Salt followed my gesture, wrenching the joystick to make the chopper circle back around.

"You got ten minutes flying time, love," he told me. "If we don't find Ash in that time, that's it, okay? I don't fancy bein' up here any longer than I gotta. Deal?"

"Deal." My grin hurt so much I thought my face would break.

The digital clock threw a greenish glow over the instrument panel. We were eight minutes in. Every movement of the blades felt like a guillotine hanging over my head, and then we saw it.

"What the hell is that?" Salt kicked the searchlights up a notch, and I held my breath.

Below us, Bitten appeared to be slowing. I was worried he was tiring or lost when something more solid than the churning ocean appeared like a speck on the horizon. Spotlights seized on whiteness in the night. Vegetation matted together with sand. Beach spinifex. Milky pools of brackish water. Pearls of shallow reef braceletting the reef.

"It's an island," I breathed. "A tiny little cay."

"Huh?" Salt cleared his throat. "I don't come out this far in the *Sea Change*, and it's pretty far from the shipping channels. Never noticed this one before."

"Down there." I sat bolt upright, pointing. "Down there."

The searchlight picked out the dark lines of letters drawn in the sand.

SOS.

And the dream dropped around me like a veil.

He was there, face down on the sand, his feet in the tide. His back sunburned, his legs scored with sores and slashes, and his body—his motionless body—abandoned like jetsam, thinner than a Halloween skeleton. I forced my mind to focus on the crab, on its deliberate, animatronic scuttle.

I put my hand to my mouth and cried, "No! Ash, no!"

CHAPTER 55

The helicopter shifted its weight in commiseration, and the searchlight beamed down on the body.

The toe moved, the crab inched back into the pool, the sea star washed back into the waves, and Ash Gordon turned his head to the side.

"Ash!" I shouted so loud in the small cabin that I was sure they heard the echoes back in Willow Bay.

He rolled over creakily, one bony arm flung up to shield his eyes. As the chopper dropped closer, Ash jerked up like a horror-house corpse, a skullish grin stretching his hollow cheeks.

"Ashley Christopher Gordon!" Salt hollered. "Jesus, the poor bastard looks half—"

"Dead." I finally said it. "He's not dead. Ash's not dead!" I whooped, a wild cackle of relief springing from my lips.

"You don't say." Salt wrenched the gearstick around, which tilted the chopper and forced me to clutch my seat.

"I reckon he's too weak to be winched up, don't you, Blue? Find something to hang onto. I'm gonna try and land this baby."

I waited for the impact, half afraid the dream chopper still might crash, but it wasn't jungle below, it was beach—the most beautiful beach I'd ever seen.

Like Birgit had taught me, I focussed on my breathing as the helicopter clattered down and hovered for a moment before bumping its skids on the sand. Relief flooded through me, and adrenalin invigorated my aching limbs as the roar of the blades subsided. I was out before the rotors came to a halt, crouching and running toward him, calling his name.

"Well, I'll be dammed." Salt's voice boomed from the cabin. "Looks like your dockside guarantee came good after all, girl."

CHAPTER 56

"I love this song." I sipped my hot Milo as the opening bars of Jason Mraz's "Life is Wonderful" floated out into the darkness, the acoustics matched by the dull lap of waves on the shore.

"I know. I've been listening to your playlists at home, slipping in a little rock now and then to break up the mellow," Ash told me.

"Hey, what's wrong with mellow?" I watched him from the corner of my eye as he stood and flipped open the lid of the Esky cooler. "I've had enough angst for any girl, thank you very much. Now I'll take mellow."

I thought about how much my life had changed over the past sixteen months; how happy I was studying and renting a small flat near the harbour with Ash, and how miserable, how dangerous, I'd been before.

I'd continued seeing Birgit for more than a year after Ash was found. After a while, I even started to like her. She'd used my case notes to write a paper for the AIPR—a ground-breaking new theory that individuals with a fractured sense of reality from frequent night terrors might warrant diagnosis of PTSD. It stopped just short of diagnosing precognition, but not by much. Surprisingly, after I'd recounted every dream to her in minute, emotionally distressing detail, the dreams became less frequent. I'd only had two since Ash's rescue, and neither involved fatalities.

Last Christmas, we'd flown to Melbourne so Ash could meet my grandparents. After a few too many glasses of ouzo, Yiayia reluctantly admitted she'd had the *mati* as a child, too. It had skipped a generation in Mum and Aunt Penny. When grandma met and married Pappous, her nightmares stopped. "He gave me enough else to worry about," she'd joked, patting his knee.

Maybe happiness was the answer.

I hummed along as Dylan started strumming the chorus.

"Sitting here, watching the sun go down, it's hard to believe there was ever a time when I didn't think life was wonderful," I said after a while.

"I've never doubted it." Ash returned with two cold beers, setting them down in the sand near where Dylan sat next to Jaz on a picnic rug. "Come over here." He took my mug and helped me out of my canvas chair, leading me over to the rug, ignoring the fact that it was a little cramped. "I need my arms around you," he explained, sitting behind me, resting his chin on my shoulder. "And it's closer to the fire."

"Even stranded on the island, you thought life was wonderful?" Jaz asked.

"Not all the time, but most days." He handed me back my mug. "Sometimes I thought about Drew and Troy, and about whether I'd die out there alone."

He stroked a strand of hair away from my ear and kissed me tenderly behind the earlobe. "But you can never appreciate the light until you've been lost in the darkness. It's like the lyrics say." He pulled away and cocked his head, listening.

The pain melted from his voice as he sang, his voice blending into air scented with sausages charred over the campfire and hot milk boiled in a pan.

Soon, Dylan struggled to break into the bridge. His prosthetic made his strumming clumsier, but his riffs and arpeggios were sharper than ever.

"At night, under those stars," Ash said after a while, "it was brilliant. Just me and the abyss. Nothing in between but pinpricks of light. That was when I knew I'd be okay, looking up at those stars."

His strong arms looped around me from behind, squeezing me tight. "As long as those stars were winking at me, I knew you'd be trying to find me, Juls."

I felt momentarily ashamed. Apart from that day I'd believed Renee's lies, I'd never given up on Ash, that was true, but I'd come perilously close to giving up on myself and everything else the universe had in store for me. Everything it had in store for us.

"Don't get me wrong. It was desolate sometimes," Ash added, "but something about the simplicity was stunning. The reef. The colour of the sky. When it stormed, I thought the whole thing might wash away. Same as when the wind was up, sand blowing everywhere. After a few weeks, it was like the ecosystem accepted me. All its sounds, all its secrets. It knew me, and I knew it. I miss that sometimes, feeling connected to nature in that way. I'd never have been inspired to make the album I did without that experience. So yeah, it was wonderful, just lonely without you guys."

"Lucky you had Bitten to keep you company," Dyl said between strums.

"Yep. And help me fish. I wouldn't be here without Bitten. That dolphin saved my sanity more than once, not just my life."

"And I guess Bitten wouldn't be here if Juls hadn't wrecked those nets," Jaz piped up. "Which means Ash wouldn't be here either." She glanced at Dyl, who was focussed on the guitar again.

"And then none of the cool apologies the universe has handed me since would've happened either," Ash said. "The album. The book. The dive centre." He grinned. "And so I rest my case for the affirmative. Life *is* wonderful."

"Don't forget the *Cleo* Bachelor of the Year." I rolled my eyes.

"Jealous jelly." Ash laughed and patted the top of my head.

As soon as word got out that the "Gordon kid" had been found, every news channel wanted a piece of the "castaway kid," as the *Willow Bay Bulletin* had embarrassingly labelled him. Ash, Bitten, and I found ourselves minor celebrities overnight, and when Ash released the album he'd written to keep him sane those long months on the island—memorizing the lyrics, writing them in the sand, and using coconut shells, sticks and stones to add percussion—it immediately went viral.

Within months, he'd signed with a record label that threw insane amounts of money at him to professionally reproduce it and make another album with the same unique sound.

The album wasn't the only thing generating cash. Ash's revelation that Bitten had kept him alive by herding fish into the shallows, and that the dolphin had actually led me to the island, was revealed in a lucrative exclusive with Tara Brown on Australia's *Sixty Minutes*. Ash and Bitten had completely charmed her, of course, and websites like *Mamamia.com* had jumped right on that action. Then *Cleo* magazine selected Ash as one of their Bachelor of the Year hopefuls.

Bachelor of the Year, my butt! The only criteria was that the bachelors weren't yet married, so the fact I'd saved his life and been his girlfriend for the past few years was irrelevant, especially to all the screaming tweens who'd plastered posters of Ash all over their walls and bought both his albums. I had to admit, however, that the professional photos of a shirtless Ash frolicking with Bitten in the surf were smoking hot.

Ash joked I should be thankful he wasn't asked to be on *The Bachelor*, and I had to agree. Not a month after he won Bachelor of the Year, Random House commissioned him to write a memoir.

Just Keep Swimming spent more than eight weeks at number one in the Personal Transformation category on Amazon, and the paperback edition was going into its third reprint.

"So how's the sequel coming along?" Jaz asked. "Lots of salacious gossip about us, or just more of your Zen surfer bullshit?"

"It's called *Just Keep Rakin' It In*," Dylan joked, looking up from the guitar. "It's all about how to cook crabs, make coconut milk cocktails, use shells as natural synthesizers, and make small talk with volleyballs. Right, Ash?"

Jaz laughed and leaned over to tuck a blanket tight under baby Callum's arm. I'd been waiting hours for their bouncing boy to wake up for a feed so I could dandle him. Ash and I had talked about what had happened with Renee, and I'd told him what had happened with Mum and Dad too. While we'd both decided we weren't ready for kids right away, it didn't stop me getting clucky over Jaz and Dylan's ten-month-old.

Cal was the kind of surprise that had forced Jaz to go part-time at university, which turned out to be a great move for Jazz It Up Promotions. Working from home suited her. Along with event management, she'd managed to snare promo gigs for some big name authors, Ash among them.

"Nah. I didn't need a Wilson," Ash told Dylan, bringing me back to the present. "I had a dolphin. I knew the chicks would lap that shit up."

I slapped his forearm with mock jealousy. I'd quickly gotten used to groupies fawning all over my boyfriend at the Willow Bay Dolphin & Dive Centre, where Ash did a once-weekly signing of his books and CDs. They sold like hotcakes down there, although I suppose it helped that he knew the owner, which was me.

When I told Mum the Dolphin Dayze Resort would never get environmental approval, I had no idea Ash and I would play such a big role in why. The tiny, endangered blue sea star that had washed up on the beach next to Ash was the nail in the coffin for Aldershot's "eco" scheme. An eminent marine biologist watching the *Sixty Minutes* piece recognised the extremely rare echinoderm when they did a "retrace your steps" shoot on the island. More of them were found close to the proposed development site, which was the death knell for Dolphin Dayze. That failure, coupled with Ash's return, sent Allen Aldershot yelping back to Melbourne with his tail between his legs, especially after Ash admitted on national telly he believed someone had tampered with the *Daydream*, leading to the boat taking on water and ultimately to Drew and Troy's deaths.

The day we found Ash, Bitten had disappeared from the island, and it hadn't rained for weeks. Ash was running out of coconut milk to drink and until he saw our helicopter that night, he'd counted himself a dead man. Out of all the days he was there, that was the only one when he'd truly cracked, sobbing himself hoarse and screaming, "Come save me" before passing out on the beach. In all his time there, it was the only time he'd truly doubted that he'd survive.

Since the *Daydream* was completely destroyed, Ash had no way of proving it had been sabotaged, but no one was happier to see the tail end of the Aldershot family than Ash and me. Before Aldershot left, he finally had the Anchorage cops charge me with vandalism for slashing the nets. Between that and stealing the jet skis, I was sentenced to fifty hours of community service, mostly spent clearing plastic bottles, fishing line, and assorted other trash off the beaches. I was lucky to get no conviction. Birgit put in a good word for me— diminished responsibility and all that. Given my experience with seaside rubbish collection, it made sense for me to head the Clean Up Australia campaign for Sunshine Shire a few months later and then to set up a local conservation effort to record the number of sea stars in the marine park waters.

After Aldershot left, Sarge Kendall retired from the force and ran for mayor. He won, although everyone down at the Sailor's Maid complained the two young coppers who'd replaced him were rookies. But at least they were honest.

Sarge was far more hands-on as mayor than Aldershot ever was. One of the first things he did was call a community meeting to discuss sustainable tourism in Willow Bay. Given Ash's newfound wealth, Mum's track record as a local businesswoman, and my studies in marine conservation, we put in a proposal. And so the eco-friendly Dolphin & Dive Centre was established—by locals and mostly for locals. It had half the grandeur of the original scheme, but less than half the carbon footprint as well.

When I wasn't at university, researching my current paper—"Methods of Monitoring and Increasing the Reproductive Rates of *Tursiops truncatus* in Shared Conservation Zones"—or surfing with Ash, you could find me down at the Dolphin & Dive. Salt was a regular fixture at the waterside cafe too. I was still working on convincing him to capitalise on Willow Bay's newfound popularity by flying helitours for photographers. He reckoned he'd done his time in eggbeaters.

The Dolphin & Dive's star attractions, of course, were a decidedly female dolphin named Bitten, her mate (whom we called Smitten), and their twin offspring (Mitten and Kitten). Who knew Bitten was a girl? It was another thing I hadn't seen coming. Busloads of tourists came to see their strictly once-a-day "shows" off Piers Beach, which were much less about dolphin training and much more about how to care for the ocean and respect its creatures, along with the occasional leap, flip, or tail slap. To accommodate the tourists, the council built four new self-composting amenity blocks and twelve new eco-friendly campsites by Bluff Bridge National Park, one of which, the one nearest the beach, was the one we were camped at this evening.

Windmills had renovated too, adding a new wing to keep up with demand, and Mum was right: the salon's business boomed, so much so that it felt like I'd hardly seen her for months. Then again, that could have been because of her new boyfriend, Bluey Marone. He'd dropped around to our flat one afternoon to see how Ash was doing, and he and Mum, who'd been over for a barbecue, had struck up quite the romance. Seeing my Mum in love was weird, but in a good way. Bluey took such good care of her that I'd almost forgiven him for calling off the search for Ash the first time around.

"Willow Bay's like a whole different place," Mum had expressed just last week, when she'd added a brand new day spa section to the salon.

She was right. Willow Bay was different. But somehow the influx of tourists felt right. The town was growing into itself, just like we were.

I stood up and walked to the picnic table, grabbing a packet of marshmallows from the lidded plastic box, along with the steel toasting fork. Then I settled next to Ash again, stuck a marshmallow on the tines, poked the fork in near the coals, and zoned back in to the conversation.

Ash was waggling a finger at Dylan. "Remember who pays your wages before you start joshing me about Zen surfer bullshit and drinking coconut milk."

"Hey!" I pulled the fork out and blew on a marshmallow that was already over-crisped. "You may be the major funding partner, but the Dolphin & Dive's paying its own way already, thanks. Last month we donated half our takings to Save Our Sealife, and we still turned a profit. Plus, we're selling your CDs and your book, remember, so technically we're paying *your* wages." I popped the marshmallow into my mouth. "And you better get cracking with the next," I mumbled through the sweet, sticky mess.

"Bloody hell," Ash complained to Dylan out of the side of his mouth. "She's such a taskmaster. I keep telling her to stop whipping me, but—"

"You secretly love it," Dylan said with a grin. "Once a pervert, always a pervert, Gordon."

I lightly whipped Ash a few times with the toasting fork, and he rolled his eyes in mock pleasure before taking it off me and sliding another three marshmallows onto the tines.

"Taskmaster," I *tsk*ed. "Watch yourself or you might become an actual bachelor this year. Also, you are two weeks out from the editorial deadline, and you need to send an excerpt to Jaz so she can start organising publicity."

Ash leapt to his feet and started patting his pockets theatrically, looking for the car keys. "Shit. I better go write to get you off my back." He smirked at Jaz. "It's hard to tell who wears the pants at our place, isn't it?"

Jaz snorted. "Just wait till you're married. No one wears any pants. Once you have a kid, you're lucky if you can find a pair that don't have yak all over them. As I tell Juls all the time, child-wrangling and husband-wrangling are both about positive reinforcement. Be a good man and meet your publishing deadline, and maybe Juls will be off your back and on *her* back instead." She winked. "Although, as a self-made businesswoman like me, I guess she prefers to be on top."

I wished. Jaz wouldn't believe it if I told her, but the truth was Ash and I still hadn't done "it." Not yet.

Ash was a total tease, insisting we had to wait for Yiayia to send up that embroidered silk handkerchief or we'd jinx it, and joking that no sex was part of his Bachelor of the Year contract. I wanted him worse than ever, and that alone sometimes made me desperate to see a ring on my finger, but after a while, I figured out that waiting was a good thing.

After all those despairing days that had stretched on and on without him, we now had all the time in the world. Ash had come back to me. Renee Aldershot was gone. And despite all his groupies, Ashley Christopher Gordon the First was mine. All mine. He wasn't going anywhere.

When the day came for me to step out on the sand, heading for a heart-shaped ring of surfboards, I wanted to be the best me I could be. I wanted it for Ash, but I wanted it for myself too. Waiting made me ache all over with desire, but my longing for Ash wasn't the worst thing in the world, not now that he was right here beside me.

Cal let out a wail, and Jaz cooed and eased him out of the bassinet, straight onto the boob.

"Lucky little guy." Dylan put down the guitar and leaned over to tickle the tiny toe protruding from Cal's green bunny rug. "Who wouldn't love a bit of that?"

Jaz poked her tongue out at him and flipped part of the blanket up over her gargantuan bosom.

"Poor Cal. That kid's going to be scarred for life the way you two carry on," Ash said. "You better watch out, or you'll end up with another one."

"Oh, don't pretend you two aren't jealous!" Jaz shot back.

Ash's eyes twinkled and he nudged me. "*Pffft.* We don't have time for that. No lollygagging around as a stay-at-home mum for Juls. She's got a business to run and research to do."

"*Puh-lease!* Like I wasn't an entrepreneur years before Juls. And like pushing a kid out of your vajayjay isn't the hardest job a girl will ever do." Jaz scoffed.

"Right on, sister." I leaned over and popped a gooey marshmallow into her mouth.

"See!" Jaz crowed. "Positive reinforcement."

"Give it a rest, Jaz. We're not married yet."

She laughed. "As you can see, that didn't stop us."

Ash and I had been best man and maid of honour at Jaz and Dylan's somewhat shotgun wedding a few months before Cal's presence was known. It was no secret that one day we expected them to return the favour.

"You know I *will* be event managing your nuptials when you do get married?" Jaz went on. "All that cash to splash around. It'll be a real extravaganza. Maybe you could do a James Bond-style pre-wedding trailer about how you met, like that celebrity couple that was all over the newspapers the other week."

"Bizarre!" I snorted. "Wait. You've just added book trailers to your repertoire, haven't you?" I asked. "Was that a shill?"

She shrugged. "Like I said, I'm an entrepreneur. Picture this." She spread one hand before her like a fortune-teller. "He's a tousle-haired, popular bronzed lifie. She's a slender, hairy-eyebrowed bookworm pitching a fit on a beach until one day..."

"Shark! Shark!" Dylan yelled so loudly it made Jaz and me jump, and Cal stirred and gave a little wail of surprise.

In a very lame falsetto, Dylan added, "Halp! Halp me, my hero! My friend's drowning out there because she's terrible at body-boarding!"

"Dylan Hoffstede," Jaz scolded. "One, I was excellent at body-boarding. Two, you nearly gave Cal a heart attack. And three, I'd jazz up the story a little," Jaz insisted. "Like maybe Juls is wearing a Bond-girl bikini like Halle Berry's, and she comes zooming up to the island on Bitten's back. We'd cut out all that bit about falling off jet skis, and she'd have bigger boobs and better eyebrows."

"But I love her eyebrows and her boobs." Ash pouted and cast a glance at my bikini top. "Can't we keep them?"

"Look at her." I jabbed at thumb at Jaz. "Event managing slash micro-managing already. We better remember to give her a very firm budget."

"I can't think of a better way to spend all my money."

I relaxed back into him, remembering how it felt that first day I'd met him, the day I'd lost him, and the glorious day I'd found him again. Turning, I kissed him, drawing in his scent, tasting his breath as his tongue teased mine.

"Me neither," I said when I finally pulled away. "Well, except maybe giving more to charity."

"Don't forget to organise the conch shell flutes and coconut bongos." Dylan grinned, stopping strumming for a moment to drum like a maniac on the guitar's wooden top. "Seriously, babe. Even an event planner extraordinaire like you will never be able to convince this pair of hippies to go for anything other than a simple beach wedding," Dylan reminded her. He moved into a canvas camp chair and swung Ash's guitar onto his lap.

Shortly after Ash had been rescued, Dylan and I both started surfing again. It was hard for Dyl at first, but not as hard as trying to be a one-armed mechanic, so he'd applied to the Willow Bay campus as a mature-aged student to study robotics. Money was tight with both him and Jaz studying, so we helped out by asking Dyl to teach a twice weekly "shark awareness" class at the Dolphin & Dive Centre. His talks were especially well received by school groups, the gory little buggers.

Busloads of kids on school camp, senior citizens from nursing homes, and County Women's Associations around Australia visited to learn about Willow Bay's sea life, including that endangered little blue sea star, and to see firsthand what a bull shark was capable of. It took Dylan a little time, and more than a little therapy with Birgit, to make his peace with the ocean's apex predator, but he was now our most outspoken advocate for letting sharks live in peace. Surprisingly, seeing Dylan's injuries and hearing his account didn't stop the tourists from swimming, surfing, or booking a dive tour with Ash, who'd qualified as a dive instructor in his "spare" time. Dylan liked to joke that Ash had returned to us as a merman who did indeed spend half his life underwater.

The nets were gone. It hadn't taken much lobbying to convince Mayor Kendall to ditch them in favour of an increased lifeguard presence, a shark tag and release scheme for fisherman who dragged any up in their nets, and a one-off subsidy for surfers to invest in a Shark Shield personal repellent device for their boards. Clever start-ups had begun to invest in other repellents and making eco-nets, too.

I lay back against Ash, feeling as content as I ever had as Dylan started to pick out an unfamiliar tune.

"Expect this to go viral," he joked. "Even if it sounds a bit jerky. We're working on some tech at uni that might improve my strumming. I'm just grateful I had enough of a stump to make me eligible for the trial."

Ash brought his beer to his lips and took a slug. "That thing's kind of cool, you know."

"It is, huh!" Dyl flexed the titanium fingers. "I'd never have played an axe again without it, let alone be able to give Cal a proper cuddle. Technology, eh? I feel like I've got to give something back. The better we get at making these things, the more others will be able to do with them in the future."

"No more going Incredible Hulk, though." I said with a wink. "Now you're the Bionic Man."

Dylan laughed. "Nah. I'd be Wolverine if I could just convince them to stick some claws in it." He growled and then played the opening riff of a song I hadn't listened to in years, the one Ash had written for me and burned onto a CD after our very first fight. For a moment, I wondered how Dylan even knew it.

"Which reminds me." Ash stuck his beer bottle in the sand and stood, fishing around in the pocket of his boardies.

Between Dylan's goofy grin and Jaz's head snapping up so quickly, I wondered what was going on.

I threw Jaz a WTF look, but she was settling Cal into his bassinet, shushing his cry at being shunted so unceremoniously off the nipple.

Ash put out a hand and hauled me to my feet. His palm felt clammy, and he dropped something, swore, and then got down on his hands and knees to search for it.

"Nerves?" Jaz laughed.

Heat crept up my neck. *What?*

"Yeah," Ash said. "Hella nerves. You want to do this for me, micromanager?"

"You're on your own with this one, pussy." Jaz beamed.

Still on his knees, Ash gazed up at me, and I noticed his eyes were wet. They were solemn and starry, too, as he held one closed fist straight out before him.

"I'd planned to do this a bit later on, once these fools had gone to bed," he whispered, jerking his chin toward Jaz and Dylan, "but since it's sunset, and our song is playing..."

Ashley Gordon was kneeling at my feet, staring up at me with such earnest intensity I could feel my heart beating in the hollow of my throat.

"A couple of years ago, I made one of the worst mistakes of my life," Ash said. "Instead of insisting that the most wonderful girl I'd ever met forgive me immediately and spend a night heavy petting me at Willow Bay Cineplex, I made the terrible decision to go fishing."

He grinned, opening his fist to reveal a white silk handkerchief that had been carefully wound around a small box. "I promise, as long as I live, I never intend to eat fish ever again. Or make such a stupid mistake. Juliette Evangelina Papavasilou Brewer, I'm sorry I couldn't do this sooner."

He unwrapped the white silk and handed the wisp of fabric to me. Beneath it, a blue velvet ring box rested on the palm of his hand. Flipping it open, he asked, "Juls, will you do me the honour of becoming my wife?"

Diamonds shone in the firelight, all set around a large pearl to resemble a sparkling dandelion head. It was the most beautiful ring I'd ever seen, but the joy in Ash's eyes—those gorgeous, familiar, chameleonic eyes—was infinitely more wonderful.

"Oh, Ash!"

He prised the ring from the box and carefully slid it on my finger, a perfect fit. "Sorry it took so long." Ash stood to admire the ring, then bowed and kissed the back of my hand. His breath was warm, and his eyes were misty when he looked at me. "So that's a yes, right?"

I squealed, realising I hadn't said it. "YES! That's absolutely a yes." I beamed. "*Finally! YES!*"

Ash whooped and lifted me into the air, spinning me around until we were both dizzy. When he set me down again, the warmth of his kiss went all the way down, right to my toes.

"You approve?" He flashed my hand at Jaz.

"Don't tell me Jaz micromanaged this?"

She waved both hands. "Nope. Honestly, I gave Ash's design the tick of approval, but that's it. Given that friggin' pearl was the reason you had to wait so long to get a ring, I figured I'd better make sure it was worth it."

I squinted at Ash, confused. "Huh?"

"What's the only other thing in the ocean that comes close to being as precious as you?" He asked. "Apart from Bitten. I knew I had to get you a pearl, but since someone"—he pinched my cheek—"started making such a fuss about ensuring marine industries are sustainable around here, and pearling's pretty exploitative, I decided to commission this cultured one from Lustre in Anchorage instead."

He pulled me close. "I organised it right after I got back, as soon as I got paid for that first article. Didn't realise it would take sixteen months to grow, did I? You can guess how many nights I've regretted *that* decision!"

He pressed against me and said huskily, "Only every damn night. But I asked Jaz, and she said it was very romantic to grow a very precious thing from nothing."

He gestured to Callum sleeping in his basket. "I think it was her way of telling me she was up the duff with Cal, but whatever. Maybe you and me can do it too someday soon—grow something precious together."

Tears welled in my eyes.

"Hey, don't cry, gorgeous." Ash took the handkerchief from my hand and dabbed at my eyes. "My plan from now on is to make you so happy you'll never cry again."

A kiss said all I needed to say about that.

The pop of a cork made Callum stir in his bassinet, and Jaz squeezed in on our embrace, holding two plastic glasses of champagne out to the side so they wouldn't spill. "Here's to the ball and chain," she said. "But don't you dare go all Bridezilla on me. Definitely no pre-wedding trailer." She rolled her eyes. "That's so lame."

"Hey, hey, not so fast." Dylan finished the song and strode over to clap Ash on the back. "As the best man, there's still the matter of the bachelor party. It better be good. You are the *Cleo* Bachelor of the Year, after all. I'm thinking a boy's weekend in Oahu for the championship in November."

"November? No way." Ash's eyes were fixed firmly on my face. "That's way too far away. I speak on behalf of my new fiancée when I say we want a short engagement. A very, very short engagement."

CHAPTER 57

We married within six months. The day the sea had taken Ash away more than two years ago was now the same day it had finally given him back. For good.

The morning of the wedding, Ash and I went on dawn patrol, paddling out to the break off Point Hanrahan. We each carried a wattle wreath, one for Drew and one for Troy. It felt right to change the tone of that day, to make it a day to be joyful, not just sad.

We fought back tears as the wattle flowers bobbed away. Once the wind picked up, Ash poured all his guilt and grief into the waves, his too-thin body leaning into the wind, careening down the face of some of the best barrels I'd seen since Ash had returned. It was almost as if Drew and Troy had willed the charging surf into existence, just for him. And maybe they had.

I was getting better at surfing again, remembering it like a lover after a long absence, finding my balance, reconnecting. Bitten sometimes came with us, leaping out of the waves whenever we successfully pulled off a manoeuvre. Only when our arms and legs were aching, our hair was plastered to our salt-specked shoulders, and Bitten had left us for the day, did we make our way back to the beach.

I stood with Ash's arms around me, excited by the thought that in ten hours we'd stand here together as husband and wife.

"Juls," he muttered. "There's something I've been meaning to tell you."

He said it so seriously that for a moment I held my breath, praying it wasn't a love-child, or a history of violence, or an admission that he was a reptilian alien or something.

"When I decided to propose," he went on. "I wanted to do things the traditional way, but it wasn't like I could ask your dad's permission. Your mum helped fine-tune the ring, so I knew she was cool with it, and she told me you spent a lot of time hanging with Salt while I was away. Salt told me how worried he was about you, how he came to think of you as almost like a daughter. So I asked the silly old bugger for his permission instead. He gave me his blessing, of course, but he also said he'd walk you down the aisle if you wanted him to." Ash bit his lip, looking hopeful. "Dyl and I had him measured for a tux when we got ours done, just in case. Salt reckons he looks pretty sharp for an old guy who hasn't worn a penguin suit in more than a decade. I know he's not your dad, but..."

Tears sprang to my eyes. Salt wasn't Dad, but he was the next best thing. Maybe even the best thing.

"Hey!" Ash's touch was tender as he wiped a tear from my cheek. "No crying, remember. Not anymore. Don't make me put it in the vows. Salt bawled like a baby when I asked him. I've never seen him shed tears before like that. Gotta admit it was kind of awkward."

I didn't tell Ash I'd seen Salt cry. Those old wounds—the empty, aching days the world had mourned for Ashley Christopher Gordon the First—had almost healed. But I knew all too well that some of Salt's wounds never would. In the time that had passed since Salt saved both our lives, I'd managed to get Salt to tell me her name, his dockside guarantee. It was Wendy.

Never say never, Salt.

The way he'd chewed his sun-chapped bottom lip after her name slid out, I could tell it hurt him to say it. I told myself that after the wedding I'd drag her last name out of him too, over lunch at Cafe Conch or a beer down at the Sailor's Maid, and then I'd Google her, see if she was on Facebook. Maybe Wendy was a widow by now. Maybe the US of A hadn't worked out for her after all. There weren't any guarantees. But if my fairy tale could come true, then perhaps Wendy dreamed about that old Peter Pan pirate Connor "Salt" McGuire every day, too.

CHAPTER 58

The ceremony was just as I had dreamed it would be. Except this time, I could see his face: that handsome, grinning, surf-bronzed, soulful face I had come to love so much. And this time, it was really happening.

We both cried during our vows, and Mum definitely needed more than one hanky. Afterward, Salt had another surprise in store.

If I'd been told Ash and I would be in a chopper again together so soon, or that Salt would be at the controls, I totally wouldn't have believed it. But Ash was determined to do everything he could to make our wedding night memorable.

"Don't worry," he whispered as we clambered into the chopper on the beach, waving goodbye to guests still dancing around the bonfire. "I've made damn sure there won't be any fishermen tonight."

Salt leaned over and refilled our glasses from a bottle of half-open Veuve Clicquot. "I'd like to welcome Mr and Mrs Ashley and Juliette Gordon aboard honeymoon class on Salt Airlines. I don't know how your new husband managed to convince me to get back in a bird so soon, but flyin' time is approximately forty-five minutes. Settle in. And cheers."

Ash and I clinked our flutes together as he fired up the rotors.

I soon knew where we were going. I'd figured it out well before we arrived. The most beautiful, secluded beach I'd ever seen. The beach that had kept him for me, saved him for me.

"Anyone would have thought you'd have had enough of this place," I said with a laugh.

"To be fair, it wasn't quite so luxurious last time I was here." Ash pointed to a white silk tent billowing on the sand, ringed by torches. A double futon rested beneath it, and a small, glass-fronted fridge was set near the bed, plugged into an ARK battery box to keep everything cool.

"Salt's been a busy beaver, ferrying everything out here in the *Sea Change* yesterday. I was praying it wouldn't rain and ruin everything."

"I put a few goodies in the fridge for the next few days too," Salt added. "Some meals the Conch whipped up for you guys, king prawns, croissants, ham, strawberries, chocolate, whipped cream. Something tells me you'll be working up an appetite." He winked. "I'll be back to pick you up in a coupla days, in a boat this time, not in this bloody thing." He jutted his chin toward the open door of the chopper. "No good for anything but mustering scrubbers." But there was a strange gleam in his eye, and a bouncing spring in his step when he turned off the rotors and helped me out.

"Thanks, Cap'n." Ash saluted him, following it up with a bear hug. Then, smiling like a man who'd just come home, he held his hand out for mine.

I followed my husband up the pristine, private beach, along a walkway they'd lined with shells, flowers, and candles, which Ash stopped to light with the engraved golden zippo I'd given him as a wedding present. He wasn't a smoker—even Dyl had given that up now—but Ash and Birgit had taught me how important it was to always keep a light on in the darkness, and I'd instructed him to keep it with him at all times.

He stopped and pulled me close. "You like it? It's not a five-star hotel, but it's the best of everything nature has to offer."

"Ash, it's beautiful," I whispered. "It's perfect."

He stroked my cheek. "Just like you, Mrs Gordon. Simple perfection. Just like you."

CHAPTER 59

We barely touched the champagne Salt had left in an ice bucket in the fridge. Our mouths found other pleasures as soon as the hum of the departing chopper faded. Our hands moved upon each other carefully but with the urgency born of years, and the waiting made it all the more sweet—even sweeter that it was here, in this place that knew Ash's body as well as I did.

"You'll never understand how often I dreamed of this," he whispered, moving my long curls so he could unlace my bridal corset. "All those nights I lay here under the stars, I dreamed of this."

The waves were the only sound as our secrets finally revealed themselves. I drew him into me, breathed him in like the sea air. I dug my nails in his back and tugged him to me like an undertow. My thighs encircled him, and his arms lifted me to some breathless space where each touch reassembled us the way his resurrection had reassembled me. Ash bent his head, and we slid naturally into our promise, gasping at the abrupt, pleasure-spiked pain. Then passion smoothed the rough edges until all that was left were the hollows only another person could fill.

What the sea wants, the sea takes.

I took it, all of it. All of him.

Ash's jaw tightened, and a dark channel of desire formed in those eyes as he rode the unstoppable swell. His eyelids flickered like the candles around us and, with one final thrust, he cried out and floated away, carrying me with him.

I threw my head back, dizzy with love and joy. The silk canopy above had been folded back, and the stars stretched into blurs of light and motion.

He collapsed on top of me, exhausted, his lips warm on my face. "You're mine," he panted close to my ear. "Finally."

I put my hand up to Ash's beloved face, tracing his square jaw, high cheekbones, dimples, smooth brow. My wedding ring shone against his tanned skin, and his eyes gleamed with the light that had guided us back here, to each other, to safety.

"Forever," Ash mumbled, pressing his lips to mine.

Out in the darkness of sea and space, I was sure I heard the ocean sigh, I was sure I saw the heavens wink. And even if all of those twinkling stars weren't actually there anymore, I finally knew they were real.

So real.

"Stars, babe," I murmured as we drifted off to sleep.

THE END

I appreciate you taking the time to read *What the Sea Wants*; I hope you enjoyed it. If so, please consider leaving a review on Amazon, Goodreads, Apple or your place of purchase. I would love to know your thoughts. You can also join my mailing list at http://eepurl. com/vk_bP to be the first to hear about new releases and special offers, follow me on Facebook at www.facebook.com/KarinCox. Author or on Twitter @Authorandeditor, my blog www.karincox. wordpress.com.

ACKNOWLEDGMENTS

As always, I couldn't have done this without the support of my family and friends. Special thanks also go to those who helped me refine, rewrite, fact check and proofread this story, including Mint Bkk, Emma Jameson, Leslea Tash, Tara West, Greg James, Dan McCarthy, Allison Edwards, Kirsten Gittens, Anna & Chloe Horsfield, Jess Cox, Helen Robertson, Iva Rajic, Michele Perry and Bev Cox. I'm ever so thankful for Theo Fenraven's attention to detail and editorial assistance. And, of course, I'm forever indebted to my fabulous and ever-encouraging indie author groups and my wonderful fans, who continue to support me even when I take my sweet time and juggle genres on them, and who visit my Facebook page to offer their advice and friendship.

STRINE GLOSSARY

ankle-biters kids
Akubra a type of wide-brimmed hat worn by country Aussies, made of rabbit fur
arvo afternoon
a roo loose in the top paddock A kangaroo loose in the crops means you're not quite all there mentally. A synonym is "a couple of beers short of a six pack".
bubble and squeak rhyming slang for Greek.
berley a mix of fish parts, bread and chicken feed thrown into the water by fishermen to attract fish
bitch's box On farms or cattle stations with several working dogs to help muster sheep or cattle, when a female dog (bitch) comes into heat, she is locked up in a high box or a kennel known as a bitch's box, to prevent the male dogs from mating with her
black stump A fictional place reference in Australia. The black stump is just some point where the country begins. This side of the black stump is usually the city or the coast. Similarly, Australians use "Woop Woop" as a fictional geographic marker. So "He lives out past Woop Woop" or "Lives out beyond the black stump" means that a person lives in the middle of nowhere.
blotto drunk
bogan welfare or working-class, rough around the edges Australian, who probably drives a commodore, drinks VB, wears a wife-beater (blue singlet) and stubbies (shorts) and has a mullet (bad haircut).
bommie a mass of coral just off the beach
chook chicken
clicks kilometres
cobber friend, mate
Kombi van a combination VW van with seats in the front and space in the back for surfboards

convo conversation

creaming soda a pink and very sweet soda pop (or soft drink, as Aussies call it) commonly sold at fairs or "shows" and beloved of children

cute as Aussies took the common idiom "Keen as mustard" which came from ads for the product Keen's Mustard, and applied it to just about everything, dropping the final noun. So cute, becomes cute as. Keen becomes "keen as" and drunk becomes "drunk as".

doona quilt, eiderdown, coverlet, duvet or bedspread—depending on where you are from

dunny paper toilet tissue

Esky cooler (or chilly bin for Kiwis). This was a popular brand, and the name has entered the vernacular.

fairy bread a much-loved food for Aussie kids that is common at children's parties: fresh white bread, spread with real butter, and sprinkled with hundreds and thousands.

fairy floss cotton candy

firie/firey fireman

gutted devastated

ham sanga "Sanga" is short for sandwich, so this could be either a ham sandwich or a slang term for a vagina, depending on the context.

holy dooley an exclamation of surprise, originally Irish.

icy-pole an ice block or frozen lemonade or cordial in a plastic tube

jackaroo a male cowboy or stationhand

jillaroo a female stationhand or cowgirl

Land of the Long White Cloud an idiomatic name for New Zealand, since it is often covered in cloud. Aussies call New Zealanders "Kiwis" but also sometimes affectionately call them "sheep-shaggers" (even if Australia has more sheep than NZ does) or call New Zealand the "Land of the Long White Cloud".

lifie lifeguard

Liverpool kiss Australia's history means that the language is a bastardisation of UK English and US English. Some idiom is borrowed from the UK, imported along with the convicts and ex-pats who have migrated to Australia. A Liverpool kiss, also something known as a Glasgow kiss, is an unexpected headbutt to the face.

Mallee bull To be as fit as a Mallee Bull in Aussie slang means to be in prime condition. The Mallee is a farming region of Australia typified by a type of Acacia (wattle) known as "Mallee".

men in grey suits   slang term for sharks

mobile phone   cell phone.

munted   ruined, broken, stuffed, buggered, fucked

nick off   leave

nippers   a surf lifesaving program for young kids, which teaches them beach fitness and how to row, surf, swim and compete in triathalons. "Nipper" is also a slang term for a young child.

Noah's ark   rhyming slang for shark

ocker   very Australian, true-blue, speaks slang or Strine

pash   to kiss

pash rash   when you've kissed so much that a guy's stubble makes your face feel chafed

pingas   ecstasy pills

putting shit on people   insulting someone as a joke, usually because you like them

rack off   colloquial form of "fuck off"

root   have sex

seppo   a slang term Aussies reserve for Americans. It is rhyming slang for "Septic Tank/Yank." Although offensive in origin, like "bastard" and "bugger" Aussies will usually use it affectionately. E.g. "How you doin', ya big Seppo bastard?" translates loosely to "How are you, my American mate." Aussies also call Americans "Yanks."

shag   have sex

shoot through   take off, leave

Strine   The word used to describe Australians' laconic drawling form of slang. It is a contraction of the word "Australian"; used to illustrate how Aussies slur words and shorten them to create their own unique language. A similar form is 'Stralyan' when you ask what nationality a person is.

surf lifesaver   Volunteer lifeguard who patrols the beach rescuing swimmer, surfers and beachgoers from rips or sharks

tarped up   Australians shorten the word "tarpaulin" to "tarp". As a tarpaulin is used to stop one from getting wet, in sexual slang, to be "tarped up" is to be wearing a condom.

torch   flashlight

Vickie   slang for "convict"

yarns   stories. A ripper yarn is an especially good story that may or may not be true or is at least heavily embellished and exaggerated

ALSO BY THIS AUTHOR

As well as *What the Sea Wants* and more than forty works of children's fiction, non-fiction natural history, Australian social history, and travel guides, Karin Cox is the author of:

Cruxim, a gothic paranormal romance/dark fantasy novel;
Creche, the sequel to Cruxim;
Creed, the final installment in the *Dark Guardians* trilogy;
Cage Life, a collection of dark literary short stories;
Crows and Other Beasts, two short, dark stories;
Growth, a book of poetry.
Hey Little Sister, an illustrated children's picture book; and,
Pancakes on Sunday, an illustrated children's picture book.

Her essays also appear in the Indie Chicks Anthologies: **Memories of Mom and Dad**, **Ms. Adventures in Travel**, and **50 First Chapters.** She lives in Australia and writes while caring for her daughter—undoubtedly her most important work.

COMING SOON...

Under Moons & Crosses
a military romance

A short sample of my latest work in progress...

If you asked me why I did it, I'd tell you I hadn't the foggiest. Not then, and not now. Likely it was some chivalrous notion that the only way to honour her memory was to join the grand old tradition, even if it robbed Farah's ancestors of the Hindu Kush for a time and taught her tongue the smooth vowels she muttered to me as she died there on the tube platform, her dark hair spread around her face like a veil.

I love you.

I'd said it back. But by then, she hadn't been listening.

Truth was, I was a landed gentry military brat who'd been fighting it for a long time. After I lost her, I simply didn't have the strength. All the fight was taken out of me, and I figured I might as well get some back. I had plenty of bottle, a shitload of pent-up anger, and nothing to live for—except Dad's Distinguished Conduct Medal winking at me from the dresser every time I buttoned up a Ben Sherman, telling me, "Go on, Son."

So I did. I went.

First, twenty-six weeks basic training at Catterick, and then another two to get me into the Parachute Regiment. Professionalism, resilience, discipline, versatility, courage and self-reliance—watchwords of the para. I lived them, and then some. Stints in Afghanistan, then the dustbowl of death that is modern-day Mesopotamia, before heading down to Sennybridge,Wales, for a forty-mile Fan Dance over the Brecon's

Beacons to become a Blade—an elite of Sabre Squadron in the 22nd Special Air Service special projects team, specialising in anti-hijacking and counter terrorism. And now, here I am in the post-insurgency sandpit of Iraq. The tip of the fucking sword.

Who's wielding it, that's the question?

When I first started at ShadowStrike, things weren't so hairy. The Coalition didn't want anymore combat boots on the ground, and no-one wanted to see Tommy Atkins with a sword to his gullet, so we stepped out in brand-new steel-caps doled out to us by a private military contractor and earned bucketloads more than the Queen's finest. If we copped it in the neck, there were no Union-Jack-draped coffins on the news, which was how everyone back in Blighty liked it.

"What you don't know can't kill you," the old saying goes.

It's bollocks.

Here in Iraq, just about everything can kill you. But if you're a fundamentalist piece of shit with the hankering to blow up a few infidel journos, whose biggest flaw is a flagrant disregard for the truth (the truth being that nothing and no-one can untangle this goddamned mess armed only with a Nikon), I'll most likely kill you myself, or die trying.

When he'd first arrived out here, Paul had been given the call sign "Fitty" for the same reason. Like a lot of the opportunists, my best mate had come to Iraq with one mission: get rich or die tryin'. Unfortunately, his call sign turned out to be prophetic. Only his widow got rich.

Me, I was here for Farah. At least, that was the lie I told myself.

On the day she died, I'd left the morgue and headed straight to the recruiting office. Got recognised at once. The recruiting officer had beamed so hard his stiff upper lip vanished into his moustache.

"A fine chap. Just like your dad." He'd clapped me on the shoulder as I signed my life away. "Proud military family, the O'Dares."

My eyes were so gritty with unshed tears I couldn't even blink as I answered, "Who O'Dares Wins." It was an old joke of Dad's, a play on the SAS motto, and I got the sense the officer would think it showed bottle.

He'd just smiled again and said, "Do him proud, lad."

I'd swallowed the ball of familial pride and patriarchal grief in my throat and nodded. I knew what a proud military tradition meant: a large family plot in Brokewood Military Cemetery.

Dad's send off, with all the regalia, had been a far cry from Farah's. I hadn't even been to her funeral. I was not her next of kin. Her father, Ajeet, hated me. He'd have killed me soon as look at me, no different from the insurgents out there on Route Irish. I was an infidel, and I'd knocked up his daughter.

I suppose you couldn't blame him.

But Farah had. After he'd disowned her, her passion for me was matched only by her hatred of everything she'd been raised to believe in, including her dad. She'd remade herself under my hands. Her poetry, her passion, her pride in being British, in being mine. But then that same hate, that same old lunacy, had risen up and stolen her away. She wasn't mine anymore. She was theirs. And nothing I could do would bring her back.

I shook my head, clearing the maudlin thoughts.

Paul. Farah. I pushed them from my mind, added their deaths to the catalogue of those who'd gone before. I sucked down the shot of guilt that followed their names on my lips and followed it with a chaser of single-malt—straight up.

I shouldn't have been drinking. I had to work tomorrow. But my philosophy was, "Tomorrow is another day." Another day that'll probably be just like today. More guts. More gore. More guns. And none of the glory. But another day, nonetheless.

There were no more days for Paul. No more days for Farah.

Suck it up, princess. I picked up my drink again. Suck it up, and sink it down, then go and get rich, or die trying.

Sign up for Karin's mailing list at http://eepurl.com/ vk_bP to be the first to hear about this exciting new release in 2016.

www.ingramcontent.com/pod-product-compliance
Lightning Source LLC
Chambersburg PA
CBHW061945170626
46813CB00006B/2533